BED OF FLOWERS

ERIN SATIE

LITTLE PHRASE

CHAPTER 1

Bonny Reed walked the main street of New Quay with a heavy basket in her arms. Pearl-gray clouds massed on the horizon and a salt-scented breeze rattled the shutters on the shops. The storm wouldn't arrive for an hour or more, but Bonny quickened her steps all the same.

Her best friend and partner in the venture that they optimistically described as a circulating library—*optimistically* being her preferred word because optimism was good and lying bad—cast her an irritated look.

Cordelia, a tall woman with few curves to round out her slim frame, moved at an unhurried stroll no matter the occasion. Keeping pace with her meant slowing down or leaving her behind. Compromise was not an option.

Cordelia was the sort of girl people called stubborn.

Instead of slowing, Bonny nipped into the chandlery. A bell rang overhead, and Mr. Shaw, a retired seaman with salt-and-pepper hair and a leathery tan, rose from his desk behind the counter. The sweet scent of beeswax wafted up from the bundles of candles on the shelves, mixed with the bitter lye of soap.

"Miss Reed!" The stern expression stamped into Mr. Shaw's

wrinkles melted away, replaced by something soft and dreamy. "Seeing you is always the highlight of my day."

Bonny blushed. Her parents didn't care one way or another about the circulating library—"I'm glad you enjoy the project" was her mother's ringing endorsement—but they did insist that she always look her best.

That morning she'd put on a simple white gown so well-worn that it would have to be retired soon. But she'd tied a red silk sash around her waist and wrapped a fichu around her shoulders— she'd crocheted it herself—with the ends tucked into her décolletage.

"You're too kind," she replied. "Is Mrs. Shaw upstairs?"

"Here!" Mrs. Shaw brandished a book as she burst through the back door, pink-cheeked from exertion. "I saw you coming from the window and nipped upstairs to get last week's novel."

The slim volume boasted a pretty cover of flower-printed cotton that Cordelia had cut from one of her old gowns. Bonny's old clothes went to her sister; Cordelia's went to her books.

Bonny tucked it into her basket. "What did you think?"

"Mr. Dickens has a sharp wit about him, doesn't he?" Mrs. Shaw propped her hip against the counter, her shoulder just brushing her husband's. "I like his sense of humor."

"Me too." Bonny offered Mrs. Shaw a copy of *The Luck of Barry Lyndon*, sheathed in pink watered silk. "This is for you. I'll mark you down for a return visit in two weeks?"

Mrs. Shaw flipped the cover. Husband and wife bent their heads to examine the frontispiece, a watercolor of a sly young man in an ill-fitting officer's uniform.

"I can see *he's* up to no good." Mrs. Shaw traced the edges of the thick paper. "Is that Mrs. Henley's work?"

Bonny beamed. Mrs. Virginia Henley, the vicar's wife, had given Cordelia the pages and contributed the watercolor. She subscribed to *Fraser's Magazine*, where the novel had first appeared, and her gifts helped to keep their little library afloat.

"You've a good eye," said Bonny.

"Tell her that if the title weren't enough to make me want to read it, the picture would be."

"She'll be delighted."

"Thank you, dear." Mrs. Shaw beckoned Bonny close for a kiss on the cheek. "It's always such a pleasure to see you."

Bonny returned to the street, where Cordelia waited on the pavement. "Mrs. Shaw liked *The Pickwick Papers*."

Cordelia already had her little black book open to Mrs. Shaw's page, pencil at the ready. A neatly ruled grid listed the books Mrs. Shaw had borrowed, the dates given and returned, and a plus or a minus sign to indicate her opinion of it. *The Pickwick Papers* got a plus.

"And you gave her the Thackeray?" Cordelia asked.

"That's right."

Cordelia finished making her notes and tucked the book into the basket. They continued on to the salter's, where Mrs. Andrews exchanged an older Ainsworth for *The Pickwick Papers*. Mrs. Bailey at the Black Lion got *Jane Eyre*.

They visited fifteen homes on each delivery day and, by delivering two days a week—on Mondays and Thursdays—managed to cycle through all their members every fortnight.

They reached the elegant townhouse Cordelia called home, just before the rain arrived. "I'll see you on Thursday? You could come over a little bit early for tea."

Bonny bit her lip. The Kelly townhouse was beautiful and well kept, but she hated to accept invitations because she could rarely return the favor.

"With cakes," Cordelia added.

"You *know* how I feel about cakes," Bonny complained.

"I'll have Cook make the ones with raspberry filling and marzipan on top."

Bonny scowled. "Who taught you to be so cruel?"

Cordelia laughed and gave Bonny a one-armed hug. "I'll see you at eleven."

Rain began to fall as Bonny reached her own front door, only a few blocks down the same street as Cordelia's. The two houses were superficially very similar. Both built around the same time, from the same materials, with similar floor plans. Only the Kelly house was prosperous and well maintained while the Reed house was... not.

Mold blackened the mortar. The paint on the windowsills had begun to peel and the wood beneath to rot. Spots of rust mottled the brass lanterns bracketing the door.

Once Bonny stepped inside though, there was nowhere else she'd rather be. Several of her sister Margot's watercolors hung on the walls—mostly pictures of young people swooning tragically, plucked from the local theater productions her sister loved. Bonny, of a somewhat different temperament, had embroidered the runners and tablecloths in bright, cheerful patterns.

Fresh flowers filled the cheap glass vases scattered around the house—a few fine bouquets from Mr. Charles Gavin, Bonny's suitor, supplemented with simpler blooms collected during country rambles.

Margot darted into the foyer. At fifteen, she was tall and gawky, all legs and knuckles and nose. In a few years, she'd be elegant. As a matron, distinguished—like their mother. But she didn't have the temper to appreciate those reassurances, especially not from Bonny.

Probably because, for all their differences, they looked very much alike. They'd both inherited their mother's creamy skin, their father's mousy-brown hair and pale blue eyes.

"Bonny!" Margot whispered. "Bonny!"

Happy to play along, Bonny lowered her voice to a whisper too. "What is it?"

"Mr. Gavin is here."

"In secret?"

"No, silly! With Papa! They're alone!"

Bonny's heart skipped a beat.

Margot leaned so close that her breath fanned the loose strands of hair floating around Bonny's ear. *"He's proposing."*

"Shush." Bonny grabbed her sister's shoulders and held her still, though it wasn't Margot who'd begun to tremble. "We don't know that."

She'd jumped to the wrong conclusion once before, two years ago. Her mother had been the one to whisper the news in the foyer: *Mr. Gavin is speaking with your father! Alone!* Bonny had been surprised, then delighted, then filled with a deep, glowing certainty. She'd been ready to become Mrs. Charles Gavin. She'd felt it down to her bones.

Then her father had emerged from his study with Mr. Gavin, and it quickly became clear that they'd been making plans for a hunting party. Nothing to do with marriage.

After that, Bonny had never quite regained her peace of mind. She had been ready. Ever since, she'd been *past* ready. If she'd seen any sign that Mr. Gavin's delight in bachelor life had begun to pall, she would have tried to bring him up to snuff. But he seemed content, so she tried not to get her hopes up anymore. It hurt too much to have them dashed.

But that was hard to explain to Margot.

"Margot, go to your room," said Mrs. Reed, bustling into the foyer. She had perfect posture and weary eyes, gray at her temples, and steady hands. Bonny admired her more than anyone else in the world.

"Bonny, why don't you come with me?" Mrs. Reed led the way. "We'll have some tea in the salon."

"In the salon?" That *did* sound serious. They reserved the salon for special occasions. With one exception, it didn't look much different from the rest of the house—a few pieces of simple furniture made locally. A few of Margot's paintings on the wall.

The exception was a large antique sofa. Made of heavy mahogany and upholstered with emerald-green silk brocade, a master woodworker had carved leaves and vines into the arms and legs.

It didn't belong in the room. It looked like exactly what it was:

an artifact of another life. A relic from the years when the Reeds had been wealthy and accustomed to luxury.

Those days were over—a devastating fire had brought them to an abrupt end—but before they'd sold all their fine things, everyone in the family had been allowed to choose one item to keep. Any item, though just one.

Bonny had chosen the painting that hung in her bedroom. Margot, who'd been five at the time, had decided on the sofa because she'd been convinced that fairies lived inside the carved foliage. Their father wanted the desk behind which three generations of Reeds had once helmed a thriving shipping concern. Their mother, exercising more sense than the rest of them combined, had safeguarded the house.

"You've been out all morning." Her mother gestured to the sofa. "Have a rest."

Bonny hesitated. Nobody ever *sat* on the sofa—they couldn't replace the silk, after all. Usually they maneuvered around it as though it were a sculpture in a museum.

Mrs. Reed gave Bonny's rear a gentle swat. "Don't be a goose."

The springs in the seat creaked as they sat, stiff from disuse. The family kept one servant, Emma, who handled the rough work, mostly cooking and cleaning. She wheeled in a rickety tea cart, and Bonny busied herself with measuring out the tea leaves, waiting for them to steep, and then pouring. She served her mother first.

Bonny's cup rattled in its saucer. She felt ridiculous and sick and terrified and tried for her most quelling tone. "It could be another hunting party."

Her mother smiled contentedly. "I put my ear to the door this time."

Bonny's breath caught in her throat.

"Breathe, dear," her mother prompted. "And drink your tea."

Bonny promptly scalded her tongue.

Mrs. Reed laughed. "Try again. By the time you've mastered the subtle art of sipping, I imagine we'll have company."

Just then the door to the salon opened. Her father and Charles Gavin entered. They made quite a contrast, standing side by side. Her father had heavy jowls and a shock of white hair, bright blue eyes and a deep, hearty voice. He'd been built stocky and thickened with age, his big barrel chest expanding in every direction while his legs remained stubby and short.

By contrast, Charles Gavin looked like he ought to be posing for a fashion plate. Tall, broad shouldered and trim waisted, he devastated the local tailors—each of whom longed for his patronage—by making periodic trips to London to outfit himself in the very latest fashions.

He'd been graced with fine features too, a high forehead and strong nose, a square jaw and perfectly straight teeth. He'd been the prize of New Quay since he was a boy: the handsomest, the best liked, and—since fortune had turned on the Loels—the richest.

He was everything a girl could want in a husband.

"Bonny dearest, Mr. Gavin would like to have a few words with you." Mr. Reed smiled at his wife. "Perhaps we should allow them a moment of privacy?"

"Just this once." Her mother stood and smoothed her skirt. She carefully positioned the door as she left, leaving it half-open. "We'll be in the next room."

"Miss Reed." Mr. Gavin strode to her. He took one of her hands and swallowed it in both his own. "How you dazzle me."

Bonny blushed. "You're too kind."

"You know that I've seen a bit of the world. I travel a great deal. I'm often in London." Mr. Gavin dropped down on one knee. "But I have never met another woman as beautiful as you."

"That can't be true."

"I assure you it is." Mr. Gavin squeezed her hand. "I confess, even a man who has everything feels the lure of a wife who will bring wealth or property to a marriage. It's not easy to turn away from the temptation. But I've given serious thought to the matter, and time after time, I reach the same conclusion. A woman who's beautiful *and* kind *and* rich will, quite rightly, set her sights on a man of higher rank than I. Though my family is good, my income excellent... I must sacrifice."

Bonny blinked. Was he admitting that, during the years when she'd patiently waited for his proposal, he'd been considering other options?

While down on one knee?

"I don't mean to be vulgar," Mr. Gavin continued, "but the fact of the matter is that I can make money without any help from a wife. Whereas I cannot make a woman more beautiful or teach her the exquisite feminine manners you display on every occasion."

"It's wonderful that you're so thoughtful and cautious," said Bonny, trying to believe her own words. "It's wise to consider all your options."

"Just so." Mr. Gavin smiled gently. "I want you to understand my thinking. It's important that we're of like minds. After all, we're talking about the rest of my life—or, should I say, the rest of *our* lives?"

Bonny pressed her fingers to her lips to stifle a startled, joyous cry. She blinked moisture away from her eyes, though the tears spilled over anyhow. Finally. *Finally.*

"Miss Reed, will you make me the happiest man in the world?" Mr. Gavin pressed his lips to the back of her hand. "Will you marry me and be the mother of my children?"

"Oh yes." Bonny threw her arms around Mr. Gavin's broad shoulders. "A thousand times, *yes.*"

CHAPTER 2

Baron Orson Loel peeled off his wet cloak as he entered New Quay's best pub. Located near the water, on the main street that connected the quays and the railway station, it attracted patrons from all over town. Before the fire in '45, it had been the Red Lion—but the flames had reached the pub's grounds and no farther, charring the western wall and leaving the rest of the building intact. The owners had bought a new roof and rechristened their establishment the Black Lion.

Mrs. Bailey, the publican's wife, bustled past with a tray crowded with frothing tankards balanced on one arm. She was an attractive woman in her thirties, comfortably plump, her reddish hair loosely pinned at her nape. She had a knack for keeping a room full of drunk men in line without ever losing her smile.

She glared at Loel with open hostility.

Loel ignored her. He approached a thin man who, despite the mild weather, had taken a seat as far away from the door as possible and huddled at the table in a thick coat with a wool scarf wrapped round and round his neck. He'd lost weight since Loel had last seen him, and the tropical sun had darkened his skin. He looked like an artist's sketch of the man he'd once been, his features exaggerated for effect.

9

Jacob Benjamin stood in greeting. Loel clapped one hand on his shoulder and pulled him close for a quick, firm embrace.

"It's been too long," said Loel.

"Three years now? And you've been here the whole time?"

"It's dull, but what can I say?" Loel gestured for Jacob to sit and took the chair across from his. "I had enough excitement aboard the *Incitatus* to last a lifetime."

"How fortunate that you can decide when you've had enough," Jacob murmured, resettling himself.

"You know you have a place here if you need it," Loel said. "Whenever you choose and for as long as you wish. I'd love to have you."

"Peace, Loel. I can't even stay the night—I have to catch the eleven o'clock train."

"Where to?" Loel signaled to Mrs. Bailey. "At least let me feed you."

"With pleasure." Jacob's smile was lopsided and easy as he toed the large wooden crate resting at his feet closer to Loel. The glass case inside rattled. "Direct from the high Andes. My notes are inside. All I'll say now is that you should order me the steak. I've earned it."

Mrs. Bailey sauntered up and directed her gaze at a point approximately an inch above Loel's head.

"Steak for my friend," said Loel. "Best you've got."

Mrs. Bailey nodded curtly and turned on her heel, skirts swishing.

Jacob's gaze drifted from Mrs. Bailey's handsome rear view to the charred western wall. "You're not very popular here, are you?"

Loel laughed without humor. "Were you hoping I'd introduce you around?"

"Honestly? If you'd let me tell them all what you did aboard the *Incitatus*—"

"No." Loel interrupted.

"Because you obviously haven't," Jacob finished. "Why not?"

Loel was saved from answering by a commotion at the door. It swung wide, and Charles Gavin paused in the threshold, the lingering light of dusk silhouetting his tall, well-built figure. A dozen men who'd been ranged around a trestle table already groaning under the weight of all the tankards and bottles arrayed across it stood in unison. They raised their glasses high.

"What's that I hear? Are the church bells tolling?" cried Freddy Morgan, a thoroughly despicable man. As best Loel knew, he worked at the brine pits—his father had been foreman for decades now. The Gavins owned the brine pits, and judging by Morgan's toadying, he hoped to inherit the job. "It's a black day, lads. Someone's passed from this earth. Who could it be?"

Charles Gavin whipped off his greatcoat as the door clunked shut behind him. "Quit your yapping, dog."

"Hark, I hear a voice!" Morgan cocked his head. "The ghostly timbre of a man I once knew. He was a dear friend to me…"

"When's the funeral?" demanded one of the other fellows at the table.

"You mean the wedding," corrected another.

"Same thing!" Morgan exclaimed.

Loel's stomach sank. "Oh, hell."

"What's the matter?" Jacob asked.

Loel shook his head. He'd hoped that Gavin's endless delays would allow Bonny Reed to realize the man was an ass.

"It will be soon." Mr. Gavin took a full, frothing tankard from Mrs. Bailey and shouldered a spot for himself at the center of the trestle table. "And none of you are invited."

The table erupted in raucous laughter.

"To a son in a year!" called one of the revelers, raising his glass again.

"Better yet—in six months!" added another.

"Now, now." Gavin winked broadly at his fellows. He stood out from his companions in every way—he was taller, for one, and much fitter. He fussed over his tailoring, making regular visits to London for fitted coats and snug trousers that flattered his admittedly enviable physique. "You know I have too much respect for the fairer sex to tolerate such talk."

The laughter this comment provoked drowned out all other conversation in the tavern.

"I'd sooner toast a swine," muttered Loel.

"So long as you don't expect me to eat it afterward," replied Jacob. He'd paid extra to bring his own rations aboard the *Incitatus*—tinned parsnips and thick stews, potted mutton and diced beef—in order to abide by Jewish dietary laws, which proscribed, among other things, the consumption of pork.

Jacob's eyes brightened when Mrs. Bailey brought the promised steak, pink at the center and crisped brown along the edges. Buttery roasted potatoes and a few boiled carrots filled what was left of the plate.

"Wine too," Loel told Mrs. Bailey.

Mrs. Bailey sniffed and flounced away.

"Now would you look at that." Jacob reached for his knife and fork. "How did the last auction go?"

"Not bad. I have your cut." Loel slid an envelope full of banknotes across the table. Once or twice a year, Jacob sent him shipments of orchids that he collected during his travels. Loel covered the cost of shipping, nursed the orchids to health, and sold the ones that survived at auction. He paid Jacob a percentage of the proceeds. "I'm breeding most of my own stock now, but I wouldn't be nearly so far along without your help."

The envelope quickly disappeared into Jacob's coat. "Every collector I meet these days knows your name—you're gaining a reputation."

"Good. I've been working hard enough."

By the time Jacob had forked the last carrot from his empty plate, the tavern had quieted. Gavin's group had left, and the few new arrivals hunched into their tables, talking quietly.

"I'm about to start a lecture tour. I loathe England because if

I'm here, I'm raising funds—if not to organize my next expedition then to have color plates printed for my next book…" Jacob sighed. "I hate dancing for my dinner, but what choice do I have?"

"It would be a shame to let your talent go to waste. One of my buyers, a man with a more broadly naturalist bent, attended one of your lectures. He couldn't say enough good. Albert Hennig?"

"I know the name—he's a donor," Jacob acknowledged. "If I have time, I'll visit again before I leave the country."

Loel scattered a few coins on the table and mimed a hat tip in Mrs. Bailey's direction. She pretended not to see, of course. He whipped his cloak around his shoulders, hefted the crate, and let Jacob hold open the door. The sky had cleared, leaving a sweet scent and slippery, rain-washed cobbles in its wake.

Jacob clapped him on the shoulder. "Be well."

"You too."

The two parted ways, Jacob toward the train station while Loel started the long walk to Woodclose His route took him past the whorehouse, a tidy, two-story building on the outskirts of town, isolated as any slaughterhouse or tannery. Thick curtains drawn over every window muffled sound and blocked even a trickle of light from escaping around the edges.

The front door opened, and Charles Gavin stood in the threshold, naked from the waist up, his trousers unfastened and hanging loose around his hips. A shadowy figure scurried past him and began retching noisily into one of the planters.

Gavin laughed, a deep basso roll. Behind him, candles and lamps blazed on gilded furniture. Gaudy paintings hung on the walls.

Bonny Reed had the kind of beauty that ought to have rendered her ancestry, her finances, even her character irrelevant. Looks alone could have won her a titled peer, a titan of industry, and she had chosen *this* man?

Loel had no right to judge. But he'd also, in a roundabout way, sacrificed to ensure her well-being. He had circled the globe. He'd known hunger and thirst, illness that dragged him right to death's doorstep and stopped just short of ringing the bell. Aboard the *Incitatus*, he'd faced trials he wouldn't wish on anyone. All ultimately at her command.

Bonny Reed's suffering—and with Charles Gavin, she *would* suffer—would cast a pall over his years at sea. Make all that he'd endured just a little more futile. But while he couldn't regret his choices aboard the *Incitatus*, he'd also discovered that heroism wasn't all it was cracked up to be. Right now, he saw no reason to interfere.

In any case, he needed to get the crate he carried out of the cold as soon as possible. So he put Bonny Reed out of his mind and walked on. He had work to do, and the most beautiful girl in New Quay didn't need his help.

∾

"I HAVE NEWS," Bonny announced, mouth watering and fork poised. Three thin layers of cake sandwiched thick lashings of rich buttercream and tart raspberry jam, all robed in marzipan. The flavors were so varied and well-balanced that every single bite was a meal, an experience, a *delight*.

She could not, for the life of her, resist this cake.

She was sitting at a dainty sofa in the Kellys' formal salon. The figured silk curtains had been tied up to let the morning sunlight in, though the ample light didn't bring with it sufficient warmth.

The salon, like every room in the Kelly house, was tasteful, well-appointed, and fundamentally unwelcoming. The same could be said of Mr. and Mrs. Kelly, though Bonny would never say anything so awful to her friend.

"And judging by your expression, it's good news."

"The best." Bonny released the giddy smile that she'd had poor luck restraining ever since Mr. Gavin's visit. "Mr. Gavin proposed!"

"He proposed!" Cordelia leaped up from the table and held her arms out. "Finally!"

Bonny jumped up to give her friend a hug. They held each other, arms clasped tight, before Bonny skipped back and began to dance Cordelia around the room.

"I'll be married!" Bonny cried.

"To the handsomest man in town."

"I'll have a house!"

"A big one!"

"You can come visit me!"

"How often?"

"Every day!"

"Will there be cake?" Cordelia asked, a sparkle in her eyes.

"All you can eat!"

They laughed and broke apart, both a little breathless.

"All right." Bonny returned to her seat, still grinning so hard her cheeks hurt. "Now that my news is out of the way—you've brought me here to discuss something important, haven't you?"

"I have," Cordelia acknowledged. "We started this project a year ago, and since then we've acquired about one hundred books and more than sixty members."

"Isn't it wonderful?" said Bonny. "I remember, at the beginning, we'd hoped for twenty or thirty at most."

"We've done well—but that's part of the problem. We can't keep adding members without expanding our catalog."

"But books are so expensive—you know I can't be buying any new," said Bonny. "And we agreed not to charge subscription fees."

"Which is why we're going to solicit donations instead," said Cordelia.

Bonny wrinkled her nose. "You mean *I* need to solicit donations."

"I do mean that, yes."

Bonny squirmed. Her family wasn't poor... but they were

close enough to make this assignment an awkward one. "I don't think it will look quite right."

"It's a good cause. You needn't be ashamed."

"I know, but…" Bonny searched for a less embarrassing—if slightly less honest—explanation. "We're not exactly handing out improving tracts."

"We're encouraging women from all walks of life to read," Cordelia said firmly. "We're showing them that books can be entertaining instead of a chore."

"If *you* explained, our prospective donors would gain a better understanding—"

"And if *you* explain, they'll empty their wallets before they've quite figured out why." Cordelia interrupted. "Bonny, you know it's true."

Bonny scowled and forked up a large bite of cake.

Mrs. Kelly interrupted the tense silence. She murmured, "Sorry to interrupt, dearest, but I wanted Bonny's opinion." She laid two fabric swatches on the table next to the tea things—a blue silk and a yellow. "I'm having a new evening gown made, but I can't make up my mind. What do you think?"

Bonny considered the two colors. "You have the complexion to carry off yellow, but I've never seen you wear it."

Mrs. Kelly grimaced. "I was afraid you'd say that."

"You'll look beautiful in the blue," Bonny assured her.

"But *you'd* pick the yellow."

"I think you'd be stunning in it."

"I suppose it's yellow—but you'll hear about it if I look sallow."

Bonny grinned. "And I'll deserve it!"

"You're always right about these things." Mrs. Kelly looked to her daughter. "You ought to take a few tips from Miss Reed yourself."

"I do," said Cordelia.

"A few *more* tips."

Cordelia's level brows and cool gaze were all the reply she

made. She didn't like to repeat herself—a trait that aggravated her mother to no end. Bonny too, occasionally.

"The young men would like it," tried Mrs. Kelly.

"I'd rather a young man who likes me as I am."

"Why must you be so difficult?" Mrs. Kelly picked up the swatches. "Thank you, Bonny. It's always so nice to see you."

"I'm sorry," murmured Bonny, once Mrs. Kelly had gone.

"It's not your fault. Let's not talk about it—that's what she wants, after all." Cordelia tapped her fork against the porcelain plate. "So can I draw up a list of likely donors?"

"You'll do it no matter how I answer."

"True."

"And I'll give in eventually," Bonny admitted.

"So why wait?"

"Why indeed?"

Bonny finished her cake—and even asked for another slice—to reward herself in advance for her good deeds.

She was grateful for her indulgence later that evening, when there was only enough meat at supper for her father and the rest of the family had to make do with gravy.

She sewed for a few hours while her sister read aloud and her mother did the accounts. Margot liked to dramatize her readings, giving each character in a novel a unique voice and acting out the dialogue.

"I heard Lord Loel was at the pub again last night," said Mr. Reed, during a pause.

"What's he up to now?" asked Mrs. Reed.

"Something suspicious?" Margot asked eagerly. She'd be a horrible gossip one day—she couldn't resist a good story, either projected on a stage or whispered in a drawing room.

Bonny listened too, the muscles in her back and shoulders tightening in apprehension. She wished Lord Loel had never returned from his travels. He'd been back for a few years now and every time his name came up in conversation, her conscience twinged.

"What else?" Mr. Reed grunted his disapproval. "He brings disreputable characters to New Quay. Lures them right into the center of town, on the main street, where decent people ought to feel safe."

"He puts all of us in danger," Mrs. Reed murmured.

"He collected another strange package," Mr. Reed continued. "Who knows what's inside those great big boxes; there's never any explanation."

"It could be anything." Mrs. Reed fretted.

"Like bars of pure gold." Margot bounced in her seat. "Or mummies!"

"I don't think the packages are big enough to be mummies," Bonny murmured. "Not if he can carry them away himself."

"Pieces of mummies!" Margot suggested. "Mummied cats!"

"There's nothing wrong with mummies anyhow," said Bonny. "We put them in museums."

"These are probably cursed."

"How do you think of these things? Margot!" Bonny shuddered. Her sister had a flair for the theatrical, but *this* image fit almost too well: Lord Loel, lean and dour, wandering his great empty house surrounded by desiccated corpses.

She tried to lighten the tone. "I doubt Lord Loel can afford a cursed mummy. They've got to be more expensive than the regular ones."

"That's why he only buys them in pieces!"

"It's not funny," warned Mrs. Reed. "One of these days, something terrible will happen. I can feel it."

"I fear you're right," agreed Mr. Reed. "I really do."

BONNY DIDN'T HAVE a mirror in her bedroom. It was one luxury that she didn't miss at all. There was a mirror on the ground floor, by the door, and she glanced at it on her way in and out. No more.

Instead of admiring—or critiquing—her own face, she did her

toilette while contemplating her painting, her one thing. *Bowl of Cherries*. It depicted, as described, a bowl of cherries. A glass of water sat to one side, with a butterfly perched on the rim.

The dealer who'd sold it to her father had said, "We call it a still life, but nothing changes more. It will mean different things to you at different times." She'd adopted the painting as her own before she really understood what the dealer meant. She'd liked it, that was all. She didn't need to know why. But over the years, she'd figured it out.

The painting didn't change, but her preoccupations did. She paid attention to different details depending on her mood—today it was the butterfly, its buttery-yellow wings a vivid contrast to the ruby-red fruit.

She often felt like the butterfly. Buoyant, letting her spirits lift her, giving her a light touch. And sometimes, like today, she felt beautiful but useless.

Her hand tightened on the brush. Not useless. She would prove it later today when she visited the first person on Cordelia's list: Mrs. Lucy Twisby, a wealthy widow who lived alone a few miles from town. They'd been acquainted in the days when the Reeds had been more prosperous and Mrs. Twisby younger and more active. She'd always had a generous disposition. Surely Bonny could coax a donation out of the old woman.

It was a fine spring day, cool enough that she could set a quick pace without worrying about arriving with a glowing red face. Inland, the scent of manure and hay replaced the coastal breezes. Curious cows ambled over to the fences enclosing their pastures, lowing warnings to one another as she walked by.

Mrs. Twisby lived in a fine old house built from ruddy-red local stone. The Twisbys were new arrivals, by New Quay standards—Mr. Twisby had bought the property some fifteen years before upon his retirement from the East India Company.

He'd arrived with his Indian wife and their three children, two girls and a boy. All three children had been baptized by Mr. Henley, given Christian names, and sent away to school. Mr.

Twisby had died not long after that, so Mrs. Twisby had been a widow for as long as Bonny could remember, living alone and not much seen in town.

Though Bonny didn't blame her for keeping to herself. Mrs. Twisby had long been a target of Mrs. Henley's ire. The vicar's wife considered it an outrage that the three Twisby children hadn't been baptized at birth—and she held Mrs. Twisby responsible. "You know Mr. Twisby never attended church," she'd say. "Why do you think that is? I'll tell you: he wasn't a Christian. Too many of our young men lose their way, tempted by heathen women… but to bring that blasphemy here? We must draw a line, I'm afraid."

Of course, the vicar's wife *would* be strict about such matters. Bonny had met Mrs. Twisby after the fire. She'd visited several times, always with gifts of food—including a sweet carrot pudding that stood out in Bonny's memory like a single ray of sunshine in a sky full of thunderclouds—and spent several afternoons with Bonny and Margot while her parents were out. Her kindness had made a lasting impression on the Reeds and many others in New Quay.

A stout, balding manservant answered the door and showed Bonny upstairs. Most of the furniture and fixtures were English, though some of the smaller and lighter items—small paintings in the Oriental style, exquisite carpets—had obviously come from abroad.

Mrs. Twisby sat beside a lit fireplace on a sort of low, flat sofa with her legs curled. She scooted off as Bonny arrived, smiling in welcome. She was compactly built, with plump limbs and thinning hair drawn into a neat bun at her nape. "Miss Reed? You must get more beautiful every day."

Bonny smiled and kissed Mrs. Twisby on the cheek. "You're very kind. But why do you have the fire going? It's nearly summer."

"Old bones." Mrs. Twisby pointed to a chair. "Stop hovering."

"A little bit of daily exercise would help with that."

"Oh, exercise." Mrs. Twisby pulled a face. "What brings you here? It's a long walk to make for no purpose."

Bonny explained the circulating library. Mrs. Twisby listened with interest, asked a few questions, and finally made her way over to the cozy reading nook tucked against the window.

After browsing for a moment, she slipped one volume out of the row and handed it to Bonny. "Perhaps this one? I doubt you already have it."

It was beautifully bound in red leather, the title printed in gold on the spine. *The Widow*, by R. E. Timothy. Bonny had never even heard of the author. Cordelia would be *thrilled*.

"This is perfect!" Bonny beamed. "Thank you so much!"

Mrs. Twisby blinked. "You know… perhaps if I join your circulating library, I could spare a few more. That way I'll get to try something new instead of reading the same books over and over again."

"But that's a marvelous idea! We'd be so happy to have you."

"I know it's a long way from New Quay…"

"So you'd best make it worth my while," said Bonny. "Will you agree to take me on a walk when I bring your books?"

"Take *you* on a walk." Mrs. Twisby snorted. "You're not fooling anyone with that talk."

"At least during the summer months," said Bonny. "It will do you a world of good."

"I'll let you ask." Mrs. Twisby plucked four more books from her shelf and handed them to Bonny. "Here, take these before I agree to anything else."

"It's a bargain." Bonny kissed Mrs. Twisby on the cheek again. "I'll be back soon."

Her route home skirted the boundary of Woodclose, the Loel estate. The gates stood open and she paused, a pleasant little idea twinkling in her mind. The Loel library had once been famous. Most of the books would be dry, dusty classics in Latin or Greek, of no interest to the library's members… but there'd be some gold amidst the dust. If she came back with Mrs. Twisby's five books and more from Lord Loel, Cordelia would be over the moon.

Besides, Lord Loel owed her. It had been eight years since the fire of 1845, long enough to know nothing would ever be the same. She didn't think of him as a bogeyman like her family or most of New Quay did. He hadn't meant any harm. But he could spare a novel or two.

On that note, she turned up the drive.

CHAPTER 3

Deep, uneven ruts scored the gravel road, treacherous even on foot. Weeds competed for dominance where once an elegant lawn had spread like a carpet over the gentle rise.

While the last Lord Loel and his lady had been alive, they'd kept Woodclose in such picture-perfect condition that one could almost believe they'd had the leaves on the trees waxed one by one to make them shine just so.

Mind, nobody had *liked* the previous Loels. The townsfolk of New Quay mostly gossiped about the endless stream of visitors to the great house, united in their disapproval of the excess and frivolity on display.

It was still sad to see the place in ruin. It had been silly and extravagant but very pretty.

Or maybe she was sad for a different reason. The Loels' fortunes had turned at the same time as her own family's and for the same reason. She hardly noticed the changes at home anymore. A life she'd once thought of as a nightmare had become normal… and good. She had no complaints, in any event.

When Orson Loel had been young, the pampered heir to a title and a fortune, he'd developed a passion for sailing. His parents had bought him a pretty little yacht, and he took it out almost every day, flitting up and down the coast alone.

One night, he'd returned home after sunset. He'd lit a lantern as he moored the little yacht, only to kick it over in a moment of inattention. It tipped and cracked—or cracked and tipped— spilling whale oil and flame. The flames caught on the bleached wood of the pier and raced to the quay. From there, the fire spread to the dockside warehouses.

Bonny's father had owned most of those warehouses. He had not owned the goods stored inside them, though he *had* been liable when they'd burned. He'd had enough insurance to escape debtor's prison, but the fire had destroyed a family business three generations in the making and he'd never recovered from the loss.

Not that the Reeds had been the only ones to suffer. Everyone in New Quay depended on the port in one way or another.

The Loels had tried to do right by the town. They stepped in to rebuild lost and damaged property at their own expense. Despite their wealth, those efforts had put a strain on their resources. All the parties and visits to Woodclose had ground to a halt.

Despite their efforts, New Quay's trade shifted north to bustling Liverpool and never came back. The damage had been done. It couldn't be undone by a bit of well-meaning renovation.

Soon after the fire, Orson Loel—who'd caused all the trouble— ran away from home. *Good riddance* had been the general reaction in New Quay. Young Loel hadn't meant any harm, but no one had sympathy to spare for a blue-blooded boy-child who'd cost most of the townsfolk their livelihoods.

A few years after he ran away, the family fortunes took another turn for the worse. Maintenance on the property stopped. Servants were let go. When Lord and Lady Loel showed their faces, they were pale and unsmiling, with dark circles under their eyes.

Then they'd died. Skimping on coal and maintenance left the great house damp and drafty enough to endanger an aging couple accustomed to soft living. They'd died from a bout of influenza.

Influenza! All the fishwives and cottagers had snickered behind their cold-chapped hands.

Lord Loel's last act before he passed had been to summon a solicitor. No one in New Quay knew the details, but his son had returned almost two years ago, and he lived like a pauper, worse than his parents ever had.

Bonny loved and honored her parents. She couldn't think of anything she wouldn't do for them—gladly—and, she suspected, that was why they hardly ever fought.

Whatever the new Lord Loel had done while he was away, it had been awful enough to complete his fall from grace. The cherished only son had become a pariah.

At the end of the drive stood a rambling structure built from the same red stone as Mrs. Twisby's, formed into branching wings with high gables and dotted with cupolas. She rapped at the front door, in vain. No one had seen her coming, and no one answered her knock. That was odd; a gentleman, even one in straightened circumstances, ought to keep at least *one* indoor servant to look after the house.

Bonny circled the building. The windows were all shut, not a single room open to the fresh air. When she peeked through the glass, the floors were bare of carpets and sheets shrouded all the furniture.

Mind, it was a large house. Without money for upkeep, it only made sense to close a few rooms.

She peeked into the windows along the front of the building and then down the side. All the same. The sheets had been in place long enough to acquire a thick coat of dust.

She continued around to the back, driven by nosiness more than anything, and found the library. It was a large, high-ceilinged room, draped and dusty as all the others. No—she mustn't jump to conclusions. Lord Loel might keep a dozen cozy rooms for himself on the opposite side of the house or the upper floors.

She reached an open yard, bounded on one side by the great house and on the other by a huge greenhouse, large as a London train station. Elegantly constructed from a mix of wood, brick, and iron lattice, its peaked roof nearly matched the great house in height.

A makeshift awning of undyed oilcloth sheltered several cords of chopped wood, stacked neatly against the exterior wall of the house. A wheelbarrow full of dark soil lay abandoned in the shade of a giant oak. Something nearby smelled strongly and revoltingly of fish.

All the energy and effort here clearly revolved around the greenhouse, not the great house. Could Loel be growing something unsavory—opium poppies perhaps? Was this why so many strangers slunk into New Quay to exchange suspicious packages?

But if the greenhouse were full of forbidden plants, wouldn't he put locks on the latches?

Her heart began to race as she inched toward the greenhouse. A piece of raw lumber kept the door open a crack. Practically an invitation.

She'd peek inside. If Loel appeared to question her, she'd simply explain her errand. She'd come with good intentions, on behalf of a charitable organization. And clearly, if all the activity on the property centered on the greenhouse, that's where she'd be most likely to find him. Perfectly innocent.

She heaved open the door. Innocently. She heaved open the door *innocently*.

And walked into a permanent spring. Not the one that waited outside—drab, inconstant, a season caught in a tug-of-war between frigid winter and fleeting summer. This was the ideal of spring, more dream than reality. A glaze of moisture condensed on her skin, wilting her dress and sensitizing her to the breeze that stirred the air.

The light had a filtered quality, as though sifted and strained until only the gentlest glimmers and sweetest rays would be let through to bathe the astonishing flowers inside.

Hundreds—perhaps thousands—of orchids filled the vast space. Some bore flowers the size of her thumbnail while others bloomed bigger than dinner plates. They sprang up from beds to either side and overflowed pots dangling from an iron lattice overhead. They came in colors as delicate as a lady's boudoir and as bold as a crime scene.

And the *smell*. Bonny breathed deep for the pure pleasure of it. Rich and heady, cool and fresh. The perfume reminded her of a summer rain or a lily pond.

Several fountains murmured in the cavernous space, all of them connected. Water flowed through a narrow trough snaking overhead to a small drop, powering a small fan as it flowed into another trough that led to another drop and another fan and so on, forming a chain that began deep inside the greenhouse and traveled the whole length of the structure. It was an ingenious system.

Right in front of her stood a table with sturdy wooden legs and a top of smooth, gray slate. Unlike the rest of the garden, crowded with flowers that draped and spilled and twined over every surface, the table and the area around it remained clear and uncluttered.

And the only thing on it... Bonny took a few steps closer, hardly believing her eyes. The only thing on it was a *weed*. A single leaf hanging limply over the side of a small squat pot full of wood chips. No flower, no color.

Bonny looked from the sad little weed to the plant bed just to her right. The nearest flower—not the most remarkable, simply the *nearest*—boasted a fringe of white petals resembling a lightly starched lace cuff, beautifully framing a fluted center the rich, saturated red of burgundy wine.

She bent to sniff at the ugly weedy thing. It smelled of chlorophyll. No perfume at all.

The strangest thing about this fantastical garden might have been the prominent place accorded to an awful little toad of a plant.

A rattling noise sounded behind her. Bonny jumped and

whirled as the greenhouse door opened and Lord Loel stepped through.

Everyone said he was dangerous. That he brought bad people into New Quay. When he came to town for market day, Bonny, like all young ladies of good reputation, kept her distance. She'd glimpsed his tall, lean figure from a distance but hadn't had a good look at him in years. She usually pictured him like he'd been the last time she'd seen him up close: tall and slim, so arrogant that he could hardly tamp down his sneer for long enough to blurt an apology.

Orson Loel had changed.

He was still tall, but he'd grown out of his adolescent grace. He was brawny now, long-legged and thick-thighed, with broad shoulders and heavily muscled arms.

He was handsome, too, but in a feral way. All his features were sharp: his cheekbones were sharp, his chin was sharp. Even his nose sloped down to a sharp point. He looked like a man who, if he tried to give a lady a kiss, would cut her instead.

Bonny had made a mistake when she came here alone. A very serious mistake.

"Miss Reed?" His big body tensed as he scanned the green-house. "What are you doing here?"

Bonny clasped her hands behind her back. Loel's gaze returned to her—his eyes were a bright arsenic green—and they were, like everything else about him, *sharp*.

Men had been looking at her with disturbing intensity since she was little. When she'd been twelve, thirteen, grown men would follow her with greedy eyes. In the years since, she'd been insulted, propositioned, and groped more times than she could count.

She would have said she hated the constant attention—she *did* hate it—but she was used to it. Loel's intensity was of a different kind, cold and penetrating. It made her feel small. And she hated that more.

Bonny forced herself to speak. "I was hoping I could enlist your aid in a project I'm working on."

"A project?"

"Miss Cordelia Kelly and I have organized a small circulating library in New Quay. We want to encourage literacy among ladies of all classes, and it is our theory that entertaining books further this goal better than purely instructional materials."

"And?"

"As the Loel library is famous, I hoped you might agree to donate a few of your books."

"No."

"No?"

"No," he said again.

Bonny admitted to herself that she was relieved. If he'd offered to donate his books, she would have had to follow him into that deserted, shrouded house to browse the library. Just the thought made her stomach twist into a knot.

"I'm sorry to hear that." Bonny eyed the door. "I'll leave you in peace. Have a lovely day."

But he didn't step aside. He watched her, silently, until she began to truly feel frightened.

Bonny tried a feeble smile. "I can't get by if you won't move."

Instead of stepping aside, Loel advanced. Bonny, startled, jumped back. Her elbow, crooked like a chicken's wing, twanged painfully as it knocked against the pot.

The pot and its weed skittered to the edge of the table, wobbled briefly, and fell. It landed on the hard cement floor with a crack. The wood chips scattered, laying the sad, sickly little plant bare to its twin root bulbs.

Bonny gasped.

"What have you done?" Loel cried roughly.

"I'm sorry!"

Loel lunged at her.

She squeaked and dodged, realizing belatedly that he hadn't been snatching at her but the *plant*. The ugly little weed.

He righted the pot and scooped handfuls of wood chips back into it, wincing as he handled the sprawl of limp greenery. Moving quickly, he laid hands on a pair of clippers—the blades lethally sharp—and a stretch of wire, cutting and shaping a skeleton of support.

"Will it be all right?" Bonny asked.

Loel ignored her, ripping a strip of linen from the bottom of his shirt and wrapping the thin wire with it.

"Is there anything I can do to help?"

"Leave," he said shortly.

"Or to make it up to you?"

"*Leave.*"

"I'm sorry to have upset you." She folded her knees and squatted beside him. "Perhaps I could replace it?"

"No."

"But—"

His cold, cold eyes silenced her easily. "Replace it? Be my guest. First find a ship bound for South America. Leave as soon as possible; you'll be gone at least a year. Upon arrival, organize an expedition into the Andes. Most likely, since you'd be unable to recognize this extremely rare species of orchid based on the single specimen you've encountered here, your search would be fruitless. If you were lucky, you might find a living flower to collect. If you were extremely—miraculously—lucky, it would survive the return voyage."

Bonny blinked. "That's absurd."

His upper lip curled in a sneer. "Get out, Miss Reed."

"But—"

"Out!" he shouted with enough force to puff out the loose tendrils of hair framing her face.

Bonny scrambled backward, crablike, then levered herself upright and dashed to the door.

~

BONNY SCURRIED DOWN THE DRIVE, her heart racing. She was halfway home before she slowed to a walk. By the time she reached the familiar narrow streets of New Quay, her fear had given way to anger.

How dare Lord Loel startle her. How dare he address her so curtly and look at her so coldly and yell at her like a common servant. She was a lady, gently raised, and he owed her courtesy and good manners. Whether she'd—innocently—intruded or not.

Bonny stopped at the Kelly house on her way home. Their footman directed Bonny to the attic nursery that Cordelia had adopted as her library and workshop. Bonny skipped up the first two flights of stairs and took the last two at a more stately pace, arriving slightly out of breath.

Cordelia sat at the small desk she'd positioned by the window, its scarred wooden surface cluttered with her book-binding materials: a deep tray for making marbled paper, razors and a bone folder, twine and thick needles.

Bookcases lined the walls, but all the shelves were empty— which explained why Cordelia had been so concerned about expanding their library's membership.

Bonny placed the small stack of new books on a shelf. "Mrs. Twisby sent these."

"How many is that?" Cordelia counted. "Five? And a few I've never heard of. Bonny, I'm amazed."

"She was very generous." Bonny paused. "Though I'm not sure we're saving time with this scheme of yours. She wants to be a member, and of course I agreed. She'd been so generous, and she must get lonely, living so far away from everyone, but it's such a long walk to her home."

"I should have expected something like that." Cordelia sighed. "I'll go with you from now on. That way I can step in before you've promised away the next decade of your life."

"Because I've already promised it to you?"

"Precisely." Cordelia grinned. "Marriage will take enough of your time."

"I'm surprised you're allowing it then."

The humor faded from Cordelia's expression. "If it were up to me, we'd have other options."

"Did someone just reject another suitor?"

Cordelia shrugged, which meant yes. She'd refused every young man her mother introduced her to. The conflict had strained their relationship near to the breaking point.

"I'm on your side, whatever you do," said Bonny. "You could turn down every duke in Christendom and I'd defend it. If you don't like a man, you shouldn't marry him."

Cordelia smiled grimly. "Don't worry, I won't."

Bonny took a peek at the book that Cordelia was in the middle of binding. "Where did this come from?"

Cordelia chuckled. "The mother of the young man I won't be marrying. I finished it last night, and it's delightful."

"So you *say*." Cordelia made no secret of her love for books, but Bonny had only actually caught her reading once—and Cordelia had put the book down immediately. It was the oddest thing. "What happens in chapter six?"

"Two good friends bicker over a topic one of them would rather not discuss," said Cordelia.

Bonny stuck out her tongue. Then, because she was indeed a good friend, she changed the subject. "I paid a visit to Lord Loel on the way back."

"Why would you do a thing like that?"

"For the library, of course. I asked if he had any books to donate."

Cordelia raised one eyebrow. "I take it he didn't impress you with his charitable spirit."

"He was very rude."

"I am shocked." Cordelia's flat tone suggested the opposite. "Shocked, I say."

"I didn't really expect any different," Bonny admitted. "But he'd left the gates to Woodclose open and I was curious."

"About what? The bodies he's buried in his yard?" said Cordelia.

Bonny laughed. "There aren't any bodies."

"Maybe you weren't looking hard enough."

"I did look," said Bonny. "The estate's deserted. It's sad to see it so neglected."

"Suspicious, you mean," Cordelia corrected. "He doesn't want anyone to find out what he's doing with all those mysterious packages he collects from the Black Lion—"

"I think he's growing orchids."

Cordelia's head snapped back. "Orchids?"

"He has a huge greenhouse full of orchids."

"Bonny, orchids are expensive. Even the commonest breeds sell for twenty shillings or more, and we all know he's poor as a church mouse. Where do you think he's getting the money?"

"There could be a legitimate explanation. You shouldn't rush to judgment."

"What do you mean, 'rush'? This is yet another piece of evidence that something odd is going on at Woodclose." Cordelia paused. "Perhaps I should say something to my father."

Her father, the judge.

A strange, unpleasant feeling blossomed in the pit of Bonny's stomach: guilt. Lord Loel had startled her, and he'd been rude, yes, and she'd been eager to complain… but not to retaliate.

If she got him into trouble—potentially very serious trouble—because she'd gone snooping about his property, she would feel awful. She'd already knocked over his plant. However sick and ugly it appeared to her, he'd gone to great lengths to acquire it. Better not add insult to injury.

"I'll thank you not to tell everyone in town that I visited Woodclose alone." Bonny smoothed her skirts. "He refused to donate any books. Leave it at that."

"If you insist."

"I do."

Cordelia slanted her lean figure into the desk, propping her head on her open palm. "How *curious*. You're the last person I'd expect to defend Lord Loel."

"I'm not defending him."

"You just want to spare him a bit of unnecessary trouble."

"Exactly."

"If you're standing between a man and the trouble headed his way, you're defending him."

"Oh, for heaven's sake, Cordelia. Do all children of judges have an insatiable urge to knot conversational threads into nooses? Or is it just you?"

"All? No. That would be highly improbable." Cordelia paused. "I'd believe half."

"Well, you're very clever. Now leave Lord Loel alone."

"Bah." Cordelia idly repositioned a few of her tools—moving a pot of ink a few inches to the right, tamping a needle into its pincushion.

Come to think of it, Bonny had made that pincushion and given it to Cordelia as a gift.

"How is Mr. Gavin?" Cordelia asked.

"Well, I'm sure. I'll know more tomorrow. He's taking me on a walk—all alone!"

Cordelia smiled, eyes crinkling at the corners. "I can't wait to hear all about it."

"It's kind of you to say so." Bonny smirked. "I, in turn, will be kind enough to spare you the details. I know you've no patience for sentimental ramblings."

"Perhaps the highlights."

"If there are any." Bonny reached for the door. "I'll see you on Monday?"

"Bright and early."

On the way home though, Bonny felt sick to her stomach. Yes, Lord Loel had been rude—but hadn't her behavior just now justified it? She'd violated his privacy and gossiped about what she'd seen, made scurrilous insinuations about him, and laughed at his impoverishment.

She had seen, over and over again, that one didn't have to *mean* harm to *do* harm. Loel had blighted her whole town by accident.

The situation reminded her, uncomfortably, of the last time she'd seen Lord Loel. An encounter that she'd kept secret for years, because she felt so ashamed of herself.

Today she couldn't stop thinking of Loel on his knees, scooping wood chips into the pot, shaping a skeleton of support out of wire. She hadn't meant to hurt him but... perhaps she had?

CHAPTER 4

Bonny woke feeling as guilty as she had before she fell asleep. She brushed her hair and contemplated *Bowl of Cherries*. The cherries were all different: Irregular spheres shading from ruby to burgundy, stems pointing in different directions. Her eye kept returning, like steel to a magnet, to the one that had bruised and begun to brown.

Bonny sighed. She lingered on the rotten cherry because it reflected her mood. She'd have to do something to clear her conscience—pay a visit to find out if the plant had survived, offer another apology.

She put on a dressing gown, tidied her room, and went downstairs. Their maid-of-all-work, Emma, was clearing away the cups and plates from Mr. Reed's breakfast. He worked as an insurance agent now, at the local branch of a Liverpool concern, and had to arrive at his office before the rest of the family had rubbed the sleep from their eyes.

"Good, you're awake." Her mother nudged a chair away from the table with her feet. "Emma's doing laundry today, so I thought we would turn the mattresses. And Mrs. Gavin sent over a basket of oranges with a very kind note welcoming you into the family. I suggest you reply today with your thanks."

Bonny, seated now and spooning baked beans onto her toast, paused to answer, "I'll do it right away."

"It was a very generous gift," continued Mrs. Reed. "What do you think about making a marmalade?"

"It would stretch the treat out."

"Just so."

Margot piped up from the doorway. "It only needs to last until the wedding. After that, Bonny's going to send us presents all the time, isn't she?"

"Of course."

"Just think." Margot slid into a seat and reached for the mostly empty pot of tea. "Once you're married, you'll have a cook. You could have cake every day."

Bonny opened her mouth to say something quelling, but the prospect of cake every day distracted her.

"She said something about having us over for dinner as well," said Mrs. Reed. "But don't mention that in your note. We'll see if she brings it up again when we see her after church."

"Mmm," Bonny agreed. "I have an errand to run this afternoon, if that's all right?"

"What sort of errand?"

"To do with the library."

"That library takes a lot of your time." Mrs. Reed sipped her tea. "I suppose Margot can help with the marmalade."

Margot grinned. "Only if I get to lick the spoons."

After breakfast, Bonny tied a kerchief over her hair and helped her mother turn the mattresses. It was a difficult, dusty chore but didn't take too long. She dressed, wrote her thank-you note, and put it in the post on her way out the door.

And returned to Woodclose, feeling the tiniest twinge of guilt about her lie. But her parents couldn't stand Lord Loel, and the mere mention of his name could send them into a dark mood that lasted hours. She'd visit, offer another apology, and put the encounter behind her. No need to start a family row over it.

A slow, rhythmic thunking sounded in her ears as she neared

the great house. She reached the yard to find the baron *himself* chopping wood. He'd stripped down to the waist, suspenders hanging loose over his thighs, the hair on his chest matted with sweat.

He settled a log upright on a large wooden block and hefted his axe, lifting with both hands. Muscles in his arms flexed with supple strength as he raised the blade high, sunlight glittering along the wickedly sharp bit. He brought it down in a controlled arc, splitting the log in two.

Bonny squeaked. She wasn't sure why—she didn't feel sorry for the firewood, for heaven's sake—but she couldn't help it.

Loel looked up from his work and scowled. Setting the axe aside, he straightened to his full, intimidating height. "What are *you* doing here?"

Bonny looked away, blushing furiously. "I came to ask after your orchid. The one I knocked over."

"It's dying."

"If I damaged your property, valuable property"—she paused, hoping that he'd contradict her, but no such luck—"then I owe you an apology, at the very least."

"Accepted." He picked up one half of the split log, set it on the block, and reached for his axe. "Is that all?"

"Is there anything I can do to make it up to you?"

"No."

"Because if there were anything—not money, I won't insult you, and in any case, I haven't any—but some assistance I could offer?"

His upper lip curled. "Do you have any experience with gardens?"

"No."

"Do you think it likely that an absolute amateur could help me care for a temperamental specimen from a family of flowers that is famously difficult to cultivate?"

Bonny knotted her hands together. People usually tripped over themselves to accept her apologies, and she resented Loel's stubbornness. She felt a revolting urge to bludgeon Loel with a smile, to make him admit that her presence alone compensated for any harm she might have done.

Not that she had wronged so very many people, but that was how they generally responded.

"I could try," she said, ashamed to have found vanity hiding behind a seemingly benevolent impulse. "What exactly does the plant require, beyond a bit of watering?"

"A bit of watering." Loel raked damp, dark hair away from his forehead and barked with laughter. The gesture set him off; he looked wild and vital and devastatingly handsome. "Come inside the orchid house. I have something to show you."

He snatched up his shirt and drew it on, raising his naked arms high. His biceps bunched; his pectorals flattened. Muscles clad every inch of his bared form, all moving together like a glorious clockwork.

Bonny crossed her arms over her chest—to show that she was unmoved—and snuck little sidelong glances as he slid his arms through the sleeves of his coat and shrugged it on.

She had seen parts of a man that she shouldn't, but it had always been horrible. Like the time a drunkard on his way back from the privy at the Black Lion had dropped his trousers and waggled his male parts at her.

But Lord Loel was putting his clothes on, not taking them off. And he was… lovely.

Bonny gestured to the axe. "Don't you have anyone to do that for you?"

"Obviously not."

He opened the door for her to precede him into the greenhouse. She had to pass close by him, breathe in the scent of sweat and sap, and it lingered in her nostrils as the warm, thick air surrounded her.

A breeze brushed her cheek, the air stirred by the fan perched by the nearest fountain. "What an ingenious system."

"My own invention." Loel strode past a hundred softly

swaying flowers to the table where the ugly weed sat in solitary splendor, much as it had the day before. A cotton-wrapped wire skeleton held the stalk upright.

"You said this is an orchid?"

"*Odontoglossum crispum Cooksoniae*." His jaw tensed. "The only one of its kind in England, perhaps all of Europe. At least until I make mulch out of it."

Bonny winced.

"Many orchids are rare by design." Loel pulled the plant closer, his keen green eyes narrowing in concentration. He had a low, rich voice and a peculiar accent, the aristocratic tones of his youth twisted by years at sea. "The flower might be common as a weed in its native land—even in England we have wild orchids—but if collectors cannot find it, harvest it, and keep a specimen healthy during the long voyage across the Atlantic, it will be a novelty here—and, therefore, valuable."

He fiddled with the wire skeleton, tweaking it minutely. "Orchid collectors sabotage their competition as best as they can. They hide the exact location where they discovered a specimen. Most try to harvest every flower they can find, *every single one*, to ensure that any collectors who come after leave empty-handed. In some cases they travel with crews of workmen who cut down the trees on which the orchids grow; they devastate whole forests."

"But that's awful!" Bonny cried.

Loel shrugged. "So? It's faster, safer, and frustrates the competition. My *crispum* hails from the Andes and grows on trees. That's all I know—and even that much information comes grudgingly."

"On trees?" Bonny asked.

"It's an epiphyte, as many orchids are." Loel gestured overhead, where flowers spilled from myriad dangling perches. "And now you know why it would be so hard to replace, were you to make the attempt."

Bonny cringed. She had been caught up in the lecture—these were fascinating, exotic plants—but Lord Loel wasn't educating her. He wanted her to know exactly how precious and irreplaceable this *Odontoglossum crispum* was so that she'd feel bad.

A great deal of Bonny's guilt evaporated on the spot. She had apologized. Several times. She'd returned to Woodclose for the express purpose of expressing regret… which, come to think of it, probably explained why he'd responded so nastily.

Lord Loel had set the whole town on fire, and no one had cared to hear *his* apologies. Now it was time to give the people of New Quay—and probably, Bonny acknowledged, herself in particular—a taste of their own medicine.

Very well. If that was what he wanted, she would oblige. Sometimes the bitter pill did the most good.

"I didn't know," said Bonny. "I understand better now, and I'm very sorry."

He squinted at her and pushed the *Odontoglossum crispum* into the center of the table so it sat equidistant between them. "Tell me, is it healthy?"

Bonny guessed. "No?"

"How can you tell?"

"I assumed, since you're so upset—"

"I didn't ask you to diagnose *me*. I asked you to diagnose the orchid."

"How do I do that?"

"If the leaves are too dark a green, the plant isn't getting enough light. Spotting might indicate rot, disease, or burning. A slight bronzing of the leaves can be a good sign—it means the orchid is ready to flower—but too much means it's suffering from overexposure to the sun."

"How would I know any of that?"

"It takes time. But—you asked about watering, didn't you? That usually comes next. Why don't you pick it up?"

Bonny hesitated. "Are you sure you want me handling the thing?"

Instead of answering, he crossed his arms over his chest and glared at her.

Bonny did not want to pick up the orchid. It seemed an invitation to disaster. But he'd asked, and as a sincere penitent, she couldn't refuse. She leaned over the table, arms fully extended, and lifted the pot a bare inch or two into the air.

It was surprisingly light.

"Good." Loel propped his hip against the thick slate tabletop. "How much does it weigh?"

"I couldn't tell you exactly."

"Is it wet or dry?"

"I don't know."

"So we've run into more trouble. You should be able to tell by feel alone."

"Which is it?"

Loel smiled wickedly. "Wet."

Bonny put the *Odontoglossum crispum* down and took a nervous step away. That smile was not proper. "So you've already watered it?"

Loel nodded.

"But—when we were outside—I thought it needed water!"

The smile vanished as quickly as it had come. "Watering the orchid at this time of day would kill it."

"What plant can't survive an afternoon shower?"

"The *Odontoglossum crispum* grows on a tree, Miss Reed. In a forest, in the shade. It doesn't like direct sunlight. And drops of water might as well be magnifying lenses. They focus the light into deadly beams that burn right through tender leaves."

"I see. I didn't know that either." He wanted her to feel ignorant, but that was all right. She *was* ignorant. If she'd known the plant was valuable, for example, she'd surely have been more careful. "When do you water the plant?"

"Dawn."

"You have too many plants here to water them all at dawn. It doesn't last long enough."

"Most need water once or twice a week. I'm usually finished before eight in the morning. If I'm delayed for any reason, I wait until after four in the afternoon. Those are the only hours when the flowers will be safe from the sun."

"What if it's rainy or cloudy?"

"And risk the clouds parting unexpectedly? It doesn't take long to do irreparable damage."

And since, even if he allowed her to lend her fumbling aid, she could never be here at the right time, she would never water the *Odontoglossum crispum.* Not today or any other day.

So Bonny told Loel what he wanted to hear, the hidden meaning behind all his lectures about the orchid: "I see I have nothing to offer."

"Good. We understand one another. Now if you don't mind." Lord Loel glanced pointedly toward the door. "I have work to do."

"Of course. Good day."

She'd almost reached the door to the greenhouse when Loel spoke again.

"I understand you're newly engaged."

Bonny looked back. "That's right."

He was still leaning against the slate tabletop, arms crossed, expression neutral. It amazed her that a man could surround himself with soft, tender things and still be so hard and unfeeling.

"Charles Gavin is not the man you believe him to be."

Bonny stiffened. "Pardon?"

"You heard me."

"You've no right to say such things."

Lord Loel shrugged.

"And besides, you're wrong," Bonny insisted. "I've known Charles Gavin all my life. He's a good man."

"I've known him just as long," said Loel. "And I assure you, he is not."

Bonny reined in her temper. Lord Loel had been jabbing at her ever since she arrived, looking for weak spots, trying to hurt her. This was just more of the same.

Maintain your dignity, she told herself. "I understand, Lord

Loel, that you are not satisfied with my apology. I wish I had more to offer. But I will not let you poison my upcoming marriage with lies."

"Lies?" His mouth flattened into a thin, grim line. "You needn't take my word for it, Miss Reed. I encourage you to seek the truth for yourself, before it's too late."

The only truth Bonny needed at the moment was that she'd made her apology and now it was time to go. Lord Loel clearly wished her ill. Let him—she had a wonderful life in New Quay, and he played no part in it.

She dipped a *very* shallow curtsy and left.

∽

APPARENTLY BONNY REED, who'd been sold at a steep discount to an insufferable pig, pitied *him*. The irony was so thick Loel could taste it.

He tugged off his shirt and flipped it over his shoulder, snorting to himself. Miss Reed might be sweet as sugar floss and pure as new-fallen snow, but she had eyes like any other woman. Maybe that was how she'd ended up with Gavin: she'd measured up his shoulders, matched them to his bank account, and decided she didn't need to know anything else.

He made a quick circuit of the stoves, checking the fires, and returned to the task that Miss Reed had so rudely interrupted. He planted trees to compensate for the ones he cut—aspen, especially, since he'd be able to harvest it again in ten years, but others as well. Ash, alder, hornbeam.

Woodclose was both his greatest blessing and greatest curse. On the one hand, most of the estate's bounty had been explicitly denied him. He couldn't lend or sell anything. The solicitors had made an inventory of the house after his father's death, down to the last teacup and saucer, and he'd be held responsible for any damages or disappearances that took place during his tenancy. He couldn't take out a loan using the property as collateral. A trustee collected the quarterly rents and deposited them in an account where the money gathered interest, and dust, from year to year. Not a single penny would ever be disbursed to him.

But he had all the rights of a tenant. Trustees drew from the accounts he couldn't touch to pay all the property taxes. One of them, sympathetically disposed, had granted him the official title of "Woodsman," which permitted him to cull the forests and fish the lake.

He'd never had to build from scratch. He saved a fortune in coal. He could afford pet projects, like his fountains, and made his own fertilizer. His expenses were minimal, and he had at least five thousand pounds worth of exotic orchids in his greenhouse. About a third of them would never make it to auction, but that was the nature of the game. He could lose about half his stock and break even, so anything more was profit. He'd do well for himself —eventually.

But all those advantages meant he couldn't afford to leave Woodclose. He couldn't escape the house, every surface coated in a film of memory. He couldn't escape the townsfolk, who loathed him. Fully justified loathing, obviously. They'd take their anger to their graves, and he couldn't blame them. Everyone would be happier if he left.

But he couldn't. And since he was in the wrong, he kept to himself. But now it seemed he couldn't spend an afternoon at home without being pestered by a big-eyed do-gooder wearing her heart on her sleeve.

Loel placed a log on the chopping block and reached for his axe. His arms ached all through the spring. He chopped firewood almost every day, stacking up piles as fast as he could so that it would season before winter. He'd run out of wood halfway through his first winter alone at Woodclose and did not intend to make the same mistake again.

Sometimes he liked chopping wood. Exhaustion blunted

nearly any emotion, good or bad. And whatever he was feeling right now couldn't go away fast enough.

He'd tried to do Bonny Reed a *favor*.

Not that he expected a thank-you. God, no. He owed her the kind of debt that could never be repaid. He'd have kept his mouth shut otherwise. He'd expected her reaction or some version of it. Horrified indignation. Wounded dignity. Veiled contempt.

Women as beautiful as Bonny Reed were, in his opinion, best kept at arm's length. Farther, actually. As far away as possible. She was stunning, enchanting, enthralling, all those words that sounded like compliments but were actually warnings. It was nearly impossible to hold on to a thought or an opinion when she disagreed with it. All she had to do was bat her eyelashes, and a man's willpower began to crumble.

A woman's too probably.

She'd been fifteen when he started the fire that burned New Quay. Back then she'd still looked like she ought to be fastened into leading strings and packed off to bed promptly at eight of the clock. That was what had made her fury so surprising, so shocking. He'd been eighteen, nearly the same age, but he'd thought of her as a child, belonging more to her sister's generation than his own.

But since he'd returned…

Her figure retained a babyish softness, as though she'd been carved out of jelly, but the shape had changed. At twenty-three, she was all dangerous dips and tempting curves—a body built for sin attached, disconcertingly, to the face of an angel. Round, with apples in her cheeks and overfull lips.

The woman could have been purpose-built to make grown men weep.

Loel paused, wiped his brow, and wondered where all the wood had gone. Had he finished already? All the better. He had no shortage of work to do.

And if he wanted to keep his mind off Bonny Reed, he'd better keep busy.

BONNY DRESSED for her walk with Charles Gavin that afternoon with special care. She told herself she was doing it to please her fiancé. In truth, she had no goal beyond thumbing her nose at Lord Loel, even though he wouldn't see and—what's more—she hoped they never met again.

You see, she thought, tying a folded scarf around her waist so that the tassels dangled enticingly down the back. *I don't believe you*.

Mr. Gavin arrived right on time, just after tea. "I'll have her home with daylight to spare," he promised, smiling to show off his perfect teeth.

Charles Gavin was very proud of his teeth.

It was their first outing without a chaperone—the fact that her parents had agreed to it told Bonny exactly how eager they were for the marriage.

A morning rain had swept the sky clean and ushered in an unusually fine afternoon, with the sun shining in a clear blue sky and a breeze blowing in from the ocean to cut the heat. Mr. Gavin led her along a winding path that followed the cliffs overlooking the quay and offered excellent views of the sea.

They crossed paths with Mr. and Mrs. Henley, walking arm in arm in the opposite direction. The vicar, tall, thin, and fair, had watery blue eyes and a subdued demeanor. His gift was his voice, deep and resonant, but when standing beside his wife—a brunette with bold features and a brilliant smile—Bonny's eyes inevitably drifted to her.

"I hear congratulations are in order," said the vicar.

Gavin stepped away from Bonny, admiring her openly. "I'm a lucky man, am I not?"

"Oh, indeed," agreed Mr. Henley.

"I was just telling Mr. Henley what a pleasure it is to see you together. You're such a handsome couple." Mrs. Henley nudged her husband. "Wasn't I just saying that?"

"You were," he acknowledged.

"Pretty as a picture," Mrs. Henley continued. "In fact, would you like it if I made a portrait as a gift for your wedding?"

"It would be such an honor." Bonny beamed. "Your watercolors are exquisite. Just the other day, Mrs. Shaw complimented the wonderful frontispiece you made for *The Luck of Barry Lyndon*."

"And you know how much I appreciate your dedication to a good cause!" Mrs. Henley returned. "How did she enjoy the book?"

"We'll find out next week."

Mr. Henley interrupted, nudging his wife along the path. "Why don't you come by for a visit when you have a chance? We need to talk about posting banns."

"We'll look forward to it," promised Mr. Gavin. "Enjoy the rest of your stroll."

Soon after, Bonny and Mr. Gavin met Mrs. Morgan, out with her two children—squabbling over a stick of rock candy. Then a trio of elegant older women, friends of Mrs. Gavin, who fussed over them for quite a while. It took well over an hour to walk the first mile of the path.

Charles Gavin dipped his lips close to her ear. "For once, I wish it were raining. I was hoping we'd have some time alone."

Bonny bit her lip as a naughty idea sprang to mind. She oughtn't voice it, but she felt bright and daring, buoyed up by all the warm words from her neighbors and the handsome man at her side who seemed so proud of her.

"Why don't we leave the path?"

"Bonny!" Mr. Gavin's tone was chiding, but his lips stretched into a wide, delighted smile. "What a shocking suggestion."

"What do you mean?" Bonny skipped away from the sandy trail, the spectacular view, into the open fields. "We're not doing anything wrong. We got lost. We don't walk this way very often, and it's so easy to get turned about."

Mr. Gavin stalked her eagerly. "The ocean's right there. How could you have missed it?"

"What ocean?" Bonny blushed. "I only have eyes for you."

Mr. Gavin swooped in on her, seizing her about the waist and lifting her off the ground so that her feet dangled in the air. For a brief, dizzying moment she was looking down at one of the tallest men she knew. She was breathless and windblown, and she could still see the ocean where it met the horizon, deep blue glazed by the sun.

"There are so many things I want to show you." He set her down, and his gaze dropped, inch by inch, to her chest. "And so many things I want *you* to show *me*."

Bonny raised her arms, shielding herself. Her cheeks burned from embarrassment... and anger. She hated when men stared at her breasts.

"So modest." Mr. Gavin cupped her cheek in one hand and tipped her head up so that she couldn't look away. "Let's start small, shall we? Say my name. Charles. Go on."

"Charles," said Bonny in a small voice.

"Not so meek, little one." Mr. Gavin—Charles—brushed his thumb across her lips. "Try again. Charles."

Little one? Had he just called her *little one?*

"Charles," she said, not at all meekly this time.

"That's better." He chuckled. "Now, how about another little step? Something we've both been looking forward to. Close your eyes."

Bonny did not close her eyes.

"Don't frown." He rubbed the furrow between her brows. "You'll wrinkle. You see how I'm looking out for you? Trust me, Bonny. Close your eyes."

Trust him. Yes. That's why she was here—because she trusted Charles Gavin. He had always been good to her, and she believed he always would be. And besides, he'd spoken the truth. She had been looking forward to her first kiss for a long time.

She closed her eyes, and he mashed his lips into hers. Hard. She squeaked and tried to pull away, but he wrapped an arm around her waist and held her in place. As though he'd anticipated her reaction and prepared for it.

Her heart raced, but she felt oddly paralyzed. Mr. Gavin pressed his teeth against hers hard enough to hurt. She peeled her lips free before they began to bleed, and for some reason this excited him. He groaned and thrust his tongue into her mouth.

Bonny tried to calm herself. It was vitally important that she enjoy this moment. It was meant to be precious, a memory for her to cherish. A foretaste of married life.

Mr. Gavin swiped his tongue around like a dog on the hunt—one convinced that a fox was hiding between her teeth. His big, wet tongue did not fit comfortably inside her mouth.

She tried to yank her head loose but couldn't. She tried using her tongue to shove his out. None of it worked. He only squeezed her tighter.

She was about to start crying and—she couldn't. She simply couldn't. This was her future. She had to accept it and, if possible, learn to enjoy it. She *had* to.

He released her very suddenly. She looked away when his hand dipped to his waistband, making some adjustment. It was vulgar. Blatantly, unapologetically vulgar.

For a brief moment, just the split second before she recognized the emotion and strangled it, she hated him.

"I've shocked you," said Mr. Gavin.

"I'm just... I'm..." Bonny tried to smile. She didn't know what to do with her hands. "So overwhelmed by it all."

"You've always been a good girl." He pinched her lower lip, tender and swollen now. "But all that needs to end soon. A man wants something different from his wife. I've no patience for missish protests—I like a bit of enthusiasm in a woman. You understand?"

"You can teach me."

"I'm looking forward to it." He took her arm and propelled her toward the path. "Your parents will be waiting."

"Yes."

She walked at his side, utterly docile. Her mind whirled, but none of her thoughts had any substance—she couldn't hold them any more than she could have captured a handful of mist, a tuft of cloud.

"My mother has expressed some reservations about this library of yours."

Bonny started. "What?"

"The library. The one that sends you and Miss Kelly all over town, talking to who knows what sort of people. I know you care about it."

"Very much."

"I can have a word with my mother. She'll back down if I insist." He nudged her, smiling conspiratorially. "And then when you can do something to make me happy, you'll return the favor. Isn't that right?"

"Of course. I'll do everything I can to make you happy."

"Good," he said and began to hum jauntily.

Bonny withdrew further and further into herself. She'd built up her expectations too high. That was all. She'd wondered for years what it would be like to kiss a man. She'd expected a—well, a fairly simple action to be infused with all of Mr. Gavin's wonderful qualities: his gallantry and courtesy and charm.

She'd have to accept that reality was different than her silly fantasies. She had to be more open to the experience, to do as he suggested and bring her own enthusiasm to it.

And yet she couldn't quench the sickly queasy feeling that had settled in her stomach. Or silence the echo of Lord Loel's warning.

Charles Gavin is not the man you believe him to be.

He kissed her again when he reached her doorstep, chastely on the forehead this time. "Place your trust in me, Miss Reed, and all will be well."

Trust him? Her whole future was at stake. The moment she

married him, she'd have no choice but to trust him with her health, her finances, her freedom of movement—the list went on. If he wanted that kind of trust *after* they married, he ought to earn it *beforehand*.

A week ago she would have said he had. Today... she wasn't so sure.

CHAPTER 5

Every other Monday, Cordelia organized the circulating library's distribution schedule for the next two weeks. Bonny joined her to double-check that Cordelia hadn't accidentally assigned the same volume to two different members or given one of their members a book she'd already read. Cordelia was careful and meticulous, but having two sets of eyes on the list prevented any errors from slipping through.

Bonny found the organizing boring and stressful. She preferred the deliveries. Especially on clear days, and the good weather had held through the night and into the morning. They set out with warm shawls and thick stockings and color on their cheeks, touched by a hint of spring fever.

"So," said Cordelia as they began their circuit. "I want to hear all about your walk with Mr. Gavin."

Bonny chewed her lip. She suspected that she wasn't supposed to discuss such intimate matters with anyone, let alone an unmarried friend. But she'd never hidden anything important from Cordelia and valued her friend's advice.

"He kissed me," she admitted.

"Was it marvelous?"

"It was..." Bonny paused. "Cordelia, it was awful."

"Awful?"

Bonny struggled to continue. It was strange how hard it was to speak the truth aloud, even to her dearest friend. "I didn't like the way he held me, like he wanted to make sure I couldn't escape. It didn't feel good."

Cordelia stopped in the middle of the street. Her eyes flashed dangerously, but her voice was mild as lukewarm porridge. "Call off the engagement."

"I can't!"

Bonny checked for eavesdroppers, but they'd reached on the outskirts of town where quaint cottages occupied generous plots of land. The only creature paying them any mind was an old plow horse, poking its head over a weathered paddock fence.

"What if it was my fault?" Bonny said.

"How could it be your fault? You've never kissed a man before."

"Exactly. Maybe I did it wrong. Maybe I was a terrible disappointment."

Cordelia, a woman of supreme fairness and decency, actually considered that argument. "Why don't you have a talk with Mr. Gavin? Surely he wants you to find pleasure in his affections."

Bonny shuddered. "He would be furious."

"Then it doesn't matter whose fault it was," said Cordelia. "If you can't talk to your fiancé about something which is, by all accounts, a necessary component of any marriage, then you've chosen the wrong fiancé."

"My family needs this connection. You know that."

"Tell your family what he did, and find out if they still want the match. They might surprise you."

Bonny wasn't going to describe kissing Mr. Gavin to her *parents*. Heaven forbid. And besides, she'd feel awful if they released her from the engagement. Like a petulant child.

"None of the other young men in New Quay have courted me. Everyone says that beautiful women can take their pick of men, but..." Bonny shrugged. "Perhaps I'm not beautiful *enough*."

"Bonny, if you're not beautiful enough, then *no one* is."

"Don't be ridiculous." Bonny silenced her friend with an abrupt wave. "Besides, it's years too late to change my mind."

"Let us be exact." Cordelia's voice sharpened on the last word. "It's too late for you to change your mind without upsetting anyone. It's too late for a change of mind to be *easy* or *painless*. But"—Cordelia narrowed her eyes—"it is *not* too late."

Bonny groaned. "You don't understand."

"You find a man's touch repulsive. Once you marry him, he'll be able to touch you as often as he wants, whether you like it or not." Cordelia slid her gaze to the horizon, her expression bland. "Quite a puzzle."

"No marriage is perfect," Bonny said weakly.

"Is that the lesson here?"

Bonny kicked glumly at the gravel road.

"Really?" Cordelia pressed.

"Can we talk about something else?"

Cordelia, true friend that she was, immediately gave the heavy basket a swing and said, "I read the books that Mrs. Twisby loaned us. There's one I found very strange—I'd be interested to hear your opinion on it. It's called *The Widow*."

"Give it to me and I'll start tonight."

The conversation shifted naturally to more benign topics as they continued their route. Bonny chattered away but with half a mind. Her thoughts turned to Mr. Gavin, to the ease with which he'd held her in place for his kiss, to Cordelia's uncompromising advice.

What if she had made a mistake? And if she had—what next?

BONNY BURNED MOST of a candle reading *The Widow* that evening. It was a novel told from the perspective of a housekeeper gathering her possessions as she prepared to leave the home of her mistress, a wealthy widow who'd recently died.

Both women's life stories unfurled as the housekeeper, Mrs. Godwin, emptied the house. The widow, Mrs. Madott, had lost her husband as a young woman and never remarried. When she died childless, the housekeeper had become her heir.

Bonny had no trouble believing that a lonely widow might leave a substantial bequest to a competent caretaker, but it soon became clear there was more to the story.

Mrs. Godwin had been working for Mrs. Madott for almost twenty years before she discovered her mistress's alarming secret: She wasn't a widow at all. She'd run away from an abusive husband and assumed a false name. Forced to support herself, she'd made a fortune selling scented bath powder. Soon after acquiring this wealth, she'd hired a housekeeper.

Mrs. Godwin remembered very clearly when Mrs. Madott first encountered her erstwhile husband. He'd tracked her down—not to demand her return, not to make amends or start a new life together, but to demand money. He threatened to expose her true identity, assert his legal rights, and have her committed to an asylum. He was physically violent.

And then he disappeared.

After reading about the husband's behavior, it was impossible to believe that he'd left of his own accord. He'd had too much to gain by insisting on his rights. And late in the novel, nearly at the end, Mrs. Godwin casually mentioned stepping over his grave.

The husband had been murdered—but who had done the deed? The housekeeper? The "widow"? The novel presented good reason to suspect both women but no definitive answer.

Bonny woke feeling tired and troubled. The gray, blustery weather suited her mood exactly. She puzzled over *The Widow* on her way to Mrs. Twisby's house. She'd liked it but... she wasn't sure they should be handing it around to the ladies in town.

She mentioned it to Mrs. Twisby when she arrived. "That book you loaned us, *The Widow*. It's very strange, isn't it?"

Instead of answering, Mrs. Twisby asked, "Have you finished it?"

"Last night."

"Who do you think killed the husband?"

"I don't know!" Bonny exclaimed. "If Mrs. Godwin had done it, she would have said so, wouldn't she?"

"Well, didn't she? When she described how shocked and relieved Mrs. Madott was after her husband's disappearance?"

"But Mrs. Madott might have been feigning."

"And Mrs. Godwin would have seen right through it."

"Hmm." Bonny bit her lip. "Perhaps. Let's take a walk."

"I don't like to walk."

"We'll make a loop around your property—"

"That's *much* too far."

"We'll walk down the drive to your gate and back." Bonny paused but, this time, received no objection. "It's dreary outside, but the fresh air will do you good."

Bonny soon had Mrs. Twisby on her feet and bundled into a warm cloak, with a thick scarf around her neck and a fur muffler for her hands. She matched her steps to the older woman's slower ones.

"Have you read any of the other the books I gave you?" Mrs. Twisby asked.

"I always give my friend, Miss Cordelia Kelly, first crack at them—I enjoy reading, but she's passionate about it and reads much faster than I do."

"Ah. So has Miss Cordelia Kelly said anything about my donations?"

"She thanked you," said Bonny. "As do I—you were very generous."

"Anything else?"

"No, not yet."

Mrs. Twisby hummed, then changed the subject. "What about this fiancé of yours? You've known one another for a long time?"

"Since we were children."

"You've made a good choice then," said Mrs. Twisby. "So

many young people think passion is the key to a successful marriage, but it's not. Friendship is far more important."

"Oh?"

"Indeed." They reached the end of the drive and turned around. "Would you like to know how I met Mr. Twisby?"

"Very much."

"I grew up in a place called Tonk, a city in the north of India. My father arranged a marriage for me to a Muslim man in good standing with the Nawab. But my mother learned, from other women familiar with this man, that he was a drunkard." She cast a sidelong glance at Bonny. "I should tell you that Muslims are less tolerant of drunkenness than the English; we consider it a serious defect of character. My mother decided I could not be married to a drunkard, and so one day when my father was away, she invited Mr. Twisby to visit and introduced him into my bedroom…"

"No!"

"Oh, yes." Mrs. Twisby nodded. "He served as a secretary to the British Agent, but he was well liked and expected to rise. She thought the alliance would be better for me and better for the family… and she was right."

"But to take such a risk!"

"Indeed it was," Mrs. Twisby agreed. "But we had no way of arranging a polite meeting, no occasions for innocent discourse… Either I married as I'd been told by my father, or I risked my honor as my mother preferred. You know which I chose."

Bonny hazarded, "It all ended well enough…?"

"That it did. But you can understand how terrified I was, married under a cloud of scandal to a man I'd never properly met. Eventually I learned that he was kind and thoughtful man, a devoted husband who earned my absolute trust, but it took time."

"Didn't he try to reassure you?" Bonny demanded.

"Of course he tried. But trust can't be forced. It takes time to develop, even between two people who are trying their hardest to hurry it along." Mrs. Twisby patted Bonny's hand. "You're lucky to arrive at the altar with such a solid foundation to build upon. I hope you appreciate that."

Bonny would have felt very smug about the conversation if it had happened a week earlier. Instead, she left Mrs. Twisby's feeling rather unsettled.

The idea Mrs. Twisby had formed of Bonny's upcoming marriage swirled like oil around her own expectations for it, thin as water.

If Bonny trusted Mr. Gavin, she would not have spent the past two years in a state of perpetual anxiety. She would have been *surprised* to learn, in the midst of his proposal, that he had been searching for a better bride.

But she hadn't been surprised, except by his tactlessness. She didn't know who he'd considered, where he'd gone searching, but she didn't need to. She knew his mind. He had to have the best tailor, the best horses, the best parties... the best wife. He wanted *the best* more than he wanted her, specifically.

And she wasn't the best. Nobody was. "Familiarity breeds contempt," as her mother liked to say. "Only strangers are flaw-less." It followed that only strangers could be *the best*.

No wonder Mr. Gavin had had such a hard time choosing a wife.

This trail of thought ended at a dark place. She knew Mr. Gavin's mind and understood his motivations. As a result of that knowledge, she had not trusted him. What did that mean for her marriage?

She was still gnawing on this troublesome thought when she reached the gates to Woodclose. She stood in the road for a few minutes, wrestling with her worst self. It would be humiliating to return after she'd stormed away, to quiz Loel about accusations that she'd condemned him for making.

Charles Gavin is not the man you believe him to be.

Lord Loel had been the first person ever to speak an unkind word about Mr. Gavin in her presence. That could mean no one else had anything ill to say... or it could mean something very different.

The Gavins held a great deal of power in New Quay and exercised it gently. They held the leases on half the homes and businesses in town. They owned the brine pits, a major source of employment—especially since the fire. They donated to charitable organizations, patronized the shops, hosted dinners and parties.

Bonny had always found the Gavins easy to like. But if Bonny went about asking odd questions, looking for slander, Mrs. Gavin would hear about it. And that... frightened Bonny.

It *frightened* her.

But she had to know what Lord Loel had meant. He would sneer, but she could swallow her pride. Whatever he told her, she would listen. If there was any truth to his accusations, she would find out.

She found him in the yard, stripped down to his shirtsleeves again as he plucked the feathers from a duck. He'd killed several —one, pink and pimpled, lay on the table beside a cleaver.

"Lord Loel."

He paused his work. "Why are you here, Miss Reed?"

"I was just chatting with Mrs. Twisby down the way and—"

Loel returned to his plucking.

Bonny trailed off. Dancing around her purpose only irritated him. "I was hoping you'd explain what you said the other day. About Mr. Gavin."

"Oh?" Loel swept his forearm across his brow, keeping his bloody fingers well clear of his face, which gave the rough gesture a dainty, feminine twist. "What did he do?"

"Nothing."

Loel snorted.

Bonny narrowed her eyes. "Nothing I'm going to tell you about."

His eyebrows shot up. "That bad?"

Yes, that bad. She wouldn't be here otherwise. But she'd do them both a favor and keep that to herself. Lord Loel's response would doubtless be smug, cutting, and unworthy of him. By averting it, she'd spare his dignity and her temper.

"Aren't you busy?" Bonny changed the subject, waving at his ducks. "If not, let me know. I could make some tea."

He swung his legs over the bench beneath his weathered worktable and stood. He slapped the dust from his trousers, not looking at her, and it struck Bonny that he was gathering his thoughts and trying to hide it.

Her stomach knotted. If a man as blunt and unfeeling as Lord Orson Loel had to brace himself before he spoke, whatever he had to say must be truly awful.

"He fathered a bastard child," Loel said abruptly.

Bonny actually staggered back a step, arms flying out to balance herself against the awful sensation that the ground beneath her feet had dropped away.

"It's not the worst thing I could say about Charles Gavin," Loel continued. "Rather the easiest for you to verify. It happened in New Quay. The woman might still be in the area."

"But…" It didn't make sense. Mr. Gavin always treated women courteously, spoke of them respectfully. He liked to say that he *revered* women. "He's a *gentleman*." Bonny clenched her jaw to stifle further protests. Lord Loel wouldn't care, and throwing a tantrum wouldn't make him take it back.

"To you or to all women?" Loel gestured for her to take the seat he'd just abandoned. "Sit. Stay as long as you like."

He disappeared into the greenhouse. Bonny breathed a sigh of relief; Lord Loel did not have a comforting presence. He hadn't seemed to *enjoy* crushing her hopes and dreams, but he hadn't seemed to mind it either. He just didn't care.

Loel spoke with such confidence, as though he'd never made a mistake in his life, but of course he had. He'd kicked over a lit lantern and burned down the quay. He was as fallible as anyone else, and that meant that he could be wrong. He could be spreading a rumor, unknowingly circulating a lie.

She would consider Mr. Gavin innocent until given proof to the contrary. She owed him that much, at least.

Thus decided, Bonny followed Lord Loel into the greenhouse. He was in the middle of repotting one of his flowers, carefully packing wood chips and moss around the root bulbs.

"I'll find out if you're lying," she said.

"I'm not."

Bonny bit her lip. "How is the orchid that I knocked over? The *Odo*..."

"*Odontoglossum crispum*." Loel shrugged. "It's not dead yet."

"That's good, isn't it?"

"That's what you want to hear. It's not what I said." He finished his task and led her to the table where the sad, stunted thing sat all alone. His mouth twisted bitterly. "Its chances of survival were never very good."

"But it *has* a chance."

"No." His expression softened into a rueful smile. "No, but thank you. Your optimism is so obviously deluded that it's clarifying."

Bonny scowled. Her optimism wasn't a delusion. It was a *choice*. She had enough experience of misfortune—as he *well knew* —to justify a repellant, gloomy outlook on life.

But she preferred not to make herself, and everyone around her, utterly miserable.

"I don't know of any English collector who's caught the knack of growing South American orchids," Loel continued. "The greenhouses run too hot; even the fans I've built aren't enough in the summer. The flowers suffocate."

"So give it to me," said Bonny.

"What?"

"Give it to me," she repeated. "If the orchid is dying and all your skill and knowledge can't save it, why not? At least I'd *try*."

"It's yours." He flicked his hand at the pot. "Take it. It'll be dead by morning."

"You sound like you'd be glad. I suppose now that you've

assumed the worst, all that remains is to wait until you're proven right and the plant dies and—" Bonny stopped herself before she made it too obvious that she was really talking about Charles Gavin.

But Loel heard the unspoken words. She could tell because there was pity in his eyes.

"Show me what needs to be done," said Bonny. "The plant can stay here, but I'll return and I'll—sing to it maybe. I've heard that plants like singing."

"You'll sing to it." The skepticism in Loel's voice was so strong it bordered on contempt. He shrugged. "Why not? Come back in the morning and I'll show you how to water it."

"I will," said Bonny, though in the back of her head she was scrambling to think of how she'd manage to get here in time and what she'd tell her parents.

"Prepare to be disappointed."

"I'd say the same back to you, but I think you already are." Bonny sniffed. "I'll see you tomorrow, bright and… now I think about it, it'll be too early to be bright." Bonny sighed. "Just early then."

CHAPTER 6

Bonny was sewing by the fire that evening when her mother walked in, a wrapped bundle in her arms. "I have something for you."

Bonny hefted the shawl in her arms. "Good, because in a week or so *I'll* have something for *you*."

Mrs. Reed laughed. "You might have to put it aside. Here, look." She untied the twine holding her bundle closed, revealing a folded square of glistening white cloth.

"Oh!" Bonny leaned forward to rub her fingertips along the fabric and gasped at the slick, smooth texture. "Is this silk?"

"For your wedding dress." Mrs. Reed began to unfold the cloth, gesturing for Bonny to hold two of the corners. "Don't even think about the price. This is a gift; it would be *rude*."

"But how? It's so dear—" Bonny pressed her hand to her chest, tears burning behind her eyes. "Oh, Mama."

"Perhaps we were a bit extravagant," Mrs. Reed admitted. "But things will be so much easier for us after you're married. Mr. Gavin promised to arrange for Margot to have a season in London; he says he can send her to his cousins in town. Once Margot's settled, we'll sell the house..." Mrs. Reed sighed. "I want you to look pretty on your wedding day. You don't mind sewing?"

"Of course not." Bonny shook the fabric, enjoying the silk's smooth ripple. "It will be a treat to work with something so fine."

"Nothing makes me happier than seeing you happy," said her mother.

"I do have a small favor to ask," Bonny said. She'd thought about what she'd say to her parents all afternoon and finally decided not to upset them by bringing up Lord Loel's name. "I'd like to make a few regular visits to Mrs. Twisby, but it would have to be very early in the morning. It's the only way that I can fit the visits in with my delivery rounds, without losing the whole day to other tasks that you need me for."

"How early?"

"She's an early riser, so if I arrive in time to take breakfast, I think it will all work out."

"It seems like an awful lot of trouble to go to—how many books did she donate?"

"It's not about that!" Bonny chided. "It could have been one, and I would still have agreed. She's interesting, actually, and I enjoy talking to her."

"I have such a good daughter." Mrs. Reed kissed Bonny on the cheek. "Sometimes I think I'm the luckiest woman in the world."

Bonny felt a little queasy as she returned the embrace. It wasn't *entirely* a lie, but—well. It was near enough as to make no difference. She was intentionally hiding information that would have provoked a very different and much less pleasant reaction from her mother.

But she couldn't justify reviving the painful memories her whole family tiptoed around for the sake of a silly squabble about an orchid. And yet, precisely because it was Lord Loel she was dealing with, she couldn't abandon her challenge for the sake of her family's feelings.

There was already so much pain and bad feeling between the Loels and the Reeds. A small offense, negligible in most circumstances, would deepen and reinforce the divide. And while no one in her own family knew it—not her mother, not her father, not her sister—Bonny had carried a secret guilt in her heart for years, ever since Loel left. It was that, more than anything, that made it impossible for her to turn her back on him now.

SHE SET out early the next morning while it was still dark and chilly outside. Walking briskly warmed her up, though, and she arrived at the greenhouse just as the sun crested the horizon.

Lord Loel was already hard at work in the yard. He'd dressed himself properly for the first time, with coat, cravat, and waistcoat covering his distracting figure. She almost thanked him, but that would have required drawing attention to his previous indecency.

Which—being a well-bred lady—she would never do. If pressed, she would have denied that she'd even *noticed* his figure, let alone the way that linen clung to his sweat-dampened muscles.

He sat on a low stool, legs spread to either side of some large, shallow, rectangular box… a planter, at a guess. He swung a hammer with one hand, steadying the planter with the other, with three nails clamped firmly between his lips.

A soft cap shielded his face from the sun and limited his field of view. Bonny took the opportunity to observe without being observed. To notice the way his cool green eyes narrowed and his mouth tightened around the nails in advance of each swing.

"Lord Loel?"

His brow furrowed as he looked up, transferring the nails from his lips to his hand. "Good morning, Miss Reed."

Bonny drew closer. "What are you working on?"

"Nothing of interest to you."

"But I'm curious." Bonny smiled brightly. "Is it for your orchids?"

His only response was a flat, unfriendly look.

"You're certainly very fond of gardening."

"That's one way to put it."

"How else?" Bonny asked. "You obviously devote most of your energy and, er, resources to the greenhouse…"

Loel squinted up at her, head tilting to the side. As though he were trying to decide if she was completely daft or only a little. "I don't grow orchids for pleasure, Miss Reed."

"You don't? But—"

"I *sell* them."

Bonny's jaw dropped. "For *income*?"

"Yes," he said with insulting slowness. "For income."

"But…" Bonny couldn't believe it. Gentlemen took professions that kept their hands clean—both literally and figuratively. A gentleman owned a farm, but he did not wield a hoe. A gentleman had an office in a bank; he never stood behind a register. A gentleman was an officer, not an enlisted man.

When her father had been at the peak of his success—when thousands of pounds had flowed through his accounts every day and dozens of dockside workers depended on him for employment—her family had still viewed the Loels as members of a class above. They might aspire to acknowledgment from their local lord, perhaps the compliment of his acquaintance, but no more than that.

Even after all that had happened, Bonny had ventured to Woodclose as a supplicant begging a favor. She'd asked the local lord to donate books to her library. It was the most natural role for her to assume.

The pampered aristocrat had fallen far, if he had to earn his bread by the sweat of his brow, to engage directly in commerce. The evidence was right in front of her, he'd said the words plainly, yet it was still hard to believe.

"Really?" she said.

"Yes." Loel was irritated now. "Really."

"But why?" And what had he done to push his parents over the edge, to make them disown him so utterly? If burning down half of New Quay hadn't been enough…

Loel sighed and set his tools aside. "Why don't we go look at the *Odontoglossum crispum*?"

"Oh! I'm sorry." Bonny winced. It had been very rude of her to pry. "That would be wonderful, yes. How is it this morning?"

"Alive, as luck would have it."

She followed him into the greenhouse. She took a deep breath of the rich, heavy air and let her gaze wander. Some places lost their magic to familiarity but not this one. She'd never seen so much purple in her life—pale as a wintry dusk, rich as royal robes.

"So," said Bonny. "How exactly does one water an *Odontoglossum crispum*?"

"Wait here." He disappeared along one of the neat stone paths that cut through the lush greenery and returned a moment later carrying an empty bowl in one hand and a strange, narrow brass tube in the other.

He held the bowl underneath the nearest fountain and gestured her toward the sad little orchid as it filled. "First weigh it again."

Bonny lifted the pot, testing the weight, and examined the leaf. "It looks the same as it did before. Is that good or bad?"

"Neither. Don't get your hopes up."

"Why not?" She put the *crispum* down. "If it makes me feel better and doesn't do any harm?"

"Suit yourself." Loel handed her a brass instrument with a wooden handle on one end and a small bulb on the other, pierced with tiny holes. He tapped the bowl of water. "Dip your finger in."

"It's warm!"

"Orchids are like Goldilocks—not too hot, not too cold. Ideally, the water should be the same temperature as the rain that falls in their place of origin." He pointed, finger tracing the course of the troughs overhead. "As the water flows from fountain to fountain, two things happen. The air warms the water, and the water cools the air. It's coldest at the source and it's warmest here, where it's traveled the farthest."

"All right."

"Now dip the rose into the water and pull back the plunger to fill it."

"The rose?"

He tapped the pierced bulb. "The tip, here."

Bonny immersed the tip. Pulling the wooden handle sucked water into the tube with a faint gurgling noise.

"You push the plunger into the barrel to expel water," said Loel. "Test it out first."

Bonny pushed as instructed, spraying a fine shower through the perforated bulb. "Like that?"

"Mmm." Loel nodded. "You water the potting material, not the orchid itself. Control the spray so that it doesn't splash on to the leaf. The *crispum* wants to be moist, never wet."

"Moist but not wet." These flowers were finicky as a fine lady. "Anything else?"

"No."

"Are you sure?"

Loel nodded.

"Because after all this preparation, I'm not sure that I'm ready." Bonny squirted a bit of water at Loel's face. "What if I make a mistake?"

Loel wiped his cheek, stone-faced. "The orchid will die, and it will be your fault."

Bonny blinked. Either Lord Loel had no sense of humor… or he had a wickedly dry one.

"Daylight's wasting," he murmured.

With a small scowl in Lord Loel's direction, she squirted a modest shower of water onto the wood chips. Then she stepped back to examine her handiwork.

"How'd I do?"

Loel shrugged.

"You may as well tell me."

"Too much splashing." Loel pulled a handkerchief from where he'd tucked it into his belt and daubed at the plant. "Like here, where the leaf meets the stem. There's always a danger of rot—"

"You're joking."

"Not at all."

"You have thousands of orchids in this greenhouse," Bonny protested. "You don't have *time* to pat each one dry with a handkerchief."

"I do things right or not at all, Miss Reed."

Bonny rolled her eyes. *Really*. She'd never heard anything so pompous in her life.

He shrugged, conceding her (unspoken) point. "Practice speeds the process."

"Well, obviously." She knew it from her sewing, if nothing else, how she worked faster even as her stitches grew straighter and smaller. "Anything else?"

"You tell me," Loel drawled, confirming that he did, in fact, have a sense of humor.

"I'm going to sing it a song," she told him. "You can stay and listen if you like, but I won't be offended if you return to your carpentry."

He left without complaint—perhaps he could sense that she would have felt awkward performing for him. She didn't know what to make of Loel, so prickly and forbidding, with his past hanging over him like a shroud... and so astonishingly tender with these flowers.

Her voice was adequate rather than fine; she could sing to an audience without feeling either embarrassment or any sense of accomplishment. In any case, the plant couldn't complain.

"Grow, grow, grow," she crooned, humming the melody to another song. The plant didn't complain, so she continued. "We grow high, we grow slow, we grow, we grow..."

So she hummed a bit, searching for a melody that caught her fancy, and then began to sing a song by Charles Dibdin, her favorite of those she heard the sailors singing as they loaded and unloaded their cargo.

> *"The breeze was fresh, the ship in stays,*
> *Each breaker hush'd, the shore a haze,*
> *When Jack, no more on duty call'd,*
> *His true love's tokens over haul'd:*
> *The broken gold, the braided hair,*
> *The tender motto, writ so fair,*
> *Upon his 'bacco box he views,*
> *Nancy the poet, love the muse:*
> *'If you loves as I loves you,*
> *No pair so happy as we two.'"*

She heard a light rattle and click—the sound of the greenhouse's glass door shutting behind Lord Loel. He must have lingered at the threshold, listening.

She took a deep breath and continued singing. The second and third stanzas described a storm that nearly wrecked Jack's ship. In the fourth and final one the voyage ended, and Jack reunited with his Nancy.

> *"The voyage—that had been long and hard,*
> *But that had yielded full reward;*
> *That brought each sailor to his friend,*
> *Happy and rich—was at an end:*
> *When Jack, his toils and perils o'er,*
> *Beheld his Nancy on the shore;*
> *He then the 'back-box display'd,*
> *And cried,—and seized the willing maid,—*
> *'If you loves I as I loves you,*
> *No pair so happy as we two.'"*

She liked the song because it had a happy ending. Not only

did Jack survive his years at sea, but he grew rich, and when he returned home, he found his Nancy faithfully waiting.

Bonny had lived in a port town for long enough to know that the reality wasn't always so rosy. But she could choose what to sing, just like she could choose to believe that the *Odontoglossum crispum* would blossom and that Charles Gavin was a good man.

Pessimists seemed to dose themselves prophylactically with pain, as though it were a poison they could develop some immunity to. Bonny could not imagine a more obviously flawed and illogical philosophy.

Outside, Loel had returned to carpentry.

"My friend told me that some species of orchids are quite valuable," said Bonny. "I suppose it must be true if you think it's worth your time to grow them."

"Rare breeds sold at auction and wealthy collectors are competitive. They'll pay dearly to own something unique."

"If you don't mind a rude question, what's the most you've ever sold an orchid for?"

"To date? Three hundred pounds."

"Three hundred?" Bonny gasped. "No!"

"And I have every chance of improving on that figure, given enough time."

"What about the *Odontoglossum crispum*?"

Lord Loel shrugged. "Don't worry about it."

"But you said it's very rare," said Bonny. "The only one in England, perhaps in Europe!"

"It's worth nothing if it dies."

"But if it *survives*, you think it might be a valuable specimen?"

"Growing orchids can be a risky business. Nature isn't as reliable or predictable as the shopkeepers of the world might like."

"Since you're not answering, I can only assume the answer is yes." Bonny bit her lip. "It would be worth that much... or more."

Loel was silent.

"More, you think."

"I had hoped," Loel admitted.

"Why did you give it to me?" Bonny demanded. "If I'd had any idea, I never would have asked. We should forget this ever happened—"

Loel interrupted. "No."

"What?"

"It's dying, Miss Reed. I know you'd like to believe otherwise, and I know why, but the truth is that the flower's chances were slim and now they are none."

Bonny sucked in a deep breath so she could give voice to her very *strong* objections.

"No need to protest," said Loel. "If the plant survives, it's yours. You'll have earned it."

That deflated her fast enough. She felt more than a little sick. *Three hundred pounds.* That was enough to survive on for a year, if one were very frugal, which Lord Loel obviously was. If she had cost him so much—even if the plant survived, she would not feel right about keeping the proceeds.

Now she understood why it had come all the way from the high Andes Mountains and why he'd placed it on a table by itself, isolated from the rest. It had been special—as valuable as the most expensive orchid he'd ever owned, or more. She must have put his whole livelihood in jeopardy.

"We'll see," said Bonny, and he didn't press his point any further. She returned home with a heavy heart.

CHAPTER 7

A storm blew in from the south on Wednesday night and held all through Thursday morning. The worst had passed by noon, though, so Bonny ventured down the street to the Kelly house. Once they'd prepared the book basket, they wrapped it in oilcloth and bundled into warm cloaks.

They began their circuit at the vicar's house, where Mrs. Henley opened the door herself. "Hurry, before the carpet gets wet," she said, ushering them inside. "I have tea all ready for you. We'll give the rain a chance to calm down and have a cozy chat."

Bonny loved many things about Mrs. Henley. Her generosity, for example; she'd donated many of her own books and magazines to the circulating library. Her strong principles, her energy… and most especially her hospitality. Her very delicious hospitality.

She made the most magnificent tea cakes, moist and rich and beautifully glazed.

They discussed all the local news: the babies who'd survived the croup, the husbands who drank too much, the new silvered glass mirror at the Black Lion. Mrs. Henley could be discreet, but she saw gossip as a sort of moral duty. She collected all the local news and shared it back out again, her information scrupulously correct and her judgments absolute.

"I hear your mother has a suitor in mind, Miss Kelly," said Mrs. Henley, when the teapot was empty and their cups nearly drained.

"She does," said Cordelia flatly.

"And what do you think of this one?"

"I hope he gives up quickly."

Bonny giggled.

"It may seem funny now, but it won't forever," warned Mrs. Henley. "Delay long enough and all the men you've rejected will find other women to marry while you'll be left all alone. I've seen it happen."

Before Mr. Gavin's proposal, that had been Bonny's greatest fear.

"Fortunately, I'm content with my own company," said Cordelia.

Bonny blinked at her friend.

"I believe your confidence is a sham, Miss Kelly," said Mrs. Henley. "What, exactly, do you have to be so proud of?"

Bonny took one look at Cordelia, her demeanor mild and steely, and realized that she'd have to step in to avert a catastrophe. "But Mrs. Henley, you've said such nice things about our circulating library—"

"I hope this modest accomplishment hasn't gone to your head."

"Oh! Look out the window. The rain has let up." Bonny bounced from her own seat to Mrs. Henley's, snuggling the older woman close in a hug. "Thank you for your wisdom, Mrs. Henley, and don't blame us too much for being silly, hardheaded girls."

Mrs. Henley melted under this embrace.

"And when will you learn, hmm?"

"We learn every day," Bonny promised. "It just happens so very slowly."

Cordelia's indignant expression said that she had no intention of changing to suit Mrs. Henley, but Bonny ignored the silent rebuke.

"Hrmph," Mrs. Henley said. "I have some primers for Claire Morgan. She's been doing so well with her literacy classes I thought it would be nice to gift her a hand. Can I send them with you?"

Bonny hugged Mrs. Henley again. "Of course."

"I expect to see you again in two weeks."

"We wouldn't miss it," Bonny promised.

On the way to Mrs. Morgan's, Bonny said, "Don't let her upset you."

"Upset me?" Cordelia asked, obviously startled by the idea.

"Any man would be lucky to have you."

"Any man would be lucky to have *you*. Most men consider *me* a trial, and the sentiment is reciprocated."

With her wide-set blue eyes, thin blade of a nose, and chiseled jawline, Cordelia was as beautiful a woman as Bonny had ever seen—and having been praised for her beauty all her life, she had definite opinions on the subject.

But while men flocked to Bonny with the bewildering single-mindedness of moths flinging themselves against a lit window at night, they utterly ignored Cordelia. Cordelia never seemed to mind—she hardly seemed to *notice*—but Bonny did.

She minded a great deal.

"Then all the men of the world are fools," said Bonny.

"Thank you for saving me from saying it myself." Cordelia smiled wryly. "Which reminds me—what did you think of *The Widow*?"

"I liked it! What a chilling mystery. Who do you think killed the husband?"

"The widow, obviously. Mrs. Madott."

"Mrs. Madott!" Bonny exclaimed. "That was my first thought, but now I'm not so sure. She was so surprised when her husband vanished."

"Mrs. Madott had the stronger motive."

"I'm not so sure of that. Mrs. Godwin would have had a hard time finding a new place if that awful man dragged Mrs. Madott to an asylum. A younger woman might have been able to start over in a new position, without a reference, but at her age…?"

"True." Cordelia hummed. "Do you think we should add it to our catalogue?"

"I… don't," Bonny admitted. "There's something unsettling about the book."

"Of course there is," Cordelia retorted. "That husband was murdered, and even if we don't know who killed him, it's obvious that neither of our suspects is sorry to see him go. That scene where Mrs. Godwin steps over his grave as though it's nothing…"

Bonny shuddered. "Though I'm not sure I'm sorry either. He was awful."

"Murder is wrong," said Cordelia, effectively ending the conversation.

Soon they reached the cottage where Claire Morgan spent the day minding her children while her husband worked at the brine pits. Bonny knew he hoped to be the foreman one day—he was always at Mr. Gavin's side.

Bonny offered Mrs. Morgan a staple-bound pamphlet, a children's story that would take a literate adult some fifteen minutes to read. "This is from Mrs. Henley."

"Please thank her for me." Mrs. Morgan returned a pamphlet whose pages had turned soft as the cotton from which they were originally made, the paper faded to a dirty gray. "This goes back to you. The children loved it as much as they did last time," she said, only a little wry. "And the time before that."

Bonny laughed. "I'm glad we finally have something new to offer."

"Oh, they'll be wanting their old favorite back before long. Once they grow attached to a story, they never seem to tire of it." There was no real complaint in her tone though. "I know someone who would benefit from your library. She's a fine woman but isolated by circumstance…"

"Exactly the sort of person who appreciates the company of a good book."

"There's something you should know about her." Mrs. Morgan lowered her voice to a whisper, though there wasn't a soul in range to eavesdrop. "She's a wet nurse. She calls herself Mrs. Rhodes, but she was never married. She takes in children—illegitimate children, that is, of wealthy or highborn parents who won't claim them."

"I'm not sure," Bonny murmured, though she couldn't help but wonder if Mr. Gavin's supposed child might have spent time in this woman's care. Lord Loel hadn't named the mother; if she existed, she could be anyone.

"She deserves a bit of kindness, Miss Reed, and it would mean so much to her," said Mrs. Morgan. "It's been more than ten years since she... made her mistake... and she's never repeated it. She mothers those poor abandoned children as if they were her own."

Bonny crumbled. "We'll pay her a visit."

Bonny Reed did not look well when she visited Woodclose on Saturday. No. That wasn't right. Beauty like hers never dulled. The whole range of human emotions could play across her face, and instead of diminishing her, the paltriest and foulest aspects of human nature would become beautiful.

Fear, hatred, guilt. Even anxiety, which he saw now, could be transformed. She'd turned pale—exquisitely pale, like ivory—and shadows as delicately mauve as the petals of an orchid circled her eyes, making them appear deep-set and profound.

It was absurd. A trick. And impossible not to be affected.

"How is Mr. Gavin?" he asked, because it wasn't hard to guess the source of her unhappiness.

Miss Reed pointedly ignored him, humming as she filled the barrel of the syringe and carefully squirted water onto the *Odontoglossum crispum*'s potting material.

"All's well?" Loel prodded. "How nice for him."

"It's mean-spirited to wish misfortune on your betters," said

Miss Reed in the prim voice she affected sometimes. He couldn't tell if she used it to disguise the fact that she was saying something rather bold... or to highlight it. Either seemed possible.

So he laughed, as intended, and her answering smile was shy and pleased.

"I haven't ignored your warning," she added. "I'm investigating."

"You are?"

"So there's no point in insulting him further," she said firmly. "You'll only make me think less of you."

"I'm surprised that's possible."

She looked at him sidelong. Her eyes were hazel, greenish near the pupil transitioning to amber at the edge of the cornea. Wide set, which contributed to her air of innocence, and lively. Every quick glance had a sparkle to it.

"Of course it is," she teased.

"Either I've risen in your estimation, or"—he swept his gaze across the greenhouse—"the orchids have won you over."

"It's the orchids," she returned, and this time her smile was wide and genuine.

He felt ridiculously proud of himself. He'd always looked down on men who made fools of themselves over women. He'd never hung on a woman's smiles, lived for her attention, shattered at her tears... and he'd felt good about that. Proud even.

Pride did have a reputation for preceding a fall.

He'd tried to resist. But there was no defense against her beauty, and—though it didn't quite seem possible—he found her more beautiful every time he saw her.

Miss Reed ducked her chin. Her hands fluttered around like a pair of nervous birds, faster and faster until she blurted, "Have you ever kissed a woman?"

Had he—?

Was Bonny Reed flirting with him? As soon as he had the thought, he knew the answer: No. She thought she was in love with the world's greatest boor. She wasn't, and he hoped she'd realize it in time to break the engagement, but in the meanwhile, she wasn't *flirting*.

"Why do you ask?"

"I wondered if you'd explain how it's supposed to happen." She tried to meet his eyes but lost her courage and scratched her nose instead. "The way you explained how to water the plant. Step-by-step."

"Tell me what's upset you and I'll try."

"Mr. Gavin is very enthusiastic—"

"Enthusiastic." Loel interrupted. A euphemism if he'd ever heard one.

Miss Reed blushed. "It's a great compliment, of course—"

Hearing Bonny Reed make excuses for her fiancé's swinish behavior filled him with a rage so white-hot it could have warmed his greenhouses for a decade.

"He was rough with you," said Loel, anger leaking into his voice.

Miss Reed licked her lips and said... nothing.

"And you didn't like it."

"I thought perhaps I might be doing something wrong or not understanding something that should be obvious..."

Good God. He couldn't listen to any more of this. "The only thing you've done wrong is blame yourself."

"I didn't ask for your opinion." She cleared her throat in that prim, chiding way of hers. "Just... your instructions. Since you seem to have a gift for describing simple actions in minute detail."

Her reaction told him everything he needed to know. Charles Gavin had made her feel small and inadequate. But give her a bit of room to express herself, the most basic reassurance, and she had fire to spare.

"Quite a compliment," he said wryly. "No doubt it's your gift for flattery that has made you beloved from one end of New Quay to the other."

"I'm an honest person who looks for the best in people." Miss

Reed clucked her tongue. "It's unfortunate that you give me so little to work with."

It would have been easy to respond in the same vein. More humor would lighten her mood. It would be safer. But who else could she talk to? How many of them were looking out for her welfare instead of their own?

She wanted to dance around the issue, but he addressed it directly. Plainly. With all the gravity he could muster.

"You should never, *ever* be frightened of a man's affection."

"I didn't say I was frightened," she said quickly.

"You didn't need to say it."

She crumbled. And he did too. He wanted, more and more, to be of use to her. But all he had to offer were these painful truths. Considering how his voyage aboard the *Incitatus* had ended, he found bitter irony in the fact that he could best help Miss Reed by hurting her.

"Desire can be sweet and gentle and mild," he said. "But sometimes it's strong and fierce—it can be, it can *feel*, overpowering. Many people would say that's the best kind."

Miss Reed's eyes went wide as saucers. "Not nice people."

Oh, the nicest. But he wouldn't convince her of that with words. He shrugged. "What matters is that any man worthy of the name learns to master himself, to control his desires. You should be able to approach as near as you like—to reach out and touch the most animal part of him—without ever feeling fear."

She shivered.

The smallest, pettiest part of him rose to the fore. It saw her fear and insisted: *I'll show you how it's done.* He extended his hand, palm up. "Give me your hand."

She skittered away. "I don't think that's a good idea."

He held still.

She promptly knotted her fingers together and mashed them against her breast. "Just my hand?"

He nodded.

"Why?"

"Why not?"

She inched her palm toward his in fits and starts. He stilled the urge to reach or grab. Kept even his fingers immobile, waiting, lest the slightest twitch scare her away. All successful gardeners learned patience.

He felt her touch through his whole body.

This would be harder than he had expected. But he'd meant what he said and he would prove it even if it killed him. He was afraid it might.

He shifted his grip so that her hand lay cradled in his larger one, both palms up. Then with his free hand he began to unbutton her glove, folding the soft leather over itself, a move that served two purposes: It bared her wrist and bound her fingers.

Instead of lifting her hand to his mouth, he bent to kiss the bared sliver of flesh at her wrist, inhaling the scent of her skin like the finest perfume.

Then he looked up to meet her eyes, because she needed to see the truth he'd wanted to hide—even from himself. Especially from himself. He burned with desire when he saw her. He burned with desire when she came close. Everything about her made him *burn*.

And still he touched his lips to her wrist as lightly as a down feather falling onto a rose petal.

It wasn't what he wanted to do. He would have preferred to strip her, to explore her secret places, to feast. That didn't matter, not at all. This was what she needed and—therefore—what she deserved.

He kissed her wrist again, tasting this time. Savoring. His greed permitted this one small liberty. He wouldn't likely get another chance.

Enough. He occupied himself with folding back her glove, fastening the tiny shell buttons, giving himself time to reel in the beast he'd unleashed. By the time he'd straightened, he'd succeeded. His feelings for Bonny Reed were back where they belonged, locked tight and buried deep.

"You know that you are beautiful," he said.

She began to shake her head, but he didn't wait for her to contradict him. He would not offer the courtesy of pretense.

"I do not think you understand how beautiful." How could she? She'd never seen much of the world. He'd circled the globe, and he'd never met another woman who could *compare*. "If you wanted a husband who would prostrate himself at your feet and worship you, you would have no trouble finding one. If you demanded this of him every day of your married life, year after year until his knees crumbled to dust, he would still get down on those ruined knees to thank God that you chose him."

Miss Reed tittered. "Don't be absurd."

He was dead serious. "If Charles Gavin has convinced you that he is your equal, he is a liar. When you chose him, it was an act of *grace*."

Her lips parted. Her pupils dilated. He'd expected horror, perhaps disgust, but he'd been wrong. She was *aroused*. He could hardly believe it, but she scrabbled at the buttons she'd just fastened, suddenly desperate to undo them again.

"No." Loel tapped his knuckles on the nearest table, jarring her back to reality. And to shame. "You are engaged to be married, Miss Reed."

She froze.

"Perhaps you shouldn't be," he added.

"I have to go," she declared, backing away, smiling a false, brittle smile. Pale again and drawn and unhappy. "I'll see you soon, I'm sure. Very busy day ahead. You must have a great deal to do."

She babbled until she reached the door. He let her go, following slowly, giving her time to reach the drive before he followed her into the open air. It was cold and real, not the artificial softness of the orchid house, but the shock didn't clear away the startling thought that rattled around in his brain.

Bonny Reed was attracted to him.

Not just attracted; he'd sensed that from the beginning. He'd assumed she simply liked a certain style of man. He and Charles Gavin fit a similar mold, physically.

But he'd been kissing women's hands all his life and he'd never before been moved by the experience. Certainly not enough to open his mouth and spout passionate, dramatic nonsense. But that's what he'd just done—and unless he badly misunderstood, her feelings had echoed his.

What if he could have her? What if he could be the man on his knees, thanking God every day until he couldn't stand? Even as he chided himself for concocting such a fanciful image, a thread of fantasy spooled out: Bonny Reed in his bed, Bonny Reed with his baby...

He snipped it. If it hadn't been for the fire, she would be wealthy and beyond his reach. And so she would remain, to him at least, because he would take no benefit from the harm he had caused.

BONNY DECIDED that nothing had happened. Lord Loel had kissed her wrist, which was quite ordinary and unremarkable. Even Mrs. Henley, renowned stickler for propriety, wouldn't have much to say against that. Being alone with Lord Loel in the first place, yes. But a chaste kiss, the kind exchanged in polite greetings almost every day? No.

So. Nothing. Bonny was glad to have that sorted in her mind because for a little while it had felt like *something*. For a little while she'd believed that she'd gazed into Lord Loel's arsenic-green eyes and seen right through to his soul. For a little while she'd been terrified—though not of him. She could have stripped naked and sat down to tea with Loel, and he wouldn't have taken a liberty that she did not grant willingly in advance.

No, she'd been afraid of *herself*. Afraid that Loel had seen into her soul as she'd seen into his. Afraid because the heat in her blood, the hunger at her core, had been for him and not the man she'd agreed to marry.

But that couldn't be true.

When she met Cordelia on Monday for their first delivery circuit to include Mrs. Rhodes, Bonny didn't mention the kiss. Cordelia would have insisted that wanting something to be untrue didn't make it untrue. Cordelia would have made Bonny examine her feelings and call each one by its proper name. By the time Bonny had finished this imaginary conversation with Cordelia in her mind, she knew better than to start it in reality.

The kiss had been nothing. It had to be nothing.

Mrs. Rhodes's small cottage occupied a large plot of land, bounded by a sturdy fence in good repair. Much of the lawn had been given over to pall-mall, with iron arches staked into the ground and colored balls lying abandoned in the grass. Swings hung from the spreading branches of ancient trees, several metal soldiers faced off against one another on a wide windowsill, and —to cap it all off—when Mrs. Rhodes opened the door, the sweet scent of freshly baked pie wafted out

"Ladies?" Mrs. Rhodes was beautiful, plump, and obviously nervous. "Is there something I can do for you?"

Bonny showed Mrs. Rhodes her basket of books. "I'm Bonny Reed, and this is Cordelia Kelly. A friend of yours, Mrs. Morgan, thought you might like to become a member of our circulating library."

"Member?" Mrs. Rhodes glanced warily from Bonny to Cordelia and back. "How much does it cost?"

"Nothing at all."

"Nothing? I'm not sure I understand." Mrs. Rhodes shook specks of flour from her bare hands. "Would you like to come in? I've just made some pie."

Bonny said, "We'd love to come in," right as Cordelia answered, "Right here is fine."

Cordelia shot Bonny a hard look. For once, Bonny responded in kind.

Mrs. Rhodes opened the door wider. Bonny stepped through, and Cordelia followed reluctantly behind. They settled in a cozy, well-lit room where a crib held pride of place. Mrs. Rhodes had to move toys off the stained, lumpy sofa to make room for Cordelia and Bonny.

"I'll only be a moment," she promised.

Once they were alone, Cordelia leaned close and whispered, "What are you about?"

"I wanted a slice of pie."

"Pie?"

Bonny nodded seriously.

"You'd send the whole town into a tizzy—for a piece of pie?"

"It smells wonderful."

"*Bonny.*"

"Worry about it later. We're already inside."

Mrs. Rhodes reappeared before Cordelia could press her case further, carrying a tray laden with cups and cutlery, a large teapot, and already-plated slices of strawberry pie. And what beautiful pie! The crust browned just so, just the right amount of ruby-red filling oozing onto the plate.

Bonny sighed happily. "Oh, thank you."

"It's easier to make the little ones eat their vegetables when the whole house smells of pudding," said Mrs. Rhodes. "Now, you say you have a library?"

"Yes, especially for women." Bonny began the familiar patter. "We acquire books that we think our members will enjoy— engaging and entertaining books rather than instructive ones. You don't choose the titles; we choose them for you. And we always ask your opinion afterward, so we can keep a record of which books you liked and which you didn't. We endeavor to match what we have available to your tastes."

"We don't yet have a dedicated facility," Cordelia added. "The library is my home, essentially, so we deliver the books by hand."

"That's right." Bonny nodded. "Every two weeks we deliver a new book and collect the old one."

"And you do this for *free*?"

"Reading for pleasure is often seen as frivolous, but I believe it ought to be encouraged," said Cordelia. "The education of women is too often neglected. I won't pretend our library is a cure—it is explicitly not—but it *is* a step in the right direction."

"I do love to read," admitted Mrs. Rhodes.

"We brought a book for you." Bonny plucked *The Tenant of Wildfell Hall* out of her basket and handed it over. "In case you'd like to give the library a try."

"Would you look at this?" Mrs. Rhodes marveled, turning the book over in her hands. "I've never seen such a beautiful binding."

"Miss Kelly binds them herself." Bonny beamed proudly. "She has an artistic eye, doesn't she?"

Mrs. Rhodes flipped to the frontispiece. "Incredible."

Bonny stood. "So we'll return for it in two weeks?"

Before they said their goodbyes, Bonny tugged lightly on her necklace. She hadn't fastened the clasp that morning, so it easily slipped loose and fell into the palm of her hand. Surreptitiously she dropped it between the cushions of the sofa.

Then, while she and Cordelia were walking down the lane away from the cottage, Bonny staggered and gasped, clasping at her breast.

"Oh, Cordelia," she cried. "I've lost my necklace."

Cordelia cast a searching eye over the dirt road. "Which one?"

"The Tahitian pearl my father gave me when I was little."

Cordelia winced.

"It might have fallen loose while we were at Mrs. Rhodes's cottage," said Bonny. "I'm going to go back and check."

"Of course."

"No, no, you keep walking." Bonny shooed Cordelia down the road. "You're too slow as it is."

"I'm not slow," Cordelia protested. "You're too fast. You scamper. It's undignified."

"You're a turtle," Bonny retorted. "Keep walking. I'll be quick

—I just want to check the sofa where we were sitting. I almost think I felt it fall, something ticklish on my neck that I took for a loose strand of hair..."

Cordelia took the book basket. "I hope you're right."

Bonny dashed back up the walk alone. She had not, in fact, lost her necklace. She had dropped it on purpose. Mrs. Rhodes raised bastard children—if Mr. Gavin had one, it might have ended up in her care. Even if it hadn't, she might know who else to ask. She might keep track of other unmarried mothers in New Quay, the same way that Bonny kept track of the girls her own age.

She hated keeping secrets from Cordelia, but their last conversation about Mr. Gavin had made her wary. If Cordelia learned about Loel's accusations, she might believe them. She might not care if the "proof" never materialized.

Cordelia could be forceful and persuasive, and Bonny... Bonny was susceptible.

A quick knock brought Mrs. Rhodes to the door again. Bonny explained that she'd lost her necklace and was allowed inside.

"I'm afraid that I've returned on a pretense." She went immediately to the sofa and plucked the glittering chain from between the cushions. "Actually, I wanted to ask you a question, but I didn't want Miss Kelly to overhear."

Mrs. Rhodes's sweet face hardened. "Ask then."

"I heard a rumor that the man I'm engaged to marry has an illegitimate child here in New Quay," said Bonny. "But I won't believe it until I've seen the proof, and I've no idea how to find the child or its mother. I thought... I thought perhaps you might be able to help me."

"The parents of the children who come to me go to great lengths to remain anonymous," said Mrs. Rhodes. "In most cases, I never learn their names—an intermediary arranges everything. I understand that many of them are afraid of being blackmailed."

Bonny wilted. "Oh."

"They mean well," said Mrs. Rhodes. "They want their children brought up properly, to have good lives. Many people, in similar situations, do much less."

Bonny shivered. Many wet nurses *said* they would care for unwanted babies while, with a sly wink, promising something different entirely. They made sure their charges died, seemingly of natural causes—babies were so frail, after all.

A single bad decision, made out of passion and weakness, could lead to so many painful choices with sorrow at the end of every branch. It wasn't right. It wasn't *proportionate*.

Mrs. Rhodes could have tried to disappear, to assume a false identity, attempting to cheat rules that must have seemed so unfair after she'd been caught breaking them. Instead, she'd dedicated herself to making sure that other women who strayed might face a dilemma ever so slightly less heartbreaking than her own.

Bonny had been afraid to visit her. Afraid of guilt by association. And it struck her, with humbling force, that Mrs. Rhodes was a braver woman by far than Bonny herself.

She hadn't done anything grand or heroic. But she'd made her life's work into a chisel strike against a stone that must, inevitably, take on a new shape. In that way, she reminded Bonny of Cordelia.

"I admire what you've accomplished here," said Bonny. "You've made a beautiful home. I didn't mean to suggest otherwise."

Mrs. Rhodes smiled a mother's kind smile. "How are you to know if you don't ask?"

"Thank you for understanding." Bonny bobbed a curtsy. "Miss Kelly will be waiting."

"Is that why you brought me the book? Was it a ruse?"

"Oh, no." Bonny squeezed all the sincerity she could into her voice. "We didn't invent the library for a stunt. The book is yours for two weeks, and there will be more for as long as you're interested. Ask Mrs. Morgan if you have any questions."

Mrs. Rhodes breathed a sigh of relief. "Good."

The baby began to fuss. Bonny took that as her cue to leave, but Mrs. Rhodes caught her at the door.

"It may be that I could help you in your search," said the woman. "What's the gentleman's name?"

"Mr. Charles Gavin."

"I know him," said Mrs. Rhodes in a neutral tone. So neutral, in fact, that it changed the meaning of her words. She knew Charles Gavin—*and did not feel warmly toward him*. She hadn't said anything against him or his powerful family, but she had withheld praise… and that was significant.

"Do you think it could be true?" Bonny asked.

"Miss Reed, I'd be astonished if it weren't." Mrs. Rhodes heaved a weary sigh. An edge of bitterness, old enough to lose most of its bite, entered her tone. "But you're looking for proof. I'll see what I can find out."

Bonny had no trouble catching up to Cordelia, who—typically—had not progressed very far down the road. She brandished her pearl necklace. "Will you fasten it?"

Cordelia obliged and they continued on, side by side, as though everything were normal. Bonny clung to the illusion; it comforted her even if she couldn't quite believe.

CHAPTER 8

Bonny felt nervous about returning, but abandoning Loel, and her *Odontoglossum crispum* would have been an admission of guilt. Since nothing had happened (if she told herself so enough times, she might even believe it), Bonny showed up at Woodclose as usual.

And felt tremendous relief when she saw no sign of Lord Loel. The orchid house was unlocked though, so she entered on her own. She'd fetch his instruments and water the *Odontoglossum crispum* herself.

She ducked under a spike of orchids the color of a dawn sky, moved a trailing vine off the paving stones to prevent a spray of gorgeous yellow flowers veined in deep violet from being crushed, dodged the profusion of leaves and blooms clogging the walkway, and collided with something large… and warm… and human.

Bonny yelped as she toppled over Lord Loel's kneeling form. She threw out her arms in instinctive reaction, and both hands landed on his back, sheathed in thin linen and damp from exertion.

She hopped back, wiping her hands on her skirt. She wished her palms would stop tingling, wished she could get the scent of his body out of her nose. It was disgusting. Completely disgusting. Sweat and stink and—oh, heaven help her, if she could have buried her nose in his armpit without anyone knowing, she absolutely would have done it.

He said nothing, neither mocking nor kind. She would have thought him stone if she hadn't seen desire in his eyes the last time she'd come, if he hadn't put his hunger on open display.

His expression shuttered quickly, but just that moment—that brief reminder of what she'd tried so hard to forget—threw her completely off-balance.

"What were you doing down there?" she demanded.

"One of the paving stones was loose."

She could have gleaned the answer if she'd bothered to look. He'd surrounded himself with mallets, tubs of sand, and mortar. She was lucky she hadn't knocked one of them over.

"Why don't you hire someone?" She had no right to be angry or to raise her voice, but she couldn't help it. "If these plants are even half as valuable as you say, you could afford a whole *army* of gardeners to help you."

He rocked back on his heels and bit out, "Who, in New Quay, would want that job?"

No one.

Bonny swallowed.

He stood, slow and deliberate, obviously trying not to spook her. The small part of her not in danger of being spooked was horribly embarrassed.

"You're looking for the rose?"

Bonny nodded.

"I'll get it for you."

She followed him to the far end of the orchid house to a clear area dominated by a large, freestanding water tank. It was at least waist high and ovoid in shape, wider than her arm span.

Loel went to a nearby table stacked with tiny cabinets and littered with bizarre instruments. The only one Bonny recognized was the rose.

She approached the tank instead. An unadorned iron pipe rose up from the basin and poured water into a trough hanging from an iron strut overhead. The trough ended in a tiny waterfall, the first in the series of cascades that ended on the other side of the greenhouse.

"Miss Reed?"

Bonny turned. Loel stood by the narrow path, rose and empty bowl in hand. She took a few quick steps, responding instinctively to the invitation in his voice, and froze when she saw the bed.

She hadn't noticed it before while she'd been facing in the wrong direction. It was a humble thing, just a thin mattress over an iron frame, white sheets tucked neatly in, the pillow perfectly centered. *He sleeps here.* Bonny looked around, all her nerves suddenly alive and prickling. *Among the flowers.*

"So I can keep the stoves burning all night," he said quietly, and the words were meaningless while the rough gravel of his voice was like a draught of some forbidden stimulant delivered straight into her bloodstream. "I have to get up every few hours to tend them."

She imagined him lying down while the stoves flared red around him, sweat beading on his brow and slowly cooling as the temperature dipped until he stirred again.

"How long has it been since you slept through the night?" Bonny asked breathlessly.

"Years." His cool green eyes roamed freely for a moment, lingering at her bodice. "Ask me something else."

Bonny shivered and, licking her lips, quickly returned to the front of the greenhouse.

Loel arrived with the bowl and the rose a moment later. Bonny took both and held the bowl to the fountain with trembling hands, still shaking with reaction.

Loel seemed unmoved, which stupefied her. He propped his hip against the table and folded his arms across his chest. The linen of his shirt pulled tight around his biceps; the twill of his trousers strained at his hips and thighs. He was beautiful.

Bonny filled the syringe in the bowl and pointed the perforated bulb at the wood chips. She couldn't concentrate on the task and wondered, hysterically, if her heart's violent beating could crack her ribs.

"Don't rush," murmured Loel. "You're still getting to know the orchid. Pick it up, take a closer look. Learn its needs, its likes and dislikes."

Bonny's cheeks burned. "Stop that."

"Stop what?"

"Saying suggestive things."

"How was what I said suggestive?"

She wasn't sure, actually. But she had a very strong suspicion that she was right.

"Miss Reed, when it comes to orchids, there is no escape from it," said Loel. "Even the name—orchid comes from the Greek. *Orkhis.*"

"I don't have any Greek."

"No? The word translates, quite literally, as *testicle.*"

"I don't know that word."

"Oh?"

"I've never heard it before," she insisted.

A wicked smile tilted Loel's lips. "You seem to know what it means."

"I don't know a thing." She firmed her tone. "And don't you dare explain it to me."

"If you should grow curious, take a look at the flower's bulbs. They bear a striking resemblance to—"

Bonny narrowed her eyes, and to her extreme satisfaction, Loel did not finish the sentence.

"If that doesn't catch your interest..." Loel's glance slid to the ranks of flowers blooming all around them, with their rippling petals and secret centers. "Perhaps you find the flowers themselves comfortingly familiar?"

"Not even a little."

"I believe you are a liar, Miss Reed."

"That doesn't concern me at all."

"Good. If you don't mind, I haven't offended."

Bonny opened her mouth to protest. Loel's smile widened in anticipation, teeth flashing.

He was doing this on purpose! Poking and prodding, insisting that she acknowledge that something had changed—and once she realized it, she had to refuse the bait.

Bonny hefted the *crispum*, as instructed, giving it a close look. The long, blade-shaped leaf wasn't quite so droopy as it had been the last time. Perhaps her singing had worked.

She began humming as she carefully returned the flower to its table and moistened the wood chips. When she risked a glance at Loel, his expression had returned to its default state, prickly and inscrutable.

She expelled the rest of the water into the bowl and weighed the plant again. This time she could feel the difference in weight— insignificant but real.

Progress.

But on her way home, she wondered if she ought to return. The obligation she'd incurred by knocking over Lord Loel's orchid had to be weighed on a balance against the risk she took by visiting Woodclose. She would have liked to pretend otherwise, but ever since Lord Loel had kissed her wrist, that balance had tipped.

The orchid wouldn't need watering for a few days. She had time to consider her options.

BONNY HEARD from Mrs. Rhodes when she and Cordelia made their next delivery to Mrs. Morgan. The harried mother slipped a square of folded paper into Bonny's sleeve with a subtlety that unnerved Bonny; where had she learned to do that?

Bonny didn't dare open the note in front of her family, because someone (most likely her appallingly perceptive mother) would surely notice and ask questions. For the same reason, she couldn't risk lighting a candle in her room at night, so she waited until the next morning to read the note.

It was brief and discreet, to Bonny's relief.

Miss Reed,

I believe you wish to speak to young Charles Dunaway who lives at 18 Crescent Court. He is seven years old.

All best in your inquiries,

Mrs. Rhodes

Bonny burned the note, then didn't do anything about it for several days. Why bother? The child, apparently, was real. Lord Loel had been right, and Charles Gavin had fathered a bastard.

Except that she couldn't stop thinking about the fatherless child. She began sewing a present for Charles Dunaway in the evenings, a small stuffed dog with a patchwork coat. He must have been named after his father, but why? Was it a sign that the relationship between Mr. Gavin and the mother had been a tender one, with affection on both sides?

Her first impulse was to talk to Cordelia. But she knew exactly what Cordelia would say. What's more, she knew how Cordelia would react if Bonny refused, again, to call off her engagement.

Lord Loel would have made a better confidant. After he'd finished gloating, she knew that he would listen and take her concerns seriously. The eagerness with which she grasped at this excuse to seek him out told her she ought to stay far, far away.

People made mistakes. If Mr. Gavin had taken responsibility for his, if he'd fulfilled his obligations to mother and child, then Lord Loel might have told her the truth but been wrong in all the ways that mattered.

Bonny decided to visit the boy. She hoped to find a happy child, loved and cared for despite the unfortunate circumstances of his birth. Of course, given his high standing in town, Charles Gavin had kept the child a secret. She couldn't blame him for that.

In fact, she appreciated this window into her fiancé's true self, the deeds he committed when he thought no one was looking. It could easily turn out that, at the end of this investigation, she thought *better* of Mr. Gavin than she had before.

Her destination at Crescent Court was a neat, well-kept cottage. Prosperous looking, on a quiet street with chicken scratching in the new grass and a shaggy pony sharing space with squawking geese in a large pen.

If the people inside were half as wholesome and charming as the home they kept...

She knocked on the door and asked the footman who answered if Charles Dunaway was at home.

"Charles Dunaway?" The footman appeared affronted. "What are you here for? Go around the back." He squinted. "What's your business with him?"

"Oh, a friend of the family knew I'd be in the neighborhood and asked me to give him a little present." Her stuffed dog, in addition to being adorable, made an excellent pretext.

"Friend of the family?" repeated the footman, voice rising in astonishment. "Do you have a card?"

A few and she didn't like to give them out, as they came dear, but she handed one over.

"Miss Bonny Reed." The footman's skeptical expression slowly transitioned to one of understanding and curiosity. "Come in. I'll send the boy up, but you mustn't take much of his time; he's not meant to be upstairs."

Bonny's heart sank as the situation came clear. She wasn't meant to use the front door, the boy wasn't meant to be upstairs— he didn't live here, he *worked* here.

The salon was lovely, like the rest of the house. Tasteful and lived-in, with personal touches scattered all about. Bonny paced back and forth, thinking of excuses. At least little Charles Dunaway had been placed in a good home instead of someplace worse. That was something.

But he was seven! Of course some families couldn't help but

send their young children out to work, but Charles Gavin was a wealthy man. He ought to be providing for the mother of his child, making sure his boy could go to school.

A handsome child slipped inside and shut the door gently behind him. He was too thin, though she wasn't sure if that was because he was malnourished or simply because growing boys shot up at such a rate. With his strong cleft chin and liquid brown eyes, he bore a remarkable resemblance to his father.

He huddled by the wall, wide-eyed and afraid. "You wanted to speak to me, miss?"

"Are you Mr. Charles Dunaway?" Bonny asked.

The boy nodded.

"You've nothing to fear. I'll only keep you a minute." She offered him the little present, wrapped in colored paper and tied with a ribbon. "This is for you, from..." She'd planned to say that his father had sent it but considering his situation, she thought better of it. "A friend."

"Oh." He took the packet. "It's very pretty."

"You can open it, if you like."

"There's something inside?" He shook the box curiously and then his expression tightened. "What do you want for it?"

"Nothing at all," Bonny said indignantly—and then, on second thought, "Though I'd be grateful if you'd answer a few questions."

"What kind of questions?"

"Simple ones," Bonny assured him. "For example: How long have you been working here?"

He counted on his fingers, mouthing the names of the months as he tapped each one. "Five months now."

"And do you see your mother very often?"

The boy didn't answer.

"Is something the matter?"

"I'm not supposed to talk about my mother."

Bonny's heart cracked. "Why not?"

"Because this is a decent house for decent people."

"I see." Bonny smiled sadly. "What about your father?"

"What about him?"

"Can you tell me anything about him?"

"I don't know anything." His little brow furrowed. "And that's the truth even if you want your present back."

"The gift is yours," said Bonny. "Would you like to open it?"

He began to pick at the present, careful not to rip the paper. He opened up the box and lifted out a little stuffed dog, made from bits and pieces of scrap—a brown nose made from wool that she'd used to sew a coat for her father, floppy ears of soft velvet left over from the cuffs of a gown for her sister, the body a masculine paisley print that had once been a waistcoat. She'd even added little leather pads to the paws.

"Oh, look." Charles Dunaway began petting the stuffed dog's soft ears. Her gift was so small, so inadequate to the situation, and yet the boy's tenderness brought tears to Bonny's eyes. "Oh, wow."

"Do you like it?" Bonny asked.

He looked up, his eyes as wide as saucers. "It's beautiful."

"I'm glad." Bonny bent and received a careful kiss on the cheek. "Thank you for seeing me, Mr. Dunaway."

The boy tugged on her skirt before she could leave.

"What is it?"

"Do you know who my papa is?"

Bonny's heart dropped into her stomach. "I do," she admitted. "But if your mother hasn't told you—"

The boy's expression turned sullen.

"I believe she knows what's best," said Bonny, devastated by her own words.

She left feeling sick at heart—not only had Mr. Gavin fathered a child out of wedlock, he'd abandoned the boy. It was heartless.

She started in the direction of home, walking at a pace that would have suited Cordelia at her most intransigent. She felt sick and… and… *scared*. After Loel had warned her about Mr. Gavin, she'd gone searching for the truth, but all she'd really wanted was peace of mind. She'd wanted to go back to thinking of Mr. Gavin as a good man and worthy husband.

Instead, her peace of mind had been shattered.

Because it turned out that Charles Gavin was neither good nor worthy. He was loathsome. And without the rosy glamour of romance, she saw their relationship for what it was: a mercenary exchange. Her beauty in trade for his money, her happiness as payment for her family's comfort.

She'd always known that money was *part* of Mr. Gavin's allure, that she admired him for his looks and his charm and his fortune. But so long as wealth had been one element that she weighed along with the rest, that hadn't seemed so wrong. Now she felt guilty and ashamed.

A warm hand landed at the small of her back.

Bonny instinctively turned into the touch. It must have been the smell that cued her, a blend of wood chips and wet stone and the gentle perfume of flowers uprooted from distant homes. Lord Loel had found her.

And she was glad.

CHAPTER 9

L oel had wandered from stall to stall at the Sunday market, a basket under one arm. Most shopkeeps in New Quay refused to sell to him, but the Sunday markets attracted vendors from across the county. They came with their fruits and vegetables, their flour and salt, and they didn't care who he was, so long as his money was good.

He could only imagine how he would have reacted if, as a boy, someone had told him that in the future, he'd have to do his own marketing. That he would care whether the onions he tucked into his basket had brown spots or know which merchants hid rotten salad greens beneath fresh ones and tried to sell them all as good.

Not well. That was certain.

And then Bonny Reed had walked by, and he forgot about produce or anything else at all. She wore pale green today, a dress he'd seen before. It flattered her—or she flattered it, more like, giving a simple gown more glamour than it had any right to.

She'd thrown a shawl over her shoulders for warmth, its tassels swaying in rhythm with her skirt, and a bonnet of some filmy fabric decorated with fresh flowers.

Someone knocked into Loel's shoulder, breaking his trance.

Loel braced himself for an insult, but it wasn't anyone he recognized. Just a passerby who'd energetically sidestepped a sticky-fingered child, running circles around his mother and brandishing a treat that oozed honey. Loel accepted the man's quick apology and let his attention swing back where it wanted to go.

But in the process he saw that half the men in the market square had stopped what they were doing to watch Miss Reed. It was like gravity. Everywhere Miss Reed went, her heavenly body became, briefly, the center of their universes. Loel's attraction wasn't special—it was dull as dirt. What could be more boring than a man's dogged fixation on a beautiful woman? Nothing.

But something about her posture nagged at him. She walked with chin down, not meeting anyone's eyes or looking about to greet her neighbors. Her shoulders drooped, her cheeks were damp—

Good God. She was *crying*.

And all alone. He made another quick survey of the square, but no one—male or female—had gone to her aid. With a muttered curse, Loel hurried to intercept her.

He touched the small of her back as he drew close, murmuring, "Allow me to escort you, Miss Reed," so that she wouldn't be startled.

"Lord Loel?" She wiped at her eyes. "What are you doing here?"

Loel raised the basket hanging from his elbow a few inches, drawing her attention to it. "It's market day."

"You do your own marketing?"

Loel sighed. "Yes."

"Oh." Miss Reed blinked and sniffled. Her lashes were wet and dark and clumped, stark black against pallid cheeks. The contrast made her hazel eyes glow.

And he was admiring her appearance again.

Ashamed of himself, Loel looked away. "Will you allow me to keep you company until you reach your destination?"

"Oh, certainly. You may take me right to the end of the earth, and then drop me off it."

Her tone was tart, but he could tell she was angry with herself, not him. He offered his arm. "We can walk but perhaps not so far. Are you sure you won't tell me what's wrong?"

She slumped, a gesture of defeat or—perhaps—relief at being able to unburden herself. He suspected the latter since she immediately hooked her arm around his elbow and leaned into him.

"You might be the only person I *can* tell."

"Oh?"

"You were right," she said. "Mr. Gavin has an illegitimate child. A boy named Charles. He's young and healthy and handsome—just like his papa. The resemblance is startling."

"You can see a resemblance already?" Loel counted in his head. He'd acquired this bit of gossip from Charles Gavin's own lips, only a few months before the fire. The girl that Gavin had dallied with—a maid, if he remembered correctly—had only just fallen pregnant.

Loel had been a newly minted eighteen. In those days, his yacht brought him into town quite often. He moored her in the harbor and, twice a week, took sailing lessons from a local. He'd usually ended a long day on the water at the pub.

Charles Gavin, only a few years older but infinitely more worldly-wise, had already acquired the habit of holding court at the Lion. He discoursed on hunting, husbandry, newspaper headlines... but mostly women.

In retrospect, it was clear that Gavin embellished most of his stories. Invented some out of whole cloth, twisted others to flatter his vanity. But at the time, Loel had been enthralled. Gavin seemed to have a new tale of debauchery every week, each more exciting than the last to a randy virgin who didn't know any better.

Loel remembered, vividly, an evening when Gavin had boiled over with real fury because a woman he'd dallied with had fallen pregnant. He'd taken the woman's condition as a deliberate insult, a malicious act of betrayal.

His rage had made such an impression that Loel walked away with a highly inaccurate understanding of human biology. It had taken Jacob Benjamin to set him straight—like any true scientist, nothing about his field of study embarrassed Benjamin. He was a naturalist who could describe a woman's monthly cycle as calmly as if he were discussing the weather.

But that had been later. Loel had left New Quay without hearing any additional news about the child. He hadn't been sure if it had survived its birth, if it had lived past its first year. So many infants didn't. And bastards had worse luck than most.

"The child should be seven or so," said Loel.

"Yes, that's right. The eyes are just alike." Miss Reed touched her own eyes, which had gone blank as her vision turned inward toward the memory. "The shape of his mouth, his complexion... I wish I could find some cause to doubt, Lord Loel, truly I do, for the boy's been put to work."

Her voice had gone high and plaintive, a sure sign that she'd seen something awful. But he still asked, "What kind of work?"

"A houseboy. I've seen children set to harsher labor—but nobody hires such young children out unless they have to. Mr. Gavin obviously isn't supporting his son at all. He ought to make sure the boy goes to school, see him set up in a trade—at the very least!"

"Yes."

Miss Reed looked up at him, expecting more, but he didn't know what else to say. She was right. Charles Gavin was a paltry semblance of a man, and his child deserved better.

She searched his expression and then looked away, blushing. With shame, he imagined. She hadn't said a word about ending the engagement.

She cleared her throat. "You said you hadn't told me the worst of it."

"Of Mr. Gavin's flaws, you mean?"

Miss Reed nodded.

"I was mistaken. What you've just discovered is worse than anything I might tell you."

They continued on toward the sea. Loel migrated toward an empty stretch of the quay, with the low tide lapping against the embankment and seagulls wheeling overhead.

After a long silence, Miss Reed spoke. "For years my family has given me a little more of everything because we all understood that, once I was married, Margot would have her turn. They've sacrificed for years without complaint. Shouldn't I be willing to do the same for them?"

"Of course," Loel answered. "So long as there aren't any better choices."

"Better choices!" She shoved away from him. "You are a cruel man, Lord Loel."

"Me?"

"You've taught me to hate the man I am engaged to marry," Bonny cried. "But have you stopped to consider what happens next? If my father's warehouses had never burned, I might have a great many excellent suitors to choose from."

Loel flinched.

Miss Reed pulled her shawl tighter around her shoulders. "But they did burn. And I don't have so many choices. If you'd shown me a man who could provide for my family, I might have thanked you. Instead, you've stolen away all the illusions that made me happy and gave me hope for the future."

"Miss Reed," he said hoarsely. "I am sorry."

"You've said that to me before."

She hadn't wanted to hear it then either.

"I'm not angry," she said. "In fact, I'm sorry that I was ever angry at you. But you knew what I'd discover here. You knew it would be awful, you knew how much it would hurt, but you chose to tell me. It was no accident. Why?"

He thought back to the moment he'd decided to warn her, wondering if he'd harbored ulterior motives.

The denizens of New Quay uniformly preferred to be spared the sight of him. To the extent possible, he obliged them. He knew a few people who would disagree—Mrs. Bailey at the Black Lion, for example—and it was true that he couldn't avoid the town entirely.

But he kept his distance. If not literally, then figuratively. He'd been strongly disinclined to involve himself in Miss Reed's problems—her mistakes, he might have called them.

So he hadn't said anything on her first visit. She hadn't endeared herself to him by damaging his most valuable orchid. Or shaking in her boots at the mere sight of him, like Goldilocks caught plundering the three bears' porridge.

He'd changed his mind after her second visit, when she came to apologize. He'd refused, of course. She owed him nothing. Nothing she could do would ever put her in his debt. Just the thought of her wearing out the soles of her only boots when it was his fault, frankly and directly his fault, that she didn't have a dozen dainty pairs, not to mention a carriage at her disposal... it infuriated him.

But his rejection had wounded her. She'd been sincere; she'd offered an olive branch. And as she walked away, he'd thought: *She is too good for that pig.*

That was when he'd decided to tell her about Gavin's child. But the true answer to her question lay further in the past.

"Do you remember what you said to me, after your father's warehouses burned?"

She folded her arms tight across her chest. "It was a long time ago."

A quelling response, but she hadn't answered no. Which meant that yes, she remembered, but no, she didn't want to talk about it.

He continued anyhow. "After the fire, I sent a letter to your father. I apologized and asked if he would permit me to visit so that I could offer my regrets in person."

He'd sent a letter like that to every family directly affected by the fire. He'd written them himself, one after the other, on what must have been the longest day of his life.

There hadn't been time for blame or recriminations while the blaze raged. Everyone scrambled to contain the flames, relaying buckets of water up from the sea, helping families evacuate their homes, clearing debris from the streets. No one had died, thank God.

The town's anger came later, after the fire was out. And so did his guilt. He'd seen the flames up close, but writing out those letters—thirty-three in all—had brought home the appalling cost of his accident.

He'd tripped. That was all. *Tripped.* And the whole town had burned.

Mr. Reed had never responded to his letter, but Loel paid the family a visit anyhow. The Reeds had started out with more wealth than most people in New Quay could ever dream of possessing, and so they'd lost more than the rest of the townsfolk combined. It would have been cowardly to send a single letter and then wash his hands of them.

And besides, he'd reasoned, he wouldn't force his presence on the Reeds. A servant would answer the door, and if the Reeds didn't want to see him, that servant could send him away.

But the household had been in disarray, all the usual rules thrown out the window.

"You answered the door," Loel continued.

Miss Reed stiffened. She clasped her hands together, fingers tightly laced.

Most memories faded over time. A few—in Loel's experience, never the pleasant ones—retained all their freshness and intensity. It had been eight years since his visit to the Reeds, but recalling it made the old wounds bleed as though they were new.

For her too, apparently.

The whole town had reeked of ash as he made his way through the streets; it stuck in his lungs. People coughed and rubbed at their noses as they swept their stoops. His horse had been frantic.

When he'd finally arrived at his destination, Miss Reed answered the door. With her plump cheeks and solemn eyes, she might have been tailor-made to sear him with guilt.

Guilt had felt different back then. It had been new and raw, and it stung. These days, guilt was more like a pair of lead shoes. Familiar, well-worn, and heavy enough to keep every part of him —mind, body, and soul—earthbound.

He'd asked to speak with her father.

She'd said no. Her voice had been firm, thick with anger, not childish at all.

He'd said please.

"Please." He stood on the pavement with hat in hand. Kept his voice soft. "If you'll just tell him I've come?"

"No," she said again—with an edge now, a hint of relish.

He stumbled then. "Did Mr. Reed receive my letter? Did he ask you to turn me away?"

Miss Reed's thin chest swelled and deflated rapidly with rising emotion, but she'd tired of repeating herself, apparently. She simply glared at him.

He didn't know what to do. "I'd like to apologize. To you too, Miss Reed. I know it won't change what happened—"

"If it won't change what happened, you can keep your apology."

"Will you at least let him know that if there's anything I can do to make this right, anything at all, he has only to ask?"

"Here's what you can do," she spat. "Leave. You can forget about us and New Quay and all of it—just so long as you go away and never come back."

Beside him, Miss Reed shuddered.

"You told me to—"

"I know."

Loel kept going, despite the interruption. She'd asked a hard question. She ought to have guessed that it would have a hard answer. "Leave and—"

"You don't need to repeat—"

"Never come—"

"*Stop!*"

Loel fell silent.

He'd decided to run away from home that very night. It had taken him a few more days to prepare—he'd packed a bag, pinched his mother's pin money, stolen a horse blanket from the stables.

He'd traveled on foot to Liverpool. Knowing how easy it would be to whip up the countryside in search of a young lordling, he'd avoided roads and towns whenever possible. He'd slept out in the open, with the horse blanket for a bed.

Once he'd reached the city, it had been easy to find a berth. The seas were dangerous and the life of a sailor full of privation. Loel knew his way around a ship, and he could read; he'd been overqualified, if anything.

Less than two weeks after Miss Reed told him to go away and never come back, he'd left England. He hadn't returned for more than five years.

Still stiff and tight, without looking at him, Miss Reed asked, "So this is your way of taking revenge?"

"No."

She shook her head ever so slightly, refusing to believe. That stung—even now she could only think the worst of him.

"You had every right to send me away without a word," said Loel. "And every right to be angry, to speak passionately. I had knocked on your door for the express purpose of hearing you out."

"I'm sorry for what I said." She interrupted. "I am so sorry."

And then she relaxed, her posture loosening, arms falling slack to her sides.

The apology rankled. She owed him nothing.

"Why? You said exactly what I needed to hear." He spoke

slowly and deliberately, because he'd finally come to the point. "Not what I wanted to hear, what I *needed* to hear."

He reframed his thoughts so he could explain. "My parents believed that rank conferred both privileges and responsibilities. They took their responsibilities very seriously—that's why they stepped forward to restore the waterfront."

He'd spent a lot of time thinking about how he'd explained his choices to his parents. He could trace a direct line between the fire in New Quay and the decisions he'd made aboard the *Incitatus*. On restless nights in his swaying berth when sleep wouldn't come, he'd searched for the right words. He'd arranged them and rearranged them like a set of puzzle pieces, certain that he'd eventually find the configuration that would make them understand.

While he'd been thinking, they'd been dying. Another lesson he'd learned the hard way.

"But they also saw themselves as the first victims of the fire," Loel continued. "They weren't angry about what I'd done to the town. They were angry about what I'd cost *them*. My parents always thought in terms of the family—and the first priority of every Loel is to preserve what he's been given so it can be passed on to the next generation. When I started the fire, I failed in my first and most essential duty to my family."

He'd understood this so viscerally that, when he'd read his father's will, it hadn't surprised him at all.

"People didn't matter to them," he said. "Feelings didn't matter. *You* wouldn't have mattered. And I would have thought the same, if things had gone differently."

"But the fire changed that."

"*You* did. You insisted that your pain was important." He sighed. "I admit that came as a revelation."

Miss Reed snorted.

Loel suppressed a smile. "It changed everything for me. In some ways—material ways, generally—for the worse. Still, I can't wish the words unsaid."

"So this is your idea of a gift?"

"I wouldn't presume," he returned. "Call it repayment of a debt. One harsh truth for another."

"Thank you for answering my question." Miss Reed rubbed at her face and pinched a bit of color into her cheeks. "My family is taking dinner at Mr. Gavin's house tonight."

"What will you do?"

"I don't know."

～

BONNY ARRIVED home just in time to change her clothes. For a dinner with the Gavins, she'd have to look her absolute best. Charles Gavin had inherited his love of fine tailoring from his mother. Mrs. Gavin prided herself on her fine taste. Along with her fine home and her fine son... she was a proud woman in general.

She had a great deal of influence over her son, and she *terrified* Bonny.

Bonny started with a plain dress in a saturated sky blue. She added an overlay of white *broderie anglaise* she'd made herself, a skirt of lacy panels in the shape of flower petals that tied at the waist, and a matching chemisette. The plain cotton for the overlay had come dear enough; embroidering it had consumed much of the previous summer.

She crossed the corridor to peer into her sister's mirror to make sure the colors contrasted nicely. Margot, who was already standing in front of the small, wood-framed oval hanging on her wall, leaped back with an exaggerated gasp.

"What's this?" she cried. "Has my sister come to engage in an act of *vanity*?"

"Hush." Bonny swatted at her sister and stood back from the mirror, rising up on tiptoes so she could see as much of the dress as possible. "I'm just checking to make sure the dress still hangs properly."

"I'm sorry to be the bearer of bad news, but it looks horrible," said Margot. "Doesn't suit you at all."

Bonny spun, trying to see her backside. "In other words, time to give it to you?"

Most of Margot's clothes were hand-me-downs. Margot never complained... but every once in a while, she did try to hurry the process along. The pink silk she wore that evening had once been Bonny's prized treasure, the fabric a gift on her eighteenth birthday. It would be still, if Margot hadn't asked for it so persistently.

"I'm just looking out for you," said Margot.

"Doing your sisterly duty," Bonny added helpfully.

"Who can be honest with you if not family?"

"The answer to that question might surprise you," Bonny murmured, pinching some color into her cheeks. Despite the fancy clothes, she looked tired and unhappy. "I think if you're coveting the dress, it must still look well enough. Do you need help with your hair?"

Margot pouted. "You don't do hair very well."

"Do you want to help me with mine?"

"I am but your humble servant, m'lady." Margot gestured for Bonny to sit on the bed so that she could kneel on the mattress behind her to get a good angle.

Margot left Bonny's hair smooth in the front, saving her efforts for a riot of curls and braids and ringlets in the back. Bonny tried to return the favor, but Margot had not lied; she hadn't much skill for styling hair.

"Doesn't she look wonderful?" Bonny asked their parents, as their father handed out lanterns on the way out the door.

"I'm a lucky man to have two such beautiful daughters," said Mr. Reed. He offered his arm to Margot. "Shall we lead the way?"

Bonny fell in with their mother. They made the trip on foot, walking arm in arm through the dusk, each with a lit lantern in one hand.

Her mother, father, and sister traded guesses about how many courses the Gavins would serve. They teased Mr. Reed for looking forward to one of Mr. Gavin's fine cigars; they wondered if Mrs. Gavin would wear her best jewelry.

The conversation grated at Bonny's nerves like sandpaper on meringue. She hadn't realized her parents so cherished the little luxuries that had ceased to be part of their lives after the fire.

Bonny wanted her family to be happy. She wanted them to have nice things, to worry a little less and enjoy themselves a little more. But why did it have to depend on *her*?

Even if she wanted to carry on as though nothing had changed, Mr. Gavin would likely sense the truth. She could *try* to treat him with warmth and admiration, as she had in the past, but doubted her acting skills would pass muster.

If she set her mind to it, she could probably fool him for a very short while—until the wedding, for example. Which begged the question: *Should* she? It would be a shabby thing to do.

The Gavins' fine mansion occupied, not at all by chance, the best plot of land in town. Far enough from the quays to escape the unsavory smells, it nevertheless commanded an excellent view of the sea. Equidistant from the church and the Black Lion, it still somehow sat on a street that received very little traffic, with one of New Quay's few public squares just around the corner.

There had once been three great families in New Quay: the Loels, the Reeds, and the Gavins. The Loels owned huge tracts of land outside of town, quarries and dairies and rich inland pastures. The Reeds, for three generations, had controlled the local shipping trade. The Gavins had been, and remained, masters of the town. They owned all the buildings along the main streets and collected rent from the tenants—everyone from the Black Lion to the bawdy house.

The fire had only affected a few of their properties, and the Gavins had built those back bigger and better than before. With the Loels financing the restoration of the quays, their investments had paid off. The family was more prosperous than ever, and they'd recently begun making new purchases, looking farther afield for opportunities to invest.

The same fire that had brought the Reeds and the Loels low had propelled the Gavins to new heights of prominence. In New Quay, they now reigned alone.

The waist-high wrought iron gate stood open. Bonny and her family crossed the narrow strip of garden surrounding the house, the shaped bushes still bare of branches.

A footman answered their knock and took their outdoor things. Mrs. Gavin greeted them with open arms, her wispy hair in an artful tangle atop her head. She wore gray silk, the color gentle enough not to compete with the rainbow of gemstones at her neck, wrists, and throat. As always, there was an inspired elegance to her appearance.

"Come in, come in, it's bitter outside!" Mrs. Gavin ushered them into the receiving room with frantic little flutters of her hands. "Just standing near the door makes me shiver. I can't believe you walked all this way! Here, we have the fires going, warm yourselves. My husband and son will be along shortly. They went out hunting this morning and came home late *and* empty-handed, if you can believe it. But enough of that—thank you so much for coming, we're so glad to have you!"

A part of Bonny sighed with pleasure as she stepped inside. Valuable knickknacks and exotic souvenirs cluttered every flat surface, and little flashes of gold foil glittered on the wallpaper, a red-and-yellow-floral print.

Wealth wouldn't bring her any closer to heaven—the opposite, according to the old parable about the rich man and the eye of the needle. Mr. Gavin's treatment of his child certainly bore out the truth of the tale. Selling the contents of this one room would have been enough to send Charles Dunaway to school and see him apprenticed to a skilled tradesman. To start him off with a business of his own.

And yet, she admitted to herself, a part of her *wanted* all of these lovely things. Just like her parents and her sister, gossiping on the walk. Just like anyone scheming for a better life, for more of the good things that gave them pleasure, for excess and plenty that meant—as much as anything else—freedom from fear.

She understood greed and covetousness. It was only natural, wasn't it? The way that Mr. Gavin's kiss had been natural. Because something could be natural without being good. Without being right or humane—or even close.

What was civilization if not a battle against nature? Against the weeds that threatened every garden, the seeping rot that crumbled castles and cottages, the indiscriminate desires that made monsters out of men?

"Thank you for having us, Mrs. Gavin." Mrs. Reed kissed their hostess on both cheeks before edging closer to the fire. "We've all been looking forward to this dinner."

"It's a treat for me too, I assure you," returned Mrs. Gavin. "It's nice to arrange something so small and intimate for a change. Dinner *en famille*."

Mrs. Reed smiled. "Well, we're about to be family, aren't we? And speaking of which—the oranges that you sent were so delicious."

"Oh, it was my pleasure—Bonny sent a lovely note, as I'm sure you know."

Mrs. Reed nodded toward the west-facing wall, dominated by two large windows. "Those must be the new windows you were talking about?"

"That's right! I've wanted to make the change ever since the glass tax was lifted, but the fire made it impossible"—Mrs. Gavin pursed her lips and huffed in apparent frustration with herself —"I'm sorry, it must seem trivial to you, but it meant so much to finally see this project through."

"Not trivial at all," replied Mrs. Reed, so naturally that even Bonny could hardly spot the lie. "I hadn't realized you'd have such a wonderful sea view from the ground floor."

Mrs. Gavin beamed. "Isn't it a wonderful surprise?"

Both the Gavin men entered, the younger first. They looked a great deal alike, both tall and well formed, but Bonny noted the differences in their behavior in a way she never had before.

Charles Gavin paused in the threshold to pose, one hand on his hip, collecting the admiring looks he both expected and received. Margot sighed so hard it was a wonder she didn't injure her lungs. Bonny couldn't blame her sister. The day's awful revelations hadn't made him any less handsome.

Meanwhile, the elder Mr. Gavin circled the room dispensing greetings. He played a perfect host, offering each of his guests a kind word while drawing ever closer to his wife. When the elder Mr. Gavin reached her side, he touched her lightly on the shoulder, offered her a special smile. It was a subdued demonstration of affection, meant for an audience of one.

Mr. and Mrs. Gavin always seemed so happy with one another. Bonny had assumed that, by accepting Charles Gavin, she'd guarantee the same connubial bliss for herself. Seeing both Gavins together made her heart squeeze. She wanted what they had.

Her attention shifted, inevitably and painfully, to her fiancé. Charles Gavin was watching her with an expression she couldn't decipher, but it was cool enough to banish her fleeting enthusiasm.

Automatically she crossed the room to greet him, to soothe and flatter. Before she could say a word, however, a servant arrived to announce that dinner was ready.

Papa Gavin offered Mrs. Reed his arm, and the assembled company formed up to follow. The dining room was, if anything, more magnificent than the receiving room. The two twin chandeliers ablaze with candles hung from the ceiling, casting a warm glow over a long table covered with two cloths—one exquisite cotton, the other fine lace. The room had been designed to accommodate a much larger party, so only half the table had been set.

Soon after the first course had arrived, a creamed celery soup, Mrs. Gavin cleared her throat in the sort of deliberate way that brought all conversation to a quick halt.

"It's really quite fortuitous that we scheduled this dinner for tonight," she said. "I thought we might have a little talk among ourselves. My husband and son came home this afternoon with very troubling news."

"That's right," said Charles. "We stopped at the Black Lion after our hunt, where nearly everyone we met told us that Miss Reed and Lord Loel were seen walking together this afternoon. Right through the center of town!"

"That can't be right," protested Mrs. Reed while Mr. Reed turned a heavy, doleful stare on Bonny.

"We thought the same," said Charles Gavin.

The elder Mr. Gavin chimed in. "Couldn't believe it."

"But everyone we spoke to told the same story. They couldn't all be wrong. I found myself forced, reluctantly, to believe."

"I take it you weren't aware, Mrs. Reed? Mr. Reed?" Mrs. Gavin asked gently.

"No, I—" Mrs. Reed took a deep breath. "Bonny, is this true?"

Bonny hesitated, but there was no sense in denying it. She'd let Lord Loel escort her right through the center of town on a market day. She nodded.

"And can you explain yourself?" Charles Gavin asked.

Bonny wasn't ready to confront him with what she'd learned about his son; she hadn't decided if she ought to say anything at all. She needed *time*.

So she hid the larger truth in a smaller one. "A few weeks ago I asked Lord Loel about donating a few books to our circulating library. It seemed the least he could do."

Her mother prompted, "You asked him... how? Where did you cross paths?"

"I was on my way home from a visit to Mrs. Twisby. The road runs right past the gates to Woodclose."

"You went to his *home*?" Mrs. Reed exclaimed. "Alone?"

"I walked up the drive," Bonny said. "I didn't go inside the house."

"You shouldn't have set foot on the property!"

"It was a spur-of-the-moment decision." She crossed her fingers under the table. "And nothing came of it—he wouldn't donate."

"What difference does that make? You've been walking out that way—" Mrs. Reed cut herself short, paled, and with obvious effort, reined in her temper. "I'm sorry. We'll discuss this later. Thank you for bringing this news to our attention, Mrs. Gavin."

Mrs. Gavin fluttered her fingers, a gesture that seemed caught between an attempt to draw attention and to ward it away. "Don't apologize. In truth, I'd hoped we could discuss this together, calmly and sympathetically. Especially because you must have strong feelings about Lord Loel."

Mr. Reed let out a brief, bitter bark of laughter. He cast his deep-set eyes from one end of the table to the other and said in a low, emphatic tone, "Do you know, he never apologized?"

Bonny flinched. Her parents didn't know about Loel's letter. They'd had so much to do after the fire—it turned out that sudden financial ruin created a great deal of work. Every day a new insurance agent knocked at the door with a list of questions, a suddenly out-of-work employee or servant needed a reference, an antiques dealer wanted a tour.

Bonny had taken on many of her mother's usual household chores, which included sorting through the mail. She'd never told her parents about Loel's letter or his visit. At first she hadn't seen the point—her parents had neither the time nor the energy to coddle a soft-mouthed lordling. Later, after Loel had gone, she'd been too ashamed.

She hadn't realized her parents noticed, hadn't imagined they cared. Her father had never said anything before. Why choose today to speak about it for the first time?

"I've heard from others that he sent letters, paid visits... but he never darkened our doorstep." Mr. Reed tipped his chin at Bonny. "That boy's a coward."

Coward was the last word Bonny would have used to describe Lord Loel.

The elder Mr. Gavin lowered his voice. "I've often thought it's a good thing that Lord and Lady Loel didn't live long enough to see what's become of him…"

"They must be turning in their graves," agreed Mrs. Gavin in the contented tone of one whose opinion, often repeated and never challenged, has acquired the shine of an established truth.

Bonny, who'd nodded along to similar comments more often than she could count, cringed. She didn't know what Lord Loel had done to disappoint his parents—but neither did the Gavins! No one did, but they condemned him with such relish.

"For a coward, he's grown bold," said Charles Gavin. "If he's taken to accosting women on the streets—one of his own victims even—perhaps it's time that we had a word with him."

"What?" Bonny spluttered. That sounded like a threat. "No!"

"No?" Gavin's eyebrows rose, then flattened. "Several of the people we spoke to insisted that you seemed very friendly with Lord Loel. Heads drawn together, speaking in confidential tones."

Bonny opened her mouth. She was supposed to say that she wanted nothing to do with Lord Loel, that he'd imposed himself on her, but the words wouldn't come.

Her mother, who'd been silent for several minutes now, began to shake her head in silent horror. She'd guessed some of the truth —and now her imagination was filling in the rest.

"What exactly was his business with you?" Charles Gavin pressed. "You spoke of a visit to Woodclose but not today's meeting. What were you discussing?"

"It was—" Bonny stuttered to a halt. She wasn't ready for this conversation! "I'm not—"

"I think you had better answer that question, Miss Reed," said Mrs. Gavin. "Hesitating only casts doubt on your own behavior."

Charles Gavin grunted his agreement. "Just so, I'm afraid. Just so."

Bonny closed her eyes and took a deep breath. It seemed that the choice had been made for her. She settled herself, squared her

ERIN SATIE

shoulders, and said, "During my visit to Woodclose, Lord Loel said something I found very disturbing."

"I won't stand for it," muttered Charles Gavin. His mother reached across the table to give her son's arm a comforting pat.

"Something very disturbing about *you*, Mr. Gavin," Bonny said sharply. "He said that you have a... a... natural child."

CHAPTER 10

The atmosphere in the room chilled abruptly. Mrs. Gavin's posture stiffened, the light in Papa Gavin's eyes went out, and a flush crept up Charles Gavin's neck.

The Reeds all felt it, drawing away from the table, glancing nervously at one another. Margot sat on her hands. The hairs at the back of Bonny's neck prickled.

"And you listened?" Charles Gavin asked in a low, dangerous voice.

"I tried not to!" Bonny's voice climbed up the register, high and thin. "I refused to believe him. I tried to put it out of my mind…"

"Have you been spreading these foul stories?" Mrs. Gavin demanded. "Is this how you recompense a man who has treated you with respect and courtesy?"

"Of course not!" Bonny recoiled. "I'd hoped to prove Lord Loel wrong—to stop him from spreading foul rumors. But instead, I discovered that he'd told me the truth."

Charles Gavin's eyes narrowed. "So you've been snooping about, behind my back—"

"Do you know what's become of your child?" Bonny demanded.

"No," Charles Gavin snapped. "And I don't care."

Bonny stubbornly continued. "He's been put to work. As a houseboy."

"So?"

Something died in Bonny right then.

Charles Gavin was not the man she had believed him to be. But he didn't fall from grace alone; she fell with him. She had been wrong. She had believed a lie.

Now she stumbled in the dark. All the lights she'd used to find her way had blinked out, and yet it was more important than ever that she choose the right path.

"I had hoped to do you a favor tonight," said Mrs. Gavin. "I thought we could discuss your misstep together, like family—it never occurred to me to view these reports from the pub in the worst possible light. But now I am forced to consider the possibility that you were committing an act of disloyalty."

"Because I wanted to know the truth?" Bonny asked.

"A wife is answerable to her husband—and not the reverse. You have no right to an accounting of my son's actions. Not now or ever." Mrs. Gavin's fingers were so tight around her cutlery they were white. "But I will offer one for your instruction. I made the mistake of hiring the strumpet who carried that child as my lady's maid—she lived under our roof, ate our food, wore the clothes we provided—and you see how she repaid us. She disgraced herself."

"Thought she'd trapped us." Charles Gavin snorted. "Greedy tart got what she deserved: nothing."

"The child is innocent," Bonny whispered.

"If so, it's only because we have prevented its dam from using her babe as a weapon against us," said Mrs. Gavin. "Just like this... blackguard... Lord Loel has tried to use it as a weapon against us. And you have abetted his calumny, Miss Reed."

Bonny sat frozen, speechless, heart pounding. She looked to her parents for support and found her father staring into his full plate as though it might whisper the secrets of the universe at him, shoulders slumped. Margot blinked owlishly, as though she'd been startled by a very bright light, and her mother...

Mrs. Reed had one hand fisted in her lap and the other propped against the table, fingers loosely curled, projecting a calm she obviously did not feel.

"Mrs. Gavin," Mrs. Reed said softly. "We've been friends for a long time; you know my daughter. She means well. The fault here is mine and my husband's. We ought to have instructed her better. Don't judge her too harshly."

Bonny couldn't believe her ears. "Mama?"

Mrs. Reed turned in answer to this plea. It was a slow, controlled movement designed to hide pain, but Bonny saw such dignity in her mother, such strength. Here was a woman who had learned to hold her head up even after her whole world had collapsed, and she'd had to carry what was left on her shoulders.

Bonny had never admired her mother more and never felt more ashamed.

"Bonny, I think you should apologize to the Gavins," said Mrs. Reed. "Thank Mrs. Gavin for her advice and for her patience."

Bonny swallowed. She couldn't refuse. It would have been ungrateful. It would have added to her mother's humiliation, and she couldn't bear that.

"I beg your pardon," said Bonny. "It seems I forgot something that I ought to know very well and believe deeply—there is nothing more important than family. I could ask for no higher calling than to love and support my family in every possible way. I'm sorry that I ever, even for a moment, forgot this most essential truth."

Mrs. Gavin's expression softened. "I confess, if you'd said anything else... but I can see you understand and that you're sincere. Charles?"

Charles Gavin let the silence linger—cruelly, in Bonny's opinion. The suspicion had not lifted from his eyes; a hardness lingered about his mouth.

In the end, he accepted her apology with a brief, gruff, "Don't let it happen again."

The rest of the meal passed slowly. Mrs. Gavin peppered Margot with questions about her drawing and her reading. Mr. Gavin and Mr. Reed discussed trade and politics, with occasional contributions from Charles Gavin.

Bonny spoke as little as possible. The courses followed, lavish and delicious, but she'd lost what little appetite she'd brought to the table. It was a relief when they finally left, one of the crisply uniformed footmen doling out their lanterns, freshly re-lit for the walk home. The temperature had chilled, or perhaps it just seemed colder after an evening in the bright and toasty rooms of the Gavin house. In any case, Bonny wasn't the only one who shivered as they walked single file along the deserted pavement.

An eerie silence held until they'd turned the corner on the Gavins' house. Even Margot held her tongue. And then, at last, the dam burst.

"Lord Loel, Bonny?" said her father.

Right on the heels of this mournful question, Mrs. Reed demanded, "What were you thinking!"

"He feels guilty about the fire," Bonny explained. "He thought he was doing me a favor."

"And you believed that?"

"I do now," Bonny said hotly. "He told me the truth."

"To what end?" her mother asked. "Do you tell every sick person you meet that they're looking poorly? Do you remind your thin friends that they need to put on weight or your plump ones that they were slimmer the last time you saw them? Truth is very easy to abuse."

"You're saying it would be better if I married Mr. Gavin without knowing who he is? What he's done?"

"It's the way of the world, Bonny," said her mother. "You can reject Mr. Gavin, but at best you'll find a replacement who hides his vices better."

Bonny's jaw dropped.

"These are hard words for an innocent to hear, I know," said her mother. "But if you insist on discussing subjects that aren't meant for innocent ears, you must be prepared for the answers."

"Are you telling me I should expect all men to behave like tomcats?" Bonny demanded. "Or that I should expect them to neglect the illegitimate children they father?"

"I'm asking you to *think*," her mother said. "Are you going to break your engagement? Is that where this is leading?"

Bonny shrugged. She didn't know.

"Because if an hour in the company of that houseboy broke your heart, explain to Margot here that you care more about Charles Gavin's bastard than your own sister."

"She doesn't," said Margot, loyally.

"I don't think you'd marry him if you were in my place," said Bonny. "I think you'd find someone better."

"You're probably right." Her mother brushed a lock of hair out of her eyes, lit from below by the swaying lantern light and looking so human, so fallible. And every bit her age. "But, Bonny, I brought an income to my marriage, family connections... I wish things had worked out so that you could have the same advantages, but they didn't."

"So Mr. Gavin is the best I'll do," said Bonny. "And you still think I should marry him."

"Yes," said her mother. "I'm sorry, Bonny, but yes."

BONNY VISITED Cordelia after breakfast the next morning. It was one of those days when her workshop was the best possible place in the world to be—cold and clear outside, and yet the heat radiating from below stairs combined with bright sunlight streaming through the windows made the converted nursery almost *too* warm.

Cordelia, accordingly, wore one of her lightest spring dresses, white muslin sprigged with bright green flowers. The pattern would have been unbearably saccharine on Bonny, but through some peculiar alchemy of character looked dashing and fierce on Cordelia. She'd set about binding a new copy of *Pride and Prejudice,* which she'd bought because the old one had fallen apart from constant use.

Bonny offered to help. Cordelia gave her a single signature, about sixteen sheets of paper with four pages printed on each side that, once properly folded, could be sewn down the middle. Cordelia had done all the folding, a process that mystified Bonny, but she could sew along a dotted line.

So she drove the slender steel needle into the stack of paper, pulled it through, turned it around, repeated the process. Watching the trail of neat stitches emerge helped her gather her courage. She might be floundering in a sea of doubt, but here, at least, was something she could do well.

"I need to tell you about our dinner at the Gavins' last night," said Bonny.

Cordelia was in the middle of cutting a sheet of thick card stock into what would become the front cover, back cover, and spine of the book. She had a lethally sharp knife for the purpose and a pumice stone to smooth the edges when she was done.

"It turned into a complete disaster because…" Bonny paused. "I suppose I should start at the beginning. I've visited Woodclose several times since that afternoon when I asked Lord Loel to donate books to the library."

Cordelia finished her cut, fingered a snag where the card stock had wrinkled, and looked up. "After what he did to you? And your family? Why?"

For the first time, Bonny told the truth. "I like him."

Cordelia wrinkled her nose. "Lord Loel?"

"He's different from any other man I've ever met," said Bonny. "He speaks plainly and doesn't mind if I answer in the same way —I talk to him as frankly as I talk to you. He listens and takes me seriously."

"That's all very nice, Bonny, but he destroyed a company that your family spent several generations building."

"I know." Bonny sighed. "I know. But the fire was an accident. Hasn't he been punished enough?"

"Oh, perhaps if he'd been living the life of a model citizen—but you know the gossip. He brings odd people to town, and they exchange mysterious boxes."

"Full of orchids," Bonny said.

"But where does he get the money for them? Have you answered that question yet?"

"You've got it backward," said Bonny. "The orchids aren't an expensive hobby, they're the source of his income—he raises and sells them to make ends meet."

"And what's more—" Cordelia paused as Bonny's answer sunk in. "Really?"

Bonny nodded.

Cordelia leaned back in her chair, her fine eyes going wide. "I knew he was out-of-pockets, but…"

"During one of my visits, Lord Loel told me that Mr. Gavin had fathered a natural child. I decided to investigate those claims, and the truth is worse than I could have ever imagined. The boy is seven years old, and he's already been put out to work. Charles Gavin doesn't support him in any way."

"My God," Cordelia whispered. "Does the man have no heart at all?"

"I'm beginning to wonder," said Bonny. "I discovered the truth yesterday, and Lord Loel happened to see me passing by in the street. I looked distraught, which I was, and we spoke about what I'd discovered… At the time, I wasn't thinking of the consequences. Of course we were seen, and of course the news was passed on to the Gavins."

"Shall I guess what they had to say?" Cordelia asked.

"Guess?" Bonny raised her eyebrows. "Go right ahead, if you'd find it amusing. I didn't."

"Something on the order of—" Cordelia paused. "Oh, I can't. It's too awful."

"It was."

"So the Gavins were furious," Cordelia prompted.

"They scolded me. It wasn't until they found out that I'd discovered the child that they were furious."

Cordelia tipped her head to the side. "I beg your pardon?"

"They accused me of disloyalty. Of—conspiring against them almost."

"Because you spoke the truth?"

Bonny's mouth twisted. "I ought to have defended Mr. Gavin. He is blameless. The mother of his child, however, is a scheming harlot, and so neither she—nor the boy—deserve a single penny from the Gavins."

Cordelia, after a short silence, spoke in a voice as hard as diamond. "You can't marry him."

"It's not that simple."

"It's exactly that simple," Cordelia said firmly. "Bad men make bad husbands, and bad husbands slowly drain their wives of energy and spirit. Unless you want to be a sad, empty shell of a human being by the time you're forty, you'll break the engagement. Simple."

"My family needs this marriage—seeing the Gavins so angry scared them. Really *scared* them."

"Did you hear me say 'sad, empty shell of a human being'?"

"He's no worse than most men."

Cordelia gave her a long, contemptuous look.

"That's what my mother said."

"Your mother is wrong."

"She'd call herself realistic."

"If your mother is right, then so am I—every time I say that women shouldn't submit to marriage under the current laws," said Cordelia. "Generally, people tell me that women are the weaker sex and we survive only through our dependence on the stronger. If that were true—which it isn't—then the institution of marriage would at least make *some* sense. But if sensible matrons are offering their daughters to cruel men of limited intellect, then the institution itself ought to be rejected."

"I want to get married, Cordelia," said Bonny. "I want a husband and family of my own."

"More women need to put principle first if we're going to change anything."

"Women who put principle first need married friends whose children they can influence," Bonny replied tartly.

"Oh, very well." Cordelia gave up with a sigh. "If you *insist* on finding a husband, I can help."

Bonny grinned. "Oh?"

"My mother's been dying to send me to London. She thinks if I meet enough young men, one of them will turn my head." Cordelia grimaced. "Sometimes I wonder if she knows me at all."

"How can you be sure one won't?" Bonny asked.

"I can't be sure," said Cordelia. "Though I believe the probability is extremely low."

"It won't be improved by my presence." Bonny didn't like to be rude, but when she and Cordelia were together, men tended to fawn over her and ignore Cordelia.

"That's the idea," said Cordelia. "I'll make my mother happy by going, you'll make me happy by keeping the men away, and hopefully by the time we're through, you'll decide that you've no further need of Charles Gavin."

Bonny blinked.

"It's an excellent plan," concluded Cordelia. "Let's put it into action."

LOEL HAD VERY NEARLY FINISHED his morning rounds in the greenhouse when the door rattled. It was the right time for Miss Reed to arrive, but he hadn't seen her in more than a week and didn't expect her now.

But there she was, a tendril of honey-colored hair slipping loose from where it had been tucked behind her ear as she bent over a *Phalaenopsis* sporting a pair of blooming spikes—the commonest of all exotic orchids, but he always kept at least a hundred on hand. They only sold for twenty or thirty pence apiece but they sold reliably, which anyone operating a business independently could appreciate. Especially pretty hybrids could fetch a good price too—and he had plans for the specimen Miss Reed had begun to reach for.

"Don't touch," he snapped.

Miss Reed squeaked and straightened.

"Touching flowers before they're fertilized shortens the bloom," he explained, once he was close enough to speak at a normal tone. "I'm surprised to see you. I thought you'd given up on the *Odontoglossum crispum*."

"I'm not sure how to answer that." Miss Reed smiled sadly. "The *Odontoglossum crispum* was just a safe way for us to carry on an argument about Charles Gavin. But the argument has been settled, and... well. Perhaps you ought to keep it."

"Because I've won, you mean?"

Miss Reed shrugged.

"What happened at your dinner?" he asked.

"Oh, nothing. I was made to feel like a villain, that's all." She traced patterns on the table with her fingertips. "Hardly worth mentioning."

"A *villain*? What could you possibly have done to give offense?"

"Paraded right through the center of town with you, for one."

Loel went cold. She'd been punished, as predictably as summer follows spring. If he'd really been concerned with Miss Reed's well-being, he wouldn't have intercepted her. He'd have left her alone.

He ought to have learned this lesson by now. He ought to have learned it several times over.

"Don't pull faces. All's not lost. I going to London with my friend Cordelia Kelly—have I told you about her?"

"No."

"She's… amazing. Fierce and uncompromising." Just thinking of her friend sent a quick, warm smile flitting across Miss Reed's lips. Loel had never been so jealous of a stranger in his life. "She thinks I'll break my engagement to Mr. Gavin once I've seen the city, where I am certain to find an endless supply of superior candidates."

So she was going to London in search of a husband. Good. That was just what she ought to do. He didn't want or expect anything else from her.

"You doubt her wisdom?" he asked.

"It's a large city, and Mr. Gavin has set a low bar, so she'll be right enough." Miss Reed shrugged. "But how am I to identify him? I can't just wander about demanding that every man kiss my hand to see if they measure up—" Miss Reed clapped a hand over her mouth, eyes going wide.

Loel, despite himself, smiled.

Miss Reed blushed red as a beet and began to babble. "I didn't think my parents would permit me to go. I couldn't have convinced them myself, but Cordelia managed it in less than an hour. She sat down across from my mother and announced the trip as though it were already decided. My mother explained why it was impossible, and Cordelia didn't say anything. So my mother explained again. She explained and explained, a little more frantic each time until she gave up and said I could leave."

"I'd have liked to see that."

"I'm not sure how Cordelia does it."

"You have a good friend."

"The best." That smile made another appearance. "So we've been making arrangements. Mrs. Henley has agreed to look after the library, so long as we give her the books in advance and a list of who should receive what. And I was finally able to sneak away from my family for long enough to reach Woodclose…"

Loel interrupted. "Sneak?"

"My parents would be horrified if they knew I'd come." She winced. "That's part of the reason why I'd hoped to give the orchid back to you. I'll miss these visits, truly I will, but with things so strained right now, I'd... like to have a clean conscience."

The answer he'd expected. If she'd been punished for taking his arm in New Quay, all her visits to Woodclose must have been made in secret. But he'd needed to hear her say it—in a sick, self-loathing way. He didn't like to think of himself as a villain, of visits to his home as a vice.

The truth hurt.

"The orchid belongs to you," he said abruptly.

"I know, but—"

He cut her off with a sharp wave of his hand. "I'll care for it in your stead, for as long as you need. But I won't take it back. If you abandon the orchid, I'll let it die."

Her face scrunched up in confusion. "But why? You said it's valuable."

Why? Because orchids could live a long time. Years after she'd said her vows with her London husband—she'd have no trouble finding one—he'd still have something of hers. He could adopt her silly quest; he could teach it to thrive.

And if Miss Reed insisted on returning the *Odontoglossum crispum*... well. It wouldn't take an Oxford don to puzzle out why he'd let the thing wither.

"Only if it blooms." He collected the rose and the bowl. "Enjoy your trip, Miss Reed. Good luck."

CHAPTER 11

Bonny made the whole trip to London in a daze. She hardly absorbed any of the sights and sounds because her mind was so wholly and inappropriately focused on Lord Loel.

He'd been so angry.

And yet it was a kind of anger that warmed her. She wanted to go back for more. She wanted to huddle up to it like a fire, at just the right distance to feel the heat without getting burned.

The impulse baffled her. She'd never been drawn to conflict or strife or discontent. And yet all day Cordelia would say something (for example: "You seem distracted. What's on your mind?"), and Bonny would mumble an unsatisfying answer and squirm because the memory of his furrowed brow and hard mouth and bright green eyes crowded out everything else.

She tried to shake herself out of her stupor when the train pulled into the station, if only so that she didn't embarrass Cordelia in front of her aunt and uncle.

Mrs. Gainsway was Cordelia's aunt, related on her father's side, and she had the family look: tall and lean and towheaded. But she lacked the hard edge that animated both Cordelia and her father. Mr. Gainsway seemed even softer than his wife, pink-faced and smiling and thick around the middle. Both embraced Cordelia warmly, and after they got a good look at Bonny, cast skeptical glances at their niece—all pointedly ignored.

Mrs. Gainsway was a social butterfly, and soon she was ferrying Bonny and Cordelia from luncheons to parties, from dinners to fetes. As expected, the bachelors flocked to Bonny—often ignoring Cordelia, even while they stood side by side on a dance floor.

Bonny had never doubted her ability to draw a man's attention, but only Mr. Gavin had ever seriously courted her. She feared the men in London would behave like the men in New Quay—full of hot looks and flattery but little more.

And she was right.

The bouquets started arriving the day after Bonny and Cordelia arrived in London. Huge clusters of roses, tulips, lilies, and peonies. Bonny paid special note to the orchids, looking for flowers that she recognized and wondering if any of them had originated in Loel's greenhouse.

When she attended a dance, her card filled immediately. Despite her best attempts at modesty, she found herself holding court at garden parties and luncheons, surrounded at all times by a half dozen or so young men eager to fetch her lemonade, help her over puddles, or render any other small service.

They did not, however, introduce her to their mothers. Nor did said mothers show up for Mrs. Gainsway's at-home hours.

Bonny was beautiful enough to enchant men for an afternoon. She was not beautiful enough to make them forget that she had neither dowry nor connections to offer.

Her spirits fell, day by day. By the end of a week, she simply hadn't the heart for another round of getting her hopes up and having them dashed. But that didn't stop Mrs. Gainsway from making plans, so she found herself bundled into a carriage and on her way to a garden party in the "country," hosted by Sir and Lady Carmichael.

Their destination was only an hour or so from Mayfair in a coach and four. A short distance, as the crow flies, but far enough to exchange the bustle of the city for a more pastoral atmosphere, with stretches of field and pasture as cushions between the burgeoning villages.

They arrived at a fine estate built in the Palladian style, small but exquisite, with well-tended grounds. Bonny disembarked, took in the idyllic scene, and wished that she were anywhere else. She would rather have spent the afternoon darning socks. At least she usually had Margot's company for the darning and a sense of accomplishment at the end of the day.

London was proving far less productive.

Mrs. Gainsway kept Cordelia close to her side, determined to introduce her to as many young men as possible. For once, Bonny left her friend to face her fate alone. She needed time to herself, to the extent allowed by courtesy.

She wandered exquisite gardens and shaded paths, a canal glittering in the distance. Birds chattered, and well-tended roses released their intoxicating scents, heavy and vulgar to a nose accustomed to the delicate perfumes of hothouse orchids. The scene reminded her of Woodclose in the days before the fire, when it had boasted a similar artificial prettiness.

While she floated idly about London, Lord Loel would be usefully employed. She didn't approve of the way he ran himself ragged, but Bonny had been poor for too long to see idleness as a virtue.

She was surprised to realize that she missed him. That she looked forward to telling him about her time in London. She could trust him to listen. If she described the young bachelors she'd met, told him her hopes and fears, he would give her his opinion in plain words.

A scream knocked her out of her reverie.

A trio of partygoers clustered around the canal had raised the alarm. A gentleman stooped and reached toward the water while two women in summer silks faced the house. They raised their arms high and waved them back and forth.

"Help!" cried one of the women. "Help!"

Bonny wondered what exactly had gone wrong, but standing around and guessing wouldn't help anyone. So she fisted her skirts and ran toward the trio.

Her lungs protested, but once she caught a glimpse of small arms thrashing in the water, Bonny picked up her pace. She was grateful, for once, for her good figure—because she wore very light stays, cinched just tight enough to smooth the lines of her dress and not enough to constrict her breathing.

She threw her shawl and bonnet aside when she reached the water. The canal, though scenic, was man-made. Instead of a gently sloping shore, the channel had been dug to a uniform depth between stone embankments on either side.

Two children had fallen into the water. Both boys small and skinny, struggling mightily to keep their heads above water. One of them had been taught to swim or at least to float. He kicked against the slow current, hollering himself hoarse, and tried to help his companion—though every time he reached for the other boy, their combined flailing caused both to sink.

"The water is so murky I can't see the bottom," complained one of the women.

"My skirts would drown me," whined the other.

"I can't swim!" cried the man.

Later Bonny might have a few choice words for the three adults bombarding her with excuses. Right now all that mattered was saving the children. She jumped before she, too, found an excuse to stay on dry land. The cold stole her breath away, despite the fair weather. She spat out a mouthful of water with a shudder. It tasted of pond scum and sewage, impossibly foul.

She used her arms to keep steady. Kicking would only entangle her in her skirts, which billowed around her in the water. They caught in the current and, like sails, began to drag her downstream.

She paddled toward the boy who couldn't swim. He grabbed hold as soon as she got close, clinging with all four sturdy limbs. The chubby arm around her neck choked her, the little legs pinioned her thighs, and Bonny began to sink.

The boy screamed and tried to climb her, shoving her under for the chance at another breath. It didn't matter that he was dooming himself along with her; he wanted to escape, he wanted to get out of the water, and he wasn't capable of thinking it through logically.

Bonny held her breath and swept her arms through the water in quick, hard strokes. It was such a short distance; a strong swimmer would have made it in a single breath, as though it were nothing. But Bonny struggled. She fought for every inch. Her lungs burned to the point of pain.

But she was a country girl. She'd grown up by the sea. She had strength and determination to spare. She feared the ocean, like anyone with sense. But she would not let a man-made canal defeat her.

The gawkers finally made themselves useful. The gentleman got down on both knees and reached for the struggling child. The women stooped on either side, and working together, they lifted the boy.

Bonny's fingers scrabbled for purchase on the slick, slimy stones of the embankment. She held on for long enough to take a few breaths and untangle her skirts, then pushed off again.

The second rescue was much easier. The boy wrapped his arms around her neck and kicked vigorously while she steered them toward safety. As soon as they were within arm's reach of the rescuers, he let go.

Bonny kept herself afloat until two gentlemen—the useless gawker and a newcomer, brawny despite the gray at his temples —knelt in tandem. Each took one of her arms and, on the count of three, heaved with all their strength. They lifted her, though only halfway—after a second count and a second mighty pull, Bonny swung knees onto the stone embankment. She crawled away from the canal, panting hard, and collapsed on the grass.

She struggled to catch her breath. Her hair had fallen out of its careful coiffure, and the tangled locks dripped foul water into her eyes and mouth. Her waterlogged dress no longer fit properly; it felt tight at the seams and loose everywhere else.

Bonny's head hung low and heavy. The polished patent leather of men's boots and the soiled hems of ladies' dresses surrounded her on all sides. A crowd had gathered, drawn by the drama and high emotion of the rescue.

One of the boys began to weep. The other coughed up water, his little chest shuddering.

Someone snickered. A whispered comment, of which Bonny caught only a few words, set her cheeks to burning. The danger was over. The time for passing judgment and cracking jokes had arrived. And Bonny was on her hands and knees before an audience of sophisticated Londoners, wearing a light summer dress rendered both clinging and transparent by the dunking she'd given it.

Two women stepped out of the crowd. Long-limbed, willowy, and almost of a height, one wore primrose pink and the other daffodil yellow. The girl in pink, pale and blond, had thin, smiling lips and a haughty tilt to her head. The girl in yellow, her skin the deep rich brown of new-poured bronze, was more watchful. She swept the crowd with jet-black eyes as she advanced on Bonny.

"Are we human beings or are we vultures?" snapped the girl in pink. "If you want to idle about and gossip, do it by the buffet tables."

"No reaction," murmured the girl in yellow. She had a slight accent, just enough to reveal that she'd been born speaking a language other than English, in a place other than England. Africa? The Indies? "How strange."

"Oh, very peculiar indeed," returned the girl in pink, voice flat with scorn.

The two women shook out their shawls and held them

outspread like a pair of lacy curtains. Acting as one, they crouched on either side of Bonny, sheltering her from view.

"Can you stand?" asked the girl in yellow.

Bonny tried to answer, but she couldn't articulate through her chattering teeth. It was a warm day, but she ached to the bone with cold.

"Do your best," said the other. "We'll make up the difference."

They linked arms with Bonny and stood. Bonny stumbled, but her rescuers held her upright—bearing her weight without a groan or a grimace, as though she were light as a feather.

The two young women marched Bonny to the house, sheltering her with their shawls the whole way, steadying her steps and chattering in bright, tart voices.

"Only a little farther." The girl in pink coaxed—and then, in a more normal tone to her friend, "Did you see those fools doting on Lilian Crowley?"

"Naturally," returned the girl in yellow. "All men know that the rule where weeping women are concerned is to give comfort first and ask questions later."

"She *is* a champion weeper," said the girl in pink. Then more sweetly, "Almost there."

The staff flocked to them.

"We need to get her out of these wet clothes," said the girl in pink. "We need privacy—and I mean *privacy*, keep any prying eyes well away—"

The girl in yellow stepped in. "And hot tea with plenty of sugar. Something warm to eat and enough water to wash the stink of the canal off."

Two footmen made for the kitchens at a trot. One of the younger maids offered to find a change of clothes in Bonny's size.

Another maid, fairly senior given her proud posture, said, "This way," and led them into the sprawling house.

Just as they reached the first flight of stairs, a uniformed maid appeared with a blanket. Bonny's rescuers reclaimed their shawls and helped wrap the thick wool around her shoulders.

They were ushered into a plainly furnished bedroom. The senior maid unfastened the buttons running along the back of Bonny's dress and picked the knot of her stays loose. Bonny's two rescuers held her in their arms while she stepped out of her skirts, lest she stumble. They didn't blush when the maid peeled Bonny's soaked chemise away from her chilled, clammy body. They simply swaddled her in the blanket and helped her sit on the narrow bed.

"Thank you," said Bonny.

"Oh, it was our pleasure," said the girl in yellow, an edge of dark humor in her voice.

It dawned on Bonny that she'd been rescued by exactly the sort of sophisticated women she ordinarily went out of her way to *avoid*. On top of being beautiful (which Bonny, of all people, couldn't hold against them), they were fashionable, elegant, and haughty. Rich too, judging by their fine clothes.

It was dangerous to draw the attention of such ladies. They knew everyone—their circumstances, their secrets—and, what's more, formed *opinions* based on what they knew. They had influence and used it, raising their favorites up and bringing their rivals low.

It was not worth risking the disapproval of such ladies in order to court their favor. Bonny preferred to avoid their notice entirely. And yet here she was, alone with two glittering habitués of high society and very much in their debt.

"Perhaps we should introduce ourselves." The girl in pink flattened one hand against her modest bosom. "I'm Olympia Swain."

Olympia Swain paused, obviously expecting a reaction. Bonny had heard the name before—it had come up in recent gossip—but she couldn't remember the context.

Bonny smiled politely. "Pleased to meet you."

"I'm Theresa Hurley," said the girl in yellow. "Though my friends call me Tess."

"My name is Bonny Reed," said Bonny. "I've only just arrived in London—usually I live in New Quay, a town just south of Liverpool."

"That was a very brave thing you did," said Tess.

"We were on our way to help, if we could, but you got there first," added Olympia. "You didn't even pause when you reached the canal!"

"I couldn't believe it." Tess shook her head in astonishment. "I'd like to think I would have saved those boys if I'd been close enough, but I'll tell you honestly: I would have hesitated."

Olympia chimed in. "We decided that if we couldn't rescue the boys, we could *at least* rescue the rescuer."

A knock interrupted them. Tess stood, ready to bar the door, but the intruder turned out to be a maid carrying a shallow hip bath. Two more trailed behind, bearing pails of water.

"Soap?" asked Tess.

The woman holding the hip bath had a cake of soap tucked under one arm. She offered it to Tess, who sniffed it.

"Rose is too heavy for Miss Reed," said Tess. "Do you have anything a little lighter? Orange blossom or lily of the valley?"

"Of course, miss." The maid positioned the hip bath by the fireplace and laid a fire. The other two poured their buckets, and all three bobbed themselves out.

"I'm not sure the scent matters," said Bonny.

"I am," said Olympia. "So you've been outvoted."

Bonny couldn't help it. She began to laugh.

"Good. A sense of humor." Olympia leaned against the wall, hips cocked, a surprisingly intimidating pose. "I'd be crushed to find out we'd rescued a stick-in-the-mud."

The tea arrived next—a huge pot of it, enough for six or seven people, along with several covered dishes and a plate of biscuits. Tess poured, not bothering to ask before adding plenty of milk and sugar to Bonny's cup.

Bonny took a sip. The warmth went right to her belly.

The maid returned with a new cake of soap, scented with

gardenia, along with towels and a fresh set of clothes. Tess approved this time and passed the soap to Bonny.

Bonny set it aside to have ready once her two rescuers left.

"What are you waiting for?" asked Olympia.

"If you don't wash now, it'll be weeks before you get that awful scent out of your hair," Tess added.

Bonny blinked.

Olympia and Tess looked at her expectantly.

Of course Bonny knew that highborn women—and men—usually bathed with a personal servant in attendance. They never had to contort themselves to wash their backs or their feet... She had not guessed that, as a consequence, they might not feel shy about bathing with company.

"You're eating," Bonny protested weakly.

"So we are." Olympia selected a biscuit from the tray and took a bite out of it. "I'll finish it after you're in the bath, to see if it tastes any different."

Bonny gave up. A film of dirt was drying on her skin, itchy and tacky to the touch, and her hair really did stink. If she insisted that they leave, she might upset them. She was afraid of appearing ungrateful and, in the process, setting them against her.

So she dropped her blanket and stood in the bath, carefully lowering herself to a seated position. Tess nudged the soap closer.

"Who did those children belong to anyway?" Olympia sipped her tea.

"I think they're related to George Trenton," said Tess. "Nephews or cousins."

"George Trenton?" Bonny asked. She didn't know that name. She didn't know any of the people that Tess and Olympia talked about.

"The gentleman on the embankment," said Tess.

"Why on earth didn't he do anything to help?" Bonny asked.

"He can't swim," said Tess.

"Oh." Bonny picked up the soap and began to lather it. "I suppose he can't be blamed."

"And he did help lift the boys out," Olympia added. "Not that it will save his reputation."

"His reputation? But if he couldn't swim…?"

"He ought to have drowned before he let a woman take a risk that rightly fell to him," said Olympia. "Swimmer or not, he'll never live down the shame."

"Is there something we could do?" Bonny asked.

"For Trenton?" Tess snorted. "Not if I have anything to say about it."

"He has frequently been unkind to Tess," Olympia murmured.

"It's Lilian Crowley and Shirley Dewitt you need to worry about," said Tess. "They're the ones who will attack you."

"Lilian and…?"

"The two ladies with Trenton," said Olympia. "You embarrassed them by jumping in while they stood idly by."

"They contributed a few squeals," said Tess.

"That's right, they did. Uncharitable of me to forget the squealing." Olympia took a bite of the biscuit. "You see? It's fine."

A sly smile curled the corners of Tess's mouth. She glanced sidelong at Bonny and explained, "Those two wouldn't ruin a new dress to save a whole cartload of little boys."

"Which anyone who's spent an hour in conversation with either of them would know."

The door burst open. Cordelia stood in the threshold, arms spread wide, chin out, ready for battle. Like an avenging angel.

"Bonny?" she cried.

"I'm here. And unclothed! Get in and close that door!"

Cordelia took in the scene before her—Tess and Olympia sipping tea while Bonny crouched naked in a hip bath—and while she closed the door as asked, her furious expression didn't change.

"Are you all right?" she asked.

"I'm fine, but you seem rather flustered. Sit down and have some tea; there's plenty."

"I've crossed the whole estate five times looking for you."

Cordelia accepted a cup from Olympia but held it at arm's length as though it might be poisoned. "I think the staff was misleading me on purpose."

"They were," murmured Olympia.

"Let me introduce you to my rescuers. These two ladies saved me from a great deal of embarrassment. I'm terribly grateful." Bonny tipped her head to the left. "Miss Olympia Swain and"— Bonny tipped right—"Miss Theresa Hurley."

"Call me Tess," added Tess.

Cordelia's eyes widened ever so slightly—obviously she recognized the names. Good. That meant she could tell Bonny who they were later.

"Olympia and Tess, please meet my dearest friend, Cordelia Kelly. We're neighbors."

"As Miss Reed's greatest admirers, we are honored to meet you," said Tess. "I don't think I saw you by the canal."

"No, I was inside—Sir John offered to show me the library."

"So you missed the rescue?" Tess asked.

"What rescue?" Cordelia asked.

Olympia clapped. "We're going to tell you all about it!"

Olympia and Tess regaled Cordelia with the story while Bonny finished washing. They exaggerated shamelessly—the canal doubled in width, the current sped up, the children very nearly expired. They talked over one another, adding asides and embellishments. By the end Cordelia had visibly softened.

Bonny reached for the towel and dried herself. Cordelia was stubborn and smart—it was difficult to lead her where she didn't want to go. But the London sophisticates had won her over.

Impressive. And a little frightening.

"So," said Tess. "What brings you to London?"

"The usual," answered Cordelia.

"We're looking for husbands," explained Bonny.

"And has the search been fruitful?"

"Not yet." Bonny began sorting through the clean clothes the maid had brought.

Cordelia put in, "Do you really want a husband who proposes to a woman he's only known for a week?"

"Stop asking silly questions." Bonny slid a clean chemise over her head. "If I don't want Charles Gavin, then yes, I do want a man who will propose to me after a week."

"Imagine it takes you a year to find a husband," said Cordelia. "So what? Your sister is young, and your family won't starve. They can wait."

"Yes, let's imagine," returned Bonny, stepping into a petticoat and hiking it up to her waist. Tess batted her hand aside and tied the ribbons. "What if I *don't* find a husband in a year? Or two years? My parents will be burdened, Margot will be furious, and I'll be desperate."

"Have you looked in a mirror lately?" Tess chuckled. "It won't take you two years."

Bonny sputtered. "It's not as easy—"

"Listen to your new friend," interrupted Cordelia. "And besides, you were never one to give up without a fight."

"I'm here, aren't I?"

"For two weeks."

"Even if I wanted to return, I doubt your aunt and uncle would welcome me back."

"Why not?" Olympia interrupted, shaking out the dress and holding it open for Bonny to step through.

"Because Bonny is too pretty," said Cordelia.

"Why did I ask?" Olympia clucked at herself. "I should have guessed."

"You can't blame them," added Tess. "I'm sorry, Bonny, but people have to be practical."

"Let me worry about my aunt and uncle," said Cordelia. "The point I'm making is: A man who's careless in his selection of a wife won't allow her to play a substantial role in his life."

"Some women don't *want* to play a substantial role in their husband's life." Bonny held still so Olympia could fasten the buttons on her borrowed gown. "Some of us would rather be protected and cherished."

"Any woman clever enough to correctly identify which of her suitors will become husbands capable of shielding her from care for a whole lifetime is a woman too clever for the idle life that husband would provide."

"Oh, now that's good," said Olympia. "Say it again. I want to be able to repeat it in future."

Cordelia hesitated, but as Olympia seemed sincere, she obliged.

"Perhaps you'd like to offer an opinion," Cordelia added. "Bonny is currently engaged to marry a truly awful man."

"True," Bonny agreed. "But he's handsome and wealthy and well liked."

"And of those qualities, which do you find indispensable?" Tess asked, a little slyly.

"His wealth," Bonny admitted.

"So find another wealthy man," said Tess. "With your looks, you could take your pick."

"So I've been told," said Bonny. "But no other man has ever courted me seriously."

"I think Charles Gavin is to blame for that," said Cordelia.

"He'd never—" Bonny caught herself. It was time to stop defending everything Mr. Charles Gavin did and said. "It's not nice to make an accusation like that without proof."

"No one else has proposed to you these past three years," said Cordelia. "What more proof could you want?"

"The bachelors in New Quay know my circumstances," said Bonny. "Perhaps that's enough to dissuade them."

"Dissuade all but the richest and handsomest man in town?" Cordelia clucked. "Don't be daft."

"You think Mr. Gavin scared them away?"

"What else?"

"I suppose he might be *that* awful," Bonny admitted. "He really might."

"You can't marry him, Bonny," said Cordelia. "It might seem like the best option right now, but marriage is forever and the law is not kind to women. If a man faced all the limitations that we do, none of them would marry. Not a one."

"If a woman wants a family of her own, she only has one way to go about it," said Tess. "So you can have your principles to keep you company in your old age... or you can have grand-children."

Cordelia stared Tess right in the eye and said, deadpan, "My principles are very good company."

Tess chuckled and Olympia *clapped*.

"They make a nice pair, don't they?" said Olympia.

"Oh yes," Tess agreed.

But Bonny didn't like cynicism, couldn't treat life as a game and people as pieces on the board. "Most men are decent. And marriage is our chance to bring out the best in them—to find the good and foster it."

"I've heard that sermon before." Olympia yawned pointedly. "Miss Kelly is right. The law gives every advantage to men. Here is *my* philosophy: It's up to us to tip the scales in our favor. I intend to find a husband so devoted that he has no desires of his own. He'll live only to please me."

Bonny remembered, with unnatural vividness, Lord Loel's growling voice as he told her that if she wanted, she could have a husband who would go down on his knees every day and thank God for bringing them together.

It had sounded romantic when Lord Loel said it. But the way Olympia Swain put it...

"I don't think I'd like that," Bonny confessed.

"Of course you would," said Olympia. "Everyone would. That's why it's so popular among royalty."

"I've lived in eight different households during the past ten years—" said Tess.

"Eight!" Bonny cried.

"My patroness places me with those whom she favors and

takes me from those who fall from her good graces," said Tess, mild and without judgment.

"Who is this patroness of yours?" Bonny demanded. "She sounds heartless."

"Queen Victoria."

Bonny bit her tongue. The Queen!

"I was given to her as a *gift* when I was very young, by a British naval captain who vehemently opposed slavery." There was enough acid in Tess's voice to etch her implied, unspoken opinion of this event onto a steel plate.

"You sound like you don't like him very much," Cordelia observed.

"I'm grateful to him, of course. He rescued me, he gave me his name, and he secured my future by placing me in the Queen's care."

Bonny noted that, while Tess sounded perfectly *sincere*, she had not said a word about liking Captain Hurley.

"You say he rescued you?" she asked.

"I had lost my family. And found myself in a… difficult situation. Ask the gossips if you must know more." Tess gave herself a small shake. Her clouded expression cleared, her posture straightened. "In the years since, I have—as I mentioned—lived in eight fine and prosperous English households. I've seen unhappy marriages up close, and not a one featured a slavishly devoted husband."

Bonny looked down at her lap.

"Cheer up, Miss Reed," said Olympia. "We're lucky, you and I. You're beautiful, and I'm rich. We have the luxury of choice. All we have to do is choose wisely."

"And those of us who are neither heiresses nor great beauties?" Cordelia asked.

"Avoid the men who drink too much," murmured Tess.

"I believe you're serious." Cordelia's mouth thinned as she turned to Bonny. "This is why, more and more, I don't think I'll marry at all."

"You dismiss your suitors too easily," Bonny told her friend. "You weigh their flaws too heavily when you judge them, their virtues too lightly."

"I want a husband whose companionship I enjoy more than the peace and quiet of my own company," said Cordelia. "Is that too much to ask?"

Bonny eyed her two rescuers and nodded minutely, which made them all laugh.

CHAPTER 12

"You know who Tess and Olympia are, don't you?" said Cordelia in the carriage on the way home.

"Tess said that she was Queen Victoria's ward," Bonny said, still stunned. "Could that be true?"

"Of course it is. If you read the papers, Bonny, you'd already know the story," said Cordelia. "Theresa Hurley is an African princess."

Bonny's mouth went dry. "A *princess*?"

"The only surviving member of her family," continued Cordelia. "She was taken captive by a rival king, after he killed her parents. That Captain Hurley she spoke of had been dispatched to rescue several British prisoners held by the same man, and when he saw the poor princess, he determined to rescue her as well."

"And you *met* her?" demanded Mrs. Gainsway.

"Yes, Aunt. She helped keep the crowd away after Bonny rescued those boys."

"Oh *my*." Mrs. Gainsway fanned herself. "They say she has a private audience with the Queen every week!"

"And Olympia?" Bonny asked.

Mrs. Gainsway gasped. "*Olympia Swain?*"

"She's incredibly wealthy, isn't that right?" Cordelia prompted.

"Rich as Croesus—rich as the Sultan on his golden divan!" Mrs. Gainsway cried. "She's the richest heiress in all of Britain and by a comfortable margin."

"Her parents must be very lax," said Bonny.

"Her parents are dead, dearest," returned Mrs. Gainsway. "And they left everything to her—mountains and mountains of money! Poor thing. She would need to be Moses to cut through the sea of suitors that surround her at all times."

"She seems up to the task," Cordelia murmured.

"Very strong willed."

"I liked them both."

"Me too," said Bonny. "I hope we see them again."

Her wish came true the very next day. They received an invitation to go for a drive, and soon after Bonny and Cordelia returned a grateful acceptance, a gorgeous barouche turned the corner on the Gainsways' sleepy street. Painted white with silver accents, drawn by four matched grays, it somehow served only to highlight the magnificence of the two young women inside—Olympia in blue and Tess in green—sitting side by side with the accordion hood folded back.

The overall effect was imposing enough to revive the nervousness Bonny had felt upon first meeting the two women. But then Tess reached out to take Bonny's hand, steadying her as she mounted the narrow steps, Olympia greeted her with a kiss on the cheek, and her fear dissolved.

"We've decided to be selfish," Olympia declared. "You see, we'd like to see more of you."

"And the only way to do that is to bring you to London," continued Tess. "Which, if we understand your circumstances correctly, won't happen unless you find a husband who spends time here."

"So we're going to help you find a husband," concluded

Olympia. "It's all for our own benefit, and we are too devoted to our own amusements to hear any protests."

"Or thanks," Tess murmured, more seriously. "And we'll be cross if you try."

Bonny, who'd had the words "thank you" on the tip of her tongue, shut her mouth.

Cordelia elbowed her in the side. "You're allowed to disobey, you know."

"Oh." Bonny beamed. "Then thank you. Thank you both."

Olympia glared at Cordelia. "Spoilsport."

Cordelia smiled serenely.

"We haven't done anything yet." Tess signaled the driver. "Let's get started, shall we?"

For the next several hours, the driver ferried them between shops and parks, sometimes waiting idly by while the girls descended to the pavement for a stroll, sometimes rolling at a stately pace through shady lanes, sometimes at speed. Whenever the conversation lagged, Olympia and Tess filled the silence with gossip—they knew *everyone*.

Bonny and Cordelia must have received a hundred introductions over the course of that afternoon. Tess or Olympia would do the honors, always adding, "You must have heard about those boys who nearly drowned? Well, it was Miss Reed who saved them. She's marvelous, isn't she? A miracle in the flesh."

In this manner, they found themselves on speaking terms with people that they would never have dared to approach otherwise. They were introduced to the most important people in London society, the tastemakers and grand dames.

"I feel very pleased with myself," Olympia declared when the barouche returned to the Gainsways' townhouse.

"We made a good start." Tess yawned. "I'm almost grateful that the choice will be made for me. It's fatiguing to conduct a search."

"It's fatiguing even when all the eligible young men come to you. I could spend whole days just sorting through the proposals

I receive, without reaching the end of them." Olympia added thoughtfully, "Though it wouldn't take nearly so long if I didn't count the ones sent by strangers."

"Strangers!" Bonny cried.

"Complete strangers," confirmed Tess. "I've seen the proposals. They're absurd."

"Tess—did I hear you say that the choice will be made for you?" Cordelia asked.

Tess nodded. "When the time comes."

"But isn't that a bit…" She didn't finish the sentence. Even Cordelia hesitated to criticize the Queen in front of her ward.

"There's no sense in complaining about the inevitable," said Tess. "So instead, I hope for the best."

"I wish I could help you the way you've been helping me," Bonny said.

"You have." Tess embraced Bonny, then Cordelia. "You see why friendship is so important to me?"

Soon after bidding farewell to their new friends, Bonny and Cordelia dressed for an assembly to which Mrs. Gainsway had obtained tickets. Mere minutes after their arrival, Bonny could tell that people were treating her differently. Men flocked around her, as they always had, but they paid attention to Cordelia, too. Both of their dance cards filled up within minutes of their arrival.

And, what was truly remarkable, the women were more welcoming as well. They sought introductions, welcomed Bonny and Cordelia into their conversations, and in the following days they paid visits.

Mothers sat down on the Gainsways' sofa and asked Bonny about her family and her fortune. These answers were disappointing, but these mothers kept up their quizzing—searching, Bonny realized, for some justification. They liked her, she realized. They wanted to approve. But with only her beauty to recommend her…

Bonny knew that if only she had *something* to offer—a relative who'd achieved some high office, a little bit of money—it would be enough. The mothers would go home to their husbands and their sons and say, "Perhaps it's not the best match, but she'll do."

Bonny began to think of the *Odontoglossum crispum* in a new light. How much was it worth? Enough to change anyone's mind?

On their last day in London, Cordelia had a wicked idea. She wrapped *The Widow* in thick paper and sent it by post to Olympia, along with their farewells and, as a postscript, "Something to talk about when we see one another next."

THE HAIRS on the back of Loel's neck rose when he walked into New Quay. The hostile glances and cold shoulders weren't anything new, but the intensity had increased. A few dockworkers jostled him as they passed, knocking their shoulders into his. A middle-aged woman with laugh lines at her lips and eyes deliberately jostled his basket, cracking the eggs he'd just bought.

Because he'd been seen with Miss Reed. She'd suffered unspecified repercussions, but she remained the town's favorite daughter. People here were proud of her, the way they might have been proud of a scenic view or a geological formation. They didn't have to be responsible for her beauty to feel blessed by it.

He would collect more blame—and, if he weren't careful, a more severe punishment. He decided to cut his marketing short and head home early. He could travel beyond the county border for supplies, if he had to.

He looked around, saw nothing, and continued along the road to Woodclose. He only made it a few steps before Charles Gavin stepped out from an alley. A few of his Black Lion cronies surrounded Gavin in a protective circle.

"You seem to have forgotten something important," said Gavin. "You're not welcome in this town."

After the fire, Loel had decided that he'd done enough damage for one lifetime. He'd promised himself that he'd never harm another soul. He'd known, even at the time, that it was an impossible oath. There was no way to live a whole human life without causing some pain. The good might overwhelm the bad, but there'd always be a scrum on the bottom, congealed from resentments and grudges, bitterness and jealousy.

But in this instance, at least, he knew what he owed to himself and to New Quay. Charles Gavin wanted a fight, however unfair. He wouldn't get it. Loel refused to lift a hand against these men, not even in self-defense.

"It's bad enough that you lure lowlife cretins onto our streets," Gavin continued. "But you crossed a line when you led one of our women astray."

"You're speaking of Miss Reed?"

"You don't say her name." Gavin swelled up with each furious word, like a cock ruffling his feathers. He was so proud of himself, and so pathetic to Loel's eyes. "You don't speak to her, *of* her—you don't go near her—"

Loel interrupted. "She deserves better than you."

For a brief, satisfying moment, Gavin froze with his mouth agape. Apparently Loel was supposed to listen quietly to a harangue before calmly accepting his beating. Charles Gavin had spent too much of his time in a town his family practically owned.

Loel wouldn't fight back, but neither would he kowtow to the bully.

Gavin scoffed. "Like you?"

"Not me." Loel rolled his shoulders, loosening them. Warming his muscles might help, once fists were flying. "But better than you. And she'll get it too."

Gavin cracked his knuckles. "Shut your mouth."

Loel shrugged. If Gavin had organized this, if he'd decided to play the brute in broad daylight, then Loel didn't need to say a word. Gavin already knew he'd lost Bonny Reed.

Loel filled his lungs. He was about to be in a great deal of pain but for the space of one breath, he'd enjoy his victory. He'd saved Miss Reed from this lout—and she would be fine. Better than fine.

"You don't know anything," Gavin snarled. "I'll show you."

The bullies at his back murmured encouragement, and Gavin lunged, aiming for Loel's face. Loel dodged, but Gavin still struck a glancing blow to his temple. It was enough to send Loel reeling. Someone kicked his knee. Someone else slugged the small of his back. He couldn't count the blows, couldn't parse the pain, and mercifully blacked out.

~

BONNY MARSHALED her arguments on the way home, but they fell apart the moment she walked through the door. Her mother greeted her with a kiss on the cheek and said, "You must have had a good time, because you're looking well. It's nice to see color in your cheeks. Why don't you go upstairs to refresh yourself and then get started on the darning?"

"I'd like to talk about—"

"Not now, dear." Her mother gave her a gentle nudge toward the stairs. "We'll listen to your stories this evening, after the work is done."

And just like that, the full head of steam that Bonny had built up dissolved into nothing. She tromped up the stairs, changed into a house dress, and went looking for Margot.

Her sister was on her knees in their small kitchen garden, planting seedlings.

"Bonny!" Margot jumped to her feet and threw her dirt-caked arms around her sister's neck. "I missed you! Did you have a marvelous time? Did you go to any plays? Did you see fine ladies wearing gigantic hats?"

"No plays I'm afraid. But the hats were remarkable. I saw feathers in colors I don't have names for—not to mention gems and flowers and ribbons that could steal your heart—"

"Oh, stop, stop! I can't bear anymore!" Margot reeled away, clutching her chest. "Just imagining the splendor will make me faint dead away!"

"Then I probably shouldn't tell you I made a friend who knows *Queen Victoria*."

"No!" Margot covered her gaping mouth. "Really?"

"She's the Queen's ward," said Bonny. "I think they see one another rather often."

"Oh." Margot slumped back against the wall with a dreamy sigh, eyes rolling heavenward. "I can't believe it. Bonny! That's amazing!"

"I'm sure you'll meet her eventually," Bonny said, then immediately felt guilty. She'd been invited into the home of two people she hardly knew—and the Gainsways had only tolerated her for Cordelia's sake. Their hospitality probably *wouldn't* extend to a second unwanted guest.

"Once you're married," said Margot in a bright but dismissive tone that Bonny knew well—a cheerful way to end a conversation that had veered into fantasy. Good things would come but not yet; until then, she'd wait.

And wait.

Bonny sighed and went inside to pick up the darning. She was the only person in the house capable of patching stockings, which ripped with a truly dispiriting regularity. She managed half the accumulated stockpile before her fingers went stiff, and then her father came home from work and it was time for dinner.

By the time she sat down to eat with her family, London seemed a world away. The bright sense of possibility she'd experienced with Olympia and Tess, the prospect of worlds opening up to her if only she'd chart a path into them, simply didn't make sense at the end of an ordinary day at home.

Margot had dozens of questions about the sights and the shops. Bonny found that she hated answering them. She hadn't been tromping around London with a Baedeker in hand, enjoying her leisure. Describing Tess and Olympia was even worse; the more she talked, the more they seemed like figments of her imagination. It was simply too good to be true, wasn't it? A pair of heroic rescuers with the funds and the connections to grant all Bonny's wishes.

She grew more and more irritated until she finally burst out with, "I want to go back. I want to call off my engagement and go back to London."

Her mother dropped her cutlery with a discordant clang. "You want." She laughed harshly and repeated, with real contempt, "You *want*."

"I think my chances are good. I was amazed to discover that even in London everyone thinks I'm really very"—Bonny lowered her voice to an embarrassed whisper—"beautiful."

Margot rolled her eyes. "That's hardly news."

"I have to agree with Margot. The only person who could be surprised by this news is you, Bonny." Her mother pinned her with a heavy, penetrating look. "When a man chooses a wife, he shows the world what he most values in a woman—be that intelligence, industry, a nurturing temperament. What sort of man chooses beauty?"

"I..." Bonny floundered. "I don't know. What kind?"

"A shallow one," answered Mrs. Reed. "A shallow—"

"Agatha," interrupted Mr. Reed. "That's enough."

"Is it?" Mrs. Reed raised her eyebrows, holding her husband's stare. "Am I wrong?"

"Does it matter what catches a man's eye first? If it convinces him to take a second look and see into her heart..." Mr. Reed gestured to Margot. "Don't get the wrong idea. Most men are good."

"They are," Mrs. Reed agreed. "But Bonny, so long as you're baiting a trap with beauty, you'll keep attracting men like Charles Gavin."

"You sound like you don't like him very much," observed Margot. "If you don't like him, and Bonny doesn't like him, why do you want her to marry him?"

"It's my dearest wish to see both of you happy. If I could give you the world on a string, I would." Her mother sighed. "But I can't. And I know you don't want to hear it, either of you, but the hard truth is that every time you ask for more, you risk ending up with nothing."

"Give it some time," urged her father. "Take a few days to think—there's no harm in that. Be sure. The Gavins are proud. If you break the engagement, there won't be any going back."

That was certainly true. And though her parents had offered harsh advice, it seemed they would leave the final decision up to her. She could choose how to proceed. She appreciated that—and she could show them just how much by acceding to her father's request.

"All right. I'll think about it."

Her parents *were* right. And she was grateful for their harsh words because they'd offered *advice*. Instead of telling her what to do, they'd trusted her to make her own decision.

And yet the conversation inspired at least one small act of rebellion. She would, as her parents asked, spend the next few days weighing her decision. But in the meanwhile, she decided she would pay a visit to the Woodclose greenhouse. To check on her *Odontoglossum crispum*.

She had responsibilities, after all. To her family... and also to the ugliest orchid she'd ever seen. And she took her responsibilities very seriously.

Didn't she?

BONNY HEAVED open the door to the greenhouse late the next morning. She stepped right into a puddle and let out an undignified squeak. The greenhouse had flooded.

The hairs on the back of her neck rose. It was midday. Gloomy, admittedly, sullen and overcast with rain threatening. But Lord Loel would *never* drench his orchid house with the sun so high in the sky.

"Lord Loel?"

The more she looked, the more she worried. Flowers that had been flourishing on her last visit drooped listlessly. Petals had begun to brown. Something had gone very, very wrong.

Her heart thumped against her rib cage. "Don't be a goose," she scolded herself—out loud for the comfort of her own voice—before removing her boots and peeling off her stockings. She'd already ruined her best boots in London, diving into that canal. She couldn't afford to lose another pair.

She paused automatically at the *Odontoglossum crispum*. It was fine; no different from the last time she'd seen it more than two weeks ago.

She followed the winding path through the orchid house and found Lord Loel flat on his back by the water tank, soaked, shivering, and sporting a pair of vivid purple black eyes.

"Lord Loel?" Bonny crouched low. She smoothed the tangled hair from his brow, only to snatch her hand back in shock.

He was burning up.

"Lord Loel." Her voice trembled. "Can you hear me?"

No response.

"What happened to you?"

A closer look revealed other injuries. He was bleeding from his nose, from a cut on his brow. His eyes were so swollen she doubted he could open them even if he wanted. And he was breathing so shallowly.

He looked—she shuddered—like a man who would not live to see the next dawn.

"I'm going to help," she promised. "I'll do everything I can."

She needed supplies. She could go home, but that would take hours she didn't have. She'd start by searching the great house. With a little luck, she'd find a cupboard or shelf somewhere stocked with infirmary items.

Quickly now. Minutes and hours might matter. She hurried to the door and snatched her shoes so she could put them back on outside and paused with her fingers on the handle.

The drenched floor made sense now. Lord Loel had known he

was too ill for his usual round of chores. He'd faced an unpleasant choice: let his flowers dry out or let the sun burn them. He'd wagered that the gloomy weather would hold, and he'd over-flowed the water tank on purpose. Gallons and gallons had spilled, and now, hours later, the air remained saturated with moisture.

The effort must have so exhausted him that, once he'd accom-plished his task, he'd collapsed on the spot.

She could have laughed—he'd put his health in jeopardy for a few flowers! Except that he'd invested months and perhaps years of effort into these orchids. He stood in danger of losing his livelihood.

The door to the great house was unlocked. Bonny entered and found herself in a large room with a checkered marble floor that must have been grand—a music room, perhaps, or a summer dining room—before it had been converted into a shed. Sheets pinned to the walls protected them from the piles of firewood stacked almost to the ceiling. Crates and cabinets overflowed with an incredible assortment of tools and accoutrements, everything from wrenches to shoe polish.

Farther in, the situation changed. Instead of clutter she saw dust and neglect, sheet-wrapped furniture and eerie quiet. She peeked upstairs too. The bedroom that ought to have been Loel's consisted of a massive suite with a sitting room and dressing room flanking the bedroom, but no one had used it in years. The carpets had been rolled up and stacked against the wall, the mattress on the huge bed was bare, sheets draped all the furni-ture. Dust coated everything.

The wardrobes were full of fine clothes, all tailored for a man shorter and thicker around the middle than Loel.

It wasn't that the rooms lacked personality. Not Loel's suite or any other. Bonny found a veritable museum of taxidermied rodents in a bedroom down the hall, voles and beavers and porcu-pines arranged in lifelike poses on wooden stands, all mangy from neglect. There were porcelain dolls in tiny, eighteenth-century finery, swords and medals from soldier ancestors hanging on the walls, a fireplace full of split geodes.

But aside from the sunny salon-turned-shed, Bonny only found one other room that showed any sign of use. A bedroom, not the biggest, but the bed had been clumsily made up with fresh linen. The few keepsakes scattered about the room had a marine flavor; pride of place, over the mantle, had been given to a beautifully embroidered cloth. Bonny had never seen anything like it; the patterns and colors were utterly foreign to her, though she appreciated the fine needlework as only someone who took pride in her own fine stitching could.

And yet she didn't think that Loel used this bedroom as his own. There was no clutter, none of the paraphernalia of everyday life—no hair tonics or shoe polish or brushes. Those things had all been downstairs in the salon-turned-shed.

The room was a mystery. The whole house was a mystery. Loel had a large and comfortable home that, as far as she could tell, he rarely entered. No one person could care for a house of this size alone… but Loel had grown up here. This was his *home*. He treated it like a tomb.

She found the stairs leading to the basement and hurried down them. She only had a glancing familiarity with great houses, but at a guess, the practical things would all be kept within easy reach of the staff.

The spacious kitchen stood at the center of a mazelike warren of connected rooms. The first door she tried was locked. Swallowing her frustration, she tracked down the key hanging from a peg in the kitchen. She searched the scullery, the laundry, the pantry, and finally struck gold in the housekeeper's room.

The cupboards contained all the supplies she could wish for. She filled a basket with rolls of gauze, a bottle of witch hazel, scissors and tweezers, needle and thread. She wasn't sure what she'd do with most of it, but she'd have it near to hand if inspiration struck.

She hurried back to the greenhouse, where Loel hadn't stirred.

Even with his bed so close, she doubted she could drag him to it, let alone lift him onto the mattress. But neither could she leave him lying on the ground in wet clothes.

After a few minutes of anxious thought, she decided to remove some of his clothes. She tugged his boots free and peeled his stockings from his feet, then dipped a rough cloth into the tank and washed his feet to cool them. She couldn't lift him to remove his coat and knew from experience how expensive it would be to replace, so she took the fine scissors and carefully snipped the threads attaching the sleeves to the body of the garment, then along the shoulder seams so she could remove the coat in pieces. She'd dry out the cloth, wash it, and sew it all back together later, good as new.

She soaked a pad of gauze in witch hazel and wiped Loel's face clean. Matter-of-factly, with all her expertise as a seamstress, she stitched closed his cuts. The fever was the real danger, she knew that. But she would fix what she could, first, and worry about the rest later.

She swiped damp cloths over his forehead and neck to cool it. She dragged him just far enough to feel the breeze generated by his ingenious fans. She dribbled water over his lips, watching to see if he swallowed.

Loel began to shiver. Had she overdone it, trying to cool him? She chewed her lip. Even though the temperature had fallen as the stoves ran low on fuel, his skin remained hot and dry to the touch.

If only she knew what she was doing.

She lifted her eyes to the glass panels overhead, but whatever prayer she'd been ready to direct heavenward died on her lips. Hours had passed since she arrived. Even if she left now, she'd be lucky to get home before sunset.

But she couldn't leave. Not yet.

Bonny returned to the kitchens. She found the meat cellar and managed to carve a bit of bone and flesh from a deer carcass. Emma did all the cooking at home, but Bonny had helped out on occasion, enough that she thought she could manage a broth.

She dropped the meat in a small pot, filled it with water, added salt, and built up a fire in the cast-iron kitchen stove. While the soup simmered, she stoked the greenhouse stoves with wood from the piles that Loel had stacked everywhere. At last she filled a small cup and brought it to her patient.

Loel roused a bit when she lifted his head onto her lap. She didn't waste any time talking—she fed him the broth sip by sip, coaxing him on with, "That's right," and "Just a little more," until it was gone.

"I'll be back tomorrow," she promised. "Try to hold on."

CHAPTER 13

I t was nearly midnight when she finally stepped through the door to her own home. Her mother must have been waiting up because she flew at Bonny, sweeping her into her arms. "Bonny! Where have you been? Why were you gone for so long? I've been sick with worry."

"I'm sorry, Mama." Bonny hugged her mother back, hungry for a comforting embrace. "I didn't mean to upset you."

Her mother pulled away, holding her at arm's length and examining her closely. "You look like you've been to the source of the Nile and back. What happened?"

"To me? Nothing." Bonny steeled herself. "I was at Woodclose."

Her mother's worried expression hardened. "Why on earth—"

Bonny barreled ahead. "Something terrible has happened to Lord Loel. I think he's been beaten!"

"All the more reason for you to *stay away*."

"But..." Her mother didn't sound surprised. At all. "You knew?"

Her mother didn't answer.

"What happened?" Bonny put her hands to her heart. "Was it

one of those strange men who visit New Quay? The ones that have everyone so worried?"

Her mother scowled. But her eyes dropped... and slid guiltily away.

"What's this?" Mr. Reed rubbed his eyes as he lurched into the hallway. "Bonny? Is that you? Where have you been?"

Bonny turned on her father. "What happened to Lord Loel?"

"Nothing he didn't deserve."

"What happened?"

Her father's expression turned mulish.

"Can't you guess?" asked her mother. "Charles Gavin happened."

Bonny grabbed the banister of the staircase to steady herself, swaying as shock and exhaustion combined to weaken her knees. "But why?"

"I should think that would be obvious."

"Because he told me about Mr. Gavin's child? And so he deserves..." Bonny couldn't finish the sentence. She couldn't believe her parents could countenance such brutality. "Cordelia had a theory that Charles Gavin had been scaring my other suitors away. Is this how he did it? With his fists?"

"Loel's a man grown," said her father. "He'll live."

"I wouldn't be so sure of that," Bonny retorted. "He's taken a fever. I was with him all day, caring for him as best I could. He's all alone at Woodclose, with no one to watch over him. He may not survive the night."

"Bonny." Her mother rubbed the heels of her palm into her eyes, sighing. "It's a lovely impulse, and I love you for having it. I do. But you know better."

"You think I should hold my own reputation at dearer than another man's life?"

"Don't exaggerate," snapped her father.

"I'm not sure how else to understand you," said Bonny. "Lord Loel helped me—"

Her mother interrupted, her voice smooth and conciliating.

"So he did. But will you consider the possibility that his motives are not all that they should be? When you have a good heart—and, Bonny, you have such a good heart—it can be hard to see ill intentions when they wear a benevolent disguise."

"So if he helped me for the wrong reasons, then it wasn't really help?"

"No, that's not—"

"Or maybe, if he wasn't *really* helping, then it's not *really* my fault that Mr. Gavin had him beaten?"

"Keep your voice down!" her mother hissed.

"Because bad people deserve whatever they get, no matter how cruel or unprovoked?"

"What's gotten into you?" her father shouted.

"What's gotten into *you*?" Bonny shook with rage. "He's sick and alone, and you hate him so much that you'd leave him to die? No. *No.* That is wrong and you know it."

Both her parents fell silent.

"I'm not marrying Charles Gavin," she said. "I'm done thinking. I won't marry a brute. I'm going to bed and"—she stuttered, then gathered her courage—"and when I wake up tomorrow, I'm returning to Woodclose. Because it's the right thing to do."

Bonny was drifting off when the mattress dipped and her sister climbed into bed beside her.

"Are you okay?" asked Margot.

"No," Bonny admitted. "I'm not."

Margot gave her a hug. "Everything will be fine. I promise."

Finally an optimist. They'd been so scarce on the ground lately. Bonny tried to thank her sister, but she was asleep before she could form the words.

BONNY DRESSED for war the next morning. Or, to be more precise, she donned an ancient dress with a stain on the bodice, a pair of old boots with salt damage to the leather, thanks to a few too many walks along the shore, and twisted her hair into a plain bun.

Every imperfection meant war. Because while her parents would *never* permit her to be seen in public like this, she'd chosen the perfect outfit for nursing an invalid.

She would return to Woodclose. If her parents objected, she would insist. If words failed, she would rush the door. Or climb out a window. Whatever it took.

She marched down the stairs with her chin pugnaciously high. Wrote a letter to Charles Gavin, requesting that he visit, and left it prominently on a table by the front door for Emma to post.

No one tried to stop her.

The floorboards creaked overhead as her father shuffled about his bedroom. He usually woke before dawn to prepare for work. He could have intervened or sent her mother downstairs to object. Why didn't he?

A vague uneasiness followed her as she gathered a few necessities from the kitchen and stepped into the fresh air. A thick marine fog blanketed the streets, pearly in the predawn, thinning gradually as she turned inland.

The cocks began to crow at about the halfway point of her journey. She reached Woodclose before the sun had fully separated from the horizon and found Loel exactly where she'd left him: lying on the damp flagstones, flat on his back. Dead to the world but still breathing.

She stripped down to her chemise, because she didn't want to ruin her clothes doing Loel's rough work, and started with the stoves. The fires she'd stoked the night before had burned down to embers. She stirred them with tongs and fed them wood.

She lifted Loel's head onto her lap, cradling it in one arm while she coaxed him to swallow a few sips of water. Just a little to tide him over while she tended the orchids.

They were fading fast. Spikes decked with flowers had begun to droop and brown. Petals littered the floor. She followed Loel's rules as best as she could, she didn't skip a single plant, and she'd hardly reached half of them before the rising sun called a halt to her efforts.

She finally had time for her patient. She prepared another pot of broth, returned to Loel, and coaxed a full cup of it into his belly. She daubed his lips with a napkin when she spilled and massaged his throat to make him swallow. She skimmed her knuckles across his stubbled cheeks, petting him, and murmured encouragement.

All the closeness made her very, very aware of his smell. He had been lying in the damp for who knows how long, unable to see to basic necessities. The results were inevitable, unpleasant, and dangerous for his already fragile health. He needed a bath. Bonny didn't hesitate for long. The stakes were too high for modesty.

She gathered a rough cloth and a bar of soap, removed his clothes—all of them, because it was necessary and she couldn't afford to be missish about it—and scrubbed Loel clean.

It was a vile task. She tried not to be embarrassed, but she was profoundly glad to be alone where no one could see her and that she wouldn't have to tell anyone what she'd done if she didn't want to.

It wasn't until she'd finished that she could really appreciate the naked male body she'd just touched so intimately, and by then she didn't care. She dried him, stripped the blankets from his bed, and draped them over him.

She didn't like to leave linens on the floor, but there was no helping it. She couldn't lift Loel. Perhaps eventually she'd think of a way to move him. If she were lucky, he'd wake and find the strength to move himself.

She had just enough time to wheedle another cup of broth into her patient before the sun dipped low enough to resume watering. It was fussy and repetitive work, but sewing had accustomed her to that. But on her feet, in the thick heat of the greenhouse... even wearing only her chemise, she felt faint by the time she finished.

She stoked the stoves as high as they'd go and checked on Loel one last time. It was probably her imagination, but she thought he looked better. The fever still burned hot, and his skin remained strangely dry, but his color had improved. He wasn't quite so terrifyingly still.

She swaddled herself in her warm clothes and set out into the gloaming. Dark thoughts chased her down the lonely road to town—she should have done more, she'd taken on a hopeless task, and she'd be grieving by the end. She almost turned around and went back, desperate to find some work, some medicine that might make a difference.

Her parents met her at the door. Margot too. Her little sister wrinkled her nose and said, "You stink," which—for some reason —Bonny found hysterical. Margot laughed too, and the tension between them all eased a little.

"Why Lord Loel?" her father complained. "Isn't there someone else you could help? Some other cause for you to adopt?"

"I know you're upset, but..." Bonny struggled to explain. "Who else can forgive him? Who else can reach out? If we don't, no one will—out of respect for *us*. And he might die."

Her father's grunt was brief and eloquent. *Let the man die.*

"Have dinner at least," said her mother. "You look exhausted."

"I am." Bonny eyed the stairs longingly. "Would you mind if I refuse? I'd rather lie down."

They allowed it. What's more, Emma brought her a tray with a bit of bread and cheese and weak tea, and Margot sat with her while she ate, repeating what she'd eavesdropped of their parents' conversations during the day.

"They're worried," said Margot. "But I don't know why. Now that you have help from Olympia and Tess, it doesn't matter what anyone here in New Quay thinks."

"They're our neighbors," said Bonny. "Of course we care what they think."

"They'll change their tune when you find a husband better than Mr. Gavin ever was." Margot hugged her. "And then you'll find one for me and everything will be wonderful."

In the morning, Emma had a basket ready for her, packed with a sealed jar of good broth for Loel and a bit of lunch for Bonny herself, if she could find time to eat it. The encouragement, however small, lifted her spirits.

They plummeted again when she reached the greenhouse. The fires in the stoves had burned low, and the fountains had stopped flowing. Even a cursory glance showed her that the flowers had suffered during her brief absence. When she reached Loel, he'd thrown off the blankets and shivered violently on the floor, naked and exposed.

Bonny blinked back a rush of tears. She wasn't a doctor. She didn't know what was wrong with Loel, and she didn't know how to fix it. Neither was she a gardener. This task was too big for her. She needed help, but who would come for the town pariah?

"Why am I doing this?" she asked aloud. Just a week before she'd been in a London. In a *ballroom*. Laughing with her dearest friend, chatting with an heiress and a princess, wondering if she should discard the fiancé she had for a better one.

Now she had broken her engagement, disappointed her parents, and she'd spent the past two days alone in a greenhouse with a dying man and his dying plants.

Calling herself the worst sort of idiot, Bonny stripped off her clothing and set to work. It was the same routine as the day before: rushing to water the orchids, stoking the stoves, feeding and bathing Loel. She learned to work the pump that filled the reservoir that kept the fountains going and worked it until her arms felt like they were made of string.

She'd never worked so hard in her life.

On the way home, she stopped at Cordelia's house. The Kellys' manservant invited her in, but she turned down the offer. She hadn't seen a mirror all day but she was sure she looked frightful. Indeed, when Cordelia arrived at the door, the first thing she said was, "Bonny? Are you all right? What can I do?"

Bonny was too tired to respond with a quip. "I'm fine. Lord Loel is sick, and I've been taking care of him."

"All by yourself?"

"Do you know anyone else who'd agree to help?" Bonny snapped, then instantly regretted it. "I'm sorry. I'm exhausted. I came to tell you that I won't be able to accompany you on the library delivery rounds"—until Loel got better or he died, whichever came first—"for a bit."

She felt bad. Cordelia already did most of the work that kept the library going. She counted on Bonny for the social aspects, smiling and chatting, that she didn't have the temperament for. Delivering the books together was fun, but it would be a thankless task all alone.

She didn't expect a complaint—Cordelia wasn't that sort of friend. But neither did she expect her best friend to say, "Of course. Don't worry about it." Or to gather her close for a hug and whisper, "You are a lamb with a lion's heart, Bonny. A lamb with a lion's heart."

The days passed in a blur. Her tasks didn't change or get any easier. She was fairly sure that a good number of Loel's orchids had died, but she wasn't confident enough in her assessment to skip them on her watering circuit.

Most seemed to be holding on. It occurred to Bonny that the technique Loel had taught her had probably been suited specifically to the *Odontoglossum crispum*, rather than intended as a universal prescription. The *crispum* had never looked better.

Loel's fever finally broke. He roused a time or two, opening his eyes and making startled noises, and convincing him to eat got easier. She wouldn't have called him lucid, but she began to think he had a real chance at recovery.

Though she still couldn't determine what infection had felled him. All the wounds that Mr. Gavin had inflicted were healing normally. She saw none of the signs that she'd learned to fear: no swelling, no discoloration, no dark threads spreading out from the site of an injury.

She was halfway through bathing him for the sixth or seventh time when the thought came to her, as though it were a revelation:

She was touching a man's naked body. She had been from the start, of course, but it hadn't seemed to matter. There'd been no room in her mind for thoughts like that.

But now, watching her own hands swirl over his flat stomach, his skin slick with soap, embarrassed her. She noticed, as she hadn't before, that his skin was golden brown above the waist, from laboring in the sun, but pale as milk below. The wiry hair she lathered and rinsed on his chest was just a little darker than the hair on his head.

She was shaking by the time she was done. Her tongue stuck to the roof of a mouth gone dry, her heart raced, her hands tingled. She didn't want to think about why. If she stopped to consider what she'd just done, what she was now feeling, she would be sick and guilty and horrified.

So she ruthlessly shut those feelings away and went looking for clothes in his size. She fled the greenhouse for the open yard, where the summer sun felt cold to her fevered cheeks, and gulped clean fresh air until her teeth began to chatter.

Then she fetched Lord Loel a pair of pants, and blushing furiously, she put them on him.

There.

Better.

A few minutes later he began to stir. His eyes opened, seeing nothing. Bonny nearly jumped out of her skin. She squeaked out, "Lord Loel?" in the guiltiest tone imaginable and, to her intense shame, quietly prayed that he'd fall back into his stupor.

He turned toward her voice, bleary eyes slowly focusing.

"Am I dreaming?" he asked, his voice gravelly from disuse.

"Yes," Bonny said promptly. "You're dreaming."

He muttered something unintelligible and sank back into unconsciousness.

Bonny breathed a sigh of relief. It had been wrong to touch him and ogle him while he was unaware. The same exact activities had been fine when she'd been subjecting herself to a vile chore she deemed essential to his recovery, but something had changed. She didn't need to examine what though. Only to make sure that nobody ever found out and it never happened again.

Thus decided, she carried on with her chores.

THE EVENING MAIL brought two letters for Bonny. The first, from Charles Gavin, proposed a time for his visit. She set it aside to answer later; she couldn't receive him in town while she was spending every day from dawn to dusk at Woodclose. She'd answer him later, once she had a better sense of Lord Loel's fate.

The other came courtesy of Cordelia, but the envelope contained a letter from Olympia Swain.

Miss Kelly,

I hereby condemn you utterly for the foul act of giving that book, The Widow, *to Tess and me. It was riveting, causing us both to lose sleep, and I hold it wholly responsible for the many arguments we've had since. Tess insists that the housekeeper killed the husband whereas I am convinced it was the widow.*

We sent a letter to the author's publisher, demanding an answer to the mystery, but have not yet received a reply. In the meanwhile, I expect both you and Miss Reed will reply in support of my theory so Tess will admit that she has made a mistake.

If you support Tess's theory, keep your thoughts to yourself!!! Unless you tell me in person—in London—as my guest. I live with my guardian —Joanna Peet, you may find her in Debrett's—in a house with many empty rooms. Should you visit, I will hear you out. Grudgingly.

This invitation extends also to Miss Reed. Though I hope she has formed the only correct opinion about your cursed book. The bachelors hereabout speak of her often and regret her absence. Ordinarily, I would recommend that you postpone a second visit until the time is ripe, right before the young men begin to forget you. Usually this doesn't take long —I have observed that young men have short memories. Better than fish but worse than dogs, at my best approximation.

I'm afraid that, as regards Miss Reed, they have undertaken to prove me wrong.

Yours affectionately,
Olympia Swain

The letter invigorated Bonny. Because she'd fished those two boys out of the canal, Tess and Clympia had introduced her around London. Because Tess and Olympia had introduced her around London, she'd gained the courage to stand up to her parents so she could nurse Lord Loel. The good deeds formed a chain, each made possible by the last.

She made the journey to Woodclose with a spring in her step. She stripped to her chemise and set about the greenhouse chores with a will, singing all the while. It might do the plants some good—or even Loel—and she felt so hopeful finally.

"Come, now." She poured Emma's broth into a mug. "I think you're losing weight."

The jostling, or perhaps the hard press of the cup against his mouth, roused him. He groaned and stirred, stretching his legs and rolling his shoulders.

"Don't thrash, please," Bonny said. "You'll knock me over by accident."

He opened his eyes. For the first time, the glossy blankness sharpened and his eyes focused.

"I didn't think I knew how to have good dreams," he said, very seriously.

Bonny opened her mouth to tell him that he was awake, that he'd forgotten his manners, but what came out was, "This is a good dream?"

"They're always bad. Nightmares." He reached up to stroke her thighs. "Except for this."

"Don't. You mustn't." Bonny used her free hand to peel his roaming fingers loose. But when she let go, he grabbed her again. His hands were hot and damp, and the feel of them on her bare skin made Bonny... hot and damp.

She pitched sideways, stretching to set down the mug of broth somewhere beyond Loel's reach. She needed to free her hands. Quickly.

He stroked her inner thighs with his thumbs. "My God, your skin is soft." His brow furrowed. "I've never felt skin so soft. Not... ever."

Bonny swallowed, afraid that the moment had come. That he'd return to himself and she'd have to explain. Instead, he sank back into unconsciousness.

Bonny stood. She trembled, head to toe, from fear and... from other things. She paced, trying to walk the jitters away. She shook her limbs and took deep breaths, but her heart only beat faster.

His thumbs had been inches away from her most private parts. *Inches.* If he'd remained awake for even a few seconds longer...

He'd wake soon and be a man again, and she had to be ready for it.

She had never touched a man the way she'd touched Loel these past few days. Charles Gavin, for all his faults, had never overstepped. He'd invited admiration, not intimacy. She'd never been able to touch him freely—not his face, not his hands, certainly not the parts his clothes covered.

But now she knew the silky texture of Loel's hair, the rough burr of his beard, the weight of his limbs. The only body more familiar to her was her own. She'd crossed so many boundaries, and she'd done it alone, without supervision... or consent.

She'd have to rebuild those boundaries on her own too. She had to ensure that when he woke, nothing had changed.

Late in the morning, Loel began to thrash. He continued in this restless, uneasy state through the afternoon. When he finally quieted, she dropped what she was doing so she could get some broth in his stomach before night fell.

He drank eagerly. The first sign of appetite she'd seen from him in days.

She finished the watering, filled the reservoir, and stoked the stoves, checking on him one last time before she left. He lay on his back, staring up at the glass roof.

She knelt by his side. "You're getting better."

"I've said the same thing to dying men."

He had? When?

Bonny smoothed a hand across his forehead. "You're not dying."

He seized her wrist. The quick movement cost him; he held her still, breathing hard, fighting to remain conscious. A battle he won.

"You're really here," he accused.

"I'm here." Bonny peeled his fingers loose, one by one. "But it would be best if we agreed that you were dreaming."

That wrinkle appeared between his eyebrows again—he didn't understand. It must have been struggle enough to sort dream from reality. Apparently a man had to be fully conscious to contemplate lying.

"I'll be back tomorrow," she promised and left with a feeling of deep foreboding.

LOEL WAS MISSING from his spot on the floor the next day. Bonny panicked, but he'd only moved to his bed. All by himself! She knelt by his side and pressed her palm to his brow.

"I think the tide has finally turned." She'd never talked to herself so much in her life, but she'd never been so isolated either. "I'll be back as soon as I've watered the flowers."

She began to unfasten the buttons of her dress... and then thought better of it. The desperate, awful days when Lord Loel had been a patient instead of a man were over. But laboring in the humid greenhouse with all her clothes on would surely make her faint. She decided on a compromise. She removed her bonnet, her gloves, her stockings, and her petticoats.

She'd covered nearly two-thirds of the greenhouse before the rising sun forced her to stop. Her speed and technique had both improved, though it was hard to congratulate herself when hundreds of his orchids had died.

Next she heated the broth that Emma had prepared. She carried it to Loel's bed, settled on the thin mattress, and lifted his head into her lap. Touching the lip of the cup to his mouth, she murmured encouragement.

He stirred and opened his eyes. His eyes gleamed in the cold morning light like sunlit absinthe, unbearably bright, but he didn't seem to see her.

She untangled herself once she'd emptied the cup. She had a few hours to herself, which she used to mend the jacket she'd cut off his body on the day she found him. Lord Loel began to stir while she was working on the left sleeve.

Quickly she set it aside.

"Lord Loel?"

He levered himself into a sitting position, sheets falling away from his bare chest to pool around his waist.

"Careful." She hurried to his side. "You'll make yourself dizzy."

He swung toward her voice, throwing out one arm for balance. Bonny caught him before he could tip, steadying him as best she could.

His gaze focused first on her face before dropping to the hand she'd splayed flat across his bare chest. She'd put it there to brace him, but now she became aware of how close they were, the springy hair tickling her palm, the fever still running hot inside him.

"Miss Reed," he rumbled.

"That's right." She steadied her voice and added, "It's good that you recognize me."

"A dead man…" He trailed off with a grimace. Bonny helped him to lie flat, and he relaxed, eyes falling shut. "A dead man would wake up for that face."

"As it happens, cemeteries are perfectly safe from me," Bonny retorted. "And you're not dead."

"Malaria," he replied. "Might as well be. Feels like."

Bonny touched her fingers to her lips, horrified. "Malaria?"

But he didn't answer. He'd fallen into the sort of deep, restorative sleep that his fever had denied him.

He'd be well soon. And that made an awful, selfish part of Bonny very unhappy.

She wrote back to Olympia that night.

Dear Miss Swain,

I have had a great deal of time for thinking in the days since Miss Kelly forwarded your letter to me, as I have been attending a sickbed. It is a dreary task, livened primarily by my memories of London—truly, the hours that Miss Kelly and I spent in your and Miss Hurley's company have sustained me at a difficult time.

I greatly anticipate the day when we meet again. Until then, I have decided that—as an homage to the author of The Widow*—I will keep my suspicions about who committed the crime to myself, sharing them with no one.*

Yours,

Bonny Reed

THE NEXT MORNING she set out with a basket filled with porridge and honey, with soft rolls and soup. Foods Loel could eat himself, without assistance.

Upon her arrival at Woodclose, he justified her confidence in his recovery. He was sitting up in his narrow bed, the sheet draped across his lap, staring at the pump used to fill the water basin with the fierce concentration of a mountain climber visualizing his ascent of Mont Blanc.

Bonny allowed herself to take in the sight of him: nude, sun-browned, with a smattering of freckles dusting his broad shoulders. Posture loose from exhaustion and illness, muscles slack, but the animating force of his personality had returned.

And it was powerful.

"I can work the pump." Bonny set the basket by his feet, quickly shedding her bonnet and gloves. "Stay where you are."

"Miss Reed?" Loel began to rise—an automatic, unthinking gesture for any gentleman upon the arrival of a lady. The sheet safeguarding what was left of his modesty slid so low that Bonny glimpsed the thatch of dark hair at his groin before he caught himself, bunched the linen around his waist, and fell back onto his haunches.

"What? You—" He groped about clumsily. Whatever he was looking for, he didn't find it. "You shouldn't be here."

"So I've been told." Bonny took hold of the lever and raised it. The first few pumps were always easy. Then water began to flow and the work took some effort.

The most peculiar cross between a blush and a scowl settled on Loel's face—chin bashfully ducked, eyes snapping fire.

"Miss Reed," he said sternly.

"It was my pleasure," Bonny said cheerfully. "No need to thank me."

The muscles in Lord Loel's jaw flexed as he ground his teeth together. Finally, begrudgingly, he managed, "Thank you."

Bonny paused, shook out her arms, and began pumping again. "You really *don't* need to thank me," she said. "It's my fault that you fell ill. Charles Gavin—"

"Didn't give me malaria." Loel interrupted. "I contracted the disease in Africa, and I'll have it for the rest of my life."

"Then it's even more directly my fault," said Bonny. "You wouldn't have gone to Africa if it weren't for me."

"I'm in no shape to argue." He glanced at his lap. "You shouldn't be here."

Bonny dropped the pump lever. Fine. She'd fought her family, and she'd been ready to defend herself against the whole town of New Quay—all for Lord Loel. Who, it turned out, also wanted her to go.

She knew when to give up.

"As you like." She snatched up her things and waved at the basket. "That's for you. It should see you through the day and perhaps most of tomorrow. Best of luck for a speedy recovery."

"Wait."

Bonny flicked him a scathing glance. He'd work himself to exhaustion, fall over—probably hit his head on the way down—and lapse back into a fever. And he'd deserve it.

"I'm thinking of you."

"You and everyone else." Bonny's anger cooled. Without it, she was just… tired. "But *I* was thinking of *you*."

"Well, stop." He covered his face with his hands, breathing hard. "Did I ask for your regard? Did I invite it?"

"No." Quite the opposite, actually. In the beginning, she'd intruded and he'd chased her away. Their encounters had proceeded more or less according to the same template ever since.

And yet she would have sworn that he was fond of her.

"Would you be more comfortable if I fetched you some clothes?" she asked. "If you tell me where—"

"Go." His head sank toward his lap. "Please."

Bonny dropped to her knees. Something like curiosity drove her, a nagging conviction that she was on the verge of an important discovery. She gently pulled Lord Loel's hands away from his face.

The torment she read in his expression startled her. He'd been sick, and now he was nearly better. He ought to be happy.

"You're upset. Why?"

"Because your kindness is wasted on me."

"How? You're better, aren't you?"

"At what cost to you?" He grimaced. "Who will punish you for helping me? How? Miss Reed—"

"That doesn't matter when your very *life* was hanging in the balance—"

"It matters to *me*."

His anger was real and growing. The harsh tone, the urgent delivery—he meant every word. And yet Bonny's impression that she was listening to a foreign language that she only vaguely understood had increased in perfect tandem.

She might have remained confused forever if something bright hadn't drawn her attention to the roof of the glasshouse. A ray of light caught on the dirt-clouded glass, then fractured into a brilliant sparkle. Bonny tipped her face up to the sky, attentive to this small miracle of nature for precisely the length of time required to identify, categorize, and dismiss it: just the sun cresting the horizon, dawn breaking into day, nothing to be concerned about.

She looked down, problem solved, and caught Lord Loel staring at her mouth. Hotly, fixedly, with a heat that struck an answering chord in her.

Oh, she thought, wondering how she'd been so stupid. *Now I understand.*

And she kissed him.

It was so natural, so obvious. An answer to everything he hadn't said, the words that swam in the shadow of the ones he'd given voice.

I'm thinking of you. He cared about her. *Did I ask for your regard?* He hadn't dared. *Your kindness is wasted on me.* Because he thought he didn't deserve it. *Who will punish you for helping me?* And valued her well-being over his own. *It matters to me.* And to her.

Their lips mashed awkwardly. Her stomach flopped in her belly like a dying fish, cold and queasy. She remembered, too late, that she had hated her first kiss. It had so upset her that she'd embarked on the investigation that had sounded the death knell for her engagement.

But then Lord Loel kissed her back, and everything was lovely. Sweet as meringue. Warm as the steam curling up from a freshly poured cup of tea. And safe—safe like home.

She'd never felt anything so pure. All the good things in life distilled into touch. When Loel clasped his hands around her waist, her arms lifted naturally to ring his bare shoulders. She thrilled at the sensation of his silky skin sliding against her own and grasped, for the very first time, that touch could be both a means to an end *and* an end in itself.

A proper kiss was a miracle. Nothing short of a miracle.

Loel pulled away, and Bonny mewled in protest. He searched her expression. His, equally troubled and fierce, made no sense at all. The discordance interrupted the siren's song playing in her heart.

But then he kissed her again. Differently this time. He teased her lips apart, he sucked her tongue into his mouth. Bonny responded with an eagerness that unnerved her, compelled by instincts she hadn't known she had.

The strangeness faded. Time itself seemed to thicken and melt around her. Every second stretched on forever; a whole drama unfolded in each one and yet she had no patience for savoring. She wanted to hurry, to find out what was next, to—

The angry, female, and horribly familiar voice of the vicar's wife shattered the peace of the greenhouse.

"Miss Reed!" snapped Mrs. Henley.

And Bonny's heart stopped.

CHAPTER 14

Bonny jerked free of Lord Loel. She stood, she smoothed her skirts—all by rote.

Part of her grasped the enormity of her situation. She'd lose her reputation, her friends, her future, her freedom. Everything. All her hopes were dead. All her plans had failed.

But this part of her was oddly... puny. She felt as though someone had placed a balloon inside her skull and filled it with air. As the balloon expanded, it pushed everything else aside. Panic and horror floated on the periphery of her awareness, unable to penetrate the thick elastic skin.

Inside, the balloon was almost—but not completely—empty. It contained one word: no. No, this wasn't happening. No, this couldn't happen. No, she couldn't believe it. No, no, no. No.

"I have no words," marveled the vicar's wife.

Bonny swallowed a burst of laughter. No words! What a coincidence! She didn't have any either.

"You are engaged to be married." Mrs. Henley's voice hardened as astonishment gave way to anger. "You, Miss Reed, a beautiful girl with a good family, a suitor who dotes on you for all the world to see—"

Lord Loel reacted to this speech, drawing away from Bonny, covering himself with his sheet.

Bonny just shook her head. No. That wasn't right. She wasn't engaged—not really. She'd decided to part ways with Charles Gavin. She'd planned to make it official, but she hadn't had time. She'd been here at Woodclose.

"No," she said in a half whisper that sounded feeble to her own ears.

"You have deceived the whole town. You—" Mrs. Henley took a deep breath and let it out slowly. "Miss Kelly told me that Lord Loel was dangerously ill and that you, Miss Reed, had dedicated yourself to his care."

But that was the truth. Bonny had spent the longest week of her life here in this greenhouse. Lord Loel had needed help, and she'd given it. Didn't that count for anything?

"She convinced me to join you in a good deed!" Mrs. Henley continued. "But here you are, playing the harlot. On your knees for the man who ruined your family. The devil couldn't devise a greater perversion."

No. Bonny shook her head again. That was all wrong. She'd known Mrs. Henley for years. They were friends. How could she possibly believe—?

"I have had you in my house!" Mrs. Henley grimaced, as though she'd tasted something foul, and turned to Lord Loel. "As for you—"

Loel interrupted her. "Spare me."

"Spare you!" Mrs. Henley cried.

"You warned me away from your husband's church. If I cannot attend his sermons on a Sunday, I certainly won't listen to yours now." With these words, Loel dismissed the vicar's wife. He turned his acid gaze on Bonny. "You are engaged to Charles Gavin? *Still?*"

"Yes, but—" Bonny cringed as an echo of the disgust boiling out of Mrs. Henley twisted Lord Loel's expression. "I haven't seen him in weeks. I'd decided to end it, but I hadn't had time—we'd have spoken tonight. Please."

"Cease your mealymouthed excuses," interrupted Mrs. Henley. "Gather your things, Miss Reed. I'll walk you home—since you can't be trusted on your own."

Bonny stooped to reach her gloves. "I'm sorry," she whispered to Lord Loel, quickly sheathing her bare hands. "I'm so sorry."

She took her bonnet and tied it round her chin as she followed Mrs. Henley out of the greenhouse.

"This is going to break your father's heart." Mrs. Henley walked briskly down the drive. "After all he's been through? But he held his head up high, and we *respected* him for it. What will he do now? And your mother?"

Oh God. Her mother.

"Of course, they bear some of the blame—and I'll tell them so," continued Mrs. Henley. "It's the innocents I pity—or is your sister like you? Does concupiscence run in the family? If I had a son, that's what I'd be wondering."

The protective bubble popped at the mention of her sister. Mrs. Henley was right. Margot would be tainted by Bonny's sin. She'd destroyed her own future... and stolen Margot's too.

Bonny's anguish turned dark and sour, reshaping itself as self-hatred. She'd been so proud of herself for defying her family, for setting herself above them. Acting as though she knew better.

She had been wrong. So very wrong.

Mrs. Henley kept a clawlike grip on Bonny's arm as she knocked at the door of the Reed residence. Mrs. Reed answered, took in the scene, and gestured for them to enter before Mrs. Henley said a word.

She looked... resigned. "What can I do for you, Mrs. Henley?"

"I'll not draw this out. I haven't the heart for it." Mrs. Henley gave Bonny a shove between her shoulder blades, pushing her into the center of the narrow space. "Your daughter is a tart."

Mrs. Reed wiped her hands on the apron tied round her waist. "That's quite an accusation."

"I know what I saw," returned Mrs. Henley. "This morning, Miss Kelly visited me for tea. I asked after Miss Reed and was told that she had devoted herself to nursing Lord Loel through an illness. I expressed my dismay, but Miss Kelly urged me to reconsider—she argued that by ministering to the man who caused her family so much woe, Miss Reed had set an example of true Christian charity that anyone familiar with her circumstances must admire.

"This argument moved me and I decided to lend my support to the endeavor. To help set an example for the whole town. So I set out for Woodclose on foot, prepared to share in Miss Reed's caretaking.

"The great house was deserted, as it happens, but I found your daughter and Lord Loel in a greenhouse surrounded by obscene flowers. He was completely unclothed—only wearing a sheet—and while he did appear ill, that hadn't stopped him from putting his hands all over your daughter."

Mrs. Reed's cool gaze migrated from Mrs. Henley to Bonny. "Is that so?"

"Miss Reed had submitted to his lust with such enthusiasm that even speaking of it is filthy." Mrs. Henley's nostrils flared. "Your daughter is a faithless liar, but worse than that, she is lewd."

"Bonny?" Mrs. Reed prompted.

But Bonny couldn't speak. She felt like a rat and wished she could be one in truth so she could flee through a crack in the floorboards.

"Mrs. Henley, may I ask? For Margot's sake?" Mrs. Reed drew in a shaky breath, but her voice never wavered. "Give us a chance to right the situation."

Mrs. Henley's prim mouth thinned. "I pity Miss Margot, especially if she is innocent. If such a thing is even possible in this den of iniquity. Miss Reed is not well. She is sick with lust, and I believe she is a danger to our community."

"I see," said Mrs. Reed. "I appreciate your honesty."

ERIN SATIE

"Your legendary composure does you no credit now, Mrs. Reed. Your daughter's fall reflects on you. Poorly."

Mrs. Reed nodded. "Yes, it does."

"Good. You understand." Mrs. Henley paused. "I'll be visiting the Gavins next, of course."

She saw herself out, closing the door quietly behind her.

Bonny, alone with her mother, inched toward the nearest wall.

"So," said Mrs. Reed. "After all your virtuous bluster, here we are. Should we expect a call from Lord Loel? Or will he disappear like he did last time and leave us to manage as we may?"

"I don't know," whispered Bonny.

The disdain in her mother's stare could have soured milk. "You don't *know*?"

"I didn't mean to—" Bonny caught herself before finishing that sentence. "I wasn't thinking."

"How long has this been going on?"

"It hasn't!"

"Are you accusing Mrs. Henley of lying?"

"No, no, of course not..." Bonny wiped at her cheeks. She wasn't sure exactly when she'd started crying, but her cheeks were drenched.

"How long?"

"Today, maybe yesterday." Bonny shrugged and sobbed at once. "I don't know!"

Her mother gave her a long, long look. "I don't believe you."

Bonny's jaw dropped. "Mama!"

"We're supposed to be a family. We're supposed to care for one another. But you've taken everything we gave you and repaid us with lies."

"You think I've betrayed you, and I have. I know I have." Bonny sniffled. "But you were going to give me to an awful man, just because he has money. Isn't that the same? Didn't you betray me too?"

Her mother shook her head in a slow, damning way that gave

Bonny chills. "We heard you out. We agreed to let you break the engagement. That wasn't enough for you?"

"It was." Bonny stared down at her feet. "I'm so sorry."

"So am I," replied her mother. "You should go to your room. I'll have to tell your father, when he gets home from work."

LOEL HAD little to show from his years at sea. There was the malaria, of course—an incurable disease that tried to kill him on a regular basis. It tended to strike when he'd already been weakened as, for example, in the wake of a severe beating.

But he'd gained something equally intangible. He had, quite literally, learned to weather storms.

A battle against nature was a battle that could not be won. Ever. Nature would never quail at a man's shaken fist. Nature did not surrender or retreat.

Almost every aspect of life at sea reminded man of his essential powerlessness. Even calm waters could kill—strong currents could send ships off course, underwater reefs and icebergs might tear the hull—and except for the new, steam-powered ships that had begun to ply the Atlantic, sailors lived and died by the wind.

Storms stole all the tools that human beings relied on to survive a crisis. Thunder deafened sailors, lashing rain blinded them, roiling waves took their balance and sense of direction. Standing still on deck during a tempest took more strength than most people would even dream of possessing—physical and mental—and yet the lowliest job aboard a seaworthy vessel required as much, and more.

When a storm rolled in, a ship's crew united with a single goal: survive. Often it seemed impossible. But by breaking this impossible goal into a series of manageable tasks, it could be accomplished. Sometimes.

In that spirit, Loel set aside for later contemplation the injustice perpetrated by Charles Gavin, the complicity of the town that had left Loel to fend for himself, the hours he'd spent limping and ultimately crawling home. He did not concern himself with the future of his nursery. He did not think of Bonny Reed, even as he dug through the basket of food she'd left behind.

He assessed his strength and judged it meager. So he chewed at the loaf of dark bread she'd brought and drank from the reservoir she'd filled, then stumbled into the yard to collect firewood.

The fresh air set his teeth to chattering.

Biting out a curse under his breath, Loel continued into the house to dress. The sun had moved appreciably westward by the time he had a full set of fresh clothes tucked and buttoned into place.

Armed against the mild weather, he began hauling firewood into the greenhouse. He had to force himself through every step of the process. Bending and kneeling made him dizzy. Carrying an armload of two logs—when usually he managed four, at twice the speed—from the yard into the orchid house left him panting with exhaustion.

By the time he'd finished, he'd drenched himself in cold sweat and his stomach felt like it had succumbed to rot. He collapsed onto his bed, groaning as the world spun around him, and reached for Miss Reed's basket of food.

He seized a jar full of amber-colored liquid, twisted off the cap, and drank. He recognized the flavor, bay leaf and thyme giving depth to a savory beef stock. It was equally delicious and revolting—because it had absorbed, as is the nature of broths, something of its environment, and now it tasted like weakness, like malaria.

His memories from the past days were hazy, at best. But he remembered Bonny Reed bending over him, wearing a gauzy shift, her skin dewy. He'd have believed he'd died and gone to heaven if her nipples hadn't been visible through the cloth, rosy pink and tempting.

"Am I dreaming?" he'd asked.

"Yes," she'd answered—without a trace of humor in her voice. "You're dreaming."

She'd lied. Why had she lied?

Why had she kissed him? He had not taken her for the sort of woman who made—or broke—promises lightly. But she'd kissed him while engaged to another man.

That... changed things.

He would have liked to ask her. He wasn't sure he could trust her to answer honestly, which troubled him, but he wanted to know what she'd say. How she'd explain herself. Unfortunately, he wouldn't have a chance. A man less thoroughly loathed could have tried an ultimatum on the Reeds: "Allow me to speak with your daughter. Depending on what she says, I might make an honest woman of her."

That wouldn't be an option for him.

As far as he could tell, he had two choices. He could leave her to suffer the consequences of their discovery alone. Or he could propose marriage.

If he left her to suffer the consequences alone, he'd never see her again. Charles Gavin might still marry her—some men, if put in Gavin's place, absolutely would—but Gavin didn't seem the type. Without her honor or a dowry, Miss Reed's prospects for the future would be dim indeed.

If Loel proposed, he'd most likely be accepted. The Reeds hated him, but even they had to admit he was better than no one. He'd then marry a woman he didn't entirely trust under extremely unfavorable circumstances.

Unfavorable because he kept his nursery growing by investing most of what he earned back into it. He sacrificed his comforts in the present for the sake of profits in the future. He wouldn't feel right making the same demands of a wife, and his nursery would suffer as a result. That had been true before his most recent bout with malaria, which had caused a financial catastrophe. He'd lost thousands of pounds worth of orchids.

Under different conditions, he might have been delighted to

wed a staggeringly beautiful woman he'd grown to genuinely like. He might have weighed the concrete sacrifices against the intangible benefits of a marriage and decided to take the risk.

Miss Reed's lies shifted those calculations. A woman who'd broken her vows once was liable to do it again, and he had no desire to live the rest of his life as a beautiful woman's long-suffering cuckold.

On the other hand, she'd saved his life. He would not have survived without her aid. If the recompense she required was marriage, he judged that fair.

Above all, she was a Reed. He had devastated the family once, by accident. They had placed all their hopes of recovery in their beautiful daughter. Now a second calamity had arrived, and he bore some responsibility for it too.

He hadn't instigated the embrace, but he'd been a willing participant. He'd had an opportunity—however brief—to push Miss Reed away before they were discovered. Instead of taking it, he'd sucked on her tongue.

That last consideration proved decisive. Whatever his wishes, in this case he couldn't put them first. He'd propose.

FIVE DAYS PASSED before he felt capable of making the round trip to New Quay. He owned about two weeks' worth of respectable clothing, for attending the London auctions, and donned his second best suit—he'd save the best for the wedding. He set out in the afternoon so that he'd arrive after Mr. Reed arrived home from work.

To his surprise, the walk invigorated him. He felt almost healthy, stronger with every step he took. The shudder that ran through his body when he set his foot on the Reeds' crumbling doorstep had nothing to do with malaria. It was the click of a lock, the tug on a knot as it tightened—the unique sensation of having come lived long enough for one of life's loose ends to curl around until, against all odds, it became a loop.

A woman with an unsettling, penetrating gaze answered the door. Her long nose and strong chin combined to make her handsome rather than pretty, and gray touched the medium brown hair at her temples.

"Mrs. Reed?" he asked uncertainly. She had to be, though she didn't look much like her daughter. Neither in appearance nor attitude.

"Yes," she answered. And said nothing further.

"I... If you'll allow me to introduce myself?" At her nod, he continued. "I am Orson, Baron Loel... of Woodclose. An acquaintance, lately, of your daughter."

"Come in." She held out her hand. "I'll take your hat."

He obeyed, entering a narrow foyer. A riot of watercolors hung on the walls, so many that the frames jostled against one another... and cleverly hid the faded wallpaper beneath. He recognized Juliet on her balcony, Ophelia in her watery grave. Melodramatic scenes, wonderfully executed. The simple hall stand where Mrs. Reed hung his hat had a bench covered in an embroidered cushion of startling fineness and quality.

Every time he'd visited the victims of the fire, he'd confronted the same awful truth: He'd hurt good people. That was why he never blamed them for their anger, or tried to defend himself against it.

He'd hurt good people. He couldn't undo the harm. His apologies *weren't* enough.

"Not one more step," barked a deep male voice, heralding the arrival of a man Loel assumed to be Mr. Reed—heavyset, older, with sad, watery eyes.

Mrs. Reed put a hand on her husband's arm.

"I don't want him in the house." Mr. Reed responded to whatever silent message his wife had conveyed with her touch. "He's taken enough—"

Mrs. Reed's gentle grip tightened to a squeeze, and her

husband fell silent. She addressed Loel in a bland tone. "Perhaps we can speak here?"

"Of course." He reviewed the speech he'd planned to make, discarding it sentence by sentence. The best thing he could do, it seemed, would be to keep the conversation short. "I'd like to ask for your daughter's hand in marriage."

"You have it." Mr. Reed jerked his chin at the door. "Come back when you have the license and a vicar in tow."

Loel hesitated. "May I see her?"

"No," answered Mrs. Reed, eyes on her husband—his lips paled to white, his neck flushed cherry red. "You may not."

Loel's anger rose up to answer his prospective father-in-law's. The Reeds ought to be more accommodating—not for his benefit but for their daughter's. If he were in their place, he'd want to see how his child interacted with her betrothed; he'd make an effort to set aside his anger in order to avoid estrangement in the future.

But he restrained himself. It wasn't his place.

"Very well." He nodded at his hat. "I'll send a letter once I have the license, to advise you about the date and time."

Mrs. Reed lifted the hat from its hook and handed it over. He tapped it onto his head and saw himself out. The whole encounter had lasted less than ten minutes.

CHAPTER 15

Bonny greeted her wedding day with relief. She'd cycled through self-pity, guilt, and fear. She'd fairly pickled herself in tears.

Every day at home had been worse than the last, because her family hated her. *Hated her.* Her father wouldn't even look at her, as though she were a wound and the sight of her might increase the hurt. Her mother spoke to her about practical matters but cut short any real conversation—she wouldn't hear a word of Bonny's apologies. And Margot... Bonny had gone down on her knees for her sister, but the last thing Margot had said to her was, "I hope you're miserable."

Whatever came next, it had to be better than this. Living with people she loved, when they didn't appear to love her back, was torture. She couldn't help caring about their opinions, craving their approval, and hurting when they denied it.

By the time Loel's letter arrived with a date and time for the wedding, she was desperate for the escape. He'd arranged for the vicar to perform the ceremony at church, right at dawn in order to avoid attracting attention from gawkers.

He arrived before her, and the sight of him stopped Bonny in her tracks. He looked... amazing. Crisp and clean in a tailored black coat with fitted gray trousers and a matching waistcoat, his collar points sharp. He wore his dark hair slicked close to the skull, the perfect frame for his angular features—starker and sharper than ever, thanks to the weight he'd lost.

His usual clothes made him look like a common laborer. They drew her attention to his body, to his size and physical strength. For once, he looked like what he was: an aristocrat born and bred, a peer of the realm.

"You can't come home," said Mrs. Reed. "Not even to visit."

Bonny started. She'd been so lost in her thoughts that she hadn't noticed her mother's approach.

"For Margot's sake," her mother added. "We can't be seen to approve of your behavior. We need to distance ourselves if she's going to have a chance."

Bonny's jaw dropped. Not from surprise—she'd been excruciatingly aware of her parents' desire to be rid of her—but at the timing. These were her mother's parting words on the day of her daughter's wedding?

"We make the best of the choices we have." Mrs. Reed kissed her on the cheek. "I hope you'll do the same."

And that was it. The vicar gestured for her to join Loel, who took her hands. She braved his piercing gaze to search his expression, afraid of what she'd find. Was he angry? Resentful? Did he hate her too? She couldn't tell.

The reality of her situation settled on her, heavier and heavier, with every word the vicar spoke. She'd spent so much time thinking about all the paths that had closed to her that she hadn't spent *any* time thinking about the ones that had opened. They all led through *him*.

Would Loel expect her to sleep in a cot in the greenhouse, like he did? How did he take his tea—and what if he wanted it so bitter it made her mouth pucker? Or so weak it had no flavor at all? Did he prefer crusty bread, which she hated, or—heaven forbid—take porridge instead of toast in the morning?

Her whole world could be turned on its head before she'd finished breakfast.

She said, "I do," with numb lips. When the ceremony ended, Loel's hand landed on the small of her back and they pivoted together, moving as one—as a married couple.

Only her mother remained in the pews. Her father and Margot had left while her back was turned.

Mrs. Reed flicked her fingers in a quick wave. The gesture, muted as it was, rocked Bonny. She saw the kindness in it, the regret. Her mother loved her. She didn't want to be cruel. And Bonny, who loved her family so much, felt a deep throb of empathy. She mouthed *I love you* as she and Loel walked down the aisle and onto the sunlit porch.

One of the vicar's sons waited in the road with the reins to a pair of horses, hitched to an antique buggy. All of Bonny's worldly possessions had been packed into two trunks, which were now lashed to the back of the buggy with a truly excessive quantity of rope.

Loel helped her onto the bench and followed after, taking the reins from the vicar's boy with a murmur of thanks. At his cluck the horses, placid and whiskery with age, ambled into the road. After they'd left town, Loel coaxed them—with no small effort—into a trot.

The rumbling and jouncing made conversation difficult. Bonny needed to talk with her new husband, not shout at him, so she kept quiet. Loel didn't speak either; perhaps he'd reached the same conclusion. By the time the buggy turned up the drive to Woodclose, the long stretch of very practical silence had her feeling like she'd been peeled.

Loel handed over the reins while he circled around to free her trunks. All the knots, solid enough to hold two heavy trunks in a precarious position over an unpaved road, unraveled at the merest tug. The signature of a sailor.

"Lord Loel—"

"Just Loel now." He glanced at her, momentarily wry. "Unless you'd like me to address you as Lady Loel?"

"No. No. Bonny, of course. My given name is Bonny." She gathered herself. "I know you didn't wish for this marriage. I'm sorry for... for what I did. For putting you in this position. But I'll do everything I can to make it up to you. To be a good wife."

Loel gently eased the top trunk into his arms, grunting as he took the weight of it. He lowered it to the ground and faced her, idly slapping clouds of dense, clay-rich road dust from his sleeves. "You might start by speaking plainly."

"What?"

"*What you did.*" Loel repeated her words, transforming them into an accusation. "You kissed me. While you were engaged to marry another man."

Bonny nodded. "Yes."

"Why?"

"I—" Bonny foundered. "I don't know."

That was a lie. She *did* know. She'd discovered something about herself that she hadn't wanted to acknowledge. And still didn't.

Loel snorted and reached for the second trunk. "So you'll do 'everything you can'. A shame that doesn't add up to much."

"That's not fair!" Bonny protested.

Loel ignored her, tipping the second trunk into his arms. He jogged it, shifting his grip, and carried it toward the house— turning his back on her and putting the bulk of the buggy between them.

Bonny, still holding the reins, circled in the opposite direction, around the horses' noses. "I'd already decided to break the engagement with Charles Gavin," she told him. "I would have done it if I'd had the time! But I was too busy here, trying to keep you alive!"

Loel sat the trunk down beside the door. "And I'm grateful."

He retraced his steps so Bonny did too, circling back around the horses. "And I'd long since lost all affection for Charles Gavin.

I think you know that. After I saw what he'd done to you, I hated him."

"So you feel free to break your promises to a man, without any warning, once you've lost affection for him?" Loel hefted the second trunk. "I'll keep that in mind."

"I'm sorry. I'm so *sorry*." Loel walked away again, so she trotted around the horses for a third time. "I did something wrong and foolish, and I regret it. But just because I did it once doesn't mean I'll do it again."

"*Say the words*. You embraced one man while promised to another. Not only that, you made me a party to it." Loel set the second trunk down squarely atop the first. He rolled one shoulder as he stood, tipping his head in the opposite direction to enhance the stretch and then repeated the gesture on the other side. The easy physicality of the gesture struck Bonny—it was the Loel she knew, hardworking and unpretentious, not the stern aristocrat who'd greeted her in the church. "And from what I've seen of the world, Bonny, you're wrong. People who stray once tend to do it twice. And thrice. And on into infinity."

Bonny's jaw dropped. "So that's it? You not going to give me a chance?"

"It is tempting"—Loel's gaze dipped to her bosom, lingered, and rose again to meet her own—"very, *very* tempting to believe that your principles crumble in my presence and no one else's. But I know better." Then, more quietly, "I *ought* to know better."

"There must be *something* I can do," Bonny insisted. "Some way for me to prove myself."

"I already told you how." Loel approached. Bonny swallowed when he came close, when he reached out, but he took the reins and shook them from her trembling fingers without touching her. "But I'll try again. While I was sick, I saw you at my side and asked if I was dreaming. Why did you lie?"

Bonny squeezed her eyes shut. Why did he only ask the questions she didn't want to answer? Her voice came out as a whisper, and even that was a struggle. Her throat wanted to close on the words, to strangle her into silence. "I was ashamed."

"Of what?"

Bonny shook her head. She couldn't explain. She *couldn't*.

"I don't mean to be unkind." Loel took her by the shoulders and gently urged her to take a few steps backward. Away from the buggy. "But you're asking me to trust you and showing me that I can't."

Bonny clapped her own hands over his, trapping them, and rose up on tiptoe. She had to make him understand, had to make him believe, and if she couldn't use words…

Loel recoiled with a curse. He covered his mouth, though her lips had never reached it, and stared at her as though she'd crawled out from under a rock.

Bonny shriveled right down to her soul.

The moment stretched. Bonny would have fled, but what would be the point? She couldn't run away from herself. Wherever she went, her shame would be waiting—with cowardice for company.

Loel set his jaw. He tensed, his nostrils flared. "All right," he said, reaching out again—for her. His fingers closed around her neck, thumb tipping her jaw up as he pulled her close for a kiss. "All right."

It was the opposite of their kiss in the greenhouse, which had made her feel so warm and safe. He plundered her mouth, tugged her lips with his teeth, stole the breath from her lungs and gave it back hotter and less nourishing. This kiss was unrepentantly angry, and Bonny ought to have been frightened.

Instead, she melted. *Melted.* Her knees turned to water, and she steadied herself by grabbing hold of him. Their bodies touched and every point of contact burned. Her breasts, crushed against his chest, ached.

The reins jangled as Loel dropped them, and a chiding *whuff* issued from one of the horses—Bonny didn't know which one because her eyes had fallen shut somewhere along the way. He wrapped an arm around her waist, and she tugged him closer, closer, closer.

Loel's fury ebbed, but the fire that fueled it remained. It had been this way from the start, Bonny realized, from the moment he'd found her snooping in his greenhouse. This draw that pulled her back to Woodclose when she ought to have stayed away, that riveted her attention, that had made nursing him so... complicated.

He felt it too. She was certain of it.

Loel pulled away. His lips, usually pale and firm, had flushed bright pink and shone wet with saliva. He composed himself but this one small part remained soft and vulnerable.

The symbolism didn't escape her.

He laughed shakily, ducking for the reins. He collected them, smoothed them in his palm, and said—directing his comment to the horses—"My God, but you terrify me."

Bonny, drunk on a small morsel of joy when it had been so scarce in her life these last weeks, smiled brilliantly. "No I don't."

"Is that so?" He laughed again, properly this time. "I have to return the buggy to Mrs. Twisby."

"Mrs. Twisby?" Bonny repeated. "You're acquainted?"

"I'm not sure how I'd manage without her," Loel admitted. "She lets me send her manservant on errands in town, sends him by almost every week. It's the only way I can buy anything from the shops since they won't sell to me."

"She's donated to our circulating library, as well."

"She's a good woman," said Loel. "Your bedroom is upstairs on the first floor. Feel free to explore. I won't be long."

SHE REALLY DID TERRIFY HIM.

Not so much the woman she was but the woman she could become. That kiss had thrown two facts into painful, blinding clarity for him. One: His new wife was only just beginning to learn how to use her beauty as a weapon. Two: Once she did, she would be unstoppable.

Her amateur efforts were devastating enough. When she wanted something, he wanted it. When she spoke, he believed her. When she made absurd suggestions, they seemed plausible. It was ridiculous, and it took more willpower than he had to defend against it.

People chided otherwise strong men for their "weakness for women." Loel wondered exactly how goddamned strong a man would have to be to resist a smile like Bonny's.

As they approached the Twisby property, the horses picked up speed without any urging. They knew when to slow too, at just the right moment to bring the buggy to a gentle halt right in front of their stable. The groundskeeper, who looked after the horses and the garden, emerged to take the reins.

Loel was surprised to see Mrs. Twisby sitting on her porch in a rocking chair, reading a book. He thanked the groundskeeper and waved his hat at the old woman as he approached.

She'd been a good friend to him since his return. She hadn't been hurt by the fire, of course, and had her own struggles with New Quay—her friends outnumbered her enemies in town, but not by much.

She loaned him her manservant and the occasional use of her horses. In return, Loel paid for the upkeep of her stable. It was more than he wanted to spend, but he thought it important to return her kindness with fairness.

"Enjoying the fresh air?" he asked.

"That I am." Mrs. Twisby grinned. "You look like a man who's got a tiger by the tail."

"I feel like one," Loel admitted. And then, gingerly—because he could feel his objectivity sailing away, never to be seen again—he added, "I'm married to the most beautiful woman I've ever seen."

"I've never seen her like either." Mrs. Twisby cackled. "She's told you about her circulating library?"

"A little."

"She came here asking me for donations, and I decided I'd give her a book. One, mind you. Books don't grow on trees—at least not directly. But once I told her I'd donate, she smiled and it was like the clouds had parted and the sun shined out, just for me. I couldn't help it—I gave her *five books*."

"The effect must dull with time," he said, thinking of Bonny's family. They hadn't seemed at all inclined to dance to her tune.

Mrs. Twisby's eyes sparkled. "Best enjoy it while you can."

Loel recognized bait, and he chose not to bite. "How's your daughter?"

"Not sending news often enough," answered Mrs. Twisby. "Hopefully she's enjoying herself too much to be bothered, but I worry."

"I could look in on her the next time I'm in London."

"I might take you up on that." Mrs. Twisby reached into her knitting basket and extracted a bell. She rang it, explaining, "I asked my cook to prepare a meal for you. Best take it home while it's still warm. Congratulations—I wish you happiness."

A manservant arrived with a slatted wooden crate half-full of dishes wrapped in towels, which Loel took. "I'll stop by again before the next auction," Loel promised, before bidding Mrs. Twisby farewell.

The walk home took fifteen minutes, which he spent thinking, inconveniently, about Mrs. Twisby's parting comments.

He had planned to postpone the consummation. It had seemed the wise decision for a host of reasons—the more comfortable they were with one another, the more likely that their coupling would be memorably good instead of memorably awkward. Not incidentally, he'd assumed that keeping his distance would give him a chance to reevaluate Bonny's character.

He glanced at the sky, measuring the sun's progress across the heavens. Not yet noon and already he could tell that he'd need a new plan.

Bonny wouldn't tolerate the delay. If only because she'd

discovered what he'd already known: Sex would cloud his wits. It would make him stupid and forgiving. What she *didn't* yet understand was that sex could solve almost any problem two sufficiently lusty people had with one another... but only temporarily.

He reached the end of the drive and circled around the house. He'd spent too much time inside in the months after his return from sea. He tormented himself with his parents' final reproaches during the day and then, at night, dreamed of Captain Royce with a noose around his neck, spewing curses.

Eventually he'd taken a closer look at the trust his parents had left, started his nursery, and begun spending his every waking and sleeping hour in the orchid house. Things had gotten... better. But some superstition had taken hold of him and he'd begun to avoid the main house.

Bonny called out, "You're back!" from an open window—she'd found her bedroom, apparently—and ducked inside.

He set the egg crate down on the table he'd dragged outside—formerly the dining table in the servants' quarters. Loel would have to repay the estate for any damages to the property—or its contents—that occurred while he resided at Woodclose. So he'd wrapped the furniture in sheets, shut up the rooms, and plundered the servants' quarters for furniture he could afford to replace.

Bonny burst through the double doors leading to the old music room, beaming. She looked—heaven help him—like the sun and stars in one, skin so luminous, eyes so bright. Breasts bouncing cheerfully.

"What have you brought?"

He began removing the dishes. "A meal, I believe."

"More than one, I think." Bonny began peeking under the lids. "There must be enough food here to last through tomorrow. How is Mrs. Twisby?"

"Good." He searched for a diplomatic term. "Bit cheeky."

"A privilege allowed to women of a certain age. And this is

really a wonderful gift." She smiled again, and this time he saw the effort in it, the edge of desperation. "How are the orchids?"

Loel grimaced.

"I'm sorry." Bonny slumped. "I did the best I could."

"Don't apologize," said Loel. "It's only thanks to you that any of them survived. But the weather's finally turned—you must have been warm inside the orchid house?"

"Aren't greenhouses supposed to be warm?"

"Some of them are," Loel acknowledged. "But not all, and I keep orchids that prefer cooler weather. A good many of those… overheated."

"You mean I killed them?"

"You couldn't have known," Loel replied. "In the winter, it's a struggle to keep the temperature high enough—but in the warmer months, heat is just as deadly."

"Oh." She sat, eyes downcast, a picture of misery. "Perhaps you can teach me to do better so it doesn't happen again?"

"Of course. It only takes a bit of practice—the proof is that the *Odontoglossum crispum* ought to have been one of the first to die, but it fared better than most."

"But it's still not healthy, is it? It's grown, what, a single leaf in the three months."

"It's a miracle that it's survived as long as it has." Loel sighed. Whatever Bonny's mistakes, they didn't stem from malice. Perhaps he was gullible, but he believed in her good intentions.

"Stay here," he told her. "I'm going to fetch the tableware and a bottle of wine. I owe you some information."

He kept china and utensils in the music room but just one set. And he usually washed them in a bucket in the yard. But he stored his wine in the meat cellar—underground for the even temperatures but no danger of accidentally poaching from the trust-protected bottles in the wine cellar—where the servants' tableware was close to hand.

It took some doing to carry the bottle and opener, a handful of utensils, plus the extra glass and plate all at once, with a few fingers free to open doors, but he managed it. He returned to the table in the yard and thanked Bonny when she carefully disassembled the stack he'd made, item by item, arranging the table.

She eyed the wine as he scored the foil with the sharp tip of his bottle opener. "Are you sure that's a good idea?"

"Why not? You're a married woman now." He peeled away the foil, twisted the screw into the cork, and pulled. "You're allowed a vice or two."

She lifted the glass he poured to her lips and sipped, pillowy lips puckering at the taste. "It's… all right."

"Hmm. Well, there are others." He downed his glass in a single quaff—he was about to explain something he very much hated to discuss—and poured himself another. "You must have wondered how it's possible for me to have access to my family's property but not my family's money."

"I'd assumed—everyone had—that your parents disinherited you, but that Woodclose had been entailed…"

"My life would be easier if that were the case. If I owned any part of Woodclose, I'd get income from it." Loel shrugged and emptied another glass. He didn't taste the wine, but that wasn't the point. "My father rewrote his will to bypass me while keeping the family's assets in the direct line."

Bonny's eyes widened. "Why? Because of the fire?"

"No." He could have explained but—no. He didn't want to talk about Captain Royce or the *Incitatus*. Not yet, maybe not ever. "He put everything into a trust for my heirs. It's designed to cut me out—but only me. If we have children, they'll inherit all the property, all the investments, bank accounts fattened by years of compounded interest. The trust will release funds to ensure that they receive appropriate care and schooling. You'll never need to worry about a daughter's dowry or a son's quarterly allowance."

Bonny's eyes widened. "And my family—my sister?"

"No. I'm essentially a tenant here—I don't own anything that I haven't bought myself. Not a single fork or plate, not even a book."

"That's why you couldn't donate to the library!"

"I had to petition the trustees to make improvements to the orchid house." He began ticking off a list. "The basin, the fountains, the hanging shelves. I had to prove that I wasn't stealing from my eventual heir. One of the trustees tried to stop me, on the grounds that commerce would devalue the property. Luckily, he was in the minority."

"What did he expect you to do?" Bonny demanded. "Starve?"

"Make a living like anyone else," said Loel. "Ask one of my competitors whether it's fair that the trust pays all taxes on the property, including the greenhouses."

"I suppose they'd say it's not."

"And ask yourself how you would have felt, knowing I had all my family's wealth at my disposal? If I'd been collecting racehorses and throwing parties while you sewed your own clothes and settled for Charles Gavin?"

"I would have been furious."

"So things are as they should be, more or less." He uncovered the dishes, and Bonny began serving—creamed spinach, roasted lamb, stewed apricots, all prepared with enough spice to prickle his nostrils. "We're on our own. But any children we might have are safe from our mistakes, and I find that makes them easier to bear."

"Oh." Bonny smiled, not so much from joy as from gratitude. "I see what you mean. Thank you."

He reached across the table and offered his hand. She took it, and he squeezed. "We can do this, you and I. We're going to be fine. Yes?"

He was surprised by how fiercely she returned his grip, by the intensity of her echoed "Yes!" And he wondered, for the first time since the vicar's wife had burst in on them, if perhaps he'd gotten lucky.

CHAPTER 16

She could feel Loel softening and it took all her willpower not to push for more. It was her instinct for self-preservation at work, the same that compelled dogs to please their masters or clerks their supervisors. She didn't just want his approval—she *needed* it.

Patience, she told herself. *Patience.*

She could tell that while Loel might be wary of her affection, he took offers of assistance at face value. She couldn't blame him for being suspicious... but nor could she stop herself from capitalizing on the one opening he left for her.

When they'd finished eating, she said, "Why don't you give me a more thorough introduction to your greenhouse?"

He agreed. Willingly. When she asked if he had tasks for her, to ease his regular workload, he answered "yes" without hesitation. He didn't trust her with his heart, but he seemed to have faith in her work ethic.

It was a start, wasn't it?

He introduced her to the iconic simplicity of the moth orchids, fan-shaped, brilliantly colored, and so modest in their demands: a bit of water once a week, good sunlight. He showed her how to recognize the *cattleyas* by their flamboyant lips; they only liked to be watered when they were very dry. She had overdone it while Loel was sick and killed most of them, leaving a large section of the greenhouse nearly empty.

The dancing ladies, on the other hand, had thrived under her inept care. These flowers formed a shape that resembled, like in a silhouette or a cameo, a well-dressed woman of the previous decade, with great leg-of-mutton sleeves and long, full skirts. They were all positioned right next to the cascading fountains, and the extra water had done them good.

The lady's slipper orchids were her favorites. Their petals formed a pouch shape that would have provided very stylish footwear to a fairy on her way to a ball. And that was only the beginning. There were star-shaped *Angraecums*, spotted *Vandas*... It was a hobby, she supposed, for people who liked to be absorbed in minutiae.

In the evening, they grazed again from the dishes that Mrs. Twisby had sent. When Bonny yawned, tired after a long day, Loel touched her shoulder.

"Not tonight."

She would have liked to whine. She'd had enough of rejection —and her husband was rejecting the part of her that she'd always believed to be most valuable; her body, her beauty.

But she checked herself. There was no judgment in his expression. His hand rested gently on her shoulder, a kind touch rather than an intimate one. Still, he'd made contact. He meant no insult.

So Bonny nodded her acquiescence and went upstairs alone. She slept now in one of the rooms that she'd sneakily explored while Loel was sick—grand and neglected, like most of the house, the protective sheets pulled away to reveal elegant furniture, spindly and feminine.

It ought to have been a lovely room, except that—Bonny realized—a lovely room must be lived in and cared for, must breathe with the soul of the people who inhabit it. A room that had sat empty for so long could only be sad.

Or perhaps her own feelings colored her perception of the

environment. Her dreams of marriage had certainly never included spending her wedding night alone. But she was tired, the bed comfortable, and she slept well enough.

The next morning, she received her first letter as mistress of Woodclose.

Dear Lady Loel,

You have acquired a title! My quill is quivering with glee. Why was this excellent news so difficult to obtain?

Miss Kelly refused to "gossip" about the recent turn of events—her unimpeachable loyalty is galling, to say the least. After I informed her that my most recent letters to you had been returned unopened, she did provide me with your new name and address.

Tess tells me that your Lord Loel is not seen often in town, which is dire news indeed. Please unravel this mystery! Better yet, show him the error of his ways. In fact, I challenge you to have him here within a month. You will introduce him to me, and I will form my own opinion. I will keep it to myself, however, until you've shared your conclusions about The Widow.

Awaiting your reply,

Olympia Swain

PS — Debrett's tells me Lord Loel is only twenty-six! So young for a peer in his own right.

Bonny immediately sat down to write back.

Dear Miss Swain,

Please accept my apologies. I never received your letters, or I would have replied earlier. I compose this reply in haste, before my courage deserts me.

I am married because I was caught in a compromising situation. It wouldn't be proper to discuss the details with a respectable young lady— a description I can no longer apply to myself—and, what's more, I find I'm unwilling to tarnish your opinion of me any more than is necessary.

I had such high hopes for our friendship. It grieves me to know that,

*through my own actions, I have brought it to a premature conclusion.
You needn't waste your time on pity; I seem to have stumbled into a
happy marriage. For my part, I will be wishing you all the good things
life can offer.*

Sincerely,

Bonny, Lady Loel

She folded and sealed the letter as soon as the ink was dry, so
that she wouldn't have to look at it, and joined Loel in the
greenhouse.

"Here," he said, pointing to a *Phalaenopsis*. "How many petals
does it have?"

Bonny counted and answered, "Five?"

"Three," answered Loel. "These three are sepals. Only the
remaining two are petals. The third petal is modified to ensure the
spread of its pollen, like so, with a lip where insects can land, a
hollow throat with something tempting inside. Perhaps a drop of
sugar water, perhaps the scent of rotting meat."

"Rotting meat?" Bonny had echoed.

"Oh, indeed. Let me show you. It's not pretty, but collectors
take an interest."

Bonny found it repulsive. Almost entirely green except for a
sort of... mouth-shaped bloom the dark, brownish red of dried
blood. She was bent over it, trying not to gag, when Cordelia's
voice echoed from the entrance.

"Bonny?"

Loel waved her away, and she hurried to meet her friend.
Bonny had been trying not to think about Cordelia—if Mrs.
Henley had done as she'd promised and spread the news of
Bonny's shame far and wide, Judge and Mrs. Kelly would have
forbidden Cordelia from ever seeing her again.

But Cordelia looked as she always did, calm and unruffled,
carrying a basket loaded with books on one arm.

"Cordelia? What are you doing here?"

Cordelia set her basket on the table and shook out her arm,

rubbing the crook of her elbow where the handle had left a red mark. "I came to ask you a question."

"Anything."

"You told me you'd have to skip our delivery rounds because you were here, taking care of a desperately ill man."

Bonny nodded.

"Did you lie to me?"

"No."

Cordelia narrowed her eyes. "Did you withhold the truth, intending to mislead me?"

"No." Bonny took a seat at the table, gesturing for Cordelia to do the same. She owed her friend an explanation.

But Cordelia remained exactly where she was, upright and uncompromising. "I don't see how that's possible. How ill could he have been?"

"Very. He suffers from malaria."

"Malaria?" Cordelia's eyes flashed. "So Mrs. Henley *lied*?"

"No."

"She couldn't have been telling the truth. Bonny, she said Lord Loel was naked, or near enough to it, and that you were... embracing intimately. To listen to her, you were on the verge of coupling out in the open."

"Perhaps she exaggerated a little," Bonny ventured. She really couldn't be sure. "He was on the mend— I had only planned to stay a little while, to bring him something to eat and make sure he could manage on his own..."

"Did he force you?"

"No!" Bonny shook her head, her hands, her whole body in instant negation—Loel was the innocent in this. "He made no advances at all... If you must know, I did."

"You," Cordelia repeated flatly.

Bonny nodded.

Cordelia's eyes narrowed. "And this had never happened before?"

"Never."

"Are you sure? You bend the truth sometimes."

"Not when the answer is so important!" Bonny cried. And then, perhaps more convincingly, "And not with you."

Cordelia finally sat. She propped her cheek on her palm and considered Bonny in her steady, unhurried way. "I was prepared to be very angry with you."

"But now you're not?" Bonny asked hopefully.

"I'm still thinking about it. Bonny, you could have gone about this *any* other way, and it would have been better."

"I know."

"You were in a difficult position," Cordelia continued. "But what does that excuse? We all are."

"And now I've made things even more difficult for you, for Margot..." Bonny blinked back tears. "I'm sorry, Cordelia. I am so sorry."

"I'm sure you are." Cordelia sighed. "Meanwhile, everyone knows about Mr. Gavin's attack on Lord Loel. Word is beginning to spread about his child. But he's as popular as ever."

"What?" Bonny gasped. "I don't believe it."

"You might be a fool... but he's a villain, and he's not sorry at all. What's worse, no one expects him to be."

"I wonder..." Bonny spoke tentatively. She didn't mean to make excuses, but she'd had a lot of time to think. To remember, to question the choices she'd made. "I wonder how I liked him so well for so long. Why was I so slow to change my opinion of him? The truth seems obvious to me now. Why wasn't it before?"

"I wish I knew," said Cordelia. "Do you remember when we met Mrs. Rhodes? We sat in her parlor, and we ate her pie, and on our way home, I kept thinking to myself that if we can't value this woman, it is our values that need changing."

"I thought the same thing."

Thought it, then had done nothing.

"Bonny, I wish I could be angry at you," said Cordelia. "It would be so much easier. But I'm not. I'm angry at everyone. The whole world."

"Then the world had better beware," Bonny teased.

"Yes," Cordelia agreed without any humor at all.

Bonny's heart swelled almost to bursting. "I am going to miss you so much."

"What do you mean, miss me?"

"Haven't your parents forbidden you to see me?"

"It's not their decision."

"But Cordelia... what if they find out you've visited? What will you do?"

"They're going to find out very soon." Cordelia gestured to her basket. "It's time for our deliveries."

"You can't be serious."

"On the contrary. I could not be *more* serious."

"I can't go into town," Bonny protested.

"I am your friend, Bonny. I'll stand by you, no matter what anyone thinks. But I can't hide from our members. Don't make me do this alone."

"All right. I'll tell Loel..." Bonny paused. "Would you like to meet him before we go?"

Cordelia agreed, so Bonny led the way. They found Loel on his knees by one of the stoves, stripped down to his shirtsleeves as usual, the cotton damp and clinging to his broad back.

"Loel?"

He stood, arching an eyebrow at Bonny as he brushed soot from his thighs.

"I'd like to introduce you to my friend—Miss Cordelia Kelly." Bonny gestured to Cordelia who, she realized belatedly, was staring fixedly at the paving stones.

"Apologies." Loel gestured at himself. "I wasn't expecting visitors."

"I'm sorry to intrude," said Cordelia.

"We have plans in town," said Bonny. "Unless you need me for something?"

"No."

"All right." Bonny steered Cordelia toward the door. "I'll be back soon."

Cordelia didn't look up until they were outside.

"That was my fault," said Bonny. "I could have guessed he'd be in his shirtsleeves."

"He just… walks around like that?"

Bonny nodded.

"All day?"

"It's very warm in the greenhouse!"

Cordelia walked at Bonny's side down the drive, oddly silent, eyes wide and as rattled as Bonny had ever seen her.

"I'm beginning to understand how you ended up in this situation," Cordelia said finally.

"What do you mean?"

"He doesn't walk around half-dressed by accident. He means to tempt you."

"Don't be ridiculous," Bonny protested. "He's spent too much time alone, that's all. Of course, eventually, he began to forget the proprieties… anyone would. And he didn't *choose* to be a pariah."

"I'm trying to say that he's handsome, Bonny." Cordelia snorted. "And that he knows it."

"So is Charles Gavin."

"And that served Mr. Gavin very well, didn't it?" Cordelia slanted a glance at Bonny. "I suppose you prefer kissing Lord Loel?"

Bonny blushed.

"Well." Cordelia blinked. "That's certainly a new reaction."

"It's like night and day, Cordelia. One word shouldn't be able to describe two such different experiences."

Cordelia's eyebrows shot up, but she didn't ask any further questions. They reached town soon enough, and conversation became difficult.

Their first stop was the chandlery. They stepped through the tinkling door, where Mr. Shaw sat behind his counter as usual.

Bonny smiled, though her stomach twisted. "Good morning, Mr. Shaw."

"Lady Loel, is it?" Mr. Shaw slapped a book on the counter and flicked it across the smooth wood. "This belongs to you. Mrs. Shaw doesn't care for another."

"Perhaps Miss Kelly could return alone—"

"Mrs. Shaw no longer chooses to participate in your library." Mr. Shaw glanced meaningfully at the door. "Unless you wish to purchase anything…"

"No. Thank you, Mr. Shaw."

Back in the street, Bonny took Cordelia's hand and squeezed. She did not think any friendship should be put to such a test—she would not have blamed Cordelia for abandoning her. The fact that they were still standing side by side was extraordinary.

Cordelia took a deep breath. "On to Mrs. Andrews."

Mrs. Andrews stepped out of the salter's before Bonny and Cordelia could enter. "Best if you don't come in." She handed over her book. "We have customers."

"I see," said Bonny. "Thank you for returning the book. Can we give you—"

"No, thank you." Mrs. Andrews interrupted. "I've had enough of reading."

They visited Mrs. Morgan's tiny cottage. She answered their knock, disheveled and tired, children squabbling in the background. But she lifted her chin haughtily as she returned her primers, saying, "I'm only opening the door to you so I can give you these—and I hope, for the good of the community, that you'll return them to Mrs. Henley."

Some of the women who cut them had dandled Bonny when she was a baby. She'd trimmed hats for them in the summer, knitted scarves for them in the winter. All those years of shared experiences, of joy and suffering and bickering and support, had come to a close. Just like that.

Even *Mrs. Rhodes* turned them away. "I'm sorry," she

explained, a baby at her breast. "I can't afford any more scandal. I have to be so careful."

At the end of their circuit, Cordelia's basket overflowed and Bonny carried a stack of books piled up to her chin. Cold-faced women watched their progress from their curtained windows. Three men peeled away from the Black Lion to trail them as they crossed the main street.

Bonny's mouth went dry. She recalled finding Loel on the floor of his greenhouse, bruised and insensible, and wondered if it was her turn.

"If anything happens," she murmured, "you should drop the books and run."

Cordelia spared Bonny a brief, contemptuous sidewise glance. "No."

"Cordelia—" Bonny hissed, but it was too late. They'd reached the green, where a crowd had gathered. Mostly men, of all ages, but a handful of young women clustered by the church with netted veils pinned to their bonnets, shielding their faces.

A boy darted out from behind a tree and shouted, "Whore!"

Bonny recognized him. He was one of Mrs. Morgan's. She'd visited his home every other week for months. Shock froze her in place, and so she made an excellent target for the clod of… of… muck that he threw at her, brown and wet and foul-smelling. It hit the stack of books, knocking them out of her arms, and then another landed on her left breast, right over her heart.

"Coward!" Cordelia cried—but not to the boy. She'd seen past him, to his father lurking in the distance. "You send a child to attack a woman and call yourself a man?"

Bonny kept her voice low. "Cordelia, don't."

Cordelia swung around, pinning one of the men trailing behind them with her diamond-hard gaze. He held a rock.

"Go on," taunted Cordelia. "Show us how brave you are."

The man actually cringed, clasping his hands over the stone he'd been ready to throw and holding it tight against his middle.

Something thudded painfully into Bonny's back. She whirled

and saw the Morgan boy had darted close again, ready to let fly another stinking missile. Had he stored a pile of them nearby?

She braced herself but didn't try to soften the blow. The boy swung his arm up and back, launched his muck... but it landed harmlessly in the grass, about halfway between them.

His aim had been perfect three times and could have been for a fourth. He'd faltered.

Still holding the boy's gaze, Bonny bent and began picking up the books she'd dropped, stacking them one by one. At least he'd hit the spines... some of them might be salvageable.

When she had them all, Bonny stood. "Let's go," she whispered. "Right now."

Cordelia didn't budge.

"The people who can hear you have," Bonny insisted, flicking a quick glance toward the women by the church—one of them had edged away from her companions and stood with her hand covering her mouth, agape in horror. When she was sure Cordelia had seen, Bonny directed her gaze toward a man who stood on his porch with his arms crossed over his chest, surveying the green with a warning glare. He was bearded, in his middle years, expensively dressed, and obviously ready to intervene.

"Please," Bonny whispered.

Cordelia relented. They plodded across the green, the crowd dispersing as they went. By the time they'd reached the other side, they were alone.

Bonny didn't know what to say when they reached Cordelia's doorstep. She'd disappointed her parents, she'd blighted her sister's future, and she'd taken her dearest friend's greatest passion, one she'd worked for years to nurture, and killed it.

She hadn't wanted any of this to happen. She hadn't intended any of it. But she couldn't fix a thing. Not a single thing.

"Cordelia, I am so sorry. I wish there was something I could do," Bonny said. "I wish I could go back in time."

"I'm glad that you can't," returned Cordelia. "I understand my neighbors now, and I'd rather see them for what they are than enjoy their company."

Bonny didn't reply because she couldn't agree, but pressing her point would have been ungrateful.

"Think about it, Bonny. Do you wish you were married to Charles Gavin?"

Bonny shuddered.

"I didn't think so. The past looks rosy because ignorance is bliss—but that's the only bliss you would have known, and it wouldn't have lasted long. It's better to know the truth."

Bonny hugged Cordelia. "I do love you."

Cordelia hugged her back, awkwardly, and then she had to go inside. Bonny returned alone to Woodclose. It meant something to know that Cordelia stood by her not just as a friend but as *Cordelia*, the woman whose judgment Bonny respected, whose courage Bonny had always tried to emulate.

But wishing she could be more like Cordelia just made Bonny feel worse, because Cordelia would never have gotten herself into this mess. She was a better friend than Bonny deserved. And though the same could not be said for the rest of New Quay, Bonny still wanted to belong. She still wanted their friendship and admiration, a place in their community.

She would never have it again. Not ever.

She turned up the drive to Woodclose in the afternoon and reached the yard right as Loel tossed an armful of rotted orchids into a wheelbarrow already brimming over with dead flowers, all headed for the compost heap. They were black and brown and slimy, with a few delicate petals fluttering in the breeze.

She walked past without a word, into the greenhouse. She stripped off her clothes, unbuttoning her ruined dress so that she could step out of it when she reached the water basin in the back. She dropped her bonnet and gloves, tossed her petticoats and stockings into a heap before plunging her arms into the water. The muck had dried while she walked home and needed to be scraped off. It fell away, but that wasn't enough; she scrubbed her arms, her bosom, filled a bucket and used it lather her hands with soap.

She hardly noticed the time passing. When Loel knelt beside her and said, "Will you tell me what happened?" she blinked past him to the glass roof, reflecting the peach and gold of a distant sunset.

"No."

"You don't have to." He helped her to stand; her knees ached from kneeling for so long. "Why don't you lie down?"

She stretched out on Loel's narrow bed, staring blindly ahead while her mind's eye recalled, over and over, a child screaming, "Whore!" and a man hefting a fist-sized rock. Eventually Loel joined her, fitting his front against her back and pulling her close. He stroked her head, sifting his fingers through her hair, offering comfort.

It felt so good. So sweet and lovely. Eventually she rolled to face him. He lay with his head propped on one bicep, eyes half-closed and sleepy, mouth soft. He didn't change what he was doing because she'd moved; just kept petting her hair. No comment, no demand.

Eventually she planted the pad of her index finger in the notch between his collarbones. He didn't react, so she dragged her finger up along the bone. His skin was warm, ever so slightly damp. She traced the curve of his shoulder, the line of his jaw—whatever she could reach without disturbing him. She was afraid to break the spell.

The arm pinned between her body and the thin mattress went numb, and she had to shift her position. Loel's gaze flicked up to track the movement and so revealed the desire in his eyes, burning with the banked intensity of hot coals.

Bonny gasped.

He ran his fingers through her hair again, the same soothing gesture he'd performed a hundred times now, but this time he held her gaze. Everything changed. Her whole scalp shivered deliciously.

The same thing… only different. But did the transformation work in reverse?

One way to find out. She reached for the notch between his collarbones, where his heart beat. She slid her finger up along the bone, to his shoulder. He made a soft noise in his throat and shifted restlessly. Bonny doubled back. It might have been her imagination, but she thought his heartbeat had accelerated.

She stopped there. She didn't know what came next. She didn't want to push.

Loel grazed the shell of her ear—she felt sparks in her throat, in her belly. He pressed the hollow behind her jaw, followed the slanting path of a tendon down her neck, and then paused.

Bonny's fingers trembled as she hooked them under the strap of her chemise and drew it down her shoulder. Loel didn't flinch or look away, so she tugged the strap all the way down to her elbow, exposing her naked breast.

This gesture precipitated the single most gratifying moment of her life. Because Loel looked as though… as though a thousand gas lamps had been lit right before his eyes, as though he'd been standing between two canons as a volley was fired… quite frankly, as though he'd been witness to a miracle.

She might have laughed at the absurdity, or from sheer delight, but she never got the chance. He cupped her breast in his palm. Shock sucked the humor right out of her. He thumbed her nipple, back and forth, back and forth, until she felt as though her skin were dissolving. A sugar shell that could crack and melt, leaving her nerves raw and exposed.

And then he kissed her. If he'd wanted to break her, he could have. She'd never been more vulnerable. But Loel wasn't mean. He had *never* been mean, not once. He had a heart of gold, and he kissed her like she deserved to hold it in her two hands.

She could have cried. After the day she'd had, his gesture of faith meant the world. She tried to show him, opening to his explorations, returning his slow, deliberate kisses with trembling, breathless ones.

Loel traced the dip in her waist, the soft swell of her belly. When he cupped her pubis, she snapped her thighs closed. She didn't speak a word in protest, and he didn't move his hand—but a battle raged silently between them. She forced herself to relax, and he moved on, skimming a light touch along her legs, her calves, before wrapping his hands around her feet and kneading until she whimpered with pleasure.

Loel began to work his way back up her legs, squeezing and massaging the resistance from her limbs, leaving her malleable as clay. The desire he'd wakened swamped her, hummed along her nerves, throbbed between her legs, tingled at the tip of her breasts —all the places he'd touched wanted more.

When he put his hand between her thighs for a second time, she rocked into the heel of his palm, into that pressure, desperate after mere seconds of deprivation. While his clever fingers petted and plucked, he fastened his lips around her nipple and pulled. She shuddered, moaned—she didn't have words anymore.

He lured her into a haze of need, a world flushed blood-red as the light filtered through the veil of her eyelids. She stiffened, jerked, her body a puppet to instincts she hadn't known she had. A scream built in her throat. She held her breath to silence it.

And then it ended. Broke. Satisfaction rocked her—first like a stormy sea and then as gently as a babe in a cradle. She felt whole again, extravagantly content.

The bed dipped as Loel shifted. He rubbed the whole length of his body against hers, chest to chest and thigh to thigh until Bonny purred. Loel fumbled between her legs, and soon something blunt and hot pressed into her. He kissed her again, but she shook free of the embrace, panting shallowly. A nervous fluttering tickled the inside of her ribs.

She had seen every inch of his body while he'd been sick with malaria, including the soft, wrinkled appendage that had lain across his thigh. She didn't understand how it could be responsible for what she was feeling now.

Loel groaned, strands of sweat-slick hair falling forward to graze at her brow as his head drooped. Bonny tried to ease the strange discomfort in her body, but Loel kept pushing, deeper and deeper until she felt, oddly, as though she might suffocate.

"Breathe," he murmured, sliding a hand around her neck, massaging her nape.

He pulled out and slid in again, making it impossible to obey. And, in any case, breathing soon seemed an unnecessary distraction. When Loel moved inside her she felt dizzy.

She'd felt something similar. On days when she went hungry for too long and finally sat down to a full plate, anxious moments when she counted the seconds until she could reach a chamber pot, or those nights when she'd stayed up too late and her eyes drifted shut whether she willed it or not. Times when some bodily need simply shoved her conscious, rational mind aside and took over.

Making love was exactly like that. And, simultaneously, utterly different. She didn't want pleasure the way she'd wanted food or sleep or a chamber pot. She wanted Loel; no other man would do. She wanted him as close as possible; she wanted him inside her and on top of her. She wanted to feel his weight, hear his desire echo hers.

When it was over and they were back where they'd started— her back nestled against his front, his fingers stroking her hair— she felt like a cloud at dawn, bathed in rose and gold. She had never been so grateful to be alive nor so full of wonder at the world.

What a gift Loel had given her. What a perfect, impossible gift.

CHAPTER 17

I t rained during the night. Loel noticed when he woke to tend the stoves, sometime around midnight, and it hadn't let up when he roused again at dawn. He yawned and stretched, careful of his sleeping wife, but his bed (pilfered, like the rest of his furniture, from the servants' quarters) was too narrow for courtesy. She stirred, rubbing sleep from her eyes, the most mundane gesture in the world—for everyone but Bonny. *She* looked like Psyche, straight from the myth... which, come to think of it, began when Cupid, an expert archer, was so stupefied by a woman's beauty that he fumbled and scratched himself on his own arrows.

Loel had never before felt such profound sympathy for a god.

Bonny made *sleep* beautiful. Her limbs sprawled gracefully, the curve of her back and the bend in her knees balancing one another in a relaxed S-shape. Just looking at her was restful.

Her lashes fluttered, and her eyes opened. "It's raining."

"Out of season but pray that it continues." He dragged the thin sheet down from her shoulder to her waist, fascinated by the juxtaposition of his work-roughened hand against the smooth, supple skin of her side—her skin had a glow to it, a depth of light, like the milky translucence of polished alabaster or the dewy freshness of spring flowers. "It's good for the orchids."

"Is it?" She shifted—straightening her legs, twisting her hips—and in an instant she'd transformed from a sleeping Psyche to a Renaissance Venus, voluptuous and sleepy-eyed. "Why?"

"They like the humidity." He tugged the sheet lower, past her hip, his mouth going dry. Her bottom had the most perfect heart shape—plump, deeply cleft and utterly devastating. "Rain draws out heat too, making it possible to control the temperature inside the orchid house with much greater precision."

"It's a shame you can't make it rain on demand."

Loel nodded absently. The urge to fill his palm and squeeze was almost overwhelming.

"Or could you?"

"Could I what?"

"Make it rain," she said. "You could build another fountain and put the spout on the roof!"

"Build a…" He blinked. God, he was hard. "What?"

"Fountain."

He dragged his gaze up to her face—which, he was reminded, could be quite distracting all on its own—and scrambled desperately for some semblance of rational thought. Would it be rude if he kissed her?

"I suppose it would require a great deal of water to cover the whole roof." A little furrow appeared between her brows. "You couldn't just dig a well."

He kissed her. She made a muffled, startled noise, and he jerked back, sat straight, met thick-lashed eyes gone wide as saucers. He was a brute. An absolute brute. He ought to listen when she spoke instead of ogling her—

She tugged his wrist, rising as he bent to her will, and kissed him back.

So… not a brute? He wasn't entirely sure. He'd think about it later. Right now her lips were soft and pillowy. Her breasts overflowed his palms, and her nipples crinkled against his tongue when he sucked. He'd been right to fear this. Touching her made his doubts about the marriage seem like petty quibbles with the persuasive force of a crumpled newspaper.

She gasped, shivered, moaned. If he'd had feathers, he would have preened like a cock. Instead, he kissed his way down her belly and nuzzled between her thighs. Her musky scent bypassed his brain and went straight to his blood. He breathed deep, and then again, clutching her tighter, spreading her legs wider. She squirmed, but her protests didn't last past the first lick. She tasted tangy and savory—human—her secret flesh slick and hot.

He groaned. He wanted to be inside her. He licked and suckled and remembered, with mounting impatience, how it felt to penetrate her. How tight she'd been at first, how by the end she'd clutched and keened and scrabbled her heels up the backs of his thighs, trying to pull him deeper.

Soon, he told himself, soon. The effort to restrain himself drove him a little mad. When she came apart against his mouth, pulsing around the two fingers he pumped into her, drenching him down to the knuckles, he froze. Like a stopped clock. And might have remained that way for who knows how long if Bonny hadn't wriggled and kicked and reached between them to take his cock in her hand.

She didn't have much of a grip, but that didn't matter. Her hand was small and soft and utterly unlike his own. It drove him wild. He let his head fall—it landed between her breasts, and he rolled his brow to either side, to feel the plump flesh. If anything could match the glories of heaven, he thought, it must be a man's last moments outside of it, when the gates have opened and the way lies clear.

"Do that again," he said.

Bonny hesitated. "This?" she asked, giving him a stroke.

He shuddered. Yes, that.

She did it again, squeezing feebly, and he couldn't take any more. He crawled up her body, met her eyes—hers were curious, ever so slightly calculating—and buried himself to the hilt.

She cried out. Her expression went vague and dreamy, eyes

falling shut as she tipped her head back, exposing her throat. He touched his lips to it, tonguing her pulse, wallowing in satisfaction. Two days ago he would not have believed that anything on earth could feel this good. Today he wasn't sure how he'd survive without it.

Her thighs tightened around his hips. He took his cue, quickly losing himself in her body—because she made it possible. Because she met desire with desire and moved like she'd been made to fit him or he'd been made to fit her.

He came hard, pleasure like a crash or a fall, shock followed by a fuzzy expanse of lost time. He returned to the present on his back, with Bonny glued to his side, tracing shapes on his chest with her fingertip.

"Did you say something about my fountain?" he asked.

"Mm-hmm."

He paused. "Would you, ah, mind repeating it?"

He felt more than heard her answering laugh, a few puffs of breath against his chest. "I said you should build a fountain with a spout on the roof," she said. "It would be like you'd made it rain on command."

He stared up at the glass roof, equally frustrated and exhilarated. It was a good idea. If it worked as intended—and he thought it might—his nursery would gain a real edge over its competitors. But he couldn't construct the sort of fountain she was describing himself. It would require cutting-edge hydraulic machinery, the sort of thing only a few specialists knew how to manufacture and install.

"Loel?"

He shook his head. Most of his profits for the year had disappeared while he was sick. "I'd like to try it—but I just lost half my stock. We can't afford an experiment on that scale right now."

Her only response was a sigh. Silent, not meant as a reproach, but he felt her lungs deflate against his side.

"We should get up." He wished he had a better answer. He didn't. "The sun won't wait."

Bonny found her chemise, drew it over her head, and began groping about on the floor for the rest of her things.

"I picked up your clothes and put them with the laundry," he told her, rising to his feet and stretching. "A laundress sends a girl every week to take away soiled clothes and return the clean."

"Oh." She stood but wouldn't meet his eyes. "Thank you."

He hesitated. He'd seen—and smelled—the mud spatters. "Will you tell me what happened?"

She shook her head.

"Is there anything I can do?"

"You can—you *have*. That's part of the problem. I'm happy here." A smile curved her lips and then fell away. "But my family... Cordelia. She founded the circulating library, the one I spoke to you about when I first visited. She devoted herself completely to it. And now, because I helped her, it's over."

"I'm sorry."

"I wish there were something I could do," said Bonny. "For Cordelia, for my family, for you... for anyone, really, so long as it helped..."

Loel had a sudden, stomach-turning memory of eight men lined up on wobbly three-legged stools, hands bound behind their backs. Of watching, hand shading his eyes from the blistering equatorial sun, as the stools were kicked away one by one and each fell to dance on the end of a noose.

"Be careful what you wish for."

But she wasn't listening, least of all to warnings. Her eyes went wide, and she cried out, "Maybe there is!"

"What do you mean?"

"I know how we could afford the fountain!" Bonny skipped close, setting her loose hair asway, and blinked up at him with her sweet full lips ever so slightly parted.

She had a siren's instinct for persuasion, matched with a puppy's talent for dissembling. Loel could only be grateful for the latter. He steeled himself against whatever request was forthcoming.

"I have something—a painting—we could sell it. Running a fountain over the roof was my idea, it's only right that I put something of mine at risk to try it."

"A painting?" He'd been under the impression the Reeds had sold all their valuables after their warehouses burned. "I don't mean to be rude, but... how?"

"We didn't sell *everything*." Her gaze skittered away from his. "We kept the house, didn't we? And I have a painting. It's valuable."

His stomach sank. He didn't know why she wanted this so badly, all of a sudden, and he doubted she'd give an honest answer if he asked.

"Wait for next year or the year after," he suggested. "A good idea will keep."

"Why wait? It isn't doing us any good right now, hanging from a wall."

"Why hurry?" he snapped. "What are you trying to hide?"

Bonny rocked back on her heels. She wavered, breath coming in short pants, then curled her soft hands into fists and said, "I had lewd thoughts about you while you were sick."

Loel froze. "What?"

"I continued to nurse you—to touch you, even intimately—after I knew it was wrong." She spat out each word as though it tasted foul on her tongue, making them as ugly as possible. "That's why I lied when you asked me if you were dreaming. Because I couldn't bear for you to know."

He snagged on that, as he was meant to. He hated being helpless. Hated losing hours and days of his life, hated being dependent. His illness had left him vulnerable, and discovering that she'd taken advantage of that vulnerability filled him with raw, bone-deep anger.

Bonny trembled like a leaf, but she kept talking. "I ought to have stopped or found someone else or insisted on a chaperone. But I was too ashamed to ask for help. I ought to have warned you before the wedding, but I was too selfish."

ERIN SATIE

"Stop!" He paced away. The closer she stood, the more intensely he wanted to do exactly as she wished, no matter how impossible. To soothe her or spoil her or rage at her.

He whirled. "Why are you telling me this?"

She winced. "Because you deserve to know."

"Why *now*?" He waited, but she didn't answer. "Because you *want* something. You want me to sell your painting."

She nodded.

And if she couldn't convince him with reason, then she'd provoke him—and hope he obliged her out of spite.

"I'd have thought better of you if you'd answered my questions when I asked instead of saving your confession for the moment when it would serve you." His voice emerged colder than he'd intended, and he hadn't aimed for warmth. "And I'd have more hope for our marriage if you'd engage in honest discussion instead of trying to manipulate me."

"I'm sorry." Tears sheened her eyes, giving the brown-green irises a startling, crystalline depth. Her cheeks flushed to a rich rosy pink. As always, emotion heightened her beauty—while her beauty ennobled her emotions, made them seem pure and true. "Loel, I'm sorry. I don't know what came over me."

He cut in. "I suggest you figure it out. You'll have time— because I'm going to do as you asked. I'll take your painting to London and I'll sell it." He paused. "You don't have to trick me to get what you want, Bonny."

Her shoulders trembled from the effort to hold back a sob. A single teardrop spilled onto her cheek. Had he gotten through to her? If she'd tell him what this was really about, talk to him like a husband instead of an antagonist, he wouldn't regret a few harsh words.

"I'll fetch the painting for you," she said and clambered off the bed.

He really did want to yell at her then—but what would be the point? An hour later, he had the painting wrapped in cotton and oilcloth tucked under one arm, a small valise in the other, and he was on his way to the train station.

BONNY'S GUILT SPIKED, and broke, like a fever. The thought of giving up *Bowl of Cherries* had been so horrible, so painful that her guilty conscience had seized on it and refused to let go. Loel's unerring ability to see right through her had only tightened the vise.

Once he was gone, she cried. She wanted to be good—no, better than that. She wanted to be the woman Loel had told her she could be, the one her husband would get down on his knees and thank God for having brought into his life. But she wasn't. She tried and failed and… she'd keep trying.

She had to be better. As much as it hurt her to sell *Bowl of Cherries*, she didn't regret the decision.

After the fire, they'd funneled all their sentiment, all their emotion, into four objects because they'd had to get rid of the rest. First they'd lost the warehouses. Then the business her father's family had spent generations building, then most of their friends had gone, the summer trips, the horses, the carriage. It had gone on and on for months. Weeping over every loss would have broken them.

Her father's decree that they could each keep one thing had been important, because it meant they hadn't lost everything. If they hadn't lost everything, they could survive and rebuild. It didn't make much sense, in retrospect, but it had *felt* true.

Just like selling the painting *felt* right. She now knew with certainty that she'd give anything to make this marriage work. Nothing barred, nothing stinted. All that remained was, well, to do it *properly*.

She never wanted Loel to be angry at her again.

She finished the evening chores in peace. Just as when Loel had been sick, caring for the orchids in his absence took all her time and energy. She even slept on his bed that night so that the chill would wake her to tend the stoves. Every time she lay down, his scent surrounded her. She breathed it in, fixated by the thought of his long-limbed body sprawled loose and easy in her place. Eventually her nose dulled and she drifted into sleep.

The next morning, after yet another night of rain, the roads had started to flood. The postman slogged up the drive with their mail, including two letters addressed to Bonny. The first was from Mrs. Twisby, asking why Bonny's visits had ceased. The second was addressed in an unfamiliar hand. Bonny opened it with some trepidation.

> Dear Lady Loel,
>
> I hope you'll forgive me for not writing sooner. I do not have the same freedom in my correspondence that Olympia does. What's more, Olympia is a champion epistolarian who finishes ten letters in the time it takes me to complete one. I confess that I sometimes rely on her talents when I ought to exercise my own.
>
> Olympia was shocked by your last letter—I was not. We met after you tossed yourself headlong into a filthy canal in order to save a pair of drowning children; you have again proven yourself to be selfless and reckless in nearly equal measure.
>
> We appreciate your concern for our reputations. However, we feel you have given up too easily. Please reply with a precise accounting of the scandal that has so altered your life—we must know what happened in order to find a way for our friendship to survive it.
>
> Address your letter to Olympia; letters sent to my home are not private.
>
> Sincerely,
> Tess Hurley

Bonny read it through three times in a row, hardly daring to believe the words in front of her eyes. Olympia and Tess weren't abandoning her? They wanted to remain friends? It was the last thing that Bonny would have expected from two London sophisticates... perhaps she'd misjudged London sophisticates. Olympia and Tess were the only two she knew.

Bonny didn't reply. If she cared about her friends, she would ignore their request. She distracted herself from this dismal conclusion with a visit to Mrs. Twisby. Cordelia had returned the widow's borrowed books to Bonny before the wedding, so she unearthed them from her trunks, swaddled herself in several layers of protective rain gear, and braved the door-to-door puddles.

At Mrs. Twisby's, all the hearths had been shoveled full of coal, cherry red glowing through the grates, generating so much heat that Bonny could have been back in the greenhouse. She handed her dripping cloak and hat to a manservant who grimaced at the wet floor and waved her upstairs.

"I should have returned these earlier," said Bonny, greeting Mrs. Twisby in her comfortable salon. "I'm sorry to be inattentive."

"Return them? I gave them to your circulating library—and I'm expecting new books, girl. It's well past time."

"I wish I had them for you, but as it happens we're not operating the library any longer."

Mrs. Twisby harrumphed. "Not very serious about it, were you?"

"We were very serious," Bonny protested. "My partner especially. But... circumstances made it impossible to continue."

"You mean you got married and decided you have better things to do?"

"No, not at all," said Bonny. "All our other members quit."

"Quit!" Mrs. Twisby seemed astonished. "Why?"

"Because..." Bonny floundered. "That is..."

"Well?" Mrs. Twisby prompted.

"Because they didn't want anything to do with me," Bonny said finally. "I thought, since you'd addressed your letter to me at Woodclose, that you might have heard..."

"Your husband told me," said Mrs. Twisby. "I suppose I

should have predicted the town's reaction. Some people really will cut off their noses to spite their faces, won't they?"

"It's a terrible shame."

"And so you haven't visited," Mrs. Twisby concluded, apparently content that she'd comprehended the situation adequately. "Well, if none of the gossips care to visit me, I don't care to heed their warnings. Can I offer you some tea?"

Bonny blinked.

"Good," said Mrs. Twisby. "Have a seat. It's nice and warm, isn't it? I hate the cold."

Tea arrived a few minutes later, along with a selection of salads, biscuits, and sandwiches. Bonny ate more than was strictly polite, because the meals she'd been able to prepare herself were not half so satisfying. Mrs. Twisby kindly didn't mention her appetite—in fact, she kept the conversation light and pleasant, discussing the weather, the harvest, her favorite summer receipts.

Bonny took the opportunity to ask about the book that she and her friends had been so confounded by. "Wherever did you find that book that you loaned to us—*The Widow*? Everyone who reads it is mad for it."

Mrs. Twisby hemmed and hawed before answering, with sly pride, "My daughter gave it to me."

"She must move in literary circles?"

"She does, yes." Mrs. Twisby nodded. "But it also happens that she wrote it."

Bonny gasped. "She wrote it!" She couldn't quite believe it. "Your daughter is R. E. Timothy?"

"Roberta Twisby—though she goes by Ruby. And her middle name is Eleanor."

"But wait—that means you know who killed the husband!"

Mrs. Twisby nodded serenely. "It does."

"You must tell me! My friends and I are all desperate to know."

"Oh, I couldn't betray her secrets. It wouldn't be right."

"I respect your position on the matter... perhaps you could

give me her address so we could write to her directly? My friends tell me they tried to send a letter via her publisher but haven't gotten a reply."

"I think I could agree to that."

When they finished their circuit of the garden path, Mrs. Twisby called for pencil and paper and wrote down her daughter's address in London. "I warn you, she may not answer your question."

The conversation so energized Benny that, upon her return to Woodclose, she replied to Tess:

Dear Tess,

Your kindness astonishes me. I admit, my first impulse was to reward it by ignoring your request. I couldn't bear it if you were punished for coming to my aid. The people I love most have already suffered disproportionately—indeed, some find themselves in circumstances far more difficult than my own.

On reflection, however, this line of reasoning serves mostly to protect my own feelings. What I can or cannot bear must not be my first priority.

What's more, I trust your judgment. If I impressed you with recklessness and selflessness, then you impressed me with your keen understanding of the social milieu you navigate with such mastery.

I rely also upon your discretion, as I will not spare you any of the details.

When I met you, I was engaged to a man who is both wealthy and well liked here in New Quay, Mr. Charles Gavin. I had discovered several defects in his character, however, serious enough to incline me against him. I ventured to London to gauge my chances at making a better match if I searched farther afield, which is how I came to make your acquaintance.

While I was away, Mr. Gavin persuaded several of his friends to join him in a physical attack on the man who is now my husband, Lord Loel. When I learned of this attack, I was more determined than ever to end my engagement. However, I was equally determined to nurse Lord Loel back to health. The latter seemed more urgent, as he had no one else to attend his sickbed.

I confess that my feelings for Lord Loel were warm even before the attack—improperly so. Nursing him heightened those feelings. The appalling truth is that I made advances on his person. I kissed him, all unprompted, and would have done more if we hadn't been discovered.

We were discovered by the vicar's wife. I had not yet ended my engagement to Mr. Gavin. I simply hadn't had time to speak with him. And so I was proved before a pillar of the community to be both lewd and unfaithful.

Instead of condemning me—as he had every right to—Lord Loel chose to make me his wife.

This is the whole unfortunate truth. All blame falls to me, and my sins have been made public. I am a pariah here in New Quay, and you would be tainted by any acquaintance with me.

Sincerely,

Bonny

P.S. — I have learned that the author of The Widow *is a woman! Her true name is Ruby Twisby. I enclose the address so you may query her directly.*

The next two days passed quietly—metaphorically anyhow. The inside of the greenhouse echoed with the sound of heavy raindrops drumming unceasingly overhead. The vast space amplified the noise better than any amphitheater; it was like living inside a waterfall.

But the orchids flourished. Leaves plumped, stems straightened, tiny flower buds sprouted with sneaky enthusiasm, springing to life the very moment Bonny turned her back. If Bonny hadn't accidentally killed hundreds of orchids while Loel was sick, she would have felt very smug—unfortunately, she knew the weather deserved all the credit.

After two days of complete isolation, she received two letters. The first was a note from Loel saying that he'd been successful and planned to return home the next day. The second was from Tess and read:

Dear Bonny,

Your new husband is a peer. Is he wealthy?
Sincerely,
Tess

Bonny replied:

Dear Tess,

He is not. What's more, he is widely loathed here in New Quay. As a young man he accidentally started a fire that devastated the town. My family was among those ruined by the blaze.
Sincerely,
Bonny

Loel returned in the early afternoon. Bonny greeted him nervously, hardly daring to speak. He'd been so angry when they'd parted. And she didn't know what to do with him in city clothes, with raindrops beading in his smooth dark hair.

He studied her, measuring and intense, and she quailed. He was still angry. He'd inspect the greenhouse, say something cutting—tell her that she'd failed—

The silence stretched. She worried that she might faint. And then Loel crushed her close and kissed her, an embrace that started politely but ended with both of them disheveled and gasping.

"You're not angry at me?" she asked when she could speak again.

He chuckled, a low rumbling sound that went straight to her core. "Do you want me to be?"

"Of course not."

He caressed her cheek with his thumb, then bent to kiss her again. Languidly this time, slow and thorough and deliberate. "I haven't forgotten our last conversation," he admitted. "But it mattered less as I missed you more."

"I'm going to to better. You'll see." Bonny rose up on tiptoes, tipping her chin up and angling for a kiss—and received a dozen, soft and scattered over her lips and nose and cheeks.

"Don't make promises you can't keep." He pinched her lower lip between thumb and forefinger, his eyes going dark, before he took a step back. "The painting was worth well more than what the engineer wanted for a pump."

"So there's some left over?"

"Almost two hundred pounds," he answered.

Bonny blinked. Two hundred pounds could go a long way.

"They'll come once it's dry—they can't dig trenches in the rain," he said, squeezing absently at her waist. "How did you manage alone?"

"Very well, thank you. Would you like a tour of the greenhouse?"

"Later. I'll take your word for it."

Bonny beamed.

"I have dinner," he added, heading for the house. "Caviar and sour cream and champagne. I thought, for one night, why not?"

"Really?"

"No, not *really*." Loel pushed through the green baize door and took the stairs down to the basement. "It'll be tinned mutton and boiled cabbage for the week."

Bonny's face fell.

Loel offered her the bags. "Here, look for yourself. Is it so hard to tell when I'm joking?"

"Obviously, it is." Bonny rummaged around in the sacks. They were full of London treats: pâté and candied chestnuts, cinnamon sticks and lemon curd, and—as promised—caviar and champagne.

"Oh!" Bonny turned the jar in her hands and admired the glossy perfection of the eggs inside. "I've never had it before."

"I remember being fond of it, though it's been years." Loel

uncorked the champagne and poured two generous glasses. He handed one to Bonny and selected a few items to carry up to the yard: the caviar, of course, a slightly crushed baguette, the sour cream—its container wet from being packed in ice that had melted—and a box of chocolates.

Bonny was contemplating the lovely, shiny chocolates when she heard Cordelia's familiar voice calling, "Hello?" from somewhere inside the house. She gave Loel a startled look and hurried upstairs, where she found her friend wearing a cloak and carrying something bulky enough to make her look round as a berry, dripping on the floor of the salon-turned-shed.

"Don't mind the clutter." Bonny reached out to unfasten Cordelia's cloak. "Let's get these wet things off you."

Bonny stowed Cordelia's outerwear in the cloakroom and then retraced her steps with a bit of toweling, wiping all the stray drops from the floor. It took long enough that when she finally returned to the shed/salon, she caught Cordelia unawares—slumped tiredly against a cabinet, dark circles under her eyes.

Bonny's heart squeezed painfully. Something had gone badly wrong in her friend's life, and she suspected that she was the cause.

"Cordelia?"

Cordelia started, straightening with some effort. She tried to look like her usual self, and the determined slant to her brows hadn't changed, but there was no hiding her exhaustion.

"I have a favor to ask," said Cordelia.

"Anything."

"I've decided to leave my family and make my own way in the world—"

"No!"

"My parents have become intolerable," Cordelia said fiercely, more emotional—more unrestrained—than Bonny had ever heard her. "From the time I was a little girl, my father taught me that it is better to be good than to be liked, that true courage lies in championing what is right, even though our fellows will object.

But they refuse to understand that I am simply following their precepts—"

"Is this because of me?"

"No, it's because they are hypocrites," Cordelia answered. "They are horrified that I want to practice what they have preached to me for so long. And I fear they'll go further."

"What do you mean, 'further'?"

"I'm not sure," said Cordelia. "A strict school? Marriage to a man who believes in harsh discipline? I believe they're contemplating some punishment which I do not choose to accept."

"I understand your anger… but don't you think you're taking this a bit far?"

"Yes," Cordelia answered without hesitation. "Yes, I am."

"Oh." Bonny relaxed. "Good. That's a relief."

"But this is the hand we're dealt, isn't it?" Cordelia continued. "Either we are compliant or we are ruined. There is no middle road."

"It's not right," Bonny agreed in a small voice. Then, more firmly, "But that doesn't mean you should leave your *family*."

"On the contrary," Cordelia returned. "That's why I *must* leave my family."

"You love your parents."

"I do love them, but they're wrong," said Cordelia. "And I'd rather make my own mistakes than theirs."

I'd rather make my own mistakes than theirs.

"I like that," said Bonny.

Cordelia snorted. "You would."

"Hey!" Bonny swatted at Cordelia. "Were you hoping to stay with us? Or do you need help to leave?"

"The one accomplishes the other," Cordelia replied. "I couldn't take a local train because I would have been noticed and followed. My parents won't let me go without a fight. I need help reaching a more distant station where I'm not known. Will you help?"

Bonny hesitated. If she helped Cordelia, her family would

suffer for it. They'd distanced themselves from Bonny, but they'd still be tainted by any scandals that involved her.

She loved her family. So much. But Cordelia had stood by her when she needed a friend, and Bonny would do the same. No matter the cost.

"Come inside," said Bonny. "Follow me upstairs… I'll find you a room, and Loel has just returned from London. We were preparing a very modest feast. You can join us."

CHAPTER 18

Bonny saw Cordelia settled and accompanied her back downstairs, where she heard voices in the vestibule—both male. She followed them to their source and found Loel at the front door she'd never seen anyone use before, speaking comfortably with a tall, rangy stranger. He wore a fine suit that had obviously seen better days and carried a large carpetbag.

The stranger glanced past Loel, whose back was turned to her, and froze, his jaw dropping.

"I was about to ask who that is," murmured Cordelia, "but clearly he's never seen you before."

Bonny scowled at her friend.

"Don't pull faces. I'm right, aren't I?" Cordelia hooked her elbow around Bonny's. "Come on, let's find out."

"Let me introduce everyone," said Loel. "Jacob, please meet my wife and her friend, Miss Cordelia Kelly. Ladies, Mr. Jacob Benjamin is a good friend from my days at sea. He's a naturalist and occasional orchid collector—he's the source, for example, of the *Odontoglossum crispum*."

Mr. Benjamin cocked an eyebrow. "You make it sound like the *crispum* is still alive."

"Last I saw it." Loel tipped his head to Bonny. "Unless something's changed while I was gone."

"Something *has* changed," said Bonny. "It's budding."

"Budding? How?" Jacob glanced between Bonny and Loel, eyes wide and brows flat—the perfect mix of curiosity and skepticism. "I had another living specimen that I sold, and it died within a week."

"I believe my wife's singing did the trick," answered Loel.

Bonny wrinkled her nose at him. "Don't tease."

Loel leaned back in his chair, palms raised in an expression of innocence. "What do you mean, tease? I honestly can't think of a better explanation."

"If you collect orchids, Mr. Benjamin, you must travel a great deal," said Cordelia.

"South America, North America. Africa. I'm bound for the Malay Peninsula in a few days... I go wherever there are beetles to be found. Collecting orchids helps to fund my excursions, but at heart I'm a naturalist—as Loel says—and an entomologist in particular. I study insects."

Bonny wrinkled her nose. "Insects?"

"You've done yourself a disservice if you dismiss them," said Mr. Benjamin. "You will find all the wonders of nature in the phylum *Insecta*—marvels of beauty, industry, and intelligence. Insects deserve respect and study as much as any of the greater apes or felines. More, even."

Bonny had no idea how to respond. As far as she was concerned, the less time she spent thinking about insects the better.

Cordelia came to the rescue. "I'm willing to be convinced."

"And he'll make a valiant attempt—but not just now. You've been traveling, and so have I. Why don't we sit down? Eat something?" Loel offered Cordelia his arm. "If that's acceptable?"

Bonny removed the protective sheets from the dining room table and chairs while Loel fetched the London delicacies. Bonny doubted that their makeshift hospitality would upset Mr.

Benjamin, a world traveler, but Cordelia was used to more comfortable accommodations.

Not that the provisions were lacking. Bonny had never eaten caviar before but discovered that she liked the look of it—black jewels on pillows of white cream—better than the fishy flavor. The eggs popped and oozed when she chewed, which complemented the fizzy frothy sweetness of the champagne.

"And to think," said Mr. Benjamin, "all this time you let me believe that you'd given up on high living."

"It's not our usual fare, I assure you."

"So what's the occasion?" asked Mr. Benjamin.

"We sold a painting." Bonny glanced at Cordelia. "*Bowl of Cherries.*"

The candied chestnut Cordelia had brought halfway to her mouth dropped from between her fingers. "No! You sold it?" Her furious glare traveled from her plate to Bonny. "For *food*?"

"Not for food!" Bonny exclaimed. "For… actually, I don't know exactly what for."

"A hydraulic ram," Loel supplied. "A kind of machine that will pump water to the roof of the greenhouse—an improvement for the nursery."

"Oh, that's brilliant," murmured Mr. Benjamin.

Loel tipped his chin in Bonny's direction. "Her idea."

Mr. Benjamin raised his glass. "My compliments—and a toast. To your insight, Lady Loel."

"No," said Cordelia. "You don't understand. *Bowl of Cherries* wasn't any painting. It was—"

"My decision." Bonny interrupted. She caught Cordelia's eyes and held them. "It was my idea, my suggestion."

"But, Bonny, you talked about it all the time. You used it to measure your moods—all your days were rotten or ripe, butterfly days or still water days."

"Everyone here has had cause to give up something precious," said Bonny. "I sold my painting; you left your family. Mr. Benjamin is about to travel to the Far East."

"But why?" Cordelia demanded.

"To start something new," answered Bonny.

Cordelia's glare melted. Her shoulders relaxed. She smiled ruefully and picked up a glass. "To burning bridges?"

Goose flesh prickled at the back of Bonny's neck, along her arms. She took the stem of her own glass between her fingers. "To burning bridges."

"May they light our way," agreed Mr. Benjamin, clinking Cordelia's glass to his own.

LOEL TOASTED WITH THE OTHERS, but he couldn't take his eyes off Bonny—who ducked her chin and looked away, a flush rising to her cheeks. She'd said the painting was valuable, but she hadn't said a word about its sentimental value. Now that it was gone, sold at her request and the proceeds spent, he discovered that it had meaning to her.

Now that he'd assembled all the puzzle pieces, they fit neatly together: She'd decided to sell *Bowl of Cherries* after her disastrous trip into town. She'd held fast to the idea through her confession and his anger. Why? Because she'd intended to punish herself.

If he'd understood, he wouldn't have done as she asked. He would have shown her more patience and more kindness... which, come to think of it, explained why she'd been so cagey and manipulative that morning in the greenhouse. She hadn't wanted patience or kindness. A woman aiming to punish herself wouldn't think she deserved either.

Miss Kelly interrupted his thoughts. She had a sharp, clear voice, hard to ignore and not entirely agreeable. "You sailed together?"

Loel nodded.

"Aboard the *Incitatus*," Jacob added.

"The *Incitatus*?" Miss Kelly glanced between them, eyes narrowing. She had pretty, clear blue eyes and perpetually looked as though she were staring down the sights of a loaded pistol. "Where have I heard that name before?"

Loel suppressed a groan. "You must read the papers."

Miss Kelly nodded, lips curving ever so slightly. She exuded a sort of bullish torpor that announced, as clear as anything, that while she hadn't come to start a fight... she'd absolutely finish one.

He did not understand Bonny's friendship with this woman at all. They couldn't have been more different.

"You read the newspaper?" exclaimed Jacob, altogether too pleased by this discovery.

"Yes," answered Miss Kelly. "I do."

"I don't meet many women who read the newspaper. I'm all admiration, of course."

Miss Kelly relaxed a bit and asked, "So what happened aboard the *Incitatus*? Something eventful if it made the papers."

"The ship was embroiled in a scheme to defraud an insurance company," said Loel. "Jacob, why don't you show everyone your lucky beetle?"

It was the wrong thing to say. Jacob *was* highly distractible; mention anything related to insects and he could start on a tangent that lasted hours... but he wasn't stupid.

"You really haven't told your wife what happened?" asked Jacob.

"It's not a pleasant story."

Jacob interrupted. "You sound like you're ashamed."

Not exactly. "Of course I'm not ashamed."

"Then tell them what happened."

Loel slouched in his chair. "Why don't you? You're the better storyteller."

"If you like." Jacob sounded mildly offended, but he quickly set it aside as he turned to the two women. He sat taller, spoke in a deeper voice; he really was an excellent storyteller. Which was probably why his lecture tours were so successful. "The *Incitatus* set sail from Valparaiso, bound for Malacca. I was on the hunt for beetles and Loel here, for orchids. We'd never met before, but we had one thing in common—and it's still true for one of us, at least"—Jacob gave the caviar a significant look—"which is that we couldn't afford to be choosy about our transportation. A berth on a ship sailing halfway across the world comes dear even if it's a leaky bucket that smells like the Thames on a hot summer day."

Bonny interrupted, "The Thames…?"

"Like human waste," said Loel, succinctly.

Bonny and Miss Kelly manifested identical expressions of horror.

"The *Incitatus* was seaworthy. Old, certainly nearing the end of her life, but fully capable of completing her journey to Malacca. And her captain, Robert Royce, had an excellent reputation. He was a big man with a great booming voice and just enough gray in his hair to make you feel quite secure on a floating matchstick. 'Here,' I thought when I saw him, 'here stands a man who has sailed around the world ten times, and his wealth of experience will get me around it at least once.'"

"As you would imagine, many sailors dream of becoming captains," Jacob continued, "but what do captains dream of? I'll tell you. They dream of owning their own ship. The difficulty is that in order to acquire a ship of his own, he must become wealthy. But how does a sea captain become wealthy? It's not impossible, but—as is so often the case—he must choose between fair means and foul, between safety and speed. Unfortunately for us, Captain Royce had chosen the latter.

"He had, in fact, entered into an agreement with the owner of the *Incitatus* to sink the ship en route to Malacca. The *Incitatus* was well insured and for his part in this nefarious plan, Captain Royce would receive a share of the proceeds. Marine insurers are wise to such schemes and investigate claims thoroughly. They can be hard to fool—which is why Captain Royce planned to sink the ship in the middle of the Pacific Ocean, several months' journey from the nearest port.

"It seemed a foolproof scheme, and no doubt many men of

indifferent morals would give it a try, but for one small flaw: sinking a fully manned ship in the middle of a watery desert where you may sit in the crow's nest with a spyglass and monitor the horizon from sunup to sundown without sighting another vessel, not just for a day at a time but for a week or even a fortnight, entails a tremendous loss of life. Counting passengers and crew, the *Incitatus* sheltered more than three hundred souls."

"Dear God," murmured Miss Kelly.

Jacob caught her gimlet glance and nodded sharply. "An affront to yours and to mine," he said. "And Captain Royce would have carried through with this plan if it weren't for Loel. He looked like a disreputable adventurer, but it only takes a short time in his company to realize he's an educated man—"

"So are you," Miss Kelly objected.

"So I am," Jacob agreed dryly. "But it was Loel's presence aboard the *Incitatus* that alarmed Captain Royce, not mine."

"Captain Royce decided to take Loel into his confidence. He explained that he intended to set the *Incitatus* on fire in the dark of night, with only a picked group of allies awake to witness the crime. Once the blaze caught, Royce and the lucky few would escape into a longboat, stocked in advance with provisions of food and water. As for the rest of us…"

"My choices were to join Royce's conspiracy or die." Loel couldn't recollect that conversation without feeling as though he'd gone back in time. An echo of the fear that had seized him then vibrated through his body even now, making his knees weak, his bowels soft.

Royce had taken a friendly tone, as though he were explaining an embarrassing problem to a friend, but Loel had seen the truth in his watchful eyes. "Royce never said as much, but he didn't have to. Only the conspirators could survive, because only fear of a hangman's noose could guarantee a secret on that scale."

"What did you do?"

"At first? Nothing." Loel paused. "Royce was clever. I guessed that he'd chosen seven other conspirators—he'd need eight to man the longboat, including himself—but I didn't know who those seven were. Men he trusted, obviously... but as Jacob said, he'd built an excellent reputation. His officers served him loyally. How could I guess which ones he'd spared, which he'd been ready to sacrifice?"

"You're saying that anyone with the authority to stop Royce was—as likely as not—in on the scheme," said Miss Kelly.

"Exactly," said Loel.

"But you stopped him," said Bonny. "If you're both here and both alive, you must have."

"I played along with Royce until he revealed that he'd decided to set the boatswain's store on fire when we were about a week's hard rowing from Easter Island," said Loel. "It's small, enclosed, frequently empty, and stocked with flammable materials like rope and tar."

"Try to picture the rope, especially," Jacob interjected. "Thick around as a man's arm, coiled in spools taller than I am—"

"We do live in a port town, Mr. Benjamin." Miss Kelly interrupted.

Loel picked up the story. "I was relatively certain that Jacob wouldn't be among Royce's seven, so I took him into my confidence. It's a good thing I did too, because I wouldn't have succeeded alone. It was Jacob who—on the very night that Royce planned to set the fire—identified the conspirators."

"The quartermaster contrived to have a triple ration of rum distributed to everyone aboard at mess," said Jacob, picking up where Loel had left off. "That convinced me that he numbered among the conspirators. I encouraged Loel to pay attention to which of the other officers drank, and how. I suspected the guilty would reveal themselves by taking their liquor too eagerly or not at all."

"The conspirators drank quickly," Loel said. "And without enjoyment."

"By the time the second dogwatch was over, and all the eating done, we were near certain that the boatswain and the first mate were innocent," said Jacob. "But we approached cautiously. We told them to lie in wait in the boatswain's store, to be ready for any mischief, but didn't speak a word of the captain's involvement."

"And then we waited," said Loel. "As near to hand as we dared, in case of trouble."

"Which arrived presently," Jacob said. "When Captain Royce was discovered, he held fast to his scheme—better to sink with his ship and hope his family profited, than to be discovered and tried for his crimes. He tried to set the boatswain's store ablaze.

"But the boatswain had taken precautions. He moved the tar and oakum into the hold, denying the fire its most dangerous fuel, and stored wool blankets soaked in seawater among the supplies."

"Royce had killed several of the sailors on watch, to prevent them from raising the alarm—so quietly that we didn't realize until the next day—but between Loel and me, we roused a handful of passengers who'd never sailed with Royce before. Working together, we were able to capture all eight of the conspirators and consign them to the brig."

"You saved everyone?" Bonny exclaimed. "But... that's wonderful!"

"Not everyone," Loel said. "All eight of the conspirators were tried and hung when we reached Malacca."

"Which is only right," Miss Kelly declared fiercely. "They deserved to die for what they'd planned."

Loel sighed. She was right. He knew it. But he'd attended the hanging. He had watched eight nooses make corpses of eight living men, and he had known that he was responsible. He'd done the right thing. Hundreds of lives had been saved at the cost of eight.

Most people who knew the story praised him. But he'd never found it in himself to be proud, and he never wanted to be in a similar situation ever, ever again. No coincidence that when he'd returned home, he'd dedicated himself to growing flowers.

"It turned out," said Loel, sidestepping the issue, "that the ship's owner was a second cousin of mine. A man by the name of Bernard Howell. He was tried and hung here in England while I was abroad. I don't know what my parents believed—perhaps they thought I'd been tainted by my involvement with the conspiracy; perhaps they thought I'd betrayed my family by exposing it—but that was the last straw for them. After Howell died, they cut me out."

"Would you have spared them?" Jacob demanded. "If the decision were in your hands, entirely, would you let men who'd planned a massacre walk free?"

"No one wants to be an executioner," said Loel.

"And yet many of us would like to take the place of a judge," Jacob returned. "Why is that?"

"My father is a judge," said Miss Kelly. "And he has often remarked that what is right and what is pleasant are rarely the same. I'm surprised that a man like you, Lord Loel, well educated and well traveled as you are, would be tempted to think otherwise."

"Captain Royce cursed me with his last breath," said Loel. "It's not an experience I would wish on anyone."

"Perhaps," interjected Bonny, "now would be a good time for Mr. Benjamin to show us his beetle?"

After a brief pause, Jacob plucked a small cube of crystal clear resin from his pocket, within which he'd trapped the remains of a rainbow-hued beetle. "I believe you're right. Here, take a look…"

Loel caught Bonny's eye and mouthed a quick "thank you." She touched her fingers to her lips and blew him a kiss, before turning attentively to Jacob's lecture.

BONNY WENT LOOKING for Loel after dinner and found him, predictably, in the greenhouse. He stood with his chin propped on his fist before the *Odontoglossum crispum*. The orchid had flourished in the rain and now sported several leaves, long tongues of green lolling about a budding stalk, but Loel's eyes were low-lidded, his gaze unfocused. He hardly seemed to see it.

When Bonny reached his side, he stirred.

"A gardener at Kew once told me that, when all else failed and an orchid wouldn't bloom, he'd drop the pot to startle it into action," he said. "I thought he was mad."

Bonny grinned. "So I saved your plant when I knocked it over?"

He slanted a look at her. "Perhaps."

"Then perhaps you owe me a favor."

"We're married, Bonny." He grimaced. "If you want something, tell me."

Bonny hesitated. "You said we had money left over from the sale of *Bowl of Cherries*?"

"A good amount. You have plans for it?"

"Cordelia will need money if she's going to have a chance on her own. If we could help… She's very dear to me. I want her to succeed."

"What do you see in her?" Loel asked. "She's judgmental and difficult—"

Bonny interrupted. "Not another word."

Loel's eyebrows rose in astonishment.

"She has more courage in her pinky finger than most people have in their whole bodies," said Bonny. "She is fiercely intelligent, scrupulously honest, industrious, principled—"

Loel showed her his palms in surrender. "Point taken. How much?"

Bonny hesitated. "All of it?"

"All right."

"Truly?"

"It was your painting. If you wanted to throw the money down a well, I'd refuse. Short of that, I'm happy to abide by your wishes."

"Thank you."

He touched her elbow, brow furrowing. "You could have told me how much it meant to you."

"And you could have told me what happened aboard the *Incitatus*."

He nodded slowly. "Why do you think I didn't?"

"I don't know." She understood his ambivalence about the hangings—she couldn't imagine carrying the burden of those deaths on her shoulders, however justified—but the people of New Quay treated him so *badly*. He deserved better. "People ought to know, Loel. If they could see you as I do—you're a good man and a worthy—"

He silenced her with a finger over her lips. "You sent me to London to sell that painting when it would have been easier and simpler just to *let me forgive you*. Why?"

Bonny froze.

Loel continued, every word a blow. "If you don't think *you* deserve forgiveness when your only crime, as far as I can tell, was to befriend *me*—"

She mirrored Loel's gesture, silencing him with a finger across his lips. They stood like that for a few seconds, arms crossed and index fingers raised like a pair of fencers, or librarians—like a pair of fencing librarians, battling to *shush* one another.

Bonny giggled.

Loel cracked a smile.

The tension broke. They lowered their arms and waggling fingers, and stood in the sweet air grinning at one another.

"I'll come to you tonight?"

Bonny rose up on tiptoes for a kiss. "Yes, please."

She returned to her room, dressed and attended to her toilette, then glanced out the window. A lantern still glowed golden inside the greenhouse. He said he'd come, but when? In a minute? In an hour? She should have asked.

She paced while the rain slanted endlessly down, pattering against her window. Her thighs were slippery. She started when the door finally clicked, then dashed across the room and threw herself into her husband's arms.

He caught her and held her, and he didn't ask questions. He speared his fingers through her hair and kissed her fiercely. He didn't make her explain what she wanted or tell him how. He bore her back onto the bed and pushed her nightdress out of the way, and she didn't have to say a word, because he knew.

He knew everything. He could see into every dark corner of her mind; he could read the desires she pretended not to understand. How else to explain it? She could not have told him that she wanted his hand rough on her thigh, spreading her legs wide, because she hadn't known it herself. She would have swallowed her own tongue before she asked him to penetrate her without pause or preliminary.

But it was exactly what she wanted. Exactly what he gave her, thrusting hard and deep and grinding his hips into hers while she hooked her leg around his waist and responded in kind. She felt twitchy and desperate, so lost to the moment that she only registered the faintest hint of shock when he flipped her over, lifted her onto her knees, and drove into her like that.

The new position was... *more*. Every stroke went deeper and vibrated out to her fingertips. When he reached between her thighs, petting and plucking, she climaxed almost instantly— she'd been so ready, right on the edge, for longer than she wanted to admit.

He followed soon after, clutching her tight and groaning softly before collapsing over her. She sighed and squirmed, just to feel him respond. Which he did, rolling to his side and fitting her against him, reaching around to cup her breast and nuzzle at her nape.

She wriggled loose, felt the spurt of moisture between her legs when she freed herself, then flipped to face Loel. She touched her forehead to his, full of emotions she didn't know how to express.

He kissed her on the lips, softly this time, and it was exactly what she wanted. Exactly what she needed. She kissed him back, brushing her fingertips over his cheek. It went on and on, kissing without any sense of urgency and almost without heat.

Almost, but not entirely. When he rolled her to her back and pushed inside her again, she welcomed him. Gladly.

She woke to warm flesh at her back, arms wrapped loosely around her, breathing in a scent that she recognized on a primal level before her conscious mind put a name to it: Loel, husband, lover.

"Wake up." He nuzzled his nose into her ear, pressed a kiss against her shoulder. "It's time to wake up."

She rolled onto her back and rubbed her eyes blearily. Loel lay on his side, head propped on his hand, his gaze roaming hungrily over her bare—

Bonny squeaked and pulled the covers up.

"Pity," murmured Loel.

Bonny turned wide eyes on her husband.

"I need to tend the stoves." He slid off the bed and stood before her, unabashedly naked but proud as if a first-rate valet had just finished preparing him for an evening out.

Bonny couldn't have looked away if she'd tried. She had touched that unblemished skin, so pale in the watery light. Those muscles had held her, moved her, lifted her. Looking at him made her feel content and smug.

"Join me if you like," he added, giving her a sublime view of his tapering back and tightly muscled rear as he strode to the door.

Bonny flopped back onto the bed with a whimper. After a few moments, however, when it was clear she wouldn't be falling back asleep, she decided to take Loel up on his offer. She dressed, drawing a cloak about her shoulders as she descended to the kitchens. She'd have liked to follow Loel but their guests would wake soon, and she wanted to have breakfast ready.

Bonny and Loel borrowed Mrs. Twisby's carriage to take Cordelia to the train station in Chester later that morning, a two hours' drive away. Loel bought the ticket while Bonny and Cordelia waited at the track, crying and embracing by turns.

"This is for you," said Bonny, folding the banknotes into Cordelia's hand. "Write when you can."

Cordelia tried to give the notes back. "It's too much—more than you have to spare. I'll be fine."

"You will let me help," said Bonny. "I won't hear any arguments either."

"But—"

Bonny put her fingers in her ears. "I'm not listening, I'm not list—"

Cordelia rolled her eyes and tucked the money into her valise. She searched through the stuffed compartment and brought out a folded note. "This is for my parents. Mail it to them, if they don't call on you soon."

"Of course."

The train steamed away with a shrill whistle, and Bonny watched it go wistfully, wondering what adventures lay in store for her friend.

"You're sorry to lose her," said Loel.

"Sorry, happy, worried." They were alone on the narrow lane, walking home, so Bonny threaded her fingers through Loel's. "Do you think I've done enough?"

"There's always more we can do," said Loel, which was true if not comforting.

The Kellys arrived in the afternoon. Bonny might not have noticed their arrival since she spent most of the day in the greenhouse with Loel and Mr. Benjamin, except that she'd dashed into the main house for tea and on her way back, the cargo she'd crowded onto a heavy silver tray rattling in her hands, she heard a banging at the front door.

She put down the tray and peeked through the nearest window. She couldn't see who waited on the stoop, but she recognized the Kellys' carriage and their poor, sodden horse, standing patiently in the wet.

She opened the door. "Mr. Kelly? Mrs. Kelly? Would you like to come in?"

It might have been an awkward moment, but the rain made them practical. They stepped inside. Bonny had removed some of the protective sheets and dusted a bit—she'd always liked dusting —so the front hall, while dim and damp and dreary, had lost its usual funereal air.

"Bonny." Mrs. Kelly untied her bonnet with trembling fingers and clutched Bonny's hand to her breast. "Bonny, have you seen Cordelia?"

"Yes. She was here last night, but she's gone already. I have a letter for you." Bonny had placed it near to the door, expecting that they'd come. She picked up the folded paper and offered it to Mrs. Kelly. "It should explain things."

Mr. Kelly took the letter. Bonny didn't see much of him; he didn't spend much time at home and hadn't much patience for frivolities, though she'd always had the impression that he doted on Cordelia. They'd been stamped from the same mold, slim and severe, and Bonny had always liked him. She saw so much of her friend in her father.

He read silently and gave the letter to his wife when he was done. Mrs. Kelly began to cry almost immediately; Mr. Kelly simply stared at Bonny with the fierce, pale gaze he'd passed on to his daughter.

"Cordelia didn't tell me exactly where she was going," said Bonny. "I can't be persuaded to reveal what I don't know."

When she finished reading, Mrs. Kelly crumpled the letter in her fist. "I blame you for this. All of it, from start to finish. You ruined my daughter."

Bonny flinched.

Mr. Kelly pried his wife's fingers loose, took the letter from her, and carefully smoothed the creases flat, all without taking his eyes off Bonny. "Why did you help her?"

"Because she asked me to."

"Don't you think you would have served her better by sending her home?" Mr. Kelly pressed.

"I trust her judgment."

"You make me sick," hissed Mrs. Kelly.

Mr. Kelly shook his head minutely at his wife. "Enough. She's telling the truth; she doesn't know." He guided his wife to the door but paused before the sheeting rain for one last comment. "You realize that your family will pay for what you've just done?"

Bonny nodded. She did. What had her mother said? *We make the best of the choices we have. I hope you'll do the same.* She'd tried.

"Doesn't that bother you?" Mr. Kelly asked.

"Very much."

"Ah." He blinked. "I wouldn't have guessed."

He shut the door quietly, politely behind him.

Bonny returned to her tea tray, picked it up, but she started shaking on her way to the greenhouse. She propped the heavy silver on her hip to open the glass door, using her foot as a stop, and almost dropped it as she slid her arms around to take a firm grip on the silver handles. She slipped inside, hurried to the nearest table, and managed to put the tray down without breaking the porcelain.

She'd kept calm while face-to-face with them, but... Mrs. Kelly? She'd invited Bonny into her home, asked for her advice about fashion, held her up as an example to her own daughter... Bonny ought to have expected her reaction but "You make me sick"?

The memory of it would *haunt* her.

"There you are," said Loel. "Are you all right?"

Bonny dredged up a smile. "Fine, thank you. I think the tea's gone cold. Should I warm it?"

Loel came closer, tipped her chin up. "What happened?"

"The Kellys visited."

"Ah." He pulled her close, wrapped her tightly in his arms, and held her. He rocked back and forth a bit, not speaking, offering comfort. It helped. "I'll heat the tea."

He left Bonny to wander the greenhouse alone, which she did —just for the relief of it, the balmy temperature and sweet scents. For a few minutes she wandered the paths in an aimless circuit, thinking about everything that had happened.

The flowers calmed her, enough that she could think clearly. Beauty was like that, she supposed. The same way that bright sunshine made one squint or dipping one's feet into an icy cold stream provoked a hiss, beauty soothed. A simple, automatic reaction.

Mr. Benjamin found her. "Tea," he said, gesturing for her to follow. Loel had cleared the table where the *Odontoglossum crispum* used to sit and placed a few chairs around it.

"You must be eager to set sail," said Loel while Bonny poured.

"Words can't describe it," replied Mr. Benjamin. "I'd rather face a raging storm than another evening soliciting donations."

"A wish Mother Nature won't delay in granting."

"No doubt." Mr. Benjamin turned to Bonny. "What about you, Lady Loel? Will this be your first trip to the auction rooms?"

"Auction rooms?" Bonny repeated.

"I told you about the quarterly auctions," Loel supplied. "I thought you ought to come, if only to see the *Odontoglossum crispum* sold."

"Sold? Already?"

"If it's budding now, it'll be blooming at the perfect time," Loel confirmed.

CHAPTER 19

The journey to London was an ordeal unlike anything Bonny had ever experienced before. First they secured all of the orchids into Wardian cases. Then they loaded the cases into a cart and drove to the train station, where they had to be transferred to the train. Loel stayed with his orchids while Bonny traveled alone in a passenger car, all the way to London—where the whole arduous process had to be repeated in reverse.

The flowers went to Stevens Auction Rooms, on King Street, Covent Gardens. The close, cramped rooms were crowded with the most bizarre collection of valuables Bonny had ever seen—colorful butterflies pinned onto pasteboard, postage stamps, fossilized eggs, and painted wooden masks.

They had to store the orchids with the auction house so that the auctioneers could catalogue all the flowers. Their experts would verify that each one belonged to the species that Loel claimed, divide them into "lots," and then prepare the catalogue.

Loel spent most of his time with the orchids. Travel stressed the flowers and they needed extra attention. Bonny had an errand of her own, however. She'd brought Tess's most recent letter to London with her; she and Olympia both posted their letters from the same address, which Bonny surmised to be Olympia's home.

The letter had been encouraging.

Dear Lady Loel,

I suspect you have formed a fairly accurate picture of your future in New Quay. You know the town and its people. But in the wider world, your scandal is among the easiest to forget and—thus—forgive.

People who marry for love are tolerated in society, most of the time. Good families with empty purses are so common that many of my acquaintance would be relieved to meet a young woman who, given the choice, preferred a titled husband to a wealthy one.

Still, it would be best to remain in the country for some little while. After a year has passed, you'll be a respectable matron whom I could meet in public without fear.

That being said, it is my observation that people generally judge others in the way that is most advantageous to themselves. They may seek the respect that is due the righteous, the affection afforded the merciful, or power gained through bribery, blackmail, and the like.

I make these observations without judgment. We are more forgiving of our friends than our foes; we overlook flaws in those upon whom we depend—as you were so tempted to do, in regard to your Mr. Gavin. It is human nature.

Most of us are happiest when our advantage and our principles align. Olympia and I did a good deed when we whisked you away from the canal. We also prevented George Trentor, Lilian Crowley, and Shirley Dewitt—three people who have spoken in the cruelest terms about my ancestry—from turning the situation to their advantage. I sincerely love my guardian, the Queen, who provides for me so generously. Convenient, no?

When we introduced you around London, we gained credit for "discovering" you, which made us seem interesting and clever.

Relationships are built on the exchange of gifts. Letters are a kind of gift—one which we have now mutually exchanged. And trust is nothing more than the bond formed by the accumulation of favors given and received, each a fragile thread on its own.

You may think me cynical. Perhaps. But a cynic who calls you friend.
Hopefully you will continue to say the same for Olympia and me.
Sincerely,
Tess

She hired a hackney to take her to the address Olympia had indicated on her letters—a large townhouse just beyond the borders of Mayfair, with a view of Hyde Park.

Bonny had never given much thought to what might happen if a young woman of twenty or so were given a large home and unlimited resources with which to furnish it. Had she pondered the question, her imagination would have fallen short of the reality.

Or at least short of *Olympia Swain's* reality.

An impossibly handsome manservant answered the door— young, square-jawed, well over six feet tall with shoulders that spanned the width of the doorway. Bonny tried not to gape as he took her bonnet and gloves, and again when—instead of carrying them away—he positioned the hat on the marble head of one of the Roman busts flanking the door. Full-length statues lined both walls of the large, high-ceilinged foyer, and they'd all been similarly outfitted, with somber gods wearing ladies' hats and an athlete's spear adapted as a hook for a bright green cloak with fanciful silver embroidery.

Opposite the door, on a large plinth, stood a headless marble nymph draped in real jewelry—beads covered her arms, chains dangled from her neck, earrings glittered in the folds of her toga. It looked like a pagan altar, draped in offerings.

An altar to what though? To wealth, obviously. To wallowing in fortune's favor. And if a young lady owed her happiness to the whimsy of chance, then she certainly *ought* to make regular offerings.

A delicate clattering jolted Bonny out of her reverie. The rapid tapping of hooves on tile heralded the arrival of a tiny, pink pig. Wearing a tiny, pink bonnet.

"Miss Swain grants her pets freedom of the house," murmured the manservant. He had a German accent. "Including Mrs. Potts."

The pig was alarming enough, but... *pets*?

Their destination was a large ballroom, the walls painted pink and covered, wherever possible, with large, full-length mirrors. Bonny, who'd been avoiding mirrors for so long that it was second nature, kept trying to look away from her own reflection only to encounter it again wherever she turned her head.

A fresco covered across the ceiling—painted as though the plaster were a mirror reflecting a ball in full swing, the whole crowd depicted from above, fanciful hairstyles and swinging skirts, couples whirling across the dance floor while others whispered in corners.

The overall effect was dizzying.

Olympia and Tess wore loose, uncorseted morning gowns and darted across the mosaic floor with more energy than dignity, whacking a felt-covered ball back and forth. An ancient cat with long white hair and blue eyes supervised the scene from a pedestal in the shape of a thick Ionic column.

The handsome German manservant cleared his throat.

Olympia whirled. The felt-covered ball went flying, and the cat hopped down to chase it, followed by Mrs. Potts. Tess trotted over and greeted Bonny with a kiss on each cheek.

"It's Miss Reed!" cried Olympia. "What brings you to London?"

"My husband's business," said Bonny. "I wasn't sure if I should come, but I thought I'd at least see if you were in..."

"For you? Always!" cried Olympia.

"Here anyhow," added Tess. "I wouldn't recommend too many public outings for you just now—but it's wonderful to visit."

"And your timing couldn't be better, as I'd invited Tess over for tennis. I'd ask you to join us, but it takes an even number of players," said Olympia. "Why don't we take you out to the garden? I'm ready for a bit of refreshment."

Olympia hooked her elbow around Bonny's and Tess mirrored the gesture. Together they marched her outside. The garden was small, with a small table under a shaded bower and a few chairs positioned around it.

The table appeared to be made of amber. Golden, translucent, full of bubbles and bits of dirt and debris on closer examination, even a few insects.

The cat followed at a stately pace, leaping onto the arm of a wrought iron chair. It began to groom itself while the pig ran circles around the chair, making desperate noises when a maid appeared with cold lemonade and dishes of candied fruit.

Olympia lifted the pig into the seat of the chair. "This is Mrs. Potts. And the cat is Aunt Emily. I like to give my pets names that might lead eavesdroppers to believe that I spend a great deal of time around nice old ladies who take naps and get indigestion."

Bonny's eyes went wide. "Does that work?"

"I think so." Olympia gestured to her companion. "It was Tess's idea."

"Here's how I think about it," Tess explained. "When an actress prepares for a performance, does she change her clothes and call it a day? Or does she add a wig and paint her face? A good disguise has layers. Like an onion."

"I see," said Bonny, who did not see at all.

"Tess's usually right about these things. And besides, I'd originally named my cat Empress Magnifique. I wasn't sorry to have an excuse to rectify *that* mistake."

Bonny tasted the lemonade—tart, sweet, and excellent.

"That's better," said Tess. "I suppose Cordelia remained in New Quay? How is she? We haven't had any letters recently."

"It's my understanding that she's in London somewhere," Bonny replied. "I'd been hoping to have news of her from *you*."

"In London?" Olympia repeated. "With whom? Where is she staying? Why hasn't she visited?"

"She's alone, as far as I know. She may have kept her distance for the sake of your reputations, as I'd thought to."

Olympia and Tess exchanged a glance. They didn't look as much alike as Bonny had originally assumed. At first they'd seemed like mirror images painted in different shades. But Olympia had a square jaw, Tess a more slanted one. Olympia's lips were lovely but on the thin side; Tess's were very full. Olympia had a broader forehead, Tess a higher one.

They were quite different in appearance. The similarity lay in their mannerisms; they had the same posture, the same enunciation, the same way of tilting their heads. They behaved like siblings without being siblings.

And, quite clearly, they could speak whole sentences to one another with a glance. Perhaps full paragraphs.

"Why don't you tell us what happened," said Tess.

"It's my fault, more than a little .. She's had a strained relationship with her parents for some time, because she's been reluctant to marry. But the final break came after she defied them to remain friends with me. The last I saw her was nearly a month ago, when she left for the train station."

"We'll have to find her," said Olympia. "How long will you be in town?"

"Only a few days, I'm afraid. My husband owns a nursery, and we can't leave it for long." Loel had borrowed a gardener from a larger nursery where he had connections, but it was a temporary arrangement. "I'm sure she's fine, but that's part of the problem… if she were less capable, I think it would be easier for her to ask for help."

"An interesting observation," said Tess. "You don't think she's avoiding us, do you?"

"I can't imagine why she would."

"Then we'll find her. And if you hear from her, will you let us know?"

"Of course," said Bonny.

They chatted for a little while longer and even tried to teach Bonny to play tennis—Olympia had taken it up after learning that French kings had favored the sport—and Bonny enjoyed herself, though she hardly ever made contact with the ball.

Bonny returned to the hotel feeling better than she had in ages. She liked Olympia and Tess. Really *liked* them. While their city polish gave them hard edges that frankly bewildered her, the sense of camaraderie reminded Bonny of Cordelia, of Margot—of all the best friendships she'd ever had.

Loel had arrived ahead of her; she opened the door to find him staring out the window. He turned and smiled at the sight of her, so naturally that Bonny's heart warmed.

"How was your visit?" he asked.

"Good. They haven't seen hide nor hair of Cordelia." She joined him by the window, opening on a street where, every few minutes, more people passed by than lived in the entire town of New Quay. "How are the orchids?"

"Most of them survived the journey." He wrapped his arm around her waist and pulled her close. "Thanks to the rain, we're in better shape than we might have been."

"It's so strange," said Bonny, trying to tease a thought that had been floating vaguely at the back of her mind into words. "In some ways my life is better than it's ever been, in other ways it's much worse. It's the middle that's hollowed out."

"I know how it's worse... but how is it better?"

"The people in my life—Olympia, Tess, Cordelia, Mr. Benjamin... you." She looked up at him. "I know you have regrets, but I don't. I can't. I am so happy to be married to you. Everything you say, everything you do increases my admiration. I only hope that one day you might say the same—"

"That day came a while ago." He silenced her with a finger over her lips, then traced the outline of her lips with his thumb. "I'd stopped expecting good luck, so I didn't recognize it when it came—Virginia Henley did me the greatest favor of my life. Marrying you is the best thing I've ever done."

"Yes!" Bonny rose up on tiptoes, peppering his cheek and jaw with kisses. "Yes! It is!"

He picked her up by the waist, and whirled her away from the window, feet dangling in the air and skirts fluttering. The impromptu dance ended by the bed.

She cupped her hands around his jaw, blinking as moisture welled in her eyes. She felt alive like she never had before, as though the infinity of time were balanced on a pin that pressed its sharp tip right into the present moment.

His lips touched hers. She shivered, arching instinctively and deepening the kiss. He teased and sucked at her bottom lip, gentle and controlled. Bonny mimicked the gesture, rising up on tiptoes, exploring textures both familiar and strange: the way the velvety softness of his lips gave way to the slippery slickness of his mouth, the scratch of his stubble against her own smooth upper lip and jaw.

He made her feel weightless, cared for, and cherished. Like one of his orchids—fed by the stoves and the sun until heat prickled along her skin and sank to her core and compelled her to reach and twine and bloom.

"I love you," said Loel, his eyes the deep clear green of a mountain lake.

"You do?" She had to blink to clear her head, as though she were waking up from a particularly deep slumber, and she could see that it was the same for Loel—his expression was open and befuddled, touched with wonder. "Is that what this is?"

"I hope so."

She looked into his eyes, the deep clear green of a mountain stream. Everything she felt was reflected in their depths. "I love you," she said, and it felt so good, so right. "I love you, Orson Loel."

He reached for the buttons of his jacket.

She covered his hand with her own. "Let me."

He raised his eyebrows in question.

"I remember... I think it was the second time I visited Wood-close. You were chopping wood, and I interrupted you, and you put on your jacket so angrily. As though you couldn't believe I'd put you to the trouble of dressing."

"That's exactly what I was thinking."

"I'd never seen anything so shocking." Bonny slipped the buttons loose and swept her hand underneath the heavy cloth, against the damp linen of his shirt. "It was outrageous."

He drew in a sharp breath.

Bonny leaned in, filling her nose with his scent.

"I would accuse you of planning it, of teasing me on purpose, except that you couldn't have known I'd turn down the drive. You couldn't have known that I'd return."

"No," he agreed.

"But I couldn't stay away," she confessed. "Because I couldn't stop thinking about this…"

Loel laughed and kissed her neck. She shivered and held him tight; he bore her back onto the bed. By the time they roused and looked at the clock, it was almost time to leave for the auction rooms.

Time to find out, at last, what an *Odontoglossum crispum* was worth.

STEVENS' Auction Rooms were crowded, the corridors packed and buzzing with people clutching catalogues and murmuring urgently at one another. The auction room itself, a narrow auditorium, was by contrast almost eerily quiet.

A velvet curtain parted to reveal a stage, shallow, with only two props—a podium of dark wood and a low table. A slim man with close-cropped hair and spectacles carried a large, leather-bound book to the podium, a gavel tucked against his palm.

He laid down the book with enough care to qualify as ceremony and opened it, turning leisurely to the desired page. The silence took on a deeper quality, expectant, that held until the man tapped his gavel against the podium.

"Welcome to our September auction of orchids, exotic, attractive, never-seen-before orchids hailing from all corners of the globe. Over two hundred lots each guaranteed to tempt and delight, beginning with number one, ladies and gentlemen feast your eyes on..."

His voice wasn't loud, and yet it carried to every corner of the room, even the very back, as though it had been projected by magic. He spoke quickly, his enunciation so crisp that Bonny caught every word.

As each lot was introduced, a pair of assistants would carry out the orchids on offer, contained in their Wardian cases, and rest them on the low table beside the podium.

Buyers had had the opportunity to examine the flowers in advance. The sight of them now, in the auditorium, was meant to entice. To stir covetousness and jealousy. The auctioneer first read the description and then opened bidding—for these first flowers, introduced at the beginning to warm the crowd up, it was often a very modest sum.

"Ten shillings for a *Phalaenopsis amabilis*. Who would be the proud owner of a healthy pink *Phalaenopsis amabilis*, guaranteed to bloom for years to come? Ten shillings, do I have fifteen?"

The air fairly crackled with anticipation, and yet every individual seated inside the room schooled their features to bland indifference. They bid with minute gestures; a raised finger or a lifted chin seemed to be enough. Bonny found their restraint convincing; the auctioneer did not. He sniffed out their desires, playing the crowd and driving prices ever higher.

The resulting cadence had a power of its own. The auctioneer named a price, it climbed until the lot sold, to be replaced by the next lot, its starting bid slightly higher than the previous. By this means the bidders were gently, inexorably accustomed to prices that would have seemed outrageous if they'd been named from the outset.

The experience reminded Bonny of nothing so much as the old adage about a frog settled into a pot of cold water. Place the pot over a stove, and raise the temperature so gradually that the frog died before it realized it was in danger and hopped out.

And so many of the flowers were unfamiliar! Bonny had imagined—foolishly, as it turned out—that her time in Loel's greenhouse had given her a certain expertise on the subject of orchids. But the auctioneer smoothly reeled off the names of genera Bonny had never heard of; the assistants ushered flowers onto the stage in shapes and sizes so unfamiliar that they still had the power to stun her. Speckled spider orchids, orchids that looked like clouds of buzzing bumblebees, potted white *Cymbidiums* blushing pink on the lip and right at the tips of their delicate petals.

Loel's orchids amounted to twenty lots, a respectable percentage of the total. Bonny knew them all; they'd survived Loel's bout with malaria, and he'd babied them ever since, coaxing every last bit of growth he could from them.

"Hailing from Madagascar, this *Angraecum sesquipedale* is guaranteed to bloom through Christmas. Herald the holiday with an orchid recalling the whitest northern star, starting at twelve guineas…"

The tension flowing through Loel jumped to her; she grew short of breath, damp under her armpits. The *Angraecum sesquipedale* sold for twenty guineas. A good amount—more than some people earned through a year of labor—but Loel displayed neither pleasure nor frustration when the gavel closed the bidding.

Bonny didn't approve of gambling, but she thought, a bit hysterically—the tension in the room had her in a noose—that it was a shame Loel hadn't taken up cards instead of gardening.

The dancing ladies came next; she'd miss them in the orchid house. Loel had cultivated seedlings, but they wouldn't bloom for another year or so. They sold well, at ten guineas each.

By the time the auctioneer reached Loel's last lot—the *Odontoglossum crispum*, of course—the sales of previous lots had accumulated to at least six hundred guineas. That was a substantial sum, more than enough for a family to live on for a year, if they avoided the city whirl and accepted a few economies. If Loel attended several of these auctions every year—and considering that his sales for *this* quarter had been diminished by his illness—their circumstances were far more hopeful than she'd realized.

"We are hiring a cook," she told him in a whisper.

He slanted a glance at her.

"And a boy to help with the greenhouses," she added. "And—"

"And now, the moment we've all been waiting for," intoned the auctioneer. The *Odontoglossum crispum* was brought out, still in its case, the blooms fully open now.

They were beautiful. Five petals formed a perfect star shape, snowy white marked with spots of red—like drops of fresh blood —and a vivid yellow center. The petals, lip, and throat of the flower boasted delicate ruffles, as though the edges had been crimped for decorative effect. The flowers grew from a spike that trailed horizontally off the pot, clustered like pearls on a necklace.

"A flower never seen north of the equator, collected from the misty rainforests of South America at risk to life and limb, our most talented experts and gardeners have tried and failed to make this glorious *Odontoglossum crispum Cooksoniae* thrive, but only Baron Orson Loel has achieved this remarkable feat. This one-of-a-kind orchid can be yours. Starting at one hundred guineas…"

One hundred guineas! Bonny's heart lurched in her chest. She seized Loel's hand and squeezed hard.

"One hundred guineas." The auctioneer pointed with his gavel at a woman with a feather in her hat. "Do I hear one hundred and five?"

Bonny's knees went weak. She had expected the *Odontoglossum crispum* to fetch a handsome sum; Loel had always told her it would. She had expected the hush in the room, the craned necks, the watchful glances shooting like darts from one buyer to the next.

But to hear the auctioneer raise the price not in increments of shillings or even by a guinea at a time, but *five guineas*? It gave her a whole new notion of what they were dealing with.

Five bidders entered the competition, and the price climbed quickly. Bonny's own head spun at the numbers; it astonished her that the principals could keep up, when the prospect of losing so much money ought rightly to have made them sick.

"Three hundred fifty, but I already see a hand raising in the corner," said the auctioneer. "Three fifty-five, but the competition is fierce, three sixty…"

"I am going to suffocate if this continues for much longer," Bonny whispered.

Loel squeezed her hand. "Stay."

Bonny gritted her teeth. She was in real danger of fainting. She would have fled the room if she were any less confident that Loel would catch her if she fell. But he wouldn't let any harm befall her, so she gathered her courage and controlled her breathing. Slowly in, slowly out, filling her lungs each time.

"Four hundred seventy, who will take the prize? Four hundred seventy-five…"

Bonny's knees weakened. Loel propped her against his side. The two remaining bidders were the lady with the feather in her cap and a gentleman, balding and portly, with a large ruby in his cravat and a neatly waxed mustache.

From what Bonny had observed thus far, the bidding didn't generally last long after it narrowed down to two—the prospective buyers took the measure of one another, assessed the situation, and one or the other would withdraw.

This lady and gentleman did not follow the pattern. They glared at one another, hardly glancing at the auctioneer as he announced the bids. The price climbed to five hundred, then six. Even the bidders seemed a bit wild by then, both red-faced, the whites of their eyes showing, as though they'd been thrown onto the back of a galloping horse and didn't know how to dismount.

"Six hundred forty, do I hear six hundred forty-one?" asked

the auctioneer, slowing down to coax every last shilling from the bidders.

The gentleman twitched his raised finger.

"Six hundred forty-two?"

The feather in the lady's cap wagged.

"Six hundred forty… three?"

A tense stillness followed, broken when the auctioneer said, "Sold to the lady with a feather in her cap for six hundred and forty-three guineas. Moving on to lot one hundred and eighty, one of the largest orchids in existence, feast your eyes on the yellow petals and chestnut spotting…"

The iron bands around Bonny's chest relaxed. She could breathe again but felt dizzier than ever.

"Let's go," murmured Loel. "It's crowded in here, and that was the last of ours."

He ushered her out of the room, and she tottered along. Busy clerks bustled back and forth in the corridor, bidders clustered in corners chatting easily, windows let in the last of sunset.

"Six hundred and forty-three guineas," she said finally.

Loel looked down at her. He opened his mouth, but no words came out.

"*Six hundred and forty-three guineas,*" she repeated. Her mind, like a finicky baby slapping away unwanted food, kept rejecting the information. She simply couldn't believe it.

"I've never heard of anything like it," said Loel.

Bonny bit her tongue. *Six hundred and forty-three!*

"Half as much, maybe," he said. "I thought it was just possible —if we were extremely lucky—that it might fetch half as much."

"What if the buyer backs out?"

"She can't."

"That poor woman."

There had been something compelling, almost magical in the auctioneer's voice, the steady lighting, the mutual agreement among everyone present to be excited about spending outrageous sums on orchids, to look with jealous awe upon those who "won."

But it all seemed different now, when the spell of the auction room had been broken.

"That was Martha Highland," said Loel. "She's a well-known collector—a wealthy widow."

"And the man?" Bonny wondered. "They seemed to know one another."

"The Earl of Angridge. Another collector."

"So they do this regularly? Come to auctions, spend incredible amounts of money on orchids…?"

"Several times a year."

Bonny shook her head in astonishment.

"Forget about her," advised Loel. "Think about hiring a cook. Where shall we look?"

Bonny plucked the answer out of the air, as though it were a butterfly that had been floating about her, hoping to catch her eye. "From a Magdalene Asylum."

"A Magdalene Asylum?" Loel frowned. "But why?"

"It's a place for women like me, isn't it? The ones who weren't lucky enough to fall for men like you."

"Flatterer," he said. "All right."

CHAPTER 20

The Magdalene Asylum was large and grim, a brick building several stories high that took up most of a city block. The nuns who greeted them wore blue, with large straw hats, and treated both Bonny and Loel with tremendous suspicion.

But eventually, through much effort, they were convinced to release two women: a cook named Frances Taylor, broad-faced with soulful eyes and a five-year-old son in tow, along with a gently bred and heavily pregnant former governess, Penny Evans.

They made quite a procession, taking up a whole cabin in the passenger train on the way back to Woodclose, then overflowing Mrs. Twisby's carriage, with empty Wardian cases packed into a wagon trailing behind.

Bonny helped the two women settle in before dressing in her plainest clothes, donning a bonnet with a wide brim, and making the trip, alone, to New Quay. She hadn't been back since her disastrous final book delivery. A part of her quailed at the prospect of returning alone; she hoped that if she kept her face hidden and steered clear of the Black Lion, that she'd avoid another confrontation.

Crescent Court was her destination. Instead of visiting the

cottage she'd entered only once before, she remained on the street. She fed a few carrots to the shaggy pony, then sat on a fence with a book she'd brought back from London.

Eventually little Charles Dunaway skittered out from one of the rear entrances to the property.

"Miss?" He watched her nervously from big brown eyes. "You're looking for me, aren't you?"

"I am," Bonny admitted. "I have a proposal for you. I want you to know that you're free to turn it down. I won't mind."

"What... proposal?" He pronounced this last word carefully, breaking up the three syllables into distinct chunks.

"I live with my husband not far from town," she explained. "He owns a business, raising orchids to be sold in the city. He could use some help. It would be a job, and we'd pay you—you'd learn about gardening and plants, and if that interests you, you'd leave with skills that other families or institutions might value."

"I don't know... gardening? Aren't house servants paid more? I make ten guineas a year here."

"Then we'd pay you twenty," said Bonny. "But what's more, we have a governess in our employ. She'd tutor you in the midday, which are the slow hours in our nursery. You'd learn reading and writing and some other things as well."

"How much would that cost?"

"Nothing at all. Our cook has a child, so we hired the governess to look after him. But you should know that most people in New Quay don't think well of me or my husband. His name is Lord Loel. It's quite possible that you'll have a difficult time here, if you come to work for us."

"I don't know..."

"That's all right. You shouldn't answer right now." She quickly gave him the directions to Woodclose. "Now you know where to find us, if you decide you're interested."

He arrived two days later—both arms wrapped around a lumpy pillowcase stuffed with odds and ends, the patchwork puppy Bonny had gifted him peeking out the top. The footman who'd answered to Bonny's knock so long ago walked at his side, a carpetbag in one hand.

Bonny suppressed the urge to greet him with a hug. Instead, she dropped to one knee in the yard, to meet him at his own level, and spoke soberly. "Good morning, Mr. Dunaway. Have you decided to accept our offer of employment?"

The boy blushed crimson. "Yes'm."

"I'm so glad to hear it. I prepared a room for you upstairs, just in case. Would you like to see it?"

"Yes'm."

She looked up at the footman. "And how can I help you, Mr. …?"

"Michaels." He hefted the carpetbag. "I offered to help young Mr. Dunaway carry his things. I'll take them up, if you don't mind."

"Not at all. Come right along."

Since the servants' quarters were nearly empty and likely to remain so for a while, Bonny had told Mrs. Taylor and Mrs. Evans to use the space as they pleased—which meant that each of the occupants had a room to him or herself. Charles Dunaway was thrilled, opening each empty drawer in the dresser and exclaiming over the view from the small window, but Mr. Michaels eyed the unused rooms with suspicion. When he thought Bonny wasn't paying attention, he murmured low, "Remember, Mrs. Harris said she'd have you back at any time. You don't have to stay if you don't like it."

While Bonny admired the man's protective instincts, she had no intention of losing Charles now that he'd come. So she introduced the boy to Mrs. Taylor, Mrs. Evans, and to five-year-old Hugh Taylor, who greeted the newcomer with such an excess of gratitude and admiration that Mr. Michaels sighed to himself, smiled ruefully, and finally bid farewell to little Charles.

She left Loel to talk the boy through his new duties while she returned, again, to New Quay. She had a painful task ahead of her, and she hoped that pride she'd felt while introducing Charles Dunaway to his new home would bolster her through it.

For all that, she dragged her feet as she reached her destination, streets so familiar that she recognized every planter, every lantern, every crack in the pavement. Her shoulders tightened, her stomach cramped. Either the passersby whispered behind her back or she imagined it; every blank windowpane seemed a hostile eye.

She kept her gaze averted as she passed the Kelly residence. She stood trembling on the doorstep of the house that she'd called home for almost the whole of her life, wondering if Loel had felt a similar mix of shame and determination when he knocked all those years ago.

Wondering if her reception would be as painfully hostile as the one she'd offered him. She'd deserve it.

She rang the bell.

Her mother answered, a kerchief shielding her hair and an apron around her waist, a sure sign that she'd been interrupted in the midst of cleaning. For a moment, a smile lit her handsome face. Bonny choked back a sob and swayed close, desperate for a welcoming embrace she hadn't dared expect...

Mrs. Reed took a quick step back. No explanation except for a quick shake of the head, a glitter of moisture at her eyes.

"I know. I shouldn't have come." Bonny spoke quickly, because it would have been too painful to hear her mother say the words. "I brought you something. I'll give it to you and go, if that's all right?"

Mrs. Reed hesitated. "What did you bring?"

Bonny offered her mother the folded bank draft she'd carried clenched between thumb and forefinger. "Two hundred pounds— so Margot can have a season in London. Let her do what I'd hoped to try."

"We can't have you over for dinner," said her mother, fond

and exasperated in a way that made Bonny's heart ache. "What makes you think we can take your money?"

"You know her chances will be better somewhere else. That's my fault; let me help fix it." Instead of waiting for her mother to take the paper, Bonny bent and placed the bank draft on the ground between them. "It would be foolish not to."

"Foolish," repeated Mrs. Reed, dry as dust.

A breeze whisked by, making the paper flutter. Before the draft could blow away, Mrs. Reed stepped on it. She slid it across the threshold under the sole of her shoe.

"Thank you," said Bonny. "And one last thing…"

Her mother's eyebrows notched up. "I thought you were going to give me something and go."

"Shut the door if you feel you must."

"I ought to," said Mrs. Reed—but she didn't.

Bonny heaved a deep, fortifying breath. "Loel did visit us, after the fire. He sent a letter asking if you'd receive him, and I threw it away without showing you. Soon after, he came in person to offer his apologies. Instead of listening, I insulted him. He left New Quay soon after, partly because of the awful things I'd said, and I was so ashamed that I never told you. But you should know —and you should tell Papa. Loel is a good man, and I'm lucky to have him. I hope one day you'll be able to see that."

Mrs. Reed nodded once, thoughtfully.

"I love you, Mama," said Bonny. "You and Papa and Margot. And I'll stay away from now on. But if you ever need me…"

"I love you too," said Mrs. Reed.

Bonny heard the deep emotion in her mother's voice—and the finality, as well. She said farewell and tried not to flinch at the sound of the door shutting behind her as she walked away.

She reached Woodclose just in time to catch Loel in the yard, a fishing pole propped on one shoulder. "Charles is tending the stoves, so I'm headed to the lake. Care to join me?"

"To catch supper? Should I let Mrs. Taylor know?"

"No, for the orchids. Fish bones and scales can be ground into fertilizer. Do you think Mrs. Taylor would want the meat?"

Bonny burst out laughing. The orchids came first; niggling details of sustenance second. "I believe so, yes. You really like this work, don't you?"

He paused, eyebrows furrowing. "When I left home, I went to Liverpool and started searching for work that would take me away from England as quickly as possible. I accepted the first job I was offered, as an assistant to an orchid collector."

"And you took to it?"

"I did—though it's hard to stomach the waste. For every thousand flowers we'd collect, perhaps ten would reach England alive. And disease isn't a risk, it's an inevitability."

"So you're happier staying in one place, with your nursery?"

"I'm happier now that you're here," he said gruffly. And then, "Are you coming or not?"

"Give me a minute to change, and tell Eleanor you might catch supper, and find something to read—"

"Speaking of reading, a letter arrived while you were out," Loel said. "From London."

"Bring it along."

Once their preparations had been made, they tromped through the woods to a large lake with a small rowboat beached along the sandy shore. Loel held Bonny's hand as she climbed inside, then he shoved the boat into the water and leaped nimbly after her. The boat rocked and then settled; it was only just large enough for the two of them.

Loel rowed them into the deep water and began fiddling with his fishing pole. Bonny twisted and turned on the narrow, hard bench, searching for a comfortable position. Eventually she gave up and opened her letter instead. It was from Olympia.

"Read it aloud," suggested Loel.

"I didn't think you'd be interested," said Bonny.

Loel shrugged. "I won't find out unless you read it."

Dear Bonny,

I am about to make you very jealous. Are you ready? Cordelia, Tess, and I have just had tea with R. E. Timothy. As an homage to her excellent book, I have decided not to tell you anything about her. You will have to come to London, meet her, and judge for yourself.

(Revenge is sweet, is it not?)

I won't withhold news of Cordelia, however. She was rather easy to track down, which is a problem we're trying to solve at present. I hired a detective and suggested that he start his search at popular bookshops. He found her within a day.

She seems well, in good spirits, and has promised to write to you very soon. In the meanwhile, I hope that I've eased some of your fears in addition to stoking your jealousy.

Yours most sincerely,

Olympia

Bonny lowered her parasol and tipped her head back so she could see the sky past the shade of her bonnet. It was a mild day, the sky a deep saturated blue. A light breeze kissed her face. She might have been jealous, but it was such a perfect day. She was so happy to be right here, in this place.

"I wonder what they're getting up to," said Bonny.

"Something alarming, at a guess. Do all women talk to one another like that?"

"Just Olympia." Bonny grinned. "She's flighty, I'll grant you, but smart enough to take Tess's advice."

"Do you wish you were there? I can't leave Woodclose... but you could spend more time in town."

"Once you've trained Charles Dunaway, we'll make trips together. Right now though... I'm exactly where I want to be." Bonny smiled and pointed at his line, bobbing in the water. "You've got a bite."

Loel caught six fish before rowing back to shore. On the way home, walking side by side, he said, "We'll bring a cushion for you next time."

Bonny savored that "next time"—the acknowledgement that she belonged, that she was welcome. That he'd enjoyed the time they spent together.

She had too.

They returned to find Charles and Hugh shouting and laughing in their piping voices as they ran in circles around the yard, playing a game of tag. Charles drew up short when he saw them, bowing and mumbling an apology.

"Take these to Mrs. Taylor." Loel handed Charles his basket of fish. "And I'll make sure all's well in the greenhouse."

Charles dashed inside, Hugh trailing slowly behind.

"It might be a while before we can think of traveling," Bonny murmured.

"Mm-hmm."

She followed him into the half-empty greenhouse. The plants that they hadn't taken to auction were young, ailing, or dormant. The sweet perfumes and vivid colors were gone. But the fountains remained, the bright chuckle of water and the sharp scent of chlorophyll. Not much for a new apprentice to injure, luckily.

Bonny clicked the padlock closed around the inside latch. "Close your eyes and count to ten."

"What?"

"Count slowly."

Loel hesitated, then obeyed.

Bonny ran down the narrow path into the center of the greenhouse, removing her bonnet and gloves and tossing them onto the empty table where once her *Odontoglossum crispum* had rested in solitary glory. She worked the fastenings of her dress and draped it over the back of a chair.

By the time she reached Loel's little bed, she was naked.

She shivered, despite the heat. So long as she was beautiful, she was valuable. So long as she was beautiful, she was afraid. The two had gone hand in hand all her life.

Men saw her and wanted her. She'd relied on their desire as

much as she'd resented it. But everything she knew about right and wrong had been upended these past months. She'd been taught propriety for the benefit of men like Charles Gavin, who'd treated her like a piece of candy, a treat made for his enjoyment, not a person in her own right

She'd unlearn it for Loel. Loel, who was earthy and physical and patient. Who'd given her time and space to bloom, like one of his flowers.

He approached slowly, without speaking, and brought her hands to the button of his coat. Because she'd told him once how it moved her to watch him dress, or undress, and he remembered. Because when she gave him a gift, he gave one back—weaving the threads that bound them together as husband and wife.

She slipped the buttons loose from his coat and drew the thin wool off his shoulders, trailing her hands over his linen-clad shoulders, his hard biceps. She repeated the process with his waistcoat and tugged his shirt loose from his trousers. He obligingly lifted his arms so she could pull it off, leaving him bare from the waist up.

She leaned close to breathe in his scent. She caressed the silky smooth skin along his ribs and arms, raked her fingers through the hair on his chest, followed the trail of it down to the waistband of his trousers. She dug the heel of her palm into his erection, thick and straining against the cotton.

"They say," said Bonny, sitting on Loel's bed and working the clasps of his trousers, "that we must lie in the bed we make. To tell us we will get our just deserts, though I've known since the fire that wasn't true, and in any case, how many of us make our own beds?"

"I've made mine for years," said Loel.

"So you have. Here in your greenhouse, where it's always warm and comfortable and you can never get enough sleep. But that's going to change."

Loel's eyebrows lifted a notch.

Bonny settled on the thin mattress and reached for him. "For now, I will lie in the bed you made, and let you make love to me."

"And what will that prove?" Loel wondered, working off his boots.

"Nothing at all." Bonny grinned. "But it will feel very good."

AFTERWORD

Thanks for reading *Bed of Flowers*! If you have a chance, I hope you'll leave a review—or share your thoughts wherever you like to talk books. Word of mouth is the best way to help other readers find the books they'll love and avoid the ones they won't.

I don't yet have a release date (or even an estimate) for the next book in the Sweetness and Light series, though I can tell you that Cordelia Kelly will be the heroine. If you want to make sure you don't miss the news, sign up for my newsletter. You'll be the first to hear.

If you want to drop me a line, you can email me at erin@erin-satie.com, chat with me on Twitter @erinsatie, or look me up on Facebook.

If *Bed of Flowers* was the first book of mine you've read, consider giving my No Better Angels series a try. It's a series about women who fight for themselves and what they want, even if that leads them away from the high road… and the men who love them just as they are.

If you're curious, turn the page to read the first chapter of *The Secret Heart*, which is free at all major retailers.

THE SECRET HEART, CHAPTER 1

Sussex, England
Autumn, 1838

Midnight struck as Caroline Small crept through the moonlit corridor. A chorus of bongs and chimes sent her ducking into the shadow of a tall clock. Her skull vibrated with the noise.

Imagining the maintenance required to synchronize so many clocks made her shudder—did the Duke of Hastings employ a servant just to wind his clocks? All day, every day, in an endless circuit? But then, it stood to reason that the Duke would find a way to broadcast his importance even in the dark of night.

Not that she'd ever met him. Hastings spent most of his time in London and rarely visited Irongate, the seat of his duchy. Caro's invitation had come from the old Duke's ward and niece, Daphne.

Silence settled over the house again. Caro brushed the dust from her wrapper and resumed her slow progress. The ballroom, when she finally reached it, was bigger than the entirety of Caro's London home. Decorative plasterwork framed tiers of arched windows, sculpted whorls and curlicues that shone dully in the moonlight. Gold leaf, probably, though she wouldn't be sure until she saw them in the light. Overhead, thousands of crystal droplets dangled from three massive chandeliers. The whole room smelled soothingly of beeswax.

Her foot slipped on the glossy floor as she advanced, allowing her to pinpoint the odor's source: a fresh coat of polish, applied with a heavy hand.

Too slick to dance on.

She tiptoed up to one of the French doors set into the west-facing wall, positioned to squeeze every last drop of sunset into the room. She flipped the latch and advanced onto a wide terrace. Beyond lay a garden in the French style, all paved walkways and bushes pruned into rigid geometric shapes.

All the windows on this side of the building were dark. Even the servants had cleared away. And a waist-high balustrade of white marble circled the terrace. It would serve her as a *barre*.

Caro lit the lamp she'd carried down from her bedroom and dropped her wrapper. Beneath she wore her usual practice uniform, a bodice and knee-length skirt of white muslin with a black sash tied at the waist. Her bare arms prickled with goose-flesh, but she wouldn't feel the cold in a few minutes.

Her instructor, Giselle, always told her ballerinas pray with their legs. If so, *An Elementary Treatise upon the Theory and Practice of the Art of Dancing* was their Bible. *Every obstacle is surmounted by perseverance and reiterated exercise*, wrote the great instructor Carlo Blasis. Caro dropped into a *plié*, heels on the ground, bending at the knees, legs turned out. *Remain not, therefore, twenty-four hours without practicing.* It had taken almost two days to reach Irongate. She couldn't let her first night here pass without finding a place to dance.

Forty-eight *pliés,* and then she moved on to the *grands batte-ments.* For these, she extended her leg, raised it as high as her hip, and beat it quickly. *All the lessons he takes, when widely separated one from the other, can be of no service toward making him a good dancer;*

and are little else than a loss of so much time. After sixty *grands batte-*
ments on each leg, she stepped away from her makeshift *barre* and
repeated the whole routine.

Lots of girls hated the *barre* exercises. Giselle said the talented
ones often tried to avoid them. Caro loved them. She loved the
repetition. She loved the precision. She loved the feel of her body
doing what she told it, when she told it, how she told it. Obedient.
With her leg turned out, her arm bent just so, her head turned up,
she felt like she'd transcended her own flesh.

Which was why, after she finished her exercises, she rehearsed
her favorite passage from *La Sylphide*. She became the sylph, a
soulless air spirit, pantomiming her erratic, teasing advances
toward a besotted woodsman with skills built from the most
earthbound qualities of all: discipline and perseverance.

By the time she finished, sweat dampened the hair at her
temples and bloomed on her bodice. She gulped air. Her legs
trembled, and she swayed like a sailor in a tempest as she skirted
the balustrade and stumbled down the steps onto a gravel path
leading to a three-tiered fountain.

Human again.

Caro drank, reaching out for more. Water filled her cupped
palms, spilled over, cool and plentiful. Her cheeks were so hot.
She could heat a small orphanage through a mild winter with the
body heat she was generating.

"You must be Miss Small."

The clipped, aristocratic voice sent her whirling around,
choking a little as she failed to stifle a shriek. She saw a heavily
muscled man dressed in warm flannels, well bundled despite the
mild autumn weather, lips thickened and split, one eye swollen
shut.

Two choices: one, she could scream. Someone would come
running, maybe even in time to save her from being violated. If
she were lucky, the scream might even frighten her attacker away.
But he didn't look like the sort of man to frighten easily. He *did*

appear strong enough to throw her over his shoulder and carry her away before help arrived.

Her second choice? Run. Just run.

The stranger had a broad chest, too solid to be called lean, his legs thick as tree trunks. Beautifully made, impressive, but not tall —though he still towered over her. Fine male specimens of his kind couldn't run with any speed. If she dug into her reserves, she'd make it through the doors before he'd gone two paces.

"I think you have the advantage of me, Mr...." Caro backed away toward the gap in the balustrade as she spoke, angling for a straight shot at the door.

"You don't recognize me?" He spoke in a tone of mild curiosity, not affront, in the purest accent she'd ever heard.

A prickle of unease raised gooseflesh along Caro's arms.

A stray moonbeam skated along his pale, sweat-dampened hair. According to the portraits she'd seen on the walls, the dukes of Hastings had for generations boasted uniform, and unusual, coloring—blond hair and light brown eyes. What if this ragged, beat-up figure of a man were a member of the family?

What if he lived at Irongate?

"I'm sorry, I don't." Caro smiled nervously. "You have my permission to introduce yourself."

She took another step toward the door, moving as lightly as she could, but the gravel crunched beneath her heel.

The stranger's gaze dropped straight to her feet. "Running won't do you any good."

"Well, of course *you'd* say that," Caro snapped. "*I* think I'll take my chances."

To her surprise, he smiled. Not much—his mouth was too swollen to stretch. Even the attempt opened the split in his bottom lip and sent a thread of fresh blood dribbling down his chin.

Caro's stomach turned, and she shuddered.

"Go on, then." He scowled. "Go back to your room. Lock the door. In future, try to remember that rules are made for a reason.

Young ladies who stay in their rooms at night don't have to worry about encountering bloody brutes in a dark garden."

She couldn't tell if terror or disgust kept her guts liquid, only that some devil had decanted strong liquor into her belly, and it would serve her as fuel. But his last sentence, the unabashed *bitterness* of it, gave her pause.

She tipped her head to the side. Softened her voice a bit. "Do you live here?"

He only glared, and in the silence she heard his labored breathing. Each inhale quick and shallow, then a catch before the slow exhale. He wasn't winded. He was in *pain*.

Of course he was in pain. He looked like he'd been pulped.

He took a single, deliberate step toward her. And then another.

Her pity fled as quickly as it had come. She forced steel into the exhausted, stinging jelly of her legs and sprinted for the door. She flew across the gravel and took the stairs in a single bound.

Then tripped over the oil lamp she'd left aglow on the terrace. She twisted as she fell and landed on her side, but the impact knocked the wind out of her. She gasped, sucking air faster than her lungs would take it, until her breaths settled back into a regular rhythm. Oh, she'd ache in the morning.

A shadow, a deepening of the blackness all around her, startled her. The stranger. He'd followed her to the terrace.

He was even harder to look at from up close. Pinpricks of blood welled in the raw skin of his forehead and cheeks. Black blood ringed the inside of his nostrils.

"Are you all right?" he asked.

She nodded.

He bent to pick up the lamp—the glass shade had cracked, but it hadn't shattered or leaked. "Lucky little fool," he muttered, then held out his hand.

It was a big hand, with thick, stubby fingers and bulging, reddened knuckles. She cringed away from it and, before he could get any closer, scrambled to her feet and through the open French door. She closed it, flipped the lock, and ran to the safety of her room.

Want to keep reading? The Secret Heart is free at all major retailers. Or jump straight to the Complete No Better Angels Box Set. Priced at $9.99, it's cheaper than buying each book in the series individually.

www.ingramcontent.com/pod-product-compliance
Lightning Source LLC
Chambersburg PA
CBHW020239180626
46810CB00006B/2278